EPITAPH

Christopher Bradbury

As ever,
for Sally, George, Ellie and Frankie

1. Chaddleworth

Clarissa Benson-Haines was a first-class bitch. Everybody knew that she was a first-class bitch, even her husband, the late and not particularly lamented Sir Sean Haines (she had insisted on retaining the family name, much to his chagrin).

Sir Sean had tolerated her because he knew upon which side his bread was buttered. Clarissa was his spine, a cast-iron spine that was, as his own spine crumpled when it all became too much, strong enough to support both of them.

Not that Sir Sean was a weak man, far from it, but he was not a killer. He could not kick someone when they were down. Clarissa was able to deliver a *coup de grâce* without flinching and frequently did.

Of course, she restricted her activities merely to the social. Her enemies were those whose *soirées* outshone hers by a single candle, those who arrived late or too early, those who broke dinner dates or refused to give way to her on the various local committees upon which she sat. She was ruthless. She knew everything; she knew of the affairs (most of the servants at the club, that hub of ex-pat life, were in her pocket), the drinking problems, the marital problems, the drug problems, the lesbians and the homosexuals who tried to disguise their predilections behind a thin veil of marriage and ended up as susceptible to blackmail as a murderer.

There were also those whom she saw as a threat to her husband. If they were a threat to him, then they were a threat to her and she would set about them, regardless of status, class (though only one class mattered), rank or lineage. No one was too big for Clarissa Benson-Haines.

Rumour had it that she had driven Cherry Miskin-Townes to suicide with the slow, steamy revelation of her relationship with a local. Her husband, Harry Miskin-Townes, in line to take Clarissa's husband's place as Ambassador and making no secret about it, had left the island in shame, on the same plane which had carried his wife's coffin back to Heathrow.

Nobody would be permitted to perforate Clarissa's bubble, would be allowed to intrude upon her comfort zone, would be allowed to edge her husband aside in favour of good looks and youth.

To her, Sir Sean was little more than a pet. She loved that pet, as anyone would love their pet, but if he stepped out of line, she would knuckle his snout and send him under the table. He would later emerge compliant, a lapdog, with no more say in its life than a shaking Chihuahua.

He had died only a couple of years previously. It had been a quick death, cancer of the pancreas. It had devoured him from the inside out and left him resembling little more than a Japanese prisoner of war; all bone, jaundiced, dimly lit, with sunken eyes.

Long before that, they had bought the small estate upon which they had lived, Chaddleworth, a bungalow atop the hills overlooking the Baie de Dieu, a stretch of beach along which lay white sands across a mouth of turquoise water that licked lovingly at the bay, for fifteen years. They were to retire on Saint Quintian in comfort, the perfect relics of a diminishing empire. The ex-pats *di tutti ex-pats*. Chaddleworth had become a hub of social activity, a well of schemes and social climbing. Clarissa had become the Hedda Hopper of the ex-pat scene. Those whom she liked, rose, with all the benefits. Those she had decided were expendable, well, they just sunk.

Upon Sir Sean's death, Clarissa had decided to stay

on Saint Quintian. Now she tended the gardens of Chaddleworth, atop the hills overlooking the bay. From there, she could survey all she had once owned. People came and went, appointments changed, politics shifted like the swell of the ocean and she was left adrift upon unfamiliar seas. Sir Sean was a memory, in her mind alone. As with all these things, when a vacancy appeared, the world filled it. What came before no longer was. The world erased that which no longer served a purpose.

Clarissa Benson-Haines knew that she would soon disappear altogether. The feeling had become almost overwhelming lately. It scared her, the thought that she would no longer exist; it blackened her mood. She had also began to smell her late husband's Old Spice after-shave and thought that sometimes she could see him out of the corner of her eye. She told him to go, that she was not yet ready, but his presence grew greater every day.

So, in an attempt to drive these thoughts away, she lost herself in her bell-flowers and her hibiscus and her anthurium and encouraged her vireos and her mango hummingbirds, doves, pigeons and fly-catchers. She would take tea with anyone kind enough to visit her, but they would seldom come back because, with her outdated, outmoded attitudes, she simply drove people away. She stood upon a pedestal of jingoism which no one was prepared to share with her.

Eventually, the world turned away and she was left alone.

Henrick, her sole servant, apart from his wife who came daily to clean, emerged from the shadows of the bungalow into the bright kaleidoscope of the garden. He had grown old with her and his short, black hair was now frosted with age. He had remained loyal to her, despite her, and took pleasure in ensuring her comfort and safety in the absence of others.

He wore the same dark suit which she had always insisted he wore, down to the black tie and impeccable white shirt. Inside the house, he did not have to wear the jacket (although she insisted on sleeve garters to avoid soiling his cuffs), but outside, where he might be seen, or when the odd rare visitor dropped by, he was required to wear it, for appearance's sake.

On this day, he had, balanced on his fingers, a silver salver, upon which lay a single letter next to a silver letter-opener. He presented it to Clarissa with a courteous lowering of his head.

She removed a pair of gardening gloves and swapped them with the letter on the salver. Henrick waited as she ran the letter-opener the length of the envelope, then replaced it on the tray next to her gloves.

She then turned away from Henrick for privacy and sauntered a few feet towards the splendid view below her while removing the letter. She paused as she read, intent upon the page.

From behind, Henrick thought he saw her totter slightly. He made a move towards her, but she steadied herself and read on. When she had finished the letter, she put it back into the envelope and slipped it into a pocket of her slacks.

Thank you, Henrick,' she said steadily, without turning around.

Henrick dropped his head minutely and headed back into the cool darkness of the bungalow. He looked back out upon the lush lawn and the blaze of colour that edged it and saw that Clarissa hadn't moved. She looked old to him now. Since the death of her husband, he had watched her age, seen the dullness in her eyes, the stoop in her shoulders and the slower, strained gait.

She held no fear to anybody anymore. Part of him missed that firecracker, that fearless jackal of a woman who brought her prey down before they even knew she was there, but he loved what he saw now, a vulnerable elderly lady - always a *lady* - whose claws had been removed and was left to rely upon that small piece of humanity that had been submerged by the beast for so many years.

Still she gazed out to sea, her hands in her pockets, white wisps of hair fingered by the warm breeze.

Her mind seemingly made up, she turned and walked into the bungalow.

'I shan't need you or your wife any more today, Henrick,' she said, not even looking in his direction. 'Please, take the rest of the day off.' She went to her handbag and took seventy-five dollars out of her purse. 'Here,' she said, holding the money out to Henrick. 'Please, take your lovely wife out to the cinema and for a nice meal.'

Henrick was taken aback. 'Madam? Are you alright, Madam?'

She put the money firmly into his hand. 'Please,' she repeated. 'Take it. I have plans for the rest of the day. You and Evie get such little time together. It would make me happy.'

Henrick took the money and quickly put it in a trouser pocket, as if embarrassed to have touched it at all.

'Thank you, Madam. If you're sure...'

'I'm sure. Go on, off you go. Spoil that lady of yours.' Henrick hesitated. 'Go on now. It's fine.'

With a bow of his head, Henrick retreated.

Clarissa Benson-Haines, that first-class bitch, went to a bureau in the corner of the room and took out a revolver. She checked to see that it was loaded, put it into her handbag, then went to the front door and without a backward glance, closed the door behind her.

The bungalow fell into a dark silence.

2. Breaking News

The *Saint Quintian Gazette* had been around for eighty-five years. It had started as a colonial rag but was now established as Saint Quintian's finest newspaper, even if the headline was more often than not about stolen bikes or the sighting of (perhaps) a Reef Shark - well beyond the reef - where it might have attacked an innocent on an airbed, but actually did not.

It contained a list of the deaths on the island that week and a list of marriages, with the occasional pronouncement of a birth, but it provided little more than local gossip and an entertaining twenty-minute read.

The Editor sat at his desk and proof-read every article. He had to watch out for slander and unsubstantiated tittle-tattle. The paper had once been taken to court for declaring that a Mr Adio Baptiste had indulged in inappropriate sexual behaviour with a ghost. It was a very superstitious island, all Voodoo and zombies and it took the subject very seriously. The paper was fined one hundred dollars and told to pay Mr Baptiste two hundred dollars in compensation. The paper had not fought the case, but had taken a less 'speculative' approach since.

But, inevitably, crime had come to the island. There had been an economic downturn at the cusp of the eighties because of the demand for beet, the fall in the popularity of sugar and a concomitant fall in the price of sugar cane. It was a small island, a product of colonialism in the early nineteenth century, dependent on its one resource, sugar cane, and it was kicked hard when the world began to compete.

Unemployment had gone hand in hand with an increase in crime, to the extent where murder had become, if not commonplace, then certainly less rare, even though the murderer, island-bound, had nowhere to run to. Outside investment increased as the tourist board and the Board of Trade had worked to introduce new business. Clothing had become a source of investment as what were essentially low-paid sweat-shops blossomed like nettles over the island to sell large amounts of shirts and dresses and shoes to fat chains in Europe at an exorbitant mark-up.

The people were grateful however. It was still better-paid and less back-breaking than cutting cane and, even if they had short nights and long days, they could now afford to at least eat.

Crime fell. The tourist industry boomed and with it came the security of jobs within the grand hotels, the restaurants and the coast-associated businesses such as scuba-diving, big-game fishing and glass-bottomed boats.

The *Gazette* was there to record it all. Even it, with all its trivia and gossip, thrived. Where there was a new hotel, there was a story. Where there was a palm-tree-fringed wedding, there was a story. Success bred success and now, as the eighties began to cast its dubious, shallow, money-driven shadow across the world, it was a fine island to be on.

At his desk in the *Gazette*, the Editor contemplated that week's stories with the usual mix of amusement and dismay. He really had very little choice when it came to what to accept. They were little more than crows pecking at road-kill, picking the tasty from the wasted, but there was, generally, for him at least, an element of delight in the job.

However, that was not all he was there to do. The previous editor, a very amiable man called Stephen (with a – *ph*) had suddenly gone on 'sick leave', stating stress, overwork and personal issues as motives for his relief.

The owner of the paper had drafted in the new temporary Editor to carry on his excellent work, while Stephen (-*ph*) spent a few months back home in West Sussex with his elderly parents and a schnauzer called Gerald.

Where this Editor had come from, nobody knew, but he was amiable, intelligent and open to ideas, which always pleased the journalist. If they could push the boundaries a little, then all power to them; the only man to take the rap would be the man at the top, with EDITOR on the door. They could say what they wanted within limits and bugger the consequences. The boss could always pull the story.

The hive of industry was buzzing on this particular day. It was the high-season and tourists everywhere were creating stories with their cocky ineptitude; the bends from gaping at a moray eel for too long, stuck on a cliff when they should have taken the steps down, lost in the forest when they should have stuck to the path, despite the fact that they had progressed no more than two hundred yards in four hours, stung by a rogue jellyfish, mugged by a homeless wanderer, regardless of the fact that their travellers cheques had become thinner than one of the local dogs and there was no way they would ever leave their hotel room without further funds. It was all fraudulent, incompetent and above all, amusing reading. As long as they paid for it, the tourists could be as stupid as they wanted.

He was though looking for just one thing among all the print; an advertisement. It was to be a carefully worded advert, agreed by a small group of people, which would do a little more than simply alert the media. It would rattle the cages from Saint Quintian to London and cause a flurry of activity not seen since wartime.

As he flicked through the final layouts for the week, he stopped, went back a page, paused and looked again at one particular advert.

'WANTED –
A LODGER TO SHARE THE BILLS EACH

WEDNESDAY. PHONE - 610-121495.

Christ! That was it. He stared at it a little longer than he should have, almost willing himself to have misread it, but that was it. For sure, that was it. A frost ran up his spine as what these few casual words had set in place raced through his mind.

He pushed back his chair and ran to the door. 'Barkley!'

A young man with immaculate hair and serious glasses leapt from his chair and walked briskly to the office door.

'Who put this advert in?'

Barkley looked at the proffered paperwork, then returned to his desk and took a large ledger out of a drawer. He shuffled and ruffled the pages until he found the one he wanted, then ran a finger down the page. As soon as he had found what he wanted, he returned to his boss.

'No name, boss. They paid their buck-fifty and that's it.'

His boss bit his lip. 'Okay, Barkley. Thanks. Listen, don't let anyone disturb me for at least half an hour. Something's come up. Quite important.'

'Hush-hush, boss?'

His editor smiled eagerly at him, a light of mischief in his eyes. 'Very hush-hush.' He put his finger to his lips, retreated into his office and closed the door.

The hubbub of the newsroom returned; the tappety-tap of typewriters, the urgent ring of the phones, the raised conversations between desks.

Barkley returned to his typing, but out of the corner of his eye, he saw the heavy, wooden newsroom door open. Through them came a stern and determined Clarissa Benson-Haines. She marched towards the Editor's office, almost oblivious to the organised chaos around her.

Upon seeing her, Barkley leapt from his chair. He wavered in front of her.

'Madam, stop, please. The boss does not want to be disturbed for at least half an hour.'

She continued walking as if she had not heard him. Barkley's hands hovered about her, daring him to lay them upon this fearsome woman who had for so long been the object of all their fears, the source of all their gossip, but he could not touch her, it was more than his job was worth.

Clarissa reached the Editor's office door and barged in, slamming the door behind her.

Barkley stood at the glass staring in.

'How dare you!' screamed Clarissa. 'Lawrie! How dare you!'

Stunned by the violent intrusion, Lawrie gaped at her, the phone in his hand, about to talk. He put the receiver down onto the desk and leaned back in his chair.

Clarissa opened her bag, fumbled for a moment, then withdrew the revolver. Lawrie barely had time to react before two bullets crashed into his chest and he was knocked from his chair.

Outside the office a silence fell as all stared through the glass at the small, grey-haired woman with the large gun in her hand.

She turned towards them, her face horrified, as if she had no control over what she had done, only that she knew what she had done, then pulled back the hammer on the gun and raised the weapon to her temple.

Without hesitation, she fired.

3. The Dull Season

It was the dull season, the worst time of year, when suicides were supposed to be at their highest; that post-Christmas lull, when all the anticipation and excitement had faded and all that was left was a stack of bills and the brick wall of normality.

Normality. The staid straitjacket that always seemed a little tighter after the holidays had gone. With a large part of January, February and a potentially raging March to get through, with little more than the promise of snow, floods and high winds, it was bleak indeed.

Mike Ward's Christmas had been quiet. He had been on duty over Christmas Eve night, monitoring and sifting calls from overseas that threatened to light a fire under the world. However, the world had taken peace to its heart over holiday period and produced little more than the usual drunks and nutters on the line, ranting unintelligibly about the end of the world and nuclear catastrophe. There had been some genuine calls, from those who were required to call in on a regular basis, but their short calls had done little more than reinforce the sugary, temporary world love-in.

He had spent New Year's Eve at the Dickens Club, not because he particularly wanted to be at a party, but he didn't want to be alone as the seventies died and the new decade rolled in. He had a good meal, some excellent wine and people-watched. The people he would have liked to have been with were now gone and he hadn't managed to fill the vacancies. He left just after midnight, leaving the sounds of Auld Lang Syne and clinking champagne glasses to drift onto the streets then to fade as he made his way back to his flat.

Now, two weeks later, he walked with heavy feet into that grey, anonymous building in Grosvenor Square, Century House, which listened to the heartbeat of the world for twenty-four hours a day and diagnosed its health with all the subtle skill of a doctor deciphering signs and symptoms with fingertips and a stethoscope.

It all conspired to leave Ward feeling jaded and bitter, feeling sorry for himself, something that he had grown to despise, which made him even more annoyed.

His office, submerged in the stunted, muddy mid-winter light which seeped through his single window, greeted him coldly.

He knew what his problem was. It had nothing to do with Christmas or the weather or anything else to which he might glibly attribute his malaise. The truth was, he was bored.

When you had done what Ward had done, seen what Ward had seen, the mundane was not enough. He realised that it was some sort of addiction, that the routine was not enough, that helping to solve problems was not the same as solving problems, but he also realised that he was only a small part of something greater, that he had to remain subservient to the will of the state.

Of course, he had seen the department psychologist who, after much meandering and, frankly, bullshit, had been of the same opinion. He had been to the weapons classes and to the self-defence classes, but they had simply served to stimulate his appetite; to remind him that he was a killer with skills.

So, a desk barely sufficed. The act of living vicariously was never enough. He needed to be out there, his adrenalin high, his brain constantly on the edge. The mundane was for office workers and salesmen and supermarket workers. He didn't want safe; he wanted alive.

He sat at his desk and pulled the 'in tray' towards him. He knew that every scrap of paper in that tray was vital to someone, just not to him. He would go above and beyond for this alone, the isolated, those that no longer had the power to control who and what they were but, for him, it just wasn't enough. He needed to fight for his life, just to know that he was still alive. God bless his job. God bless the twisted soul that it had left in the shadow of Mike Ward. He wondered sometimes if enough would ever really be enough.

He rummaged through the 'in tray'. It was an epitaph to the mediocre; it was meetings and updates, it was 'just to let you knows' and the ordinary. The *ordinary*. What had *they* done to him that the ordinary, the shopping on a Thursday night, the poker game at the club, the occasional movie, the losses...the losses...meant so little to him.

Had he become a killer without remorse? Without regret? With nothing to offer the world but his trigger finger and his soul? Was that the sum of the man? Did he really do good among the chaos or did he simply cause the chaos to perpetuate?

Such was the oppressive cloud that fell upon him in that darkened room.

The phone rang as he waded his way through a small pamphlet about how to pick out a 'honey-trap'. How gullible men were, to fall for the fluttering lashes of a pretty woman. Or, maybe, how lonely they were, how egocentric, how shallow, how desperate, how very, very human.

He picked up the phone.

'He wants to see you.' Mrs Thornton's voice was a stern as ever. Ward smiled. She was the Chief's fortress, his Hadrian's Wall past which no one would pass without her austere eye upon them.

'Good see me or bad see me?' quipped Ward.

Mrs Thornton hesitated before answering. She always had to summon her patience in the face of flippancy. 'With you, Mr Ward...Well, who knows?' Another pause. 'Now, please.'

She hung up and Ward put the phone down. It could be anything, he said to himself. He might have bungled some paperwork, failed to register a call, forget to attend a self-defence update...

He hoped though. He hoped it was more. He hoped desperately that it would be something to take him away from the drab, the sameness, something to loosen the knots.

He straightened his tie and took the stairs up a couple of floors, then walked along the corridor, flanked by anonymous, unlabelled doors. He actually had butterflies. The same thrill he always felt when going to the Chief's office began to surface. His spine tingled and he felt the sweat on the back of his neck. If it ended in disappointment now...Oh God forbid!

He opened the door to Mrs Thornton's office, that anti-chamber to the King. She didn't look up but carried on typing as if he had merely been a passing spirit.

'Good morning, Mrs Thornton,' offered Ward.

'Good morning, Mr Ward. He will see you now.'

Ward went to the solid door that separated them form us and knocked.

'Enter.'

Ward opened the door and stepped tentatively into the room. As ever, the Chief was absorbed in paperwork. His morning was almost ritualistic; in by eight, tea, a discussion with Mrs Thornton to sort the wheat from the chaff, then a couple of hours dedicated to every piece of paper that crossed his desk, then tea and two biscuits ('sugar for the brain, nothing for the waist') at ten-thirty, followed by more paperwork until twelve-thirty.

Ward stood before the Chief until told to sit. The Chief continued to browse his papers, occasionally throwing an impatient green tick at the work or worse, a cross, until signing off with the traditional green 'C'.

'Sit down, Mike.' The Chief still didn't look up, but Ward knew this was a good sign. He never used 'Mike' unless there was something good to come.

Ward sat. At this point he usually, with permission, lit a cigarette, but he had given up smoking as part of a rather feeble new year gesture, not because of the awful tradition of self-denial that traditionally followed the first of January, but because he was fed up with being a slave to the sticks. He was at an age now when the breathlessness could creep in and the heart problems begin to take hold. He still had some years left on active duty and didn't want to compromise that precious time. The doctor was a finicky, wily man and would notice the slightest decline in, well, a heartbeat.

He could not deny that at this moment he would have ripped his own face off for some nicotine, but the devil and the angel on each shoulder would have to fight it out without him. He would simply drink more.

'Something amusing you?' The chief had pushed his paperwork aside while Ward daydreamed.

'No, sir. Just daydreaming.'

The Chief grabbed his pipe and began the rite to his first fill of the day. 'I hope she was worth it.' He almost smiled. He held the pipe up. 'You don't mind, do you? I know you're trying to stop...'

'It's fine, thank you,' said Ward, resisting the urge to grab the pipe and launch it through the nearest window.

He waited as the Chief went through his routine and, after what seemed an eternity, finally lit the pipe. The Chief took a couple of puffs and used the delay to form the words he wanted to say in his head.

'Do you remember Lawrie Stuart?'

Ward smiled fondly. 'Of course, sir. He was the one that got me into this mess.'

The Chief leaned forward in his chair and rested his

hands upon his desk, as if bracing himself. 'I'm afraid he's dead.'

Ward shifted uncomfortably. 'I'm sorry, sir. I didn't mean...What happened?'

The Chief, a little greyer at the temples and with the lines of worry and age mapped upon his face, considered the question. 'He was shot.'

Ward was at a loss. He couldn't think of anyone who would want to kill such an amiable man, but the business they were in was fickle. When he had taken over as high commissioner after the death of Alec Trelawney on that rather beautiful, strategically vital island in the Indian Ocean a few years ago, he had been a man in a coat of many colours. It was one more role he'd had to play among many. He had been a diplomat and a spy and he had melded the two together with aplomb. His decency had gone hand in hand with his duplicity, his diplomacy had danced with the hardness required to endure a war colder and more bitter than any that had gone before. Out of all of this shone his humanity and decency. Ward had liked him tremendously and forgiven him for being the one who reeled Ward into this cat and mouse game.

'Why,' asked Ward flatly.

'I simply don't know,' said the Chief. 'He was awaiting a signal from a defector when, apparently, into his office came a rather bitter old woman called Clarissa Benson-Haines; accused him of goodness knows what and shot him twice in the chest.'

'For no reason?'

The Chief shrugged his shoulders. 'As you well know, all calls into the department are answered instantly by a permanently-manned desk and recorded.'

He reached out and played a cassette. It had little to say, merely Clarissa's initial tirade and then the gunshots.

Ward listened intently. He quickly concluded that it wasn't the noise that mattered, but the silences in between.

The Chief switched off the machine. 'Well?'

Ward took a deep, considerate breath. 'Well, there were three shots. I'm going to assume that two were for Lawrie and, judging by the delay, the last one for her.' Ward waited a moment and considered. 'Lawrie doesn't say a thing. No 'please, Clarissa, be reasonable', no 'don't shoot, I'll do as you say'. Nothing. You can hear the receiver fall upon the desk and click as our end picked up. I think he said nothing because he wanted us to listen.'

The Chief looked at him through narrowed eyes as if Ward had declared check-mate. 'Yes. That's what I thought.'

The Chief's pipe had died, so he relit it, using the full length of the match to do so, until the flame caught the end of his finger. He shook it away. Thinking time.

'But I don't think that's the reason he called,' continued Ward. 'He was in the middle of making a call to MI6 when this woman burst into his office. His silence says that he wasn't expecting her, at the same time warning us to listen. There are two questions, sir. Why did Lawrie try to ring us and why did she shoot him? I'm not sure there's a connection. It might have been coincidence. Bad timing. Call it what you will. But he was about to spill the beans on something important and she had...well...she had chosen an unfortunate time to barge in, the cause of which is unknown.'

'I agree,' said the Chief. He paused long and met Ward's eyes. 'Listen, Mike, it's a little awkward, but this is a little personal.'

Ward's lips rose a little. 'Oh, yes? You knew the lady?' He regretted it immediately

'For Christ's sake, Ward, jump down from your libido for a moment, would you!'

'Sorry, sir.'

The Chief leaned back in his chair and returned to his pipe. 'As a matter of fact, Clarissa Benson-Haines was well-known to the ex-pat community, and not just in Saint Quintian. They had been to KL, Kenya, Mauritius...'

Ward raised a knowing eyebrow.

The Chief continued. 'Even spent some time in Simla. She didn't like it, apparently. Too cold in winter, too hot in summer. So, he applied for transfers until she was happy. He eventually ended up in Saint Quintian and by all accounts was a first-rate diplomat and a second-rate husband.' The Chief frowned wisely. 'It's often the way. Anyway, she became the keystone of the social scene and manipulated her husband's career, by hook or crook, until he became High Commissioner,'

Ward winced at the words. 'What is it about High Commissioner's wives?'

The Chief grunted. 'Anyway, once his time was done, they settled there, quite successfully by all accounts. Of course, the old empire began to wither and with it so did they. He retired with a top-notch pension and spent their days in a bungalow on the island, called *Chaddleworth*. He died two or three years ago and left her to see her days out in the place.' Mentally, the Chief closed the buff folder which he had recently absorbed. It was his turn to shuffle a little uncertainly in his seat. 'There is one other thing I thought you ought to know.'

'Oh, yes?' said Ward.

The Chief fiddled with the bowl of his pipe, holding it between thumb and index finger, letting go, then repeating the cycle.

'The thing is, Lawrie Stuart was my cousin. We were like brothers. We went to Cambridge together. I studied Medieval History and he studied the classics. In all honesty, they weren't much good to either of us, but we had a good time.'

'You were recruited at Cambridge?' asked Ward. It was a facile question, but he was curious.

The Chief smiled at the memory. 'Yes. Him first, of course, he was always the more intelligent, but then he basically said, 'hang on, I've got this cousin...', and there you have it.'

'I'm sorry, sir,' offered Ward, a little emptily.

'Thank you, Mike. I'm sorry to bore you with an old man's history, but I thought...'

Ward smiled. 'I ought to know.'

'Precisely.' The Chief relit his pipe and pondered. 'On a professional level, and that is what matters here, is that a colleague of ours was killed in the line of fire. I need you to tell me why. I want to know why. I want to know that...well...it wasn't all a waste. Could you do that for me?'

It all raced through Ward's mind; the tape, the gunshots, the hysterical woman, the Chief's relationship to the victim. None of it mattered. He liked the Chief, very much, and could see that he was vexed and in pain. 'Of course, sir.'

The Chief leaned back in his sumptuous leather chair, at last able to relax. 'Thank you.'

Ward's eyes narrowed. 'It's business, sir. Somebody killed one of ours. That's all there is to it.' He knew that the Chief would like the detachment, the shedding of the personal for the general good. It justified the expenses.

Ward could see the relief upon the Chief's face. He wasn't just judged by results any more, but by how much it all cost. 'Good. Mrs Thornton has a ticket for the 16.15 to Saint Quintian from Heathrow for you.'

Ward smiled. The Chief had known all along that the rat would not resist the cheese.

The Chief got up from his chair and went to the

window. Outside the drizzly day had barely evolved from night. 'I had hoped you would accept the mission,' said the Chief. 'I can't think of anyone better.' He turned around and stared at Ward. 'Find out who was behind this, Ward, then do what you have to do.'

Ward stood and buttoned his jacket. 'Yes, sir.' He turned to go. 'First class, is it, sir?'

'Baggage,' said the Chief. 'Cuts. You know?'

4. Hôtel Hibiscus

As Mike Ward stepped onto the tarmac from the British Airways 747, he could not believe how much different it was now to his first flight abroad. The 707 that he had taken in the early sixties as a very junior reporter, had been cramped; it wasn't until all these years later, when he travelled on a 747, that he appreciated just how confined the 707 had been, but what a marvel it was; at the time, the sleekness of the 707 was new, right down to the sail-tail and that sleek, cigar-shaped body.

Now, the 747 with its cephalic head and unashamedly large torso was the height of luxury. No more numb limbs due to the lack of leg-room, a cabin in which you could, almost, walk along normally, instead of craning your neck to avoid head-injury, seats that allowed a bit of movement rather that cramped hips. The world had moved on in its barely noticed but significant way. Ward guessed that it was only in hindsight that people realised how massive the strides taken were. Tomorrow, the world would see what the 747 had achieved, but perhaps only in hindsight, but today it was merely another first-world delight, a toy, a means to an end, no questions asked.

Saint Quintian was an island in recovery. In the late seventies it had struggled mightily between the appeal of communism and the freedom of democracy. It was normal for a teething nation to bite down on the first thing that the world shoved into its mouth. The world developed so quickly, especially after the introduction of satellites and world-wide media, that it had developed and identity crisis. Small, unestablished nations, whether within the commonwealth or set free from the greedy grasp of imperialism, had to find themselves a place not only in the world, but in their own minds. Telstar had started the TV revolution in the early sixties and now it was almost impossible for any free country to remain opinion-free and uninfluenced by bias.

Saint Quintian had been through its own problems. It was close enough to the United States to feel the heat generated by the growth in science and technology and afraid enough of those advances, and the frightening amount of money and responsibility that came with them, to push the country towards a theoretically simpler life, where equality ruled over finance. 'Four legs good, two legs better' or was it the other way around. No one seemed sure any more.

It was the schizophrenia of the developing world, induced by the heady drugs of modernism and reward, and the stasis and certainty of the old ways. One was safe, the other dangerous, but which was which? Who knew?

In the end, after rioting and bloodshed and death and the manipulation of the so-called superpowers, democracy won. Either way, they ended up as slaves to the masters, such was the way of the world, but they got their factories and their jobs and their TV and movies and supermarkets and a wage which, only a few years ago, would have seemed unattainable for the ordinary man, never mind the fact that inflation ate away at those profits like piranha and the more you had, the more would be taken away.

Beneath the surface of the body whole though, lay a constant itch for change, and it would forever be the same, until man crawled back into the sea.

Ward had asked that attention not be drawn to him on arrival. He wanted simply to be another anonymous, tired, stressed traveller who longed for clean sheets and a mini-bar. The fewer people who knew that he would be there, the more chance he had of taking people off-guard.

He had been booked into the Hotel Hibiscus, an apparently comfortable three-star hotel which Mrs Thornton said came within the budget, but only just.

Even though it was warm, noticeable enough once you stepped off the plane, it was not unpleasant. He had arrived in what was the Saint Quintian spring, so the temperatures were mid-eighties and it didn't have that oppressive humidity which other countries could have, which sucked the water from your body and left you bogged down in your own soggy clothing.

After an uneventful trip through customs, Ward found a cab outside the airport and made his way through the usual concrete clutter that surrounded every airport in the world until they crossed an invisible barrier into the barren heart of the island. There were cacti of various sorts thriving on parched, sandy ground and beyond, lush hills covered by trees and above them, the ever-present clouds that sat like silver on sapphire as the sun fought for a way through. There were still areas of sugar cane to be seen, those tall hybrids of grass with the appearance of bamboo. The villages they passed through could be described as glorified shanty towns, concrete, multi-coloured bungalows that had seen better days, occasionally interspersed with the local shops which had adverts for Sprite or Coco-Cola nailed colourfully to the eaves.

Every now and then they would see the factories that kept the villages alive, all simply named for the purpose for which they were built: L'Usine de Chaussures, L'Emporium de Chemise, even T-shirt City and Jeans Genies. However they described themselves, there was little disguising the fact that they were a-buck-a-day mills dedicated to maximum profit with minimal cost. The people could afford to eat. Well, they had to, didn't they, otherwise they wouldn't have had the energy to work.

When he had been a journalist, Ward had been on the merry-go-round of exposing all the major clothing labels.

Some had changed their practices, some had simply disguised them. Although he had never been to Saint Quintian, he had seen it all before.

The Hotel Hibiscus was about fifty miles from the airport, on the island's west coast. The road into the resort had clearly been smartened up for the tourists. It had been freshly tarmacked so that, unlike the rest of the island, there wasn't the constant, bone-shuddering jolt into a pothole. It was lined by palm trees and a multicoloured, vibrant variety of shrubs.

When they pulled into the apron of the hotel, they rounded a central reservation, topped by the most vivid, probably dyed, grass, again with the ubiquitous palm trees, and with the name of the hotel spelled out in, naturally, hibiscus.

Ward was astounded by the difference between it and the villages through which he had just passed. It must have been a Mecca for work to the locals and they must have felt a complex mixture of emotions as they walked the couple of miles from their homes to this paradise each day. Were they filled with envy or pride? There was no doubt that the resort will have paid more than the factories, but to have your poverty rubbed in your face each day must have been hard to take. It was easy to see why socialism and its less-beneficial 'associates' would find seed in this scorched land.

Ward paid off the driver and walked into the hotel foyer. The air-conditioning was immediately noticeable; not only was the temperature consistent and pleasant, but he could smell the slightly artificial odour of the AC, that mix of air in a can and the attempt to disguise it with hidden scents, mostly, of course, the Hibiscus. The floor was a parquet floor, brightly shone with that welcome patina of wear and care. The lighting, welcome after the blinding outside, was subtle.

Ward walked to the desk.

'Good evening,' he said. 'Mike Ward?'

The girl, pretty, straight back, efficient, welcomed him with a practiced smile. 'Good evening, Mr Ward, we've been expecting you'.

Ward had a moment of déjà vu. 'That's comforting,' he said.

The girl smiled at him. 'Room 234, second floor.' She laid a flat hand towards a bellboy. 'Pierre will be happy to guide you.'

Ward smiled as a lad, who can't have been more than sixteen, grabbed his bags. Luckily, Ward travelled light.

'Thank you, Pierre.' Ward smiled at him. 'Old enough to drag bags but too young to drink, eh?'

The boy smiled at him. '234?'

'234,' confirmed Ward. He turned to the pretty girl behind the desk. 'Any messages?' He expected nothing.

The girl turned at looked at the 234 pigeonhole. 'Yes, sir.'

Ward's heart fell. Nobody was supposed to know he was on the island.

The girl handed him the message. He opened it. It was simple and to the point.

'LA FOLLE, 11 AM.'

Ward tucked the message into his pocket. Who the hell knew that he was here? In fact, who the hell knew that he had arrived before he had?

The hairs on the back of his neck prickled. 'Thank you,' he said to the girl. He looked at her name tag. 'Marianne. Do you know who this was from?'

'No, Mr Ward. It was by telephone.'

Ward cursed quietly. 'Okay, thanks. Could you send some food up to my room?'

The girl picked up a pen and laid it ready upon a

notepad. 'What would you like?'

'Anything,' said Ward flatly. 'You choose, but throw in a good bottle of whisky with it, would you?'

'Yes, sir.'

'And could you arrange for a driver for me? I'll need to get around. The same driver each day, if possible.'

Marianne smiled warmly. 'The hotel has a pool of drivers, Mr Ward, no problem. We can dedicate one to you for your stay.'

As he turned to go, he hesitated and turned back to Marianne. 'La Folle?'

'A restaurant in Saint Jeanne, the capital. Very good; very expensive.'

'Thank you.'

He hoped that whoever had made the arrangements was paying.

Ward followed Pierre to the lift. He was shattered and needed food, drink and sleep; even a couple of hours of deep sleep would refresh him.

Once Pierre had gone, Ward went through his bags and took out a small bug detector. He scanned the room inch by inch until, to his deep disappointment, he detected a small listening device behind an oil painting of some hibiscus and another in the room's phone. He sat on the edge of the bed and shook his head, wondering if it would make any difference at all if he asked to move rooms. Probably not. Every room would be taken except the other one that they had set aside for him. Hr ripped away the device behind the painting and crushed it underfoot. Who was at the other end of that? he wondered. Maybe it was just a recorder, noiselessly recording all that happened, to be examined later. He half-hoped that there was sweaty little man in a darkened room filled with cigarette smoke and misery.

A knock at the door took him out of his thoughts.

'Yep?'

'Room service, Mr Ward.'

'Come in.'

The door opened and a waiter in a bright yellow jacket with white trousers and highly polished black shoes came into the room. He parked the trolley at the only table in the room.

Ward tipped him and he left. 'Thank you, sir. Please enjoy.'

Ward could see that there was a table and chairs outside a set of French windows, so opened them and pushed the trolley outside.

He looked at the contents of the trolley. Marianne had thought of everything; Lobster, griot - cubes of pork marinated in chilli, onion and citrus juices - fried chicken and rice and various sorbets.

Most pleasing of all was the bottle of Johnnie Walker Black Label. He cracked it open and poured out half a tumbler of the dark, smoky liquid. He didn't bother with ice and water, merely drank half of it, put the tumbler down and picked a sample of everything from the trolley. It was all delicious, the griot in particular, and the lemon sorbet cleansed his pallet wonderfully; he wasn't a lover of citrus, but it was perfect, especially with the whisky to finish it off.

He went to the outside table and sat on a chair with his feet up.

He could not get over his initial disappointment. It was not a good start to the trip. His anonymity had been compromised, perhaps the whole mission, whatever *that* was, compromised too.

The Chief had been in the dark about what he was going to find or even what Lawrie Stuart had been up to, although he must have been up to something. Ward had a murder and that was it. The local police would have trodden all over the office where he died, so there would probably be nothing to find there.

He had to be philosophical about it all. He had been found out sooner rather than later, so he had to take advantage of that. His element of surprise might have been lost, but that merely gave him freer rein; no need to hide in the shadows.

In the morning he would go to the High Commission in Saint Jeanne. Then at eleven o'clock he would go to La Folle for his mysterious meeting. It might be a trap, it might not, but he didn't think that it was a meeting he could afford to miss.

He had a shower and then slipped naked between the cool sheets.

He fell asleep instantly.

5. The High Commissioner's Strife

Ward's allocated driver was a grumpy bastard. He had the gnarled face of a walnut and a personality to match. His thick, black hair was combed back in an attempt to bring out the rock and roller in him but it had fallen limply and simply accentuated the misery within and the hard shell without. Ward had been told that his name was Jacques and that he was the hotel's best driver.

Ward was alarmed to see that the car he had been allocated was an orange, three-door 1977 Ford Pinto. They had a reputation for exploding due to a fuel-tank fault and at that time Ford were in all sorts of trouble because they had known about the problem all along. People had died. Even the smallest rear-ender had been enough to cause a fireball. The Pinto had been made to be cheap and it lived up to it but the 2.8 litre V6 engine had a tidy swiftness about it. Ward knew that he was in for a hell of a ride and hoped that the miserable Jacques was as good a driver as claimed.

They reached the High Commission's offices, a typically grey, bland government building, at nine o'clock. Ward asked Jacques to park around the corner and then walked the short distance to the building. He was met at the gates by a rather surly individual with a rifle slung loosely over his shoulder and sweat bands at his armpits. Ward took an instant dislike to him.

He held up an ID card. 'Tell the commissioner Dragonfly is here,' he demanded.

'Who?'

Ward leaned in towards his booth. 'Dragonfly.'

'What's your first name?' asked the guard as he scratched at his two-day-old stubble.

Ward felt himself twitch. 'That's it,' he said. 'Just Dragonfly.' He waited as the man paused. 'Do it now.'

The guard picked up the phone and mumbled into it. He put the phone down and raised the gate. 'Thank you, Mr...Dragonfly.'

Ward walked through the gate to the embassy. He wondered if that was the best defence Britain had; a sweaty, overweight man with a rifle hung loosely around his sloping shoulders, two-day-old stubble and a jobsworth attitude.

Once inside, it was assumed that he was now safe, never mind the fact that he had merely outwitted a mollusc.

He was shown to the High Commissioner's ante-chamber and asked to take a seat. The room was high and airy with sash windows open wide and the smell of floor polish, the same smell that Ward had encountered at school. It still nauseated him. A fan, slightly misaligned, chuck-chucked around with the constant threat of flying loose and decapitating anybody nearby.

Eventually, the door to the High Commissioner's office opened and Ward was greeted warmly by the man himself.

'Mr Ward. Welcome to Saint Quintian. I hope your company can find something in common with the island which allows you to do business.' The man held out his hand. Ward took it. It had a firm grip. 'I'm Bill Buckley. Do come on in.'

Ward followed the man into the office, a cool piece of acreage. He studied the HC. He was in his mid-fifties with a round, ruddy, amiable face and the jowls of a faithful hound. His red hair was grey at the temples and his stomach overhung his belt in a way that, on him, looked comfortable and right.

Ward liked him immediately. He had the kind of easy-going nature that put people at their ease, but his steel blue eyes never smiled. Buckley studied the person in front of him and made his assessment as he talked. He'd been too long in the game to take anyone at face value.

The HC didn't sit behind his desk, but invited Ward to sit in a cane chair, one each of which was parked next to a cane, glass-topped table. 'Can I get you anything? Tea? Coffee? A flagon of beer?' He smiled.

'I'm fine,' said Ward. 'Thank you.'

Buckley nodded. 'The room's clean. It's swept twice a day, before I come in and when I leave. Anyone eavesdropping deserves the credit. What can I do for you, Dragonfly?'

'Mike will do. I need some help,' admitted Ward.

'I'm aware of that,' said Buckley. 'The Chief had a word.' He chuckled. 'We were told to do nothing unless you contacted us, and now, here you are. So, how can I help you?'

Ward crossed his legs and relaxed a little in his chair. 'What do you know about the Lawrie Stuart murder?'

Buckley sighed, crossed his arms and grunted. Touchy subject, realised Ward. 'It has been dealt with by the local police. We tried to get our snouts in there but were told quite firmly to back off. Naturally, I protested, what with Stuart being one of ours, but I wasn't even allowed to examine the scene.'

Ward's brow furrowed. 'How hard did you try, if you don't mind me asking?'

'I went to the top, to The Prime Minister, Perry Abadie; had a meeting with him.'

'And?'

Buckley frowned. 'He declined my 'help' and said that it was in the hands of the police. He said that to interfere with police business could be considered political abuse, an intrusion by government in the workings of the law.'

Ward stuttered a laugh. 'That's a handy revelation! Since when had decorum become a part of the way of justice in this part of the world?'

'It can when it suits them,' said Buckley firmly. 'I did point out that Saint Quintian was a part of Her Majesty's Commonwealth, but he simply shrugged. It doesn't have the weight that it used to.'

Ward sighed heavily. 'And Mrs Benson-Haines, what of her?'

'I was allowed to see her. That was unpleasant, I can tell you.' Buckley shook his head at the memory. 'She had no family, so I was next in line, so to speak. We'll take her home and bury her with her husband.'

'Were you able to see her house?'

'Oh, yes. There was no problem there. We were given the keys straight away.'

'Any servants?'

'A butler, Henrick Chery, and his wife, Evie. He'd been with her for years. He buttled and she cleaned and occasionally cooked.'

'What was going on between her and Lawrie?'

'We found nothing to say that they had any sort of relationship. Lawrie was parachuted in to do some sort of top-secret work at the *Gazette*. The regular editor was sent on leave, all paid for by Her Majesty of course, while Lawrie, for whatever reason, took over the ship. He was only meant to stand in for a few months apparently, until whatever it was that he had to do was done.'

Ward tugged at an ear lobe in mild irritation. This was getting him no closer to the truth. 'She called him Lawrie.'

'I beg your pardon?'

'On the recording we have of the event. We record all calls in and out of the communications room. She came into the room and said, 'How dare you! Lawrie! How dare you!' and then shot him twice. She sounded like a woman betrayed. And Lawrie is an intimate term. She didn't say 'Mr

Stuart' or call him 'Editor' or any one of the list of insults usually aimed at journalists. It was just 'Lawrie'.'

'I see,' said Buckley. This was all beginning to drown him. He and Ward were both at the point where they felt saturated.

Ward looked at his watch. 'I have to be somewhere at eleven o'clock. Is there any chance I could take up a few of your precious hours later?'

'By all means. The Chief made it clear that you are a priority. I'll clear my diary for the next couple of days, get someone junior to offer my apologies. They can practice their diplomatic skills.'

Ward stood and held out a hand. 'Thank you, High Commissioner.'

The High Commissioner reciprocated. 'Bill's fine. I don't mind all that formality on state business but, to be honest, it just makes me cringe.' He walked Ward to the door. 'I haven't liked this whole business from the start, Mike. What with Stuart playing his cards so close to his chest and the frankly obstructive behaviour of the police and Prime Minister...well...it's all caused me a bit of internal strife, I can tell you.' Buckley opened the door. 'Just pop back at your convenience. I'll make myself available.'

Ward stepped out of the office and wandered through the wood-lined halls and decorative cornices that threw the passer-by back into the old Empire.

He understood the reluctance to change it all; there was a safety to be found in the myth of the pink, but times had moved on; the Empire was no more. The nation could no longer hide behind titles and possessions when those possessions were gone and the titles had become little more than words.

6. La Folle

There were few what you would call grand buildings on Saint Quintian. There were large buildings, some modern, some an elaborate remnant of the Victorian era, but La Folle was set inside a *grand* building.

Within walking distance of the High Commission in Saint Jeanne, it was part of an impressive edifice that stretched along one side of the Rue Anglais which had been part of the administrative centre of colonial rule. It was built to impress, a sign of power as well as wealth, and it certainly did that. Now it had become a catacomb of businesses; boutiques, salons, a market, jewellery shops, book shops, music shops and restaurants.

The finest of the frontages belonged to La Folle. It was inordinately, unabashedly French, aimed at the small percentage of wealthy on the island, the ex-pat colony and the tourists. It had a red, white and blue awning (à *La Marseillaise* as opposed to *God Save the Queen*) that stretched along its entire length and exposed some of those eating inside through four huge panes of glass which were boxed in by Corinthian columns, all of which supported a fine stone edifice pierced by a series of sash windows. From the outside, especially in the sunshine, the inside was mysteriously dark.

Ward walked through the large wooden doors, held open by unseen, substantial door hooks between them and the walls.

At the entrance, a local in a smart pair of buff trousers and matching jacket gave a little nod to those entering and those departing and opened the car doors of those who found the effort too much.

Ward was greeted by the wide smile of a sharply attired girl - white blouse, black trousers with straightened shiny black hair that fell freely across her collar bones - on the front desk, a thick, bound reservations diary in front of her.

'Good morning, sir. May I help?'

Ward looked around the restaurant, all square tables, white linen and glinting silver. 'I hope so. My name's Ward...'

'Ah, yes, Mr Ward. Follow me, please. We have a table for you.' She grabbed a menu and walked away without hesitation.

Impressed by the girl's preparation, annoyed by his name being known once again, he followed the girl.

Ten feet away, he saw a black cat dart underneath one of the tables. He wasn't even certain that he had seen it; maybe it had been some sort of *trompe l'oeil*.

'Did I just see a cat in here?' asked Ward.

'House cat,' said the girl, as if it was normal for an expensive restaurant to house a cat. Sure enough the cat reappeared and ran under the cover of another table.

Ward was led to a table for two, hidden behind several pots of chilli plants - red, green and yellow - the same colours as the Saint Quintian flag, which created a colourful barrier and gave privacy to those behind them. The table itself was a standard, square table big enough for two, frosted with a crisp white table cloth and bejewelled by overwrought cutlery. It was very nouveau, very late Victorian in its presentation, very fitting with the environment, but like everything he had seen in Saint Jeanne, it lent nothing to modernity. The temporal stasis might well have appealed to those who felt the need to step back in time and pretend that the madness of the twentieth century had not yet passed.

The girl invited him to sit. 'My name is Mirlande. I will be your waitress today, Mr Ward. I shall give you a few moments to choose your beverage.'

Ward looked at the wine menu and gasped internally

at the cost. The Chief would be apoplectic. 'Can I take it that I'm the guest?'

Mirlande smiled. 'Of course, sir. Please, whatever you want.'

'And who *is* paying?'

'I have no idea, Mr Ward.' The girl maintained her well-rehearsed smile.

'So, you have no idea who booked the table?'

'Only the name in the diary, sir.'

'So, who would know?'

The smile never left her lips. 'I'm afraid I don't know.'

Ward clenched his jaw. 'Fine.' He looked at the wine menu. He honestly did not have a clue what he was looking at, some of the names were famous and familiar, but knew that he preferred red and so went for one halfway down the list. 'I'll have that one,' he said.

Mirlande raised her eyebrows. 'A very good choice, sir. I shall leave you with the food menu and return when you are ready. The sommelier will bring your wine.' She hesitated a moment. 'You won't go wrong with the steak. That red will complement it beautifully,' she said. 'Or I would recommend the snapper. It's light, but meaty, with some Creole roasted vegetables. Not too heavy for lunch.'

'I'll take your word for it,' said Ward, 'but I'd rather have white wine with fish. Any suggestions?'

'You can't go wrong with a chilled Sauvignon Blanc.'

Ward closed the menu. 'Then I'll have snapper and sauvignon. Alliterively pleasing if nothing else.' He smiled tightly. 'I'll take the wine straight away.'

Mirlande returned his smile. 'Certainly, sir. I'll send the sommelier.'

Ward watched her as she left and disappeared behind the chilli plants. She had a confidence born of experience.

Never mind the food, she knew people, but he wouldn't have trusted her an inch.

The sommelier came quickly and decorked the bottle of Sauvignon in front of Ward. He filled the glass and inch, expecting Ward to taste it, but Ward just indicated that he should fill the glass. The sommelier's glare told Ward that he believed him a philistine. Ward shrugged within. The sommelier was probably right. He liked what he liked and did not worry too much about refinement when it came to his choice of food and drink. He put it down to his time in the army, where food had been grub and intended to sustain, and then living alone for so long after his divorce, as he travelled rapidly and relentlessly from one place to another as a journalist, when food became a snatched necessity rather than a pleasure.

The sommelier, satisfied that he could no more for Ward, left him too it.

Ward tried the wine. It was tinged with citrus and refreshing. The alcohol oozed into his veins and he felt a little tension drain away. He should go steady, he thought. There was a long day ahead.

To his surprise the cat jumped onto the chair opposite. It sat with wide, green eyes and pondered Ward.

'Hello, Kitty,' said Ward. 'Do you think you should be there? Unless of course, you're the one paying the bill.' The cat stared impassively. 'No, I thought not. Well, you'll have to go when my food comes. If you're not paying, you're not sharing.'

It took only a few minutes for the snapper and Creole vegetables to appear. It smelled amazing; a blend of spices that teased at his nostrils, settled on his tongue and enraged his appetite.

The only thing Ward didn't like was that the fish had been presented whole. He disliked the curled gills and frosted eyes of the corpse, the tiny, sharp teeth inside the gaping mouth and the rigid, blackened tongue. He didn't want to be reminded that his food had had a previous life. It was like having a cow dumped on your plate and trying to enjoy your steak.

The cat had not moved. Ward picked up a side plate and put it on the floor. It jumped down in anticipation. 'This is your lucky day, Kitty. I hope you like dead head and eyeballs.'

As if understanding him, the cat sat primly and licked its lips. Ward carefully prised the head from the rest of the fish and put it on the plate.

Without thanks, the cat dived in. Ward watched as it walloped down the treat. As it did so though, it began to gag on the food and then to struggle for breath. Quite suddenly, it collapsed, writhed and shuddered, then vomited. Within seconds it was dead.

Ward stared at the cat in disbelief, then at the fish on his plate. He leaned forward and cautiously sniffed it. He could smell nothing other than the powerful collection of spices.

What the hell? Was this supposed to be his last supper?

He shook with fear and rage and disgust and could feel beads of sweat begin to roll down his face and chest. Was that why he was seated there? So that he wouldn't be seen to collapse by anybody and could be removed at leisure? How could he have been so stupid as to fall for such a childish trap?

He gulped down some more wine - at least he knew that was safe - and gave himself a minute to find some composure. How he would have killed for a cigarette!

He saw the head of a waiter bob by the chilli plants and jumped up. 'Excuse me.'

The waiter turned towards him. 'Sir?'

'I seem to have lost my appetite. Could I have this to take away please?'

The waiter looked at him quizzically. Ward stood between him and the table, so that he didn't catch sight of the cat. 'Anything will do,' he pressed. 'Tupperware, perhaps?'

'I will do my best, sir.'

The waiter went off in search of Tupperware.

Ward quickly hid the cat under the table and covered its pool of vomit up with a dropped napkin. The fewer questions he had to face and the less time he had to spend in La Folle, the better.

A few uneasy moments later, the waiter returned with a Tupperware pot. He intended to carefully place the meal in as presentable order inside the container as he could, but Ward deflected his hand.

'I'll do it,' he said. He picked up a spare napkin and held the edge of the plate with it. Without any ceremony, he scraped the contents of the plate into the plastic tub, followed by the knife and fork. 'Don't worry,' he said to the bemused waiter. 'I'll bring them back.' He pushed the Tupperware lid very firmly into place, then reached under the table and dragged out the corpse of the cat.

The horrified waiter gasped and stepped back as Ward tucked the dead animal under his arm. 'Claude?'

So that had been his name.

'Pudding,' said Ward.

He walked past the waiter and through the restaurant as calmly as he could, all the time resisting the urge to run outside and throw up on the pavement.

As he strode towards the door, past a river of silence that grew longer with each step he took, he became aware that Mirlande was no longer anywhere to be seen.

7. The Bureau Des Affaires

Ward was shown into Buckley's office. Buckley's secretary, very aware of the dead cat under Ward's arm, gingerly opened the door and then retreated.

'How was your meeting?' asked Bill Buckley without looking up as he absently flicked through some paperwork at his desk.

'Toxic,' said Ward flatly. He dropped the Tupperware and cat on Buckley's desk. 'Do you have access to a lab to take a look at these? Urgently and quietly.'

Buckley reeled as he saw what Ward had deposited in front of him. He nodded slowly. 'I won't even try to understand.' He pushed a button on his intercom.

'Don't let anybody touch it,' warned Ward. 'I don't know what it is, but whatever it is causes instant death.'

Buckley nodded as the phone at the other end was picked up. 'Miss Grace, would you get the chemical hazards team over to my office please?' He waited as Miss Grace spoke. 'Yes,' he said casting an eye over the cat and the pot. 'Quite serious.' He put the phone down and glared at Ward. 'What's going on?'

Ward helped himself to one of Buckley's myriad of drinks from a nearby cabinet and sunk into a chair. 'A cat died.'

Buckley followed suit. 'I can see that.' He sat down opposite Ward and waited for him to speak.

'I think someone tried to kill me,' said Ward. 'No, I'm certain someone tried to kill me. If it hadn't been for that cat, I would've died.'

'Where?'

'La Folle.'

'La Folle?'

'Yes,' said Ward. 'I'm going to give it a poor review.'

Ward explained what had happened. He was shaken, he had to admit. There was something to be said for a man with a knife or a gun, at least you knew where you stood, but to find yourself prey to an invisible killer was a step too far. He felt more vulnerable now that he had ever felt. It was impossible to fight something you couldn't see. It was Sarin gas and Soman and Cyanide. It was the monsters that crawled unseen though the dark.

The chemical hazard team arrived. They cautiously took the Tupperware and bagged it, placed the cat into an airtight bag and left Ward and Buckley in silence.

'Fancy a trip out?' asked Buckley.

'A bit of a distraction?' Ward smiled thinly.

'It can't hurt.'

'Sure, where to?'

'The Benson-Haines' place.'

Ward perked up. 'Sure.'

Buckley grabbed his jacket from the back of his chair. 'Is your driver still around?'

'Grumpy? He's parked outside.'

Buckley rubbed his hands together. 'Good. We'll use him. It's a little more subtle than taking the Jag with a Union flag on the wing and HC1 on the number plate.'

'That's fine by me.'

Buckley made for the door. 'I've asked someone to meet us there, by the way.'

Ward looked sharply at the High Commissioner. 'Oh? Who?' He wasn't sure that he wanted anybody else in on this. On the other hand, it seemed that most of the island already knew he was here.

'Don't worry,' reassured Buckley. 'They're a friend.'

'Well,' said Ward resignedly. 'God knows, I could do with more of those at the moment.'

'She was a piece of work, you know,' said Buckley as Jacques negotiated yet another pothole.

'Benson-Haines? In what way?' asked Ward.

Buckley looked out of the open car window. The breeze on his face was warm and offered little relief. 'Well, far be it from me to speak ill of the dead, but she was, by all accounts, a bit of a bitch.'

'Don't worry,' said Ward. 'She can't hear you. In what way was she a bit of a bitch?'

'Well, it was before my time, I've only been here a couple of years, but in the late sixties and early seventies there was a very large ex-pat community here. Very cliquey. You know how it was, the tail-end of the Empire, its light burning brightly before it finally died...'

'Oh, I know,' said Ward.

'Simply put, she was the queen bee. Her husband, Sir Sean Haines, was a little too laissez-faire for her. I mean, he was good at his job, always had been, hence the knighthood, but he wasn't one for the, what should I say? Social life? He was happy to do what he did for the job, but never really wanted to be the one to hold the soirées or the poolside drinks parties or even bother with the social ladder-climbing, at which his wife excelled. Those who knew him said that he was a diplomat; those who knew her said that she was an assassin.' He sighed deeply, as if exasperated by the people about whom he was talking. 'That's often the way it is with couples, don't you find? One is liked, the other either loathed or feared. In her case, I think perhaps she was both loathed and feared.'

Ward grunted. 'I never understood that mentality, but you're right.' He became pensive. He had been caught in that web before. 'So, what went wrong?'

'The same as usually happens. Their star faded when he retired, he died and she fell out of favour.'

'What happened to him?' Ward's mind flicked back to the deep green eyes of the dead cat. It had become symbolic of the whole shambolic non-meeting, the kind of thing that would snap back into his mind as he wandered the supermarket on a random summer day.

Buckley threw up out of the car window. Ward looked at him in astonishment.

'I'm sorry,' said the High Commissioner. 'I always get car sick in the back seat. Usually travel up front in the Jag.' He took out a handkerchief and wiped his mouth.

Ward wanted to laugh. It was one of the funniest things he had seen in a while and was the perfect tonic.

'Go ahead,' said Buckley, as if sensing Ward's thoughts. 'It's alright to laugh. It always amused my wife.'

Ward broke, but only a little. 'I'm sorry. I had no idea. You could have sat in the front with Jacques.'

He saw Jacques' eyes in the rear-view mirror. They were thunder. He would have to clean and polish the car now.

'No,' said Buckley. 'It's done now. Once is usually enough. Funny thing is I'm alright on aeroplanes. It's just cars.'

There was a moment's silence. 'Wife?' asked Ward eventually.

Buckley didn't look at him at first. It was clearly quicksand upon which Ward was standing.

Buckley cleared his throat as if to purge the words. 'She killed herself. Overdose.'

'Christ, I'm sorry,' said Ward. 'I didn't mean to...'

Buckley put a hand on Ward's arm and stopped him. 'It's okay. I've grown...used to the idea. She was a very unhappy woman, not because of me or anybody else. She was just one of those people born with a hole in their soul which they could never fill.'

'How long ago?' asked Ward.

'Three years. We were in Sri Lanka at the time.' He let out a shuddering sigh. 'I suppose, in hindsight, it was inevitable, but I loved her and hoped that she might outlive me, perhaps find something...anything...'

'I'm sorry, Bill,' said Ward.

Buckley straightened himself up. 'Don't be. I've learned that nobody was at fault, except perhaps for Mother Nature. She's the biggest bitch of all.'

The Pinto, with a final lurch through a crater in the road, which made Ward wince as he thought of the petrol tank, pulled into Chaddleworth's driveway. It was a steep climb, thankfully along impeccable tarmac, that took itself between carefully nurtured foliage.

The Baie de Dieu was at the north-west of the island. It was becoming a hub for tourists as hotels began to spring up. This part of the island was the hottest by far, but it also tended more towards cloud in the afternoon and you were pretty much guaranteed a five-minute shower at three pm most days as the weight of the water seemed just too much for the sky to hold. Within minutes, it would pass, the sun would turn it all to steam and the cycle would start again.

Chaddleworth sat four hundred feet above all the new buildings going up. Its view of the bay was unimpeded by any of the work, which seemed to have gone on forever, and the absolute peace that surrounded the property, which almost cocooned it, was paradisiacal.

Ward could see how it had appealed to them, an old married couple seeing out their retirement with plants and birds as children. 'How lovely,' he said, almost to himself.

It was exactly the sort of place in which he wouldn't have minded spending his final years, away from the rat-race, away from the smog, away from the unions and the masters, away from the cold, the long nights and short days.

Then he thought of the pleasure of a summer evening at the pub, the smell of beer wafting through the back door into the garden, where people chatted happily and ate their scampi and were more than content with the English summer. There was nowhere in the world, and Ward had seen a lot of it, that beat the English summer. It was the horrors of winter which made it perfect, so perhaps the winter was worth it, just for that.

'I was thinking of buying it,' said Buckley suddenly. 'One might as well die here as anywhere.'

'I can't say I'd blame you,' said Ward. 'Let me know if you want a house-boy. I wouldn't cost much.'

Jacques pulled the car up outside the bungalow. It was a surprisingly simple affair. It was flat-roofed to minimalise the impact of hurricanes but, apart from that, very much like any small bungalow you might find dotted about West Sussex. The gardens were the real star of the place; immaculate lawns edged by a whole host of colour and a view that Ward could have sat and stared at from dawn to dusk.

Buckley removed the house keys from his pocket and unlocked the front door. Inside it was as typically functional as most of these places were. The front door gave onto a small hallway. Straight ahead was the living room and to the left a rather splendid kitchen, presumably for her ladyship to be the hostess with the mostest.

Buckley led Ward into the living room. It was bigger than he had anticipated with large French doors leading to a small, paved area with table and chairs, the garden and *that* view.

The furniture in the living room was clearly not cheap. Ward guessed that they would have had it shipped in at great expense.

The living room was divided from the dining room

by a moveable lattice screen, composed of light-coloured Caribbean Rosewood, suspended from runners on the ceiling.

There were three bedrooms, all much of a muchness but, once again, dressed expensively. No doubt these would have been a part of the house tour when new initiates arrived.

It was odd though, walking through a dead house. There were still pairs of glasses lying around and half-read books, slippers and a teacup with the last half-inch of tea still in it, clinging to the sides of the cup as it turned. They were now all orphans, their fate undecided, almost certainly unwanted.

'As far as we can tell,' said Buckley, 'the only thing missing was the revolver she used to shoot Stuart with. It's difficult to tell, obviously, because the only people that really knew the place were the butler and his wife.'

Ward walked over to the bureau where the gun had been kept. 'I take it they've been questioned.' He began to sift through various bits of paperwork.

'Yes. She had given both of them the afternoon off. She gave Henrick some money to go to the cinema and for a meal. Actually, she gave them seventy-five dollars.'

Ward whistled softly. 'That must have been a month's wages for both of them.'

'It was more than a trip to the flicks and a meal, that's for certain.'

Ward pulled a letter out of an envelope and scanned it. It was a bank statement. A very healthy one. 'Was that out of character?'

'Completely,' said Buckley. 'She paid them a good wage and provided uniforms, but that was about it. By all accounts, she had never shown any more feelings towards them than as employer to employees, despite the years they had both worked for her.'

'But there were no problems with the relationship? Henrick couldn't have stolen that money and then claimed she had given it to him?'

Buckley considered the question, sidled to the French windows and opened them. A warm sea breeze embraced him. 'It's possible, I suppose.'

'Could we see their bank account?'

Buckley laughed cynically. 'These people would no more trust a bank than you or I would trust a cobra. Everything is cash. All part of the grey market. I doubt very much that they even pay any tax on their earnings. It would be different in the big factories and the businesses, of course. The employees would have to pay taxes. The companies have to present their accounts every year, but this sort of domestic arrangement is very casual and very little attention is ever paid to them. The grey economy keeps small businesses going which in turn helps keep the national economy ticking over. Nobody really wants to upset the apple cart.'

'Can I take all this?' Ward waved a hand at the paperwork inside the bureau.

'Sure, but it is now the property of Her Majesty's Government, so don't steal it or lose it.'

'Thanks,' said Ward. 'Did the police look through the papers?'

Buckley shook his head. 'Not as far as I know. I accompanied them as they went round the place, it only took them a few hours, and I never saw them look inside that bureau.'

'There are unspent bullets in here,' pointed out Ward. 'Wouldn't they be important evidence in the murder, at least linking her to the gun?'

'The gun was in her hand at the murder scene, Mike. She shot herself with it. As evidence goes, that's rather conclusive.'

'Fair comment,' agreed Ward reluctantly. 'All the same...What about what was on her at the time? Any belongings?'

'She had the clothes on her back, a gun and a set of car keys.'

'Car keys?'

'Of course, how else would she have got to Saint Jeanne?'

Ward felt like an idiot. Of course, that was how she had got there. He hadn't even asked himself how she had managed to get from the north west of the island to the capital. What was the matter with him?

'Where's the car now?'

'The impound at the Saint Jeanne police headquarters. We were meant to have collected it by now and brought it here, but we just haven't got round to it.'

'Could you get it for me?'

'No problem. I'll send someone over, tell them to park it in the HC car park and leave the keys on my desk.' Buckley came back inside. 'I'll find something to put those papers in.'

'Who were we meant to be meeting here by the way?' asked Ward.

Buckley snapped his fingers. 'Of course.' He went to the front door and beckoned someone in.

A moment later Jacques came through the door.

'Mike, meet Detective Sergeant Jacques Sanon. He's one of ours.'

8. Jacques of All Trades

Sanon had been a British plant in the police for years. 'The only condition,' said Buckley as they came away from Chaddleworth, 'was that he didn't rise too high in the ranks; that might have compromised his position. So, he's done a very good job of mixing insolence with excellence and staying in the lower ranks.'

'So, Grumpy actually turns out to be the Prince?' It was a little cynical, but Ward couldn't resist.

'If you want, yes,' said Buckley, perhaps a little defensively on Jacques' behalf.

'Why?' Ward thought that perhaps he already knew the answer, but a good conversation might distract him from the fear of a Pinto explosion.

'This island, as you well know, went through some rocky times a few years back. We thought the communists were about to pull another Cuba by poking at the fires; you know the sort of thing, rich versus poor, slavery versus freedom...'

'That's a bit extreme,' interrupted Ward.

'Not if you're the slave,' countered Buckley. 'Sure, people were paid for their work, but they were paid a pittance, barely reaching subsistence level. That's a hotbed for change, especially when all they had to do was turn a couple of corners and they were face to face with the grand houses of those who paid them; those who owned them. They had no choice but to go back, day after day. They had little or no education, little more to offer than their hands, and so they were trapped.'

The car shuddered as it's undercarriage was dragged through another pothole.

'You don't think the change might have done them good?' asked Ward. He was playing Devil's advocate, he knew that.

'We both know that's not true. They would simply be swapping one form of colonialism for another, only the other would have been more oppressive, more violent, less democratic. Look at Castro. Cuba is rife with poverty. Repression against minorities is practiced to the point of imprisonment and murder. There is no freedom of speech or movement.'

'But health and education are excellent,' said Ward. 'Infant mortality is less than in the United States and they have far more doctors than the US.'

'That's because the doctors have no choice about where they work. They aren't allowed to leave. And when does education stop and indoctrination begin?'

Ward sniffed. 'Batista was no angel.'

'No, he most certainly wasn't and he was equally guilty of repression and murder, maybe more so; he turned Cuba into a police state, murdered about twenty thousand people, but that doesn't justify replacing one monstrosity with another.'

'No,' conceded Ward. 'It doesn't and I appreciate your passion, Bill. We're not too far apart, I can assure you. Whenever I get off a plane in these places, I always find the journey from the airport depressing. The Hotel Hibiscus is an oasis, only not everyone can drink from it.'

'They have elections here, Mike. They have freedom of thought and speech. The freedom, or the golden handcuff, of capitalism is within their reach. It's a choice that they should be allowed to make.'

'What do you say, Jacques?' asked Ward.

Jacques shrugged. 'The people are irrelevant. Like Cuba, it's about East versus West. The USA doesn't want communism on its doorstep, the USSR wants to camp on America's porch. I know which I would prefer but, like everybody else, I am irrelevant. All I can do is choose and support the best option, but, in end, the best option is simply a matter of perspective.'

Ward thought of the clash between unions and government that constantly rattled the cages at home; the trivial, often petty, first-world problems that were as nothing next to the trials of others.

'I'm sorry, Jacques, that was flippant of me.'

For the first time since he had met him, Jacques smiled broadly. 'No, Mr Ward. You're the first person to ask me. Thank you, sir.'

'Jacques,' said Buckley, 'has been priceless. Every communist insurrection and breath of wind has been stopped since he came to us. He sees things and hears things than none of us would. The hotel is a wonderful source of information. His employers think he's working undercover against the drug trade and he brings home enough information to make him worth their while. It's dangerous work, but he's pretty well compensated by HM. He will actually be able to retire, unlike most of his fellow countrymen.'

'Yes,' said Jacques with a hint of sadness, 'but not here. I will go to Bermuda. If I stay here, someone will cut my throat. The local man who retires stands out.'

'Can I then assume,' said Ward, 'that Marianne allocated you to me and that therefore..?'

Buckley put a finger to his lips. 'Hush now, Mike. Let us not speak of such things,' he said with a wink. 'You have more friends than you realise.'

Ward gazed out of the Pinto's window. He'd had friends in the past and they had sold themselves to the Devil. Trust was hard to come by.

'I'll check through this paperwork as soon as possible,' said Ward, clutching a shoebox filled with all the paperwork from the bureau. 'You never know, there might be something.'

'Let me know if anything comes up,' offered Buckley. 'We're open twenty-four hours.' He chuckled. 'Well, after a couple of G and Ts, someone at the office is available.'

'That sounds fair enough,' said Ward. 'You've earned them.'

Ward looked in the rear-view mirror. 'Jacques, come and get me at six-thirty. I'll treat you to a night out.'

*

Ward was on the balcony when Jacques called for him. The sun was setting, leaving behind a bruised sky and a rippling finger of red pointing from the horizon to the land.

With the knock on the door, he put on his lightweight dark blazer and checked that his faithful Browning Hi-Power was properly concealed at his waist.

'Come in,' he called.

Jacques entered. He wore flip-flops, a red T-shirt, which had seen better days and a pair of age-polished black trousers. He looked at Ward in his expensive slacks, blazer and black loafers. 'I feel underdressed, Mr Ward,' he said.

'And now I feel overdressed,' retorted Ward.

'Where are we going, sir?'

'Dinner first, I think. Somewhere local with good beers. Can you think of anywhere?'

Jacques frowned apologetically. 'Not until you lose the school tie and gun, sir.'

'That obvious, is it?' asked Ward.

'The tie or the gun, sir?'

'I take your point.'

He would just have to go out without the gun. It

probably wasn't necessary anyway.

He changed into some jeans and a T-shirt. That way he might at least pass for a tourist being shown the town.

Jacques dipped into his back pocket. 'Before we go, sir. One more thing.' He handed Ward a piece of paper. It was the report from the laboratory about poor Claude and the fish.

'Bloody hell!' said Ward. 'Tetrodotoxin?'

Jacques nodded gravely. 'You were lucky.'

'Poor Kitty,' said Ward. He put the report in a drawer. 'Where do people get that poison from round here?'

'Tetrodotoxin, TTX, is common, sir; the puffer fish. People die accidentally each year from eating its balls and its liver.'

'Then why not leave it alone?'

'It's very tasty, sir,' said Jacques, as if that was obvious. 'But very expensive. Sometimes people catch their own fish, prepare it badly and...' He ran a finger across his throat.

'Any chance that it could have been accidental?'

'No, sir. You were eating snapper.'

Ward winced. 'That was a stupid question, wasn't it?'

'Not your best, sir.'

Ward slipped a billfold full of notes into his pocket. He wouldn't chance his wallet. 'Okay, take me somewhere to eat. And you'd better stop calling me sir.'

'Yes, Mr Ward.'

The streets of Saint Jeanne hustled and bustled as people went out and tried to forget the hard slog of the day. They wouldn't, couldn't, spend much, but they could sit outside the rum-joints and chat away the night with only a couple of drinks and good company.

Jacques pulled the car up and parked it in a dark corner of the street, away from the anaemic streetlights.

'Some people are very nosey,' he said, by way of an explanation.

He and Ward walked onto the main street and were greeted by all shades of the spectrum, each colour falling from an open doorway to yawn onto the street.

Jacques led Ward to what looked like little more than a hole in the wall. 'Best food on the island, Mr Ward.'

He stepped inside and Ward followed. It was like the Tardis. The place was full and loud and cheerful. It smelled of sweat and rum and spices. There must have been fifteen tables, all square and unpretentious, covered in gingham tablecloths, with various condiments in the centre of the table and four very aged wooden chairs around each. The padding had clearly left them some time ago and all that was left was a shiny, faux-leather dip.

Above the smell of rum and sweat however, the air was filled with fried onions in butter and spices and lightly-scorched flesh, whether it was goat, beef, pig or fish.

Nobody turned to look at the tourist who had just come through the door. The owner gave a friendly wave to Jacques and pointed out a table.

'I take it they know you,' said Ward, his voice raised slightly above the jazz-tinged Creole music that emanated from a couple of large speakers at either side of the room. Ward liked the sound of it. It had a bit of Jimmy Smith's Chicken Shack style of jazz blended with reggae and very distinctive drums, that always just about managed to stay in time as they wandered off on their own way before returning home before the door was locked on them.

'I come here a lot,' said Jacques. 'I sometimes bring tourists, as a guide, you know? They appreciate the business.'

Ward raised his eyebrows in appreciation. It was all good so far. 'Well, be my guide and choose my food. Let's avoid the snapper though, eh?'

Jacques rough-hewn face softened as a smile crossed its tough terrain. 'Blowfish it is then.'

He raised a hand and a couple of beers were brought over to them.

Ward looked at the label. He hadn't heard of it. 'Local?' He took a sip. It was extremely good; dark brown and malty and with a kick, but it had the lightness of a lager.

A waitress came over. She greeted Jacques and Ward with a beam and spoke in Creole to Jacques. They chatted a bit and eventually Jacques ordered, along with a couple more beers.

'So, what have we got coming to us?'

'Conch chowder to start, too good to miss even if it goes with nothing else on the menu, and Pepperpot.'

'Pepperpot?'

'It's a Caribbean dish,' explained Jacques. 'A thick stew with many different vegetables, cornmeal dumplings and goat. We could have had any meat, but I hope you don't mind my choice.'

'Not at all,' said Ward.

Jacques scrutinised Ward. 'So, what's this about, Mr Ward?' Ward looked around the room to see if anybody was taking an interest. 'It's okay,' reassured Jacques. 'Nobody cares.'

'The girl at La Folle.'

'Mirlande?' Jacques had a good recall.

'Could you find her?' He gave Jacques a description of the girl. 'It's almost impossible, I know, but she's a lead, if nothing else.'

'Sure,' said Jacques. 'I have friends at La Folle. I'll see what they have to say.'

'Thanks.'

They both cleared their arms from the table as the conch chowder arrived. It was a perfect light pink. Ward could smell the rich, creamy soup with a hint of the sea in the steam that rose from it. He tried a bit. It was slightly salty and tasted a bit of clams and crab. There was also a touch of Scotch bonnet, not enough to be unpleasant, but enough to add a bit of an edge to the dish. It was all steeped in garlic and fruity peppers and lardons, along with celery and onion. This was one course Ward never wanted to end.

Jacques broke into his daydream. 'And what else, Mr Ward?'

Ward took a long sip of beer. 'Where would the TTX on the snapper have come from? I mean, who could have prepared it in such a way?'

'Anyone who knows what they're doing,' shrugged Jacques. 'A good fisherman can dissect one, but I'm not sure I'd chance it.'

'A specialist then.'

Jacques considered the question for a moment. 'To extract the required amounts from the correct organs, yes. It's not only dangerous for the target, but for the person preparing it. Then it would have to be delivered to, for example, La Folle, and applied carefully to the food and then that food would have to be delivered to you. That's quite a chain.'

'I'm proud to have been worth the effort. So, who on the island could do something like that?'

'Let me check,' said Jacques.

When they had finished the chowder, the Pepperpot arrived. It was as good as it had sounded and Ward felt like he had eaten the best meal he'd had in some time.

Jacques dropped Ward back at the Hotel Hibiscus. Ward had grown to like him. It seemed that Grumpy had depth, even a sense of humour. He could believe thoroughly in the 'insolence and excellence' tag which Buckley had used to describe him.

It was still before nine, so Ward went to the hotel bar for a quiet drink. After that he would spend a couple of hours going through the shoebox of paperwork he had brought back from Chaddleworth.

He felt like he was walking through quicksand; the more steps he took, the more he seemed to become bogged down. There were so many facets and possibilities and unknowns.

He wondered briefly how much the Chief had kept from him. He didn't begrudge him playing it close to his chest, everything was need-to-know, but this was the second time in Ward's short career in the SIS that Lawrie Stuart had turned up, first in the Indian Ocean and now in the Caribbean. He was a trouble-shooter, pure and simple. He cleaned up other people's messes.

So, in this case, whose mess was he cleaning up and whose trouble was he shooting?

Ward drained his whisky and went back to his room. Perhaps he could find the answers in the paperwork.

When he entered the room, it was as if a high wind had passed through it. Clothes were everywhere, lights were thrown to the floor and broken, the mattress and pillows had been gutted, his tailored, code-locked, Samsonite suitcases had been hacked at, but remained intact.

He quickly shut the door and locked it.

There was only one thing that can have been of any interest to whoever had done this. He crossed the room and went to the balcony. He looked under a chair and was relieved to see that the shoebox with the paperwork was still there.

Next he went to his large suitcase to make sure that all was intact, especially the secret compartment. Nothing had been touched, but the latch had been scratched and hacked in an effort to get in. The Browning hadn't left its cosseted sponge cradle. His other suitcase was in much the same state. Whoever had done this seems to have lost control; a heavy glass ashtray had been smashed against the lock, to point where it had fractured and shards of glass were strewn on the floor around it.

He sat on the edge of the bed and surveyed the devastation.

It had been quite a day.

He went to the phone to get in touch with Buckley. Gin and tonics or not, he wanted him to see this. Unfortunately, somebody had severed the phone wire.

'Well, that was pointless,' he said aloud.

'Not really,' said a voice. 'It means that you can't phone for help.'

9. Broken Noses and Bloody Hearts

Ward threw the receiver to the floor. He knew the voice and, unfortunately, he also knew the name.

'Hello, Mirlande.'

'Hello, Mr Ward. I'm sorry about the mess, but I need those papers and now that I know where they are...' She glanced at the balcony.

Ward turned around and looked at her. She was as pretty as he remembered; her glossy, black hair down about her shoulders rested on a dark red shirt, her wide brown eyes could have enticed a ship onto the rocks and her long legs seemed to go on forever in a fetching pair of black slacks.

The only unattractive thing about her was the gun in her hand.

He got himself a drink from the mini-bar and poured it into a plastic hotel tumbler. 'Would you like one?'

She curled her lip. 'No.'

Ward sat down on the bed again. 'What's so special about those papers anyway?'

Mirlande shook her head. 'I have no idea. I was told to find them. That's all.'

'By whom?'

'By the person who pays me.'

'And that is...?'

Mirlande smiled spitefully. 'A genie in a bottle.'

'Did he also tell you to poison my food?'

'No, that was my idea.'

'Why?'

'You're in the way, Mr Ward. They need you gone, by any means possible.'

'It's a bit rude to poison a man's fish, wouldn't you say? Couldn't you have just shot me?'

She gestured with the gun. 'I'm getting to that.'

'Why didn't you just break into the bungalow and steal the papers?'

'They were apparently not important then.'

'But now *I'm* here...'

Mirlande shrugged. 'I guess so.'

Why had his appearance on the scene made so much difference? Had the police intentionally left the papers, as if to play down their importance? Or had the police really been unaware of their significance? Were they to be picked up at some later date, when they had been forgotten about? Perhaps it was hoped that, once the bungalow had been cleared of everything Benson-Haines, they would simply be thrown away and never be seen again. Certainly, as Ward had browsed them at Chaddleworth, he had seen nothing about them that drew his immediate attention. It had just seemed odd that they had been left undisturbed in the bureau. Everything was evidence. He was beginning to suspect that Clarissa Benson-Haines had been a little more than a good-time party gal.

'Well, come on then. Get it over with. Take your best shot.' He pointed at the gun in Mirlande's hand. 'That's a Baby Browning. You'd better be a good shot. Those tiny, tiny bullets would have trouble penetrating a leaf.'

Ward downed the whisky and tossed the empty cup onto the floor across the other side of the room.

For half a second, Mirlande's eyes followed it as it spun through the air.

Ward took advantage of her distraction and rolled quickly from the bed and towards her.

The gun fired, a cracker in the thunder. He felt a searing pain as a bullet seared his shoulder. It burned ferociously as his muscles naturally contracted and were then forced to take on the burden of his roll.

He caught Mirlande in the midriff. The air gushed

from her as she was slammed against the wall. Ward righted himself and before she could pull the trigger again, he punched her in the nose. The back of her head slammed against the wall and she slid to the floor, unconscious.

Ward had clearly broken her nose. It was at forty-five degrees to the rest of her face.

He rolled her over, pulled his belt swiftly from his trousers and bound her hands. Blood pulsed from her nose onto the carpet. He turned her onto her side so that she wouldn't choke. Her breathing was laboured but steady.

The pain began to eat into Ward's shoulder. The baby only had tiny teeth, but when it bit, it bit badly.

There was suddenly an urgent knock at the door. Ward felt dizzy with the pain, with the whole event. He tried to get to the door, but his legs had gone. He thought he had spoken, some sort of invitation to come in, but all that fell from his mouth was nonsense.

There was a metallic rustle as a key turned in the door.

He turned and looked. There was someone he recognised. Female. Young. From somewhere, long, long ago.

'Mr Ward?'

Ward's lips felt like they had been bee-stung. 'Marianne? Is that you?'

'It's me, Mr Ward. Don't try to talk.'

His head reeled. 'Complaints about the noise?'

Suddenly he couldn't breathe. His throat began to close and his head throbbed as if it was going to explode. He vomited as his entire body seemed to lose control and crumpled into a heap.

*

Ward had very little recollection of what followed. He recalled the weight of his body on the floor, his hunger for air. Somewhere there was a never-ending scream and someone trying to smother him. His name was called over and over again, his face slapped, his sternum rubbed, forcefully, as if a blunt knife were being used to cut him open. There was a garden hose – it seemed like a garden hose – pushed down his throat and the soothing sound of some distant someone inviting him to sleep.

He awoke, at some unknown time, to the sound of footsteps and mechanical beeping, to muttered voices and to the smell, strangely, of toast.

His throat was very sore and he was thirsty. His left shoulder throbbed with every beat of his heart.

He opened his eyes and saw the concerned face of Bill Buckley. 'How are you doing, Mike?'

'You tell me,' said Ward, his voice raspy, his eyes not quite able to focus.

'Well, you're not dead.'

'Bonus! What happened?'

'You were shot. In the shoulder.'

'By what?' He winced as the very mention of it seemed to focus the pain. 'An elephant gun?'

'Actually, no. Just a Baby Browning. The bullets, however had been dipped in Tetrodotoxin. If it had been more than just been a flesh wound...'

Ward caught a snapshot of Mirlande with her broken nose. 'What's the matter with that bloody woman?'

'I think she wants to kill you. Don't take it too personally though. She was, after all, only doing it for someone else.'

'Well, in that case, no hard feelings,' said Ward. 'Where is she?'

'In the basement at the HC. We have a small medical

unit. It's going to hurt like hell when she sneezes for the next few months.'

'Good,' said Ward. 'Have you questioned her?'

'As much as we can. She's sedated after surgery to stop her nose bleeding, you managed to tear the nasal artery or whatever it is, and to try and correct the misalignment. She's probably scarred for life.'

'Even better,' said Ward. He sat up and took a long drink of water. 'What do you know about her?'

Buckley looked triumphantly at Ward. 'Quite a lot now, thanks to you.'

'I did very little except for nearly getting killed.'

'Fair point,' agreed Buckley.

Ward feigned offence. 'You could at least argue the point a little.'

'I never argue with the resurrected,' smiled Buckley. 'She's an interesting lady. Full name, Mirlande Rose Guerrier. Aged twenty-seven, born in Haiti, a product of the constant unrest which that country seems to constantly put itself through. Her father was a bauxite miner and her mother a domestic. They were, as far as we know, good people. Her father died of bauxite associated sarcoidosis when she was thirteen. This left her and her mother to fend for themselves, her mother bringing in only a domestic's wages. Mirlande turned to crime. As usual, to start with, it was the petty stuff; theft, burglary, ripping off gullible tourists, then she found she had a talent for, and indifference to, murder.

She joined the famous Kè San gang - the Bloody Hearts - and quickly worked her way into the enviable position of their number one killer. In Haiti it's not uncommon for the gangs and the government to work together, either for financial benefit or to achieve a common goal. Duvalier is, shall we say, flexible in his outlook. He will kill anyone who disagrees with him or who he sees as a threat.

He's murdered thousands of his own people, no doubt, some of them at least, with the help of the Kè Sen and their best assassin.'

A doctor came into the room. He knocked at the door but didn't wait for a reply. 'Excuse me, gentlemen. Good morning, Mr Ward. Still alive, I see.' He grinned broadly and cast an eye over the medical paperwork pinned to a clipboard at the end of his bed. He seemed to be happy with what he saw. 'I'm sure the High Commissioner has explained what happened to you. You're very lucky. There is no antidote to Tetrodotoxin poisoning. All we could do was help you breathe for a few hours and treat you symptomatically. How do you feel?'

'Sore,' confessed Ward. 'But fine.'

The doctor seemed satisfied. 'Okay, Mr Ward, you're free to go whenever you want. I shall leave you in the safe hands of Mr Buckley. Try to take it easy for a couple of days though, eh?'

'Thanks,' said Ward. 'For everything.'

'Sure, but please, don't do it again. It scared the hell out of me.' He laughed heartily and left.

Buckley waited until the doctor was out of earshot and started again. 'Eventually, Mirlande went freelance. Earned herself riches beyond the dreams of the ordinary young Haitian. She has various bank accounts dotted around the islands, most of them untouchable unfortunately.'

Ward wasn't sure whether to be impressed or repulsed by Mirlande. 'So, where do I fit into all of this?'

Buckley looked pensive. 'I'm not sure. Jacques went to the restaurant and did some checking. Mirlande was casual labour. Someone had phoned in sick and she had turned up in their place. It's not uncommon apparently. As long as the work's done, no one really cares. Whoever steps into the sick person's shoes gets that day's wage from the absentee on pay day.'

'Whose place did she take?' asked Ward.

'I don't know. Why?'

'She's probably dead. I can't see Mirlande negotiating this sort of thing. She will have watched her for a couple of days, followed her home and done the dirty when it suited her the most.'

Buckley sighed. 'I'll get Jacques onto it. I hope you're wrong, I really do. It would mean things are spiralling. Once innocent bystanders are dragged into this sort of thing...'

'They always are, somehow,' said Ward. 'And on this occasion, it seems that I might be the cause. For some reason, my appearance lit a bonfire under someone. What about the paperwork?'

'With Marianne, in the hotel safe. I thought perhaps she could give you a helping hand with it. She's a bright young thing.'

'Sure,' said Ward. He didn't like other people doing what he could do. He trusted his eyes alone. Others came at things from different angles, with different agendas, but it would be good to have some company. 'Is she available later?' He looked at the window. Bright sun filtered through some blinds. 'I don't even know what time it is.'

'I'll make her available. It's twelve-thirty by the way.' Buckley hesitated. 'Are you sure you're ready to leave your sick-bed? You've had quite a time of it.'

'Of course. If Jacques wouldn't mind collecting me in an hour...'

Buckley raised a hand. 'Wouldn't hear of it. I'll give you a lift. Don't worry, not in HC1. I've borrowed the Pinto. It's a bit less ostentatious.'

'Okay,' agreed Ward. 'I'm grateful.'

Buckley chuckled. 'Not as grateful as I am. I got out of the most dreadfully dull meeting thanks to you.'

'Glad to have been of help,' said Ward, not without a little irony.

10. Hiding in the Moonlight

Ward had been right. Buckley had advised the police to go to the missing girl's house and they had found her.

She had been suffocated, undoubtedly poisoned, but the blowfish rammed down her throat was unequivocal; Mirlande had not expected to be captured and so left a calling card. She wanted credit for her work. She had finished her grisly show by withdrawing the blowfish far enough from the girl's throat for the spines to become lodged in her palate and even to pierce her cheeks.

Superintendent Raphael Moise stood next to Bill Buckley in Ward's hotel room. He had his hands in the pockets of his grey uniform. He hung his head as the details of the murder were revealed by a sergeant who had attended the scene.

When the sergeant had finished, he dismissed him. The three of them were left to stand in silence in the room. It was difficult to know what to say in the face of such premeditated, sadistic brutality.

It was the Superintendent who broke the silence.

'I need to know what's going on, gentlemen. We can't have this indiscriminate violence. If you are mixed up in this, I need to know. The fact that Bill called me about the girl tells me that you know something.'

Ward was not inclined to involve the local police. He was already concerned by their superficial search of Chaddleworth and by the Prime Minister's dissociation from what the police did or didn't do. Their refusal to let anyone from the High Commission attend the scene of Lawrie Stuart's murder also rankled him.

He crossed his arms and waited for Buckley to make the first move.

'Come on, Rapha,' pleaded Buckley. 'We don't even

know what's going ourselves yet.'

'Well,' said Moise. 'Clearly, you do, otherwise you wouldn't have phoned me in the first place.' He turned to Ward. 'And you, Mr Ward, what are you up to?' He pointed at the wall and floor where Ward had tackled Mirlande. 'I'm pretty sure that's not an old gravy stain on the carpet there. Your room service needs to do better. I believe you came in on a tourist visa. I'm not sure that it will stand up to scrutiny. What do you think?'

Ward didn't answer. As it stood, he might as well pack up and go home now. The Chief wouldn't like it, but he would understand. If the local police were going to start interfering, then everything would be blown; whatever *everything* might be.

However, he didn't want to go home empty-handed. That would niggle at him for ever and a day. He also felt that he would be letting the Chief down. He had asked him to come here and look into the murder of his cousin, almost as a personal favour. The Chief was never one to use the department for his own needs; he would have felt it was morally wrong and against his own ethics. And the accountants went through everything with a fine-toothed comb. He had to justify the expenses of every trip. It wouldn't look good in the report that Ward was obliged to write after every mission; it would look like a quick trip to paradise and back.

'My problem,' he said to Moise, 'is that I don't entirely trust the police.' He laid out his reasons. Moise listened attentively, making no sort of reaction to what might have been interpreted as a slight upon his leadership and his force.

When Ward had finished, he sat down and considered what he had been told. Ward thought that Moise appeared a little thrown by what he had said, but he might just have been a good actor.

'Do you feel the same, Bill?' asked Moise.

Buckley nodded. 'Pretty much. I have trouble understanding why I was kept away from the *Gazette*'s office when Stuart was killed.'

'It was a crime scene,' countered Moise.

'So was the bungalow,' said Buckley, 'but I was allowed to trample all over that. God knows what evidence I could have removed had I been involved in Stuart's murder. I still haven't seen a post-mortem report on either him or the Benson-Haines woman.'

'We're not obliged to show you.'

'I have put three requests to the coroner's office and received no reply. I am Her Majesty's representative in this country. There are courtesies to be observed, especially when the deaths of two British Nationals are involved. Never mind the fact that you might well be breaching the Vienna Convention.'

'Mr Ward, what is your role?' asked Moise.

Ward shrugged. 'I'm just an interested party.'

'And I'm the girl of your dreams. Could we have a little honesty in the room, please?'

'He's MI6,' said Buckley. Ward shot him an angry stare. 'Come on, Mike, it's not like he doesn't know that already, is it now.'

'I do now,' said Moise.

Ward flung his arms up. 'For Christ's sake! This is turning into a farce!'

'I agree,' said the Superintendent. 'Not because of anything either of you have said, though.' He stood up. 'You're right, Mr Ward. Things are definitely awry. I had no idea and I apologise. To you too, Bill. I did not know that you had been kept away from the *Gazette* or what had gone on at the bungalow. Neither did I know about the post-mortem reports. I'll have that rectified by end of business today.' He paused to let what he had said settle in. 'Now, I understand that Jacques Sanon already works for both of us.' Buckley's jaw fell. 'So, I'll give him to you for the duration. He's about as honest a policeman as I've ever met.'

'How did you know about him?' asked Buckley.

'I told you,' said Moise. 'He's honest. As soon as you drafted him in, he asked for my permission. Naturally, I said yes. It was too good an opportunity to miss.'

For the first time, Ward felt the atmosphere lighten.

'I will look into both of your concerns,' reassured Moise. 'If I find any substance, I'll take action. Mr Ward, keep playing the tourist. Bill, it's a bit late, but you're welcome to have a nosey around Stuart's office. Now, I'd like to see this Mirlande woman.'

'Who?' asked Buckley coyly.

Moise pointed at the floor. 'Bill, I know that isn't a gravy stain on the floor. Mr Ward, I know that you were poisoned by TTX. My maths is not so bad that I can't put two and two together. Now, *we* don't have her, she's not running around the streets with the damage it appears might well have been inflicted upon her.' He looked them both in the eye. 'So why don't we pop down to the medical unit in the High Commission so that I can cast an eye over her and perhaps throw in a question or two?'

Ward was exhausted. With an effort he agreed to the visit to the HC. There was clearly nothing to be hidden from the wily Superintendent Moise. The fault with the rag-tag end of the Empire was that it still thought itself better than anyone else. The thing was that it had trained so many people to be better than it and they had succeeded. There was little they could do about dirty, corrupt government, but the men behind it had taken the best from the best and rejected the worst from the worst.

The High Commission loomed like depression on the skyline. It was by now six pm. The sun was beginning to fade. Long shadows threw themselves recklessly against tall buildings and squatted mercilessly against the small. Night, whether they liked it or not, was not far off.

They entered the HC compound with a salute from the fat man and parked in the single, golden, reserved space.

The journey had been muted. Buckley wondered how he was going to explain having an international assassin in his basement. Ward wondered how he could keep the assassin as the world inexorably turned towards sympathy for the Devil. Buckley wondered when his next G&T would be.

They got out of the Pinto. Jacques immediately took control of it. He was clearly peeved that it had been borrowed, but the surreptitious thumbs up from the Superintendent gave him the cue that all had gone well. He got back into the car waited.

The building, by now forced to hide in moonlight, half-lit, stood like a castrated Colossus. It made Ward yearn for what had been, at the same time grateful for the redress.

The High Commissioner flashed his pass and all three entered the government-standard, air-conditioned building.

Buckley walked on like a man possessed. Ward imagined that this was how King Charles the First walked on the way to his execution; brave yet full of dread, finally aware that he had been found out and ready to accept the consequences.

He took the lift down. There was an uneasy silence. Even though Buckley had essentially, by now, admitted to the presence of the 'ward', it felt as if he was exposing Santa Claus as a fraud. The presence of the secret ward, the *shame* of the ward, was just too much. His country had spent so long condemning human rights and now, here he was, caught in the act.

The lift 'pinged' and the doors opened. The ward lay before them. There were no pretensions of corridors or expensive signs blu-tacked to the wall, it was just a semi-lit lair for the guilty and the hurt.

When they found the bodies of the medical officer and the nurse, draped across the nurse's station, Ward's heart fell. The medical officer wore his scrotum in his mouth. The nurse's throat and abdomen were open. She had spilled. The stench of faeces and blood was almost too much for any of them to bear.

Mirlande was gone. Her restraints were cut. There was a single spot of blood upon her pillow.

Ward scanned the devastation angrily. 'What the bloody hell…?'

11. More Questions Than Answers

Ward sat in the Pinto with Jacques. The engine was off. Jacques smoked a cigarette and blew the smoke out through the open window.

'Can I have one of those?' asked Ward.

Jacques looked in the rear-view mirror. 'No.'

'No? Why no?'

'You have given up cigarettes, Mr Ward. I'm not going to be the one to help you start again.'

Ward was impressed. 'How did you know I'd given up?'

Jacques sighed patiently. 'Because if you hadn't given up, you wouldn't have asked me for a cigarette. You would have had your own.'

Ward rolled his eyes. 'Bloody coppers!'

'I am that,' said Jacques with immense satisfaction. 'What happened in there?'

Ward rubbed his eyes. He would give anything for sleep. 'She escaped.'

Jacques puffed his cheeks out. 'That's a whole bag of shit right there, Mr Ward.'

'Yes, Jacques. A whole bag. Any idea where she might go?'

Jacques blew out a grey plume of smoke and laughed. 'The airport?'

'Not so helpful, Jacques,' said Ward.

'Listen, Mr Ward, there's only three ways off this island; by plane, by boat or by swimming.'

'Bit of a swim to Port-au-Prince,' said Ward.

'Boat it is then.' Jacques dithered. 'Although…'

'Yes?'

Jacques' smile waned. 'Mr Ward, would you leave a job half-done, what with professional pride and all that?'

Ward thought back to the conversation he had had with himself earlier in the day. Getting on the first plane home was not always the right move. 'No, Jacques, I wouldn't.'

'Well, there you go.'

'Meaning?'

'Meaning, she has friends on this island; somewhere to hole up until she can do what she came here to do. It's not just the money she risks losing, Mr Ward, it's her reputation, and that's worth a lifetime of dollars. You have to die, Mr Ward. I'm sorry, but you have to die.'

Ward jiggled in his seat. Too much discomfort. 'Any ideas?' he asked again.

'Not a one.'

'Because?'

'Because I don't know who or why someone wants you dead.' Jacques began to sway in the front seat as he suddenly started to sing along with the radio. *There are more questions than answers. Pictures in my mind that will not show. There are more questions than answers. And the more I find out the less I know. Yeah, the more I find out the less I know.'* He laughed aloud. 'Yeah, Johnny Nash!'

'So, I have to sit and wait until she comes for me?'

'No! Duck and dive, Mr Ward; that's what you have to do. Duck and dive!'

'Well, let's assume that I'm already ducking and diving, Jacques. You're the local copper. What would you do?'

Jacques lowered his tone and thought seriously for a moment. He could tell that Ward was losing patience. 'Listen, Mr Ward. I'll be honest. We have nothing. The one thing we did have has taken flight to who knows where.' He threw the cigarette stub out of the window. It hit the ground in a shower of sparks and rolled into a storm drain. 'Okay, back to basics. Let's look at the paperwork you took from Chaddleworth and then take a trip to the *Gazette*. A thorough midnight search; no one there to interfere, just us and the silence.'

'And Mirlande?'

'She'll turn up. That's her nature.'

'That doesn't instil confidence,' said Ward.

'Sometimes you have to be the rabbit, Mr Ward, if only to see the dog.'

Ward sighed wearily. 'Reader's Digest?'

Jacques snickered. 'No, just me.'

He turned over the Pinto's engine and revved away from the High Commission towards the mirage of the Hibiscus Hotel.

*

Marianne was already in Ward's room going through the paperwork. She had a rum in one hand and a piece of paper in the other. She sat on the floor in a paper ring, each compass point of the ring piled high with sheets of paper.

She looked delectable in a white cotton dress. Her legs were crossed, her long blue-black hair swaying with each turn of her head as she looked from pile to pile.

As Ward came in, she looked up at him and smiled. 'Hello, Mr Ward. I've managed to boil things down to date, time and subject matter. The difficulty is trying to find…' She searched for words.

'The connection?' offered Ward. He sat and helped himself to a large glass of Marianne's John Watling's Amber Rum which she had brought with her. It was very smooth, with a background of vanilla and oak, probably due to the oak barrels in which it had been stored.

'Yes,' said Marianne. 'I know, I *know*, that there is a

paper trail in there somewhere.'

'Is that just wishful thinking?' It was a bit harsh, but Ward couldn't be bothered with the hopscotch of politeness.

Marianne's forehead creased. 'I don't think so, Mr Ward…'

'Call me Mike, please. Why don't you think so?'

'Okay,' she slapped a hand down. 'This pile here is household bills. Nothing untoward but for a ridiculous alcohol bill, which was no doubt put down to expenses.'

'Okay.' Ward dragged a chair over and sat down next to the sacred paper circle. He could tell that Marianne had an administrator's mind.

She put her hand on another pile. 'Wage slips, P60s et cetera. Dull, but in combination with…' Her hand hovered over and then snatched at some wrinkled papers, 'this pile of bank statements, it's a good indicator of whether lifestyle meets income.'

'And that pile?'

'More bank statements.'

Ward's senses prickled. She was working up to something.

'Look at this.' She plucked a paper from the other pile and held it out to him.

Ward took the paper and compared it to one from the first pile of statements that she had shown him. They were similar, but each had a different account number.

'I really don't know what I'm looking for,' admitted Ward. 'I can see that this one has a different account number but, other than that, they both just look like run of the mill bank statements. I mean, one could have been his account, the other hers or one could have been for personal expenses, the other for expenditure in the line of work.'

Marianne carried on excitedly. 'Okay.' She took another swig on the rum. She had clearly been at this for a while. 'What about you, Jacques? What do you see?'

Ward passed Jacques the paperwork. He self-consciously took out a pair of reading glasses and scanned the two pages. 'Say nothing,' he warned. 'I feel old enough.'

He examined the statement wordlessly and carefully, his eyes darting from side to side as he made comparisons. 'Boring. This one is the shopping. You see, always from the same shops where the ex-pats go.' He paused as he scanned. 'I would say that they drank more than they ate. There were items that can be claimed back from the British government as expenses in his role as High Commissioner. It amounts to anything and everything, from alcohol, to club membership, to…' He waved a hand at the paper and slapped it. 'Tobacconists and music shops and food shops. Very indulgent.' He tossed the list aside. 'Its irregularity makes it genuine. It's a mess.'

Marianne drained her glass and handed Ward the empty. He refilled it. 'And the other statement?' she asked Jacques. 'In your experience,' she added with bite.

Jacques glanced at her, his lips raised in a slight smile.

He scrutinised the statement some more, ran a finger down the page, counting, making mental notes as he went. Whatever was on the page had him like a fly to a fish.

'I see it,' he said at last. He lifted his head and beamed at Marianne. 'I see it.'

'What do you see?' asked Ward.

'Patterns,' said Jacques. He took an empty glass, filled it a couple of inches with Marianne's rum and lit a cigarette. 'It's clever,' he said at last, to no one in particular. 'Have you got more from this account?'

Marianne grabbed a sheaf of papers. 'These go back ten years.' She picked a few out and handed them to Jacques. 'Some go back earlier. They kept them all.'

Jacques took them to a table and spread them out.

'Same purchases on the same date each month and a large payment made into the account on the same date each month. But…' He compared the sheets again, just to be sure. 'The purchases are not just for one thing; they are for many different things, from different places, but still the same thing on the same date each month. It never varies.'

'Is that suspicious?' asked Ward.

'It's not necessarily suspicious. But, in my *experience*,' he eyeballed Marianne, 'patterns suggest habits and habits can be either good or bad.'

'What about the bank they were with?'

Marianne took the question. 'They were with Barclay's until they came here.' She scrabbled through the papers and picked one out. The headed paper was familiar. 'This is the confirmation from Barclay's that their account was closed and the funds transferred to the Caribbean Islands Bank.' She looked at the date on the letter. 'That was eighteen years ago. That was when they opened their original account with the CIB. The one we're looking at now was opened twelve years ago.'

Ward walked over to Jacques and looked at the papers on the table. He could see the pattern now. He felt ridiculous because he hadn't seen something so obvious. 'What about after Sir Sean died?' he asked Marianne.

'The account was shut down. That was about three years ago. After that it is only the original account which remained open and it's apparent that she lived a pretty frugal life after his death. After he retired six years ago, you can see the gradual decline in their social life. They wouldn't have been able to claim expenses anymore because he was no longer attached to the High Commission, so the statements are smaller, shorter, than before. Their lifestyle became far less extravagant when they had to pay for the drinks themselves.'

'It's all a bit sad really,' said Ward. 'Marking people's rise and decline on a bunch of old papers.'

'Forensic accounting, Mike. It brings out the ghosts.'

'Is that what you do?'

Marianne tilted her head. 'Among other things.'

'I get the feeling that you and Jacques are a bit of a team.'

'I'm the intellectual, he's the heavy.'

Jacques snorted.

'So, in conclusion,' continued Ward, 'did the income support the lifestyle?'

'Oh, absolutely,' said Marianne enthusiastically. 'He was on a very good wage, had a very good government pension and they were basically subsidised by the British government when it came to playing the part of HC and wife which, as you can see, could pay for almost anything.'

'Were they making false claims?'

'Probably not, no, but they were stretching the boundaries.'

'So why the other account? Why, six years after they got here, did they suddenly feel the need to open another account? It's not like they even hid the fact of it. Are there any transfers between the two accounts?'

Marianne shook her head. 'None that I've seen.'

'So where did the money come from that was paid each month into the other account? Who's paying it and how much?'

It was Jacques' turn to speak. 'It was the same amount as his government pay and it was paid in by a company called Denimes Internationale.'

'Never heard of them,' said Ward. 'Have you?'

Jacques and Marianne shook their heads.

'How is it possible that this went unnoticed?' asked Ward.

Jacques looked at him with incredulity. 'Are you serious? He was in the club. *The* club. He was a part of the pink and even as late as the seventies it was almost untouchable.' Ward could not disagree. He had served. Rules were bent. Crimes went unjudged. Jacques carried on. 'The British Empire relied upon integrity and trust and the reason it fell was because, when it mattered, it lacked both. No matter who you were, you skimmed, you bent the rules; sometimes you even got away with murder.'

'Jacques!' Marianne's sharp rebuke shattered the fragile air. 'Enough!'

Jacques drained his rum and stubbed his cigarette out with force. 'I'm sorry. I'm tired. If you don't mind, Mike, I would like to go home.'

Ward felt like he had missed something. 'Sure, Jacques. Go and get some rest. We're all tired.'

Jacques gathered in the paperwork on the desk and handed it back to Marianne. 'Goodnight, then. I shall be available from six in the morning, Mike, should you need me.' He handed the Pinto's keys to Ward. 'One of the pool drivers will take me home. I have too much rum inside me to drive.'

He nodded courteously at them both and left.

Marianne started to gather up the papers around her, trying to make sure that they were put back in the right order.

'What was that about, Marianne?' asked Ward.

'Rum,' said Marianne flatly. 'Rum and the fact that his father was killed by the British.'

12. It Would Have Been Nice To Know That

It was one a.m. before Ward reached the *Gazette* office. The streets were quiet. Stray dogs, little more than skin and bone, battled for territory and scrounged through bins. They flitted through weak street lights and ducked into the shadows, waiting for their opportunity to take or defend.

Occasionally a stray man weaved his way unsteadily home after a night on the rum, locally fermented moonshine, sold for cents from under the counter. It wasn't about the quality, it was about the escape. He walked with his eyes closed, his flip-flopped feet skimming the uneven pavement, the hems of his baggy trousers trodden under heel.

Ward had left Marianne asleep on his bed. She had polished off her own bottle of rum, her irritation with Jacques refusing to subside, and eventually given up the ghost, foetal, a sheet over her to keep off the nightly chill.

Ward spent a moment with her as she slept. He reflected on her beauty and intelligence. Asleep, with her dark hair draped across her right cheek as her chest rose and fell in the peace of sleep, with a strip of moonlight falling through the window and across her face, he found her enchanting.

He wished she would go away. Too many times those who he had cared for had died because of him.

He brushed the hair from her cheek. Her skin was soft. She stirred a little, licked her lips, then slipped away again.

Ward had two choices about how to get into the *Gazette*'s office. He could pick the door; old locks tended to be no problem due to the wear and tear of age, but he didn't want to crouch in the street in case someone passed by. Even a moonshine drunk was a witness.

He chose the small, open window instead. He stood

on an aged bin and pulled himself in. He had brought the Browning with him, more as a 'just in case' than because he suspected any sort of trouble, and had to manipulate it and its waist holster to get in.

There was the familiar, if hideous, smell of men's toilets, made worse by the heat and the less than satisfactory plumbing.

He landed on a tiled floor and made his way to the very squeaky door.

The office was in pitch black. There was a slight smell of oil in the air where the typewriters were maintained and the slightly bitter smell of ink. He wondered briefly how many millions of words had been hammered on the heavy old keys. It was a nostalgic smell which reminded him of his days as a cub reporter. He could hear the urgency of the keys and hubbub of noise that were unavoidable in such an animated environment.

He crept forward and removed a pencil torch from his pocket. Typewriters lay like tombstones upon desks. Sheafs of paper, some tattooed, some virgin, lay next to them. The heat was almost unbearable, even at this time of night. It would have been intolerable during the day, even with the ceiling fans on.

He didn't even know what the hell he was looking for. Every shadow was a ghost, every creak of the aged wooden floor a phantom footstep.

He made his way between desks to the office. He opened the office door. The word 'EDITOR' loomed large upon the glass. There was a sash window which allowed the moonlight to fall in chequers across the room.

It had been meticulously cleaned. Ward cursed their efficiency. It shouldn't have been touched, not without him there. He felt a pang of guilt for his arrogance, but that arrogance had kept him alert and alive.

The desk, a large, dark oak affair, which would have made the Chief envious, was bereft of paraphernalia. It had been cleaned. Ward wondered if even the hundred years of patina had been scrubbed away. How many stories could this desk have told? How many secrets did it keep?

The wooden building creaked and groaned as the heat twisted its insides minutely. It was like being aboard ship.

Ward made his way to the shelves that lined the room. It was full of dictionaries and reference books, maps and stories of the Caribbean. There were giant folders which contained previous editions of the paper. They started in 1953 to the present day. Prior to that, assumed Ward, they were in the basement.

He went to the desk and pulled the drawers. They had been cleared. No doubt Stephen (with a 'ph') would be back soon enough to resume his role and lay claim to this vacant land.

Ward thought back to the final phone call from Lawrie Stuart. No one knew as yet what had caused him to pick up the phone to London. What had he been doing that caused him to make the urgent call? Ward had no idea what Stuart was doing on the island in the first place. The Chief had not shared that information. After all, Ward was only there to find out what had happened, why he had been shot. The Chief might well have thought that any other information was irrelevant or too confidential to share. Stuart was, he knew, a trouble-shooter, one who stepped in to sort out a problem and then stepped away again.

So far, Ward felt that he had only created more questions. Every step forward took him two steps back and ultimately led him down a blind alley.

He picked up the office phone and dialled a number from the directory he kept in his head.

Eventually, the phone at the other end was picked up. 'Yes,' said a tired and impatient voice.

'Dragonfly,' said Ward. He waited. He knew that at the other end he was being scrambled and recorded.

After thirty seconds the Chief's voice came through. 'Do you have any idea what time it is here, Ward?'

'Not as early as it is here,' said Ward bluntly.

'What's the matter?'

'I need to know why Stuart was here.'

Ward could sense the Chief thinking, going rapidly through all the options. He would have known that Ward would never have taken the risk of phoning him if it wasn't a matter of urgency.

'Where are you?' asked the Chief.

'In the office at the newspaper. It's about the only place I can get any privacy at the moment. It's been wiped clean. There's no trace that Stuart was ever even here. The HC hasn't even had the post-mortem report on either Stuart or the woman and he has only been permitted to see her body. All sorts of things are wrong here, sir. The local police have been behaving most strangely, being most uncooperative. Even the Prime Minister is being evasive. He basically told Bill Buckley that it had nothing to do with anybody but the local police.'

'I was afraid of this,' said the Chief. 'It's worse than we thought.'

'What is?'

'Another bloody Cuba! Only this time it's by invitation.'

'Sir, I've got some deranged woman with a bucket of poison trying to kill me; she's already escaped from our custody once, leaving two bodies in her wake, and is now free to roam the streets. And she doesn't care who she kills, as long as she gets to me. What the hell makes me so important?'

'Because they think that you're there to take over from Stuart.'

'And why would they think that, sir?'

'Because you are.'

Ward bit his tongue. Being bait was a part of the job and he knew it. He just didn't like it. 'It would have been nice to know that, sir.'

'Sorry, Ward, but we couldn't chance it. The more you knew, the more cautious you would have been. We needed you to force their hand.'

'What was Stuart doing then?'

'He was waiting to be contacted by an inside man.'

'Inside what?' asked Ward.

'The government I should imagine. It was supposed to be made through an advert in the *Gazette*. I can only guess that's why he phoned. He'd found something.'

'Something that caused an old woman to shoot him?'

'I don't even know if the two are connected. I must assume they are until you say otherwise.' The Chief paused. 'I'm sorry, Ward. I don't like to use our people this way, particularly you, but you know how it is.'

'Of course, sir. I'll have to use the hotel as my base and reach out to Buckley when necessary. We were assured by the police commissioner that we would get the post-mortem reports by end of business yesterday, so I'll look into that.'

'Look into everything, Ward,' warned the Chief. 'This is all way more advanced than any of us knew. If the Americans get involved they'll just cock it up as usual by going in all guns blazing. We don't want another Bay of Pigs, especially in a Commonwealth country. The diplomatic fallout would be horrendous. The long-standing friendship between us would mean nothing if they thought that they had reds knocking at their back door. I'd like to present them with a *fait accompli*, if at all possible.'

'But they must be aware…'

'Oh, they're aware alright, they're just not as up-to-date as us. We should try to keep it that way.'

'Fine,' said Ward. 'Goodnight, sir.'

Good *morning*, Ward.'

The line went dead.

Ward turned the torch on and looked at the issues of the paper on the shelving. He picked out the latest edition and laid the broadsheet out on the desk.

He turned to the advertisement pages and looked through each one of them. The list was interminable. There were adverts for businesses, for work, for lost cats and dogs, for restaurants. It was like looking for an unknown tree in a dark wood.

Then he saw what he was looking for:

'WANTED -
A LODGER TO SHARE THE BILLS EACH
WEDNESDAY. PHONE - 610-121495.

It was just that bit too different from all the other adverts on the page. Whoever had paid for the advert had insisted on a large font and block capitals in bold. Expensive.

Ward tore out the advert, replaced the paper in its binding and left the office.

It was two-thirty. If he was lucky, he could get back to the hotel in twenty minutes or so and grab a couple of hours sleep.

He rounded a corner to where he had parked the Pinto.

It was parked in the weak, yellow light of a street light. The light thrown consumed perhaps a couple of yards, then faded into a cloudy jaundiced mist. The Pinto sat beneath the light. The orange and chrome of the car absorbed the weak light and spewed it back as little more than shadows.

Ward wasn't sure what he was seeing at first. He squinted through the semi-darkness. There was something draped across the front of the car. He looked about. There was nothing that could have cast such a shadow. He took out the Browning and approached the vehicle slowly.

Jacques' body had been thrown onto the bonnet and left there. A trail of coagulating blood ran from the bullet hole in his head down the bonnet, to drip onto the chrome bumper and then onto the ground. It looked in the poor light like an oil leak.

Ward shone the torch on Jacques' grey face. His rough, tough exterior was petrified in death, made uglier by the blowfish in his mouth.

13. An Ounce Of Integrity

'This is a leaking ship,' said Ward furiously.

'It is no such thing,' protested Buckley. 'It's only since you arrived that we've run into any problems. You've turned this island into a cauldron.'

Ward wanted grab Buckley's lapels and shake some sense into him. 'Bill, do you have any idea at all what is going on around you? The island, the Prime Minister, of all people, are about to hand this place over to the communists. Are you sleepwalking? Do you want another missile crisis?'

'Oh, I don't think…'

'I won't disagree with that,' snapped Ward.

Buckley puffed his chest out. 'I was going to say, I don't think it will come to that.'

Ward ran his hands impatiently through his hair and pulled himself away from the window. It was a glorious day. 'How deep are you in this, Bill? Were you simply hoping that if you turned a blind eye, that it would all simply go away? For Christ's sake! You're supposed to be proactive, Bill. This has been bubbling for ages and you have failed to notice the heat.'

'Don't you dare talk to me like that…'

Ward pointed a finger. 'Don't! Don't hold up the HC card to me. It won't wash. Jacques is dead. Two of the staff in that unwindowed, dark, basement ward of this very building are dead. Some poor innocent girl has been killed just because she happened to work in a restaurant. An old lady murdered the editor of the *Gazette* and then blew her own brains out. Some lunatic tried to poison me. In what way, on this God's earth, do you think it would amount to nothing?'

'I just thought…' It was pathetic really. Buckley could see his straw house collapsing. Beads of sweat poured from his forehead as he paced the room. The back of his shirt and the armpits were dark with sweat.

'I need to know what you know, Bill, before you lose your job and your pension. I promise you, that seafront house on the private estate in West Sussex will be a dead dream.' Ward's voice became a bark. 'Now, what haven't you told me?'

The High Commissioner slumped into a chair. He looked deflated, his trembling belly adrift like a wind-filled sail, his face as pale as melted wax.

'Now, Mike, listen…'

'I am listening.' Ward pulled a chair in front of Buckley until he was only a matter of inches away.

'If the people want to choose their own government…'

Ward slapped Buckley's face. The sound echoed like a firecracker. 'What have you done?'

Buckley began to cry. 'I haven't *done* a thing.' He took a handkerchief out and blew his nose. 'I have known for some time what they were up to. I have simply…turned a blind eye.'

Ward was stunned by the admission. 'Well, why didn't you do something about it? The Prime Minister of Britain is on the other end of the phone. MI6 is on the other end of the phone. You could have simply packed your bags and left on the first plane out and gone on bended knee to London. What the hell did they do to you?'

Buckley finally collapsed. 'They threatened to kill me, Mike. They threatened to kill me!'

Ward's eyes narrowed. 'That's it? Really? That's it? Do you know what happens when someone kills you?' Ward's lips twisted in disgust. 'You die. No matter what they do to you - bullet, knife, blowfish - you die. End. Darkness. No more. The only difference between life and death is the ounce of integrity you hold in your final breath. Tell me about Mirlande.'

'What?'

Ward took out his gun and aimed it at Buckley's head. 'Tell me! How the hell did she escape? How did she manage to kill two medical workers and escape?'

Buckley cowered at the sight of the weapon. 'I helped her! I loosened her restraints and hid a scalpel under her pillow so that she could get away. I didn't think…'

'That's not one of your strong points, is it, Bill. Thinking. Every action has a consequence and every consequence has a price. Your cowardice killed two good people.' He leaned forward in the chair until he could smell Buckley's rotten breath. 'You know?' he said. 'I think she knew my every move. La Folle? Who wrote that tidy little invitation?' He could see in Buckley's wandering, bloodshot eyes that it was him. 'Listen, Bill. Listen carefully. I don't care if you live or die. I don't care if you die with a bullet in the skull or a fish in your throat. You're already dead to me and when Number Ten finds out, you'll be drinking from brown paper bags and begging on street corners; that's if they don't lock you behind bars for the rest of your life.' Ward considered for a moment. Once again, he felt as if he had taken a step away from the truth and ended up in the land of confusion. 'I'll tell you what you're going to do, Bill. From now on, you work for me. If you want that house by the sea, that expensive whisky and the Mercedes with the drop-top to drag along the A27 on a summer day, you will work for me. The only thing you have to think about is whether, at the end of all this, I kill you and drop you in the deep, blue sea and turn you into fish food or whether you live. Well?'

'I want to live.' Buckley had become pitiful. Part of Ward wanted to put an arm around him and tell him it would be alright. The rest of him wanted to pull the trigger and be done with the man.

Ward stood and pushed the chair away with the backs of his legs. It toppled over. He pointed a finger in Buckley's blotchy face. 'If you let me down again, if I even suspect that you have done something wrong, I'll kill you. For Jacques, I'll kill you.'

'Jacques wasn't such an angel you know!' snapped Buckley. 'He wasn't what you thought he was.'

Ward sighed. 'You just can't help yourself, can you. Just shut up until I leave the room. Just…shut up.'

'Mike,' Buckley was short of breath. His voice broke as he spoke. 'Now you listen to me.'

Ward rounded on Buckley. 'Why? Why should I? You're a lie. You claim to be something you are not. Why should I trust you?'

Buckley took a deep breath. It shuddered as he tried to pull himself together. His face was pale, his eyes half-closed, as if the drugs of confession had taken effect and left him in a stupor.

'Why?' Buckley smiled as if his soul had taken flight. 'Hell's bells! For all the reasons you have stated; for the house by the sea, the car, the peaceful retirement unto a sleepy death. I need redemption. I need to right the wrongs. It really is that simple.' He drew a deep, trembling breath. 'I have been afraid for ever. Fear has ruled me, from prep school to, well, today. I'm a diplomat, Mike, but I'm not a brave man. I can joust with words, but once I see the lance, I die inside.'

Ward sat down again and faced Buckley. 'Tell me about Jacques. If he was rotten, I want to know.'

Buckley ran his hands across his face. They came away wet. He wiped them down his saturated shirt as if it would make a difference. They glistened in the light from the window. The devil and the deep blue sea were never far away.

'Come on!' growled Ward. 'Your career is about to expire.'

'Fine.' Buckley held up a hand in an attempt to deflect a truth that thundered towards him like a train. He licked his dry lips, then took a sip of water from a glass on the desk next to them. 'Jacques and I were in business.'

'Okay,' said Ward. 'What sort of business? Did you make strawberry jam for the ex-pat market? Scones perhaps? For those traditional cream teas?' Buckley sat forward. Ward shoved the Browning into his chest and pushed him back. 'Oh, I *do* know,' said Ward with sarcastic bitterness. 'How about the distribution of marijuana, cocaine and heroin into the island? Why not go the whole hog? How about some speed? Some tranquilisers? Anything that could be stolen from the real dealers under the guise of police action? He turns in fifty, maybe seventy-five percent of the take into evidence, and you and he recycle the rest. How's that?'

Buckley rung his hands, but now there was a defiance in his eyes, that same insolence that lay in the gaze of a man before an execution squad. 'Pretty much perfect. How did you know?'

'I didn't. All I had to do was put a bent HC and a narc together and I ended up with you. Jacques told me that he would one day retire to Bermuda. That was a slip of the tongue. On a police pension from the island of Saint Quintian? Not a hope. Not unless all he ate was pineapple and all he drank was water. He was a drinker, a smoker and lived comparatively well. I bet, if we took a good look into his accounts, there would be more questions than answers.' He thought for a moment of Jacques half-dancing to the song in the car. 'Well? What say you, Bill Buckley?'

'You'd be right,' admitted Buckley.

'How much? How much did *you*…' Ward stabbed a finger into his chest. '*you*, make out of this?'

Buckley swallowed nervously. 'If I said that the house by the sea cost half a million, would that answer your question?'

'I think you might have to settle on a flat in Worthing,' said Ward. 'And maybe a Robin Reliant.'

'I'll take it,' said Buckley quickly.

'Not yet you won't,' said Ward. 'I want to know all about the payments into the Benson-Haines' accounts. If you lie to me, I will get Marianne to dig all the way to China to find the truth and then I will come back for you.'

For half a second, Ward hoped that Marianne was on his side. As ever, outside the Chief's office, there was nobody he could trust. Betrayal had followed him like a constant ghost and it ate away at the better part of any man. It would make a change in his devious world if Marianne was not one of those people, but there was no trust between him and anything that breathed any more.

'Marianne's a good girl, Mike. She has nothing whatsoever to do with this. Jacques wouldn't let her. He loved her, you see. That ugly, broken man loved Marianne with all his heart. I think that if anybody came near her, he would have split the island in two to find them and have his revenge.'

Ward snorted. 'It's a sob story, Bill. Tell me about Jacques. Come on. Spill it!' he ordered. 'Now.'

14. The Thin Ice

There is an absolute horror in undercover work. If you're not sociopathic, or at least iron-willed, you will crumble, deflate, fold and eventually die at the whim of another or by your own hand. To succeed, there must be no boundaries; no conscience, no morals, no ethics, no standards, no love, no hate. Families are an encumbrance, a risk, a liability. Love is fleeting, because those you love either leave, because you drive them away because of your own fears or they die because you made them a target. The only thing that matters is the survival of the fittest and the fittest must be you. The end justifies the means. Innocents must die to take down the guilty. Friends must be used and enemies held close. You must become as repulsive as those you hunt and yet you must not descend into that abyss of lost identity or moral decomposition in which those you come into contact with live on a daily basis.

Those who do it, successfully or not, are changed. The soul that they possessed when they started will have been damaged beyond repair. What they once found horrific will now fill them with a sense of invulnerability, of power, will leave them bereft of conscience. Worse still, they might feel nothing.

Once all that happens, once the decency has been suppressed and the scruples dissolved, there is little left of the person other than the occasional flicker of self-loathing and righteous, but misplaced, indignation.

Ward had felt these things. When he had lost the women he loved most due to the gross machinations of others, he had needed to steel himself for revenge, to obliterate every sense of decency and run rampant until his own soul was sated by the poison of retribution.

The problem was that you never got back what you

lost. The acid rain of life ate into the virgin statue. No matter how you tried, you would never be whole again. That which didn't kill you made you stronger? Rubbish! It simply chipped away at you until there was very little of the original you left.

Ward hadn't written anything for some years. That flair for journalism and fiction had been extracted, to be replaced by a detached flatness. Everything was now black and white. Greyness, that middle ground, that compromise, that blend of right and wrong, had gone, to be replaced by self. He had become selfish, in the most literal sense because, if he didn't, he would fail or die. Self had to be all. Self was staying alive. Self was keeping an identity. Self was a disregard of others, to the point of sacrifice.

Ward therefore understood Jacques' weaknesses. He could perhaps never get a sense of the absolute immersion into which Jacques had descended, nor the normality for which he longed. He was a man trapped under ice looking at the sun, longing for the life-saving breath of air, yet afraid to breathe in case what awaited him above the ice was no more than the lung-shattering cold of truth, but Ward, who had at some times felt irretrievably lost, realised how thin, how fragile, that layer of ice really was. It was so easy to fall through, so difficult to overcome.

'And what about Jacques?' asked Ward. 'What happened to him?'

Buckley had calmed. He had a large whisky in front of him. That was his second. If he didn't have something to eat soon he would slide away and be no good to anyone.

Ward picked up the phone. 'Miss Grace, I need some food to be delivered to the office.' He paused as she asked some questions. 'Really, I don't care. Something warm, something filling and nothing from La Folle.' He gazed sternly at Buckley as he spoke. Buckley rested the tumbler of whisky upon his belly, while his face translated every painful thought that blundered through his mind. 'That's fine,' continued Ward.' He hung up. 'I hope you like Chinese, Bill.'

'Love it,' said Buckley as he slapped slack lips onto the tumbler.

Ward poured himself another whisky. He needed to be careful. Had he still been smoking, he would not have drank so hard, but there was something missing from his life. He simply felt incomplete. He picked up the phone again. Miss Grace? I'd like a packet of Lucky Strike with that please. And a box of matches.'

He hung up and returned to Buckley. 'Jacques?' reminded Ward.

Buckley took a drink and ran a hand across his wet face. 'He was only human,' he said. His voice was slightly slurred. 'How can you stare at so much wealth, have access to such fortune, and not be tempted?' He gazed into his tumbler as if it was the fount of all truths. 'In time, he would be found out. People would eventually put two and two together and his life would be forfeit. What are these people paid? Fifty cents an hour? What's that? A few pennies? How is a man supposed to live on that, never mind die? Most of these people are on a dollar a day. A copper? Maybe five or ten. What are they supposed to do? Work like dogs, shunned by society because of their job, if they are honest, and then settle in a corrugated tin box with a kettle and a black and white TV for company for their remaining years? Jesus, how primitive!'

Ward was too consumed by the idea of a cigarette to really hear what Buckley said. He had gone so long without the drug, without the relief, without the ten contemplative minutes they offered, that what Buckley had to give was small beer. Ward scrutinised the pathetic HC. What sin cigarettes compared to betrayal, to moral weakness, to greed?

'Go on,' said Ward.

'Twenty years ago, Jacques went into the narcotics squad. He was very good at it, too. Brought in some big fish. Her Majesty's Government had not stood in the way, so long as he continued to provide it with information. I can only imagine how difficult it must have been for him. He must have split himself in two trying to combat the whole drugs scene and to continue to feed the then HC.'

'The then HC being?'

'Sir Sean Haines.'

Ward felt that he knew which way this was going. 'With what? Feed him with what?'

'With drugs, Mike.' Buckley said it as if it was obvious. 'With drugs.'

'They'd gone into business?'

'In a sense, yes.'

There was a knock at the door, then Miss Grace entered with a bag of takeaway Chinese food. She placed it on the table, along with a couple of forks, then went into her handbag and took out twenty Lucky Strike and some matches and put those next to the food.

'Thank you, Miss Grace,' said Buckley.

'Will there be anything else, sir?'

'No, Thank you.'

She looked at the cigarettes and then at Ward, as if to say, 'I dare you', then left the room.

Ward doled out the boxes of food. He dived in immediately. He was hungry. What was this? A late lunch or and early dinner? He looked at his watch. As it turned out, he was completely wrong. It was only eleven-thirty. Early lunch then.

'In a sense?' he prompted. 'That's a little elusive, Bill. Come on.'

Buckley picked at his food. He looked like a fat, sulky

child. 'As you have already guessed, Jacques didn't turn in all that he found. What he had left, he dealt.'

'And where did Haines come into this?'

Buckley's eyes wandered; he looked anywhere but at Ward. It was as if he was trying to avoid catching the shadow of truth out of the corner of his eye. 'At first? As a customer.'

Ward looked sceptically at Buckley. 'What do you mean?'

'I mean…' Buckley dithered. 'I mean that there was a certain small percentage that he put in his arm.'

'Don't be ridiculous!' spat Ward. 'Haines? An addict?'

Buckley took a mouthful of the Chinese food. 'He had been for years, even before he came here.'

'And his wife?'

'Oh, she knew, but she was happy to turn a blind eye to his habit. It made him controllable, malleable, and made her the real boss in their marriage. He became as dependent upon her as much as he did on the drugs.'

Ward thought about what Jacques had said: 'Patterns suggest habits and habits can be either good or bad.'

'And as far as the business went? How much of that was her?'

Buckley had found his appetite. Now he was shovelling in the food as if he hadn't eaten for a month. 'In the end, all of it. He was quite content to be thrown a sprat while she took in the haul. And he wasn't really capable of such affairs. He was a rather weak-minded man. Don't get me wrong, he was a brilliant diplomat, but he wasn't a strong man, not in himself. He could hide behind the flag and occasionally poke his head out over the top of it but he constantly fed upon self-doubt and the drugs were a way to hide from that. Sadly, in the end, he had to retire, before the physical effects of the drugs and a decline in his psychological state forced him out of the job.'

'And his death?'

'Probably sepsis. A dirty needle, an infected injection site. Who knows? I know that his end came quickly and uncomfortably.'

Ward put his carton of food aside and opened the packet of Lucky Strike. 'How do you know? How do you know about any of this? How can I trust you? This might just be a string of lies told to try and save yourself.'

It was difficult for Buckley to disagree. 'Jacques shared much of it with me and when Clarissa handed me the reins, she filled in the gaps.'

Ward tapped out a cigarette and pulled it from the packet. 'Why didn't she carry on?'

'She'd had enough. She was tired. Without him, there was little purpose anymore. In the end, she was as dependent upon him as he had ever been upon her. Without his weakness, she had no strength. Who knows? She might have actually loved him. Ironic, eh? She didn't need the money, that's for sure.'

Ward knew that there was more to tell. 'And?'

'And by that time she was under a lot of outside pressure.'

Ward put the cigarette in his mouth. 'From whom?'

'I'm not sure really sure, but her and Jacques had been, shall we say, taken over? Forced into partnership? A partnership which I too am forced to continue. If I don't, they will kill me and if not kill me, expose my actions, and those of my predecessors; they would tear us apart and in doing so undermine the Brit's entire hold on the island, perhaps even shed doubt upon the Commonwealth. If people knew that the HC and his wife had been on the take for all those years and that I had taken over…'

'They're going to do that anyway, Bill. You're well

and truly screwed. And who is behind it?'

Bill frowned as if it was all over. 'The commies I suspect.'

'And here? On the island?'

Buckley put his empty carton down and wiped his hands upon his trousers. They left a damp trail in their wake. 'The only thing I can tell you is that it is run by one person.'

'Go on. Who?'

'Someone called The Genie.'

Ward stuck a match.

15. A Devil's Whisper, An Angel's Wings

Ward closed his eyes and listened to a tape of Tubular Bells on his Sony Walkman. He loved it. It was monster and lover, unleashed by the liberty of new-age freedom. It broke boundaries without breaking rules. He admired its crafty cunning. Vivian Stanshall's voice broke through and gave him a start, as it always did. He smiled at the jolt.

He had laid on his bed for an hour, the mid-afternoon downpour long-gone, to be replaced by the boiled-kettle oppressiveness of its steamy aftermath. The room windows were open. Nothing stirred. The sun had fractured the clouds and had broken through, a last flourish before it succumbed to evening, that wounded end-of-day that heralded a clear night and the prospect of shooting stars and a sharp moon.

Ward turned over and looked out of the window. It was still day, but only just.

He didn't know what the hell he was going to do about Buckley. The man was a turd in a swimming pool. He was irretrievable. Yet there was something about him that Ward liked. He was an amiable man who had fallen to the Devil's whispers while clutching at an angel's wings. Perhaps he was being sentimental, emotionally and practically blind, but he believed that in his heart, Buckley really was one of the good guys, he had simply been caught in the web and longed to be free.

Was he making excuses for a clumsy, greedy, infantile man? Who was to say? He could only go by instinct, and his instinct said to give Buckley a second chance. Heaven only knew why, but underneath that cowardice and soft shell, he believed that there was a man who could atone for his mistakes.

His meeting with Buckley had concluded in a cloud of drink, particularly on Buckley's part. He had fallen asleep in the chair in which he had eaten and confessed. For a moment, Ward had wanted to kill him. There were many ways in which he could have done it and none of them would have been obvious. Buckley would just have been another well-bellied ex-pat who had over-indulged, fallen into a terminal sleep, then been stuck into the abdomen of the next jet home, to be buried with a single mourner somewhere in the home counties.

But he liked Bill. Despite his cowardice and his gullibility and his disloyalty, he liked him. He was only human, after all, and it was only by the grace of God that Ward was not the same. Lord knew, he had come close. He had come so close.

What distinguished Buckley from all those who had come before? Those who had willingly betrayed their country for self-gain? He was scared. That was all there was to it. Fear steered many men to stupidity and treachery, but his fear was the fear born of a child, who had been smacked across the face for a reason he did not understand, who had felt the sting of an umbrella across his back when all he had done was to breathe in joy. He had somehow scrambled through the brambles, torn and bruised, and come out the other side, better for it, but forever afraid of the thorns.

For some reason unknown to himself, Ward wanted to help him. He wanted to know, somewhere else, not too far in the future, that the fat kid could do some good.

That and the fact that Buckley had blown the match out. 'You don't smoke anymore,' he had slurred before drifting away.

Ward had also taken time to look through the two post-mortem reports, which had finally turned up.

There was nothing particularly surprising in Lawrie

Stuart's report. The damage done by the two shots to the chest was devastating. One bullet had caused a massive blood loss through the wall of the heart, the other had ruptured the internal thoracic artery. The poor man had not stood a chance. The only positive, if it could be seen as such, was that he would have died very quickly. Other than that he was a very fit man. He might have gone on for years.

Clarissa Benson-Haines was a different story. The first thing that surprised him was the presence of lithium in her blood, explained by the fact that she was bipolar a couple of lines down further on in the report. Her depression was, in theory at least, controlled by amitriptyline. That had all been a well-kept secret. It also went some way towards explaining her behaviour. It was a fine balancing act to control such an abominable disease.

Most alarming of all though was the mention of ma huang. The coroner had taken the time to say that this was taken from the herb *Ephedra Sinica*, something that had been used in Chinese medicine for thousands of years in the treatment of chest ailments, allergies and sinus problems. Traditionally it had been served as a tea. The coroner could not speculate as to why this substance was in her blood and could only suggest, but could not confirm, that the blood levels suggested a maintenance dose of the drug, though over how long a period was impossible to say. The problem was that ma huang was contraindicated in those with any form of psychosis and in those taking particular types of anti-depressants. It could increase delusional behaviour and perhaps make the individual concerned more prone to suggestibility, especially if the blood lithium levels were lowered.

What that all meant, Ward couldn't say; if the point of withholding the post-mortems was to protect confidentiality, then he could understand. The woman had been besmirched enough. However, there was always the possibility that the reports had been withheld for less sympathetic reasons. It would have been easier to assume that she had gone cuckoo and shot herself in the head. No one was going to question the obvious; any other information could be dismissed as irrelevant, unless you knew what you were looking for.

The room's phone rang. It was a dagger in the silence. He quickly rolled over and picked it up. It was Marianne. 'Good evening, Mr Ward. This is your wake-up call. It is five-thirty pm and your table is booked for six.'

Ward looked at his watch. It was exactly five-thirty. He had been out for the count. He made a note not to drink competitively with Buckley.

'Marianne?'

'Yes, sir.'

He rubbed his eyes. 'What time do you finish?'

'Eight o'clock, sir.'

'Cancel my table. I'll have room service at seven fifty-five. Lobster for two and whatever goes with it - something light. You choose the wine. Come to my room when you're done if you wouldn't mind.'

A moment's hesitation. 'Yes, Mr Ward.' The line clicked and went dead.

He got up and had a hot shower, as hot as he could bear. Just before he got out, he turned it to cold. It fell down upon him in bracing shards. Fully awakened, he dried and dressed himself.

He had time to slip out before his food arrived.

He went round to the car pool and picked a driver he had never seen before. He gave him ten dollars up front and got into his car. Thankfully, it wasn't a Pinto, just a dirt-brown Austin Allegro. Ward smiled at the square steering wheel, which British Leyland had touted as 'quartic' and was widely mocked, to the point where it was quite quickly dropped. That made this car at least six years old, but it looked like a relic from a different age and had clearly been well-used.

'Where to?' asked the driver as he slipped behind the wheel.

'The airport,' said Ward.

The driver ground the Allegro into gear and pulled away.

There was something that had been nagging at the back of Ward's mind. It was one of those niggles that he knew he had but couldn't place, something that he had seen somewhere at some time. He just had to look.

They left the smooth thoroughfare from the hotel and hit the pot-holed roads between the fields of sugar cane. Dusk was coming in. The sky was on fire, the wispy clouds like coals against the darkening blue. They passed the dimly-lit corrugated homes and villages where light spilled from drinking holes and small crowds milled about aimlessly, free now from their toils but having little idea what to do with that freedom other than to gossip and drink.

'Pull over,' said Ward suddenly.

The driver pulled over.

At a turning in the road, a path led to a factory, already lit for the night. He knew he had seen something, but was he now just clutching desperately at straws, seeing bats in the ink blots?

But there it was: Jeans Genies.

What had Mirlande said when Ward had asked who was paying her? 'A genie in a bottle'? Was this coincidence or had Mirlande become just a bit too cocksure, let her mouth run away, believing that by the end of the evening Ward would be dead anyway?

'Okay,' he said. 'We can go back to the hotel.'

The driver did a U-turn. The sun had now plunged into the horizon and left myriad stars behind it. He flicked on the Allegro's lights. They brought the sugar cane to life, throwing shadows as they passed.

Ward looked at the waxing moon. It was as dark as it was going to get for a while. He would have to take advantage of that.

16. Marianne

Marianne arrived shortly after the room service. She had changed out of her hotel uniform into a pair of tight-cut jeans and a white blouse. Her hair fell freely and she had a hint of perfume about her, and not the cheap kind.

'I'm sorry about Jacques,' said Ward. 'I know you were friends.'

'We had grown to be,' said Marianne.

They sat at a table on the patio next to the French windows. The night was warm but a cooling breeze from the sea made it tolerable.

Marianne had ordered salad with the lobster and a bottle of chilled Pinot Grigio. It was a perfect combination.

'I have to ask,' said Ward. 'Did you know about his side business?'

Marianne took a sip of the wine. The question discomforted her. 'No, Mike, I didn't. I had no idea.' Her eyes moistened as she spoke. She was clearly still raw.

'And what about Bill Buckley?'

Her face fell. 'What about Bill?'

Ward searched her face for lies. 'You really don't know?'

'Don't know what?'

'That he and Jacques were in business. That Jacques and the previous HC had been in business. That Clarissa Benson-Haines had been involved, the same Clarissa Benson-Haines that had marched into the *Gazette* with a gun and shot the editor and then herself.'

Marianne gave up the pretence of eating. Ward didn't; he was hungry.

'Mike…'

Ward held up a finger. 'Don't lie to me, Marianne. This isn't the time for lies. I need to be able to trust someone on this island and you're my only hope.'

'You can trust me. I give you my word. You can trust me.'

Ward examined her. Her eyes were edged with tears, but she held his stare with defiance. If she had been lying, she would not have been able to do so.

'When did you start to work for MI6?'

She seemed startled by the question. 'I was lucky. I went to university in the US…'

'Which one?' asked Ward.

'Rice.'

Ward was impressed. 'How?'

'I got a scholarship. It turned out that I was very good at maths.' Ward could tell that she was a little embarrassed. 'I mean, really good, so I was able to get in on the back of that. I had no idea that I was any good until someone pointed it out to me. It all came so easily.' She took a sip of wine. 'Anyway, I went to Rice and studied business and accounting. It was all rather easy and interesting, like a hobby, and I strolled through it all. Just before I graduated I was approached by someone who suggested that I could put my services to good use.'

'A Brit?'

'No, an American. I said no. I never saw him again.'

'Why did you say no? You could have made a fortune.'

She laughed. Thank God, thought Ward. 'I didn't want to work for *them*! I'm a part of the Commonwealth. I'm as good as British.' At last her deep brown eyes became animated. He had hit upon a vein. 'So, I wrote to the British Ambassador in Washington, completely off the cuff, and told them what had happened.'

'And?' asked Ward.

'I swear, within twenty-four hours two guys in suits

turned up and offered me a job. They wanted me to be undercover. Did you know the Brits own this place?'

Ward was astonished. 'I did not, but it explains why I'm not in a lean-to in Saint Jeanne.'

'Do they tell you *anything?*'

'Apparently not,' said Ward.

He could however verify all that Marianne said. He had contacted London that afternoon and got a resumé of her life by fax via the HC. As Buckley had snored, he had worked. Marianne had not lied about a thing. He was relieved. He liked her for her intelligence and her looks. She was now thirty years old and had dedicated herself to her work. It said a lot for Jacques that he had kept his love for her between himself and Buckley. She was quite something.

He went to the box of paperwork, searched for what he was after and pulled out a couple of pages. He handed them to Marianne.

'In light of what you now know, do you have any new interpretation of this statement?'

Marianne took another drink and studied the papers. Her face gave nothing away, but her eyes flitted intently across the pages. At last, she started to eat a bit.

'Absolutely,' she said. 'Each purchase is that of a drug. So, for example, lemonade is, don't know, marijuana. Gin is perhaps cocaine. A good whisky, perhaps an opiate. The more expensive the drink, the more expensive the drug. A quick look at the investment in each shows how much each was selling. Marijuana and coke did the best. The payments in...' she raised her eyes and looked at Ward. 'The payments in are profit. Pure and simple. The fact that they are the same as his wage is a rather flimsy way of trying to cover their steps. Should someone decide to take a closer look, which nobody would ever have done, he could simply claim that he had transferred his wage into this account. It wouldn't stand up to close inspection, for sure. You only have to look at the other account to see that nothing had been transferred. He and his wife used the money to reinvest in the trade, but I can pretty much guarantee that there is another account somewhere to take the excess.'

'Where?' asked Ward.

'It's the Caribbean,' said Marianne. 'Name a bank.'

'Could you find out?'

Marianne snorted. 'I doubt it. It's like Switzerland and the Nazis. No one really wants to talk about it, despite the fact that everyone knows about it.'

'Don't we have an 'in'?'

Marianne shook her head. 'Mike, apart from love, the only thing on this earth to drive people to lies, murder and deceit is money. I could go to every bank in this beautiful sea and come back with nothing but stuttering deniability.'

Ward finished off his lobster and downed the last of his wine. It had been the perfect meal. He made a mental note to repeat the experience.

'What do you know about Jeans Genies?'

'The clothing company?' Ward nodded. 'Nothing.'

'Do they work at night?'

'Hell, no. That would cause a real revolution. Nights are sacrosanct to those poor souls. The only time they get to see their wife and kids is in the evening. The only time they get to let off steam is when the rum joints are open.'

'So why would Jeans Genie be saturated with lights at night?'

Marianne shrugged. 'Security?'

'Exactly,' said Ward.

17. Jeans Genies

Marianne gave Ward the keys to a pool car. Most of the drivers had gone for the night, apart from a couple who remained to deal with last-minute requests.

Ward drove to the Jeans Genie factory and parked the car about twenty yards from the entrance. He checked the Browning was in place, holstered in the small of his back, where it was less obtrusive and easy to grab quickly if needed.

The short road to the building was edged by brown, patchy grass and beyond that by random scrub and eventually palm trees enveloped by high grass. There was a wire fence around the entire perimeter, so people and traffic were funnelled towards a single main entrance. An imposing set of metal gates straddled the road, secured by a chain and padlock.

The building, a remnant from the turn of the century, probably a sugar cane factory, it still had an enormous round chimney, stood solidly in a ring of spotlights that covered every inch of the front of it. The building had very much the mill look about it - high, arched windows, a shallow corrugated roof and a large, ornately hinged, double wooden door.

Ward needed to get inside, but the lights barred him from any frontal approach. If anyone was watching, he would be a sitting duck. The whole courtyard in front of the factory was ablaze. He went to the perimeter fence and followed it around. Thankfully, the bright spotlights which shone on the building merely deepened the darkness in which he moved.

The building sat on a large plot, two or three acres at least. The base of the fence was beneath ground. No one was going to slip under it. Across the top ran razor wire, coiled tightly, looping around barbed wire which was stretched tightly between posts about fifteen feet apart. It was pretty much impenetrable. The good thing was that Ward couldn't see any of the small junctions that came with an electric fence. All the same, it was overkill for a factory turning out cheap jeans by the thousand.

He crept carefully around the back of the factory. This was less well lit. It was careless but understandable. Once the average person had seen the well-lit front, they would assume that it was the same all around. A pair of jeans was a pair of jeans. There were always cents which could be turned to dollars. After all, these were the jeans for which the gullible high street stores charged a fortune. There was a certain swagger to be had from ownership. As for theft, they could stuff them in their bags, wear them out underneath their normal clothes, pay a few bucks to the van driver on the way to the boat. The market was hot. To wear the same as someone in Zurich for a few cents more than it cost to produce was a dream. However, for the casual thief, the searches and security would have been enough to put them off.

And those who were caught? Rumour was they disappeared. They were turned into zombies. They were given drugs that submerged them to the point where their pulse and breaths disappeared and they were buried alive. If they were lucky, they awoke and rang the bell from the grave as they sought to claw their way out, and they were saved, but they wandered vacant, a shadow of their former selves, bereft of soul. More often than not they were shunned; quite often they were burned alive. Superstition on the island was stronger than God because God played no part in the resuscitation of the empty soul.

But did it really need an electricity bill bigger than the entire output of Saint Jeanne to dissuade the odd bungler from theft? Ward doubted it very much. It was easy to play on fear, especially among a predominantly Catholic culture where God was little more than guilt. If you wanted Heaven, don't piss off the Lord. On the other hand, did need outweigh guilt? Did hunger outweigh fear? He doubted it. It would be so easy to trace the source who stole from the company that it wouldn't be worth the risk. A job was a job, which was better than no job at all. When it came to pride, there was no pride like food.

Ward traced the side of the fence until he reached the end. It was unforgiving and thorough. Without a set of wire cutters he would not be able to work his way through. He felt his impatience rise. Every turn was a cul-de-sac. Every idea stillborn. He'd have to come back at some other time, armed with the right equipment. He cursed his own stupidity. He should have guessed that he would need more.

He followed the fence nonetheless. There had to be some vulnerability. Everywhere had a weakness, usually down to human error or arrogance. So, where was the secret here? Where was the way in?

The rear of the building, though less lit, offered no more.

The area was well lit. There was no point in having lights that served no purpose. However, they spoke of more than the bipeds who crawled tiredly to work each day. This was the night shift. These were the people who gave not one iota for jeans. So what did they care about?

Ward's white knuckles clenched the fence. If he thought he would get away with it, he would have shaken it until it fell.

Around the back of the building, he found the same, the only difference being that there were fewer spotlights, the assumption presumably being that the well-lit front would be enough of a deterrent to any would-be intruders. That, however, didn't overcome the problem of the fence. If he could get past that, then he could probably find a way between the spotlights, where the shadows fell the darkest. If that was successful, all he had to do was find a way in.

Easy.

There was no way he could get through by using the old trick of an overhanging tree. All the trees had been pruned back to at least ten feet from the fence. If he tried to leap that, between the distance and the height, he would be lucky if he didn't impale himself on the razor wire or break both ankles and even if he was still walking, he would have to get out again, over a twelve feet high fence. Absolutely no hope.

In the distance he heard the sound of a ropey old diesel engine, throaty enough to be from a large vehicle. What the hell was it doing out this way at this time of night? Except perhaps delivering? Or taking away?

He ran as fast and as lightly as he could back to the front of the property and threw himself to the ground of the grass verge. It was dark enough here to remain unseen unless he was caught directly in the headlights.

Sure enough he heard the vehicle slow and drop a gear as it made the turn towards the factory, then saw the headlights as it turned in. It was a big old late-fifties Ford Thames Trader van, clearly exported once it had become outdated in the mother country, now seeing out its twilight years in the Caribbean.

It stopped at the gate and the driver descended. He had a key for the padlock on the gate. While he fumbled with the keys, Ward took his chance and tried the tailgate door. It gave way and he climbed in, leaving the doors slightly ajar. The van stank of chemicals, of ammonium; it was just an eye-burning haze. The van moved off again. Between the doors Ward could see the light increase. They were in the front courtyard, no doubt about that, but the van continued past this and quite clearly rounded the building towards the back. Ward opened the doors a little. The lights fell against the building in bright ovals and, in between, lay grey areas where the light failed to meet. It was the only chance he was going to get. If he didn't jump out now, he would be trapped and probably discovered. He lowered himself from the back of the truck, which can have been doing little more than ten miles an hour and closed the doors. Crouching, he ran to the least lit area he could find and pinned himself against the ground.

The van, brakes squealing, came to a stop and then, with much revving and weaving, reversed as close as it reasonably could to the back of the building.

The diver got out of the cab and opened the back doors. He stood back as the gasses dissipated, waving them away with his hand, and then thumped heavily three times on something metallic that Ward couldn't see.

In response, there was a screech and a wail as a roller shutter raised unwillingly against age and rust and coiled itself slowly against the inside ceiling. A pale-yellow square of light slowly revealed itself and drenched the van. The open doors shielded whatever was going on, but Ward could see feet moving and heard the whirr of a forklift truck as it travelled between van and building. Whatever it was shifting was heavy.

Somehow he had to get between the van and the factory and get inside. He moved further around the edge of the perimeter until he was directly behind the van.

What were the choices? He could bolt forward and hide under the van in the hope that the roller shutter would be closed before the van moved. If it didn't pan out as he hoped, he would be easily spotted and the consequences felt. They, whoever they were, had made no bones about killing him before and he had no doubt that they would take the opportunity now.

He took a chance and moved towards the building. The workmen were too busy with their business to worry about anything else. They chatted animatedly, their voices carrying through the still night air and echoing around the courtyard. To them, it was business as usual. For all they knew, they were removing chemicals which dyed clothes from the van. Or were they not so innocent? Did they know what was coming and going or did they prefer to accept the bucks and run? It was impossible to tell. Neither of them was armed, he had seen that and the relaxed conversation, foreign though it was, carried none of the tension of people breaking the law; it was all banter, all laughter. It wouldn't have surprised Ward if they had been related.

Because the lighting was less intense at the rear of the building, Ward was able to inch forward in what was the darker centre of a binocular light. If no one appeared from the back of the van, he would be fine. If no one was looking out of the windows, he would be fine. If no one decided they needed a cigarette and a cool down in the steamy heat, he would be fine.

He crept to the side of the van, his hand tucked continuously behind the small of his back should he need the Browning, then darted into one of the grey areas between halos of light.

Now he was vulnerable. Now, he would not stand a chance of he was discovered. His Browning, even at the speed at which he could draw it and fire off a shot to body and head, would not be enough. For all he knew, they were armed with rocket launchers and hand grenades and could fell him before he had taken a step. Sure, he might have hit a sternum or a head in a few seconds, but that quite possibly would not have been enough. What could he tell the world as a dead man? What truths lay in a corpse? Nothing and none.

He moved away from the van to the other side of the building. There was nothing. No windows, no doors, just light and brickwork. It was a bust. He was going to have to go back to the Hibiscus empty-handed. It wasn't a step back, but neither would he have achieved a thing. This whole suspension in a vacuum was beginning to piss him off.

Okay. It was time to take a chance. He could not go back to the hotel with nothing. He'd had enough of the inertia. He'd had enough of being the almost-victim. It was time to take control and the hell with what followed.

He went cautiously back to the entrance and waited in the shadows. If he had to, he would shoot and bury the bodies. This whole thing was really beginning to exasperate him. No matter what he did, said or thought, it seemed that someone else was a step ahead.

Within ten minutes, the van was empty. An overpowering smell pickles and vinegar filled the van.

The forklift driver then filled up the van with four pallets of boxes.

After an hour, between the chatting and smoking, the driver and the factory worker made their farewells. Ward pressed himself to the wall until he was convinced he had become invisible. The truck kicked over in a cloud of acrid smoke from the exhaust. The driver pulled away, the headlights ablaze in the opposite direction to Ward and coughed its way back to the gate. Ward watched it round the corner of the building and disappear.

He stood still and waited. He could feel his heart pound in his chest and hear it in his ears, like the rush of white water before it fell one hundred feet into the river below.

He removed the Browning and took a silencer out of his pocket. He screwed it in place and waited for five minutes.

The lights were still on and the roller shutter remained open. He guessed that the forklift driver, job done, had gone for a break. Now was as good a time as any to go in. As he was about to move, a shadowy figure stepped out and lit a cigarette. It wasn't the forklift driver. This man threw a completely different silhouette. That wasn't good news; if there were two men, there could be three or ten or a hundred. Ward cursed his caution. He could have been inside by now if he hadn't waited for so long.

Eventually the man reached the stub and flicked the cigarette away across the car park. He put his hands in his pockets and considered the dying embers, then raised his head to the sky. A meteor threaded a silver arc through the stars, then was gone. The man went back inside the building, but left the shutter open.

Ward gave him more time. He looked for shadows in the tongue of light that licked the ground from the open shutter. There was nothing. Whoever it was had clearly had enough of the stifling heat and fumes and allowed the building to breathe.

He edged forward. The light from the doorway seemed awfully bright. He peeked around the door. There was nothing. The barrels from the van were gone and the area within was no more than a carpet of red cement coated by a thick layer of red paint. There were even rubber track marks on the floor where the forklift had repeatedly carried out the same task.

The choices for Ward were obvious. Step in and take a chance, take a look around and see what he could find or play it safe and get Superintendent Moise to issue a search warrant and take the place apart. He didn't trust Moise. It was easy to admit. Past experience had taught him not to trust. It was as straightforward as that. Moise could have been batting for either side or for himself. He could have been playing the survival game, standing aside until he saw where his bread was buttered, then choosing sides as it suited him. And as for Buckley…well…he was little more than a chocolate teapot at the moment. The less he knew, the better. He was so vulnerable, it would not take much pressure from either side to sway him.

The sound of the forklift was distant; it's gas-driven engine was very quiet, but the metal bucket on top of it shook loudly. Occasionally, the forks would slide along the hard floor as it moved something, then grind away again as it moved onto the next lift.

On impulse, Ward ducked through the doorway. The place was bathed in light. Dotted about were hundreds of boxes but, most startling of all, behind a painted yellow line about twenty feet from the door, there was row upon row of small, square desks, each burdened by a Singer Futura sewing machine. There must have been two to three hundred of them. That was a big investment. The place smelled chemical, not nearly as much as the van, but it had a distinct lab odour about it. On each bench was a partially-finished pair of jeans, a sign that whoever sat at the table had bolted as soon as the whistle blew.

Ward looked in one of the boxes. It was full of denim. On the side in bold blue letters was printed Denimes Internationale. That was the name of the people paying money into Haines' account. Once again, that had to be more than coincidence. There was always the possibility that Haines had genuinely invested in the company. Jeans were big; they would never go out of fashion. Some sort of investment in a growing, overseas company would not be unreasonable. The shares and the profits from them would supplement his pension, for sure. A monthly income would be better. But weren't shares paid quarterly? Ward was sure of that, but maybe the old HC had come to his own arrangement. He wondered briefly if Buckley's accounts were similar. If the company still put the quarterly amount on the books, which amounted to the monthly payments to Haines, then that was merely jiggling figures. Yes, it was, technically, illegal, but as long as input and output matched at end of year, was anybody really going to care? Especially in this part of the world where so much finance collided that any attempt to 'officially' regulate it might cause a landslide on the Caribbean stock market. From that, the whole world might suddenly wobble. The markets were notoriously timid when it came to any sort of rumour or event. It was all built on a foundation of straw. At any time, a small gust of reality could bring it down.

The noise of the forklift increased. It was returning to the entrance. Ward ducked behind some boxes of denim and waited.

The driver pulled it up and parked it, then closed the shutter doors which fell with a nails-down-a-blackboard grind. He made final cursory check of the room and then turned out the lights.

The place was plunged into darkness. There was only the light from the spotlights, which fell through the large arched windows and yawned across half the room.

The silence was absolute. The forklift tick-ticked as it settled, but apart from that, there was nothing.

He was trapped. The shutters were his only way out and they were kissing the cold concrete floor. He could raise them again if he had to, but that would only draw attention to him.

The driver had exited a door at the other end of the room. Should he follow him? For all he knew, he might end up smack in the middle of the canteen with fifteen of his close cousins. There was just no knowing.

Yet, where had the barrels been taken? The forklift would never have made it through the doorway. Where had it gone? There had to be another area where the truck deposited its goods. And you couldn't turn out this many jeans without a warehouse somewhere. Why had there been such a strong smell of vinegar? It had been overwhelming in the back of the van and made Ward's eyes sting enough to make them water; it still lingered in the massive sewing room. The stagnant air dissipated nothing.

He tried to make sense of it. Was vinegar used in the production of jeans? What was vinegar anyway? Some sort of acid he seemed to remember. Something told him it was used to make jeans, perhaps in the dye process. He was sure that it had been touched upon in chemistry lessons long ago, but there was also something about drugs, how it was used to aid in the precipitation of certain substances.

He clutched the pistol and moved forward. He did not want to use the gun; under no circumstances did he want anybody to disappear tonight. It would raise all sorts of alarms. If anyone became aware of his intrusion, they would shut the operation down and cut all communications. That would mean bodies in the sugar cane and on the reef as those in the know were quickly dispatched.

Ward moved forward towards the door which the driver had gone through. Sure enough he found out where the forklift had gone. Between the windows and the door was a ramp, very much like the kind of incline found in a multi-storey car-park.

The light from the windows fell upon him and then dissolved as he passed through them. Even in his light shoes he could hear his footsteps upon the ground. They echoed around the factory and made him feel clumsy.

The ramp was at about one in five. In the distance, beyond the end of the ramp and to the right, Ward could see a faint light. It clearly faded as it reached the bottom of the incline, but was enough to give Ward some indication of where he should go.

He descended the ramp with his back against the wall. Even in the dull light he could see where the teeth of the forklift had bitten into the concrete as drivers had forgotten to raise the forks to account for the angle. It must have been a jarring experience. Those machines were heavy and gave way for nothing. Every driver who had forgotten about the slope would never do it again, if only for the sake of their wrists and their backs.

With the Browning in both hands and his hands held high, he reached the end of his descent. He looked right and in the distance saw the weak, white light of fluorescent bulbs. He knew that somewhere at the end of this subterranean vault lay some answers. As he descended, the smell of vinegar grew stronger. On the walls were some extractor fans which sucked in the hideous smell and shunted it into the night. It wasn't much, but it might have stopped people passing out or causing serious eye and skin irritation.

Time was money, money was power.

He approached the semi-light carefully. At any moment, a forklift or just someone taking a break might pass by, although he was pretty sure that breaks would have been discouraged.

The walls had been carved by some elementary machinery. The teeth marks of whatever mechanical monster it had been were scraped into the walls. The end of the short, for want of a better word, corridor, opened into an area lit by a dim luminescence. The entrance was round, like a cave by the sea, as if time alone had caused the breech in the rock.

At the end of the corridor he stopped and looked into the cave.

He was astounded by what he saw.

Row upon row of long, joined desks, running down the centre of the huge cavern. The air was cloudy. The people behind the desks wore face masks as they manipulated a pile of powder in front of them.

Ward turned as he heard footsteps.

'Hello, Mr Ward,' said a familiar voice. 'You seem determined to pursue your own end.'

Ward turned quickly and then dropped his weapon. Behind him were five men, all with M16A1 Rifles aimed at him. They weren't subtle, but they were very efficient.

Ward raised his hands and stepped back against the wall.

Out of the shadows came Superintendent Moise.

'The problem with the British,' he said, as his face cracked into a smile, 'is that they don't know when they're done. They've been hanging onto a dead empire for so long now that they don't even realise that it has slipped beyond their grasp.'

Three of the men converged on Ward, their rifles buried in their shoulders, their eyes along the sights, while the two brawniest men pinned him to the wall. He felt handcuffs bind him, then felt that punch-in-the-nose dizziness that led to sleep.

18. The Chimes of Midnight

Moise stood tall next to Ward's inert body. Ward had been dragged into a side room, essentially a cell, and deposited naked on the cold floor. When he awoke, it was with a pain in the back of his head, doubled by the pain in his nose. The butt of a rifle carried a mighty sting.

'Mr Ward,' Moise got down on his haunches. 'I need to know what you know. I need to know what you have passed on. If we are to save this revolution, I need to know.'

'Bloody coppers!' said Ward between broken lips. 'You're all the same. Everywhere. You're all the same. If you can take a fiver when anybody else wouldn't settle for less than a tenner, you're there. Cheap bastards!'

Moise leapt up and kicked him in the ribs. It hurt. It really hurt. The breath rushed from him.

'I don't have time, Mr Ward. Come on. What do you know? It won't save you, but it might make your death less painful.'

Ward opened his eyes. The cell, essentially little more than another cave, was dimly lit by a candle. The thin yellow light struggled for oxygen and with every one of Moise's words, flickered for life.

'Death is death,' said Ward. 'The pain will end, no matter what. I will scream and I will fight and I will lose and I will die. I don't care. As long as there are bastards like you in the world, I don't care.'

Moise leaned against the wall and crossed his arms. 'And England? What of England? What of the England that subjected the world to obeisance and pain for nearly three centuries? What of the England that with its bare hands tore apart culture and belief, all in the name of profit?'

'England will be fine. She always has been and always will be. She is an island, entire of herself…'

'She is a monster!' spat Moise. 'She and the west, where low morals and poor education and libertarian standards allow the fabric of society to be torn by a weak heart and an unsteady soul.'

'And the alternative?' asked Ward. He could feel the cold handcuffs bite into his wrists as he lay against the concrete floor. He tried to sit up, but Moise put his foot upon his back and pushed him down.

'It's obvious. The totalitarianism of the communist state. The absolute rule of the father over the child.' Moise's breath stuttered in his enthusiasm. 'The equality of the individual against the elitism of the rich. The absolute destruction of capitalism in favour of a meritocracy, where that which you earn is yours and what is yours belongs to all.'

Ward groaned as he rolled over. 'I'm sorry, Moise, but a meritocracy is capitalism. The only difference between communism and capitalism is the suppression of that meritocracy and the oppression of the people.'

Moise laughed derisively. 'Really? Then you truly do not understand the essence of the communist state.'

'Yes, I do,' said Ward. He coughed. It hurt without end as a spasm wracked his body. 'I understand that no one is born equal. I understand that the essence of human nature is to prevail. I understand that there must always be lords and serfs, no matter the century, no matter the belief. You see, that's the thing. Ultimately, human nature isn't about logic, it's about greed and survival and that will never change. Sure, you can use logic to achieve that greed, but there must always be a hunter and a victim. Always. It's about the survival of the fittest.'

'I agree,' said Moise. 'I agree completely. There is no reason whatsoever for the weak to survive. The crippled, the mentally ill, the weak, the outcasts, what purpose do they serve but to undermine the strength of a nation and therefore the world?'

'I think you miss my point,' said Ward. 'Just because they are not as fortunate or rich as others does not mean that they can't contribute. They contribute because they have thought and, right or wrong, thought makes them free. And the thing that allows that thought is compassion. Neither you nor the Nazis were able to understand the concept of compassion and that is why, in the end, they lost and you will lose. You will kill those that matter most in order to end up with an oppressed, bland, homogenous whole.'

'I am not a Nazi,' objected Moise.

'Really?' said Ward. 'Tell me, where does the oppression of the right-wing end and the tyranny of the left begin? Names don't matter really. You're all the same. You want wealth for an elite few and screw the people. Power is everything. The absolute authority of the individual is all. It's just a circle, that's it, and you all meet at midnight.'

'And where are you, Mr Ward?' asked Moise agitatedly. 'Where are you on this circle? Left? Right? At your master's bidding?'

Ward knew that he was doomed, whatever he said. 'I despise you all. I despise the right, the left and the in between. You know why? Do you *want* to know why?'

Moise held his arms out, inviting Ward to speak some more. 'Why, Mr Ward?'

'Because people like you create people like me. I wish I was redundant. I wish there was no need for armies and bombs and war. I wish that I could go back to writing my meaningless books.'

'You can, Mr Ward.'

'No, I can't, because I'm in this thing up to my neck and I can never go back. As long as I know that you and your kind exist, then I must do what I can to stop you.'

Moise laughed heartily. 'So, it's a crusade, is it?

You're doing the work of the gods, whichever god it is that happens to be sitting behind a desk in London?'

'Listen,' said Ward tiredly. 'Why don't you just do me a favour and shoot me. Put me out of your misery. I can't listen to your bullshit anymore.'

'I promise, I will,' said Moise. 'Just as soon as I know what you know. Who have you told?'

'Go to hell!' spat Ward.

'I think you'll get there before me, Mr Ward.'

'Then I'll see you there.'

Moise got down on his haunches again. He was sweating profusely. The feeble candlelight made it look as if his waxen skin was melting. 'I think it's your turn to misunderstand me. This,' his finger circled the cave around him, 'is your hell. This hot, airless little hole in the ground is your hell.'

He stood up, went to the door and pulled it open. 'Come on in,' he said.

Ward lifted his head to see who Moise was talking to. There was no mistaking who it was, even in the semi-darkness. The black eyes and broken nose gave Mirlande the look of one who had been resurrected without their soul.

19. The Iron Chair

'So, who is The Genie?' Ward shuffled uncomfortably. The uneven floor, strewn with small slivers of rock, bit into him.

Mirlande softly sang the lyrics to David Bowie's Jean Genie. '*Sits like a man but smiles like a reptile.*'

'That's meaningless,' said Ward.

Mirlande scoffed. 'Meaningless? Look at you! You are about as meaningless as it gets; naked and nothing. You see what you did to me?' She reached down, grabbed his hair and wrenched his head towards her. 'Look at me, you savage son-of-a-bitch! Do you see what you did to my beauty? Do you see the scars?'

'You'll be fine. The eyes will settle. They'll be back to their dusky devil-red in no time. Although…' Ward winced. '…that nose…'

Mirlande instinctively put her hand to her face. 'Yes?'

'I have to say,' said Ward with the faintest hint of satisfaction, 'you look like a pig. Really, you look like you've swapped that lovely little feminine nose for a porcine snout…'

She kicked out and caught Ward in the centre of his face. His neck snapped back. He reeled. Consciousness slid away from him for a second. He would have been grateful. It would have been good to just let it all go, but Mirlande's screaming fury brought him back.

'You are going to suffer!' she shrieked.

Ward spat. He could taste nothing but iron as blood filled his mouth. 'I already have suffered, believe me. A conversation with Moise is torture enough.'

She went to the door and stuck her head out. Ward heard the grate of metal against stone and then saw two burly men carry in what was clearly a weighty object. They set it down next to him, almost in the centre of the room.

It was a chair, a metal chair that, much like a colander, was full of holes. It was bulky. The lower half was covered to the ground, so that it wasn't a chair with four legs, but a chair with an iron skirt. The back of the chair, normally built for style, for elegance, for comfort, was six inches thick and straight. At the side of all of this, just below the seat, was a handle, like the handle one might find on a manual whisk, only larger.

She nodded at the two men. One of them removed Ward's cuffs, then they both dragged him from the floor. He tried to resist, to make life difficult for them, but one sharp punch to his solar plexus was enough to double him up and remove what little fight was left in him. They slung him into the chair. The metal was cold against his skin. Each of his wrists was then cuffed to the chair and a leather belt strapped around his waist. It was tight. He thought that Moise might have broken a rib or two. It was an effort to breathe.

'Would you like to know about this chair, Mr Ward?' asked Mirlande. She looked like the cat that had got the cream.

'No,' said Ward.

'I'll tell you anyway.'

'I thought you might.'

Mirlande circled him like a hyena in for the kill. 'I had this chair made. I mean, from my own costs. Nobody paid me to make this chair; it was just a part of the pleasure.'

'Let me know the name of your blacksmith. It's a fine chair,' said Ward.

Mirlande sauntered over to him. 'Have you heard of the iron chair?' she asked.

'I'm guessing it's nothing to do with picnics,' said Ward. He felt a drop of sweat fall from his brow and land in his eye. It stung. He could feel his heart rage inside his ribcage.

Mirlande clapped her hands like a child. 'Quite right, Mr Ward. Quite right.' She pressed her palms together as if she was about to pray, then linked her fingers tightly. 'In the middle ages people were put in the iron chair to make them talk. Or cry. Who cares? But it was what you might call a 'persuader'. A machine invented solely for the purpose of confession. It was simply an iron chair with spikes and it hurt.'

Mirlande walked to the handle and fondled it. 'This,' she said, 'is my iron chair. I have adapted the design to better suit my needs. Inside it is a secret that nobody wants to know.'

Ward curled his swollen lips. He was deeply aware of her sadism and had never doubted that she would practice it on him.

Mirlande grasped the handle and turned slowly.

It was an odd sensation. At first it felt like ants crawling across his back and over the backs of his thighs, nipping away at him, then it felt like they were stinging him. Then, as each tiny tooth broke his skin, he felt as if he was going to explode.

He fought the handcuffs until he thought that his wrists would break. He strained to get away from the pain, but there was nowhere to go. The thick leather belt around his waist cut into his already bruised abdomen and chest. He could feel the two ends of a broken rib grind away at each other. Whatever he did just seemed to bring on another, different pain.

'You see,' explained Mirlande as she wound the handle, 'with each turn, the spikes inside the chair get longer and, as they get longer, they eat into your skin. First they nibble at the epidermis. Then they pierce the dermis and start to hurt, because that's where they begin to tickle the nerves, and then they get to the steak, that meaty layer of subcutaneous tissue, followed by muscle. Omnomnom.' She giggled like a schoolgirl. 'What you feel now is the beginning. It's nothing. By the time I've finished, you'll be begging to die.' She rubbed pensively at her chin. 'The difficulty I have is to not let you exsanguinate. If that happens, well, it'll be over and none of us will get what we want. So long as the pointy bits plug the holes, you'll be fine, but if I should happen to turn the handle the wrong way then, whoosh, blood city.' As if to emphasise the threat, she wound the handle the other way. 'But we're not quite there yet. That was only,' she chuckled, 'scratching the surface.'

Ward felt the pins withdraw and then the warm stickiness of his blood as it seeped between his skin and the chair. The spikes can only have gone in perhaps a couple of millimetres, and thankfully hadn't invaded his groin but, as with many of these things, the anticipation of what was to come next heightened the terror and the pain. If this was only the beginning, what would the end be like?

Mirlande dragged a wooden chair in from outside the room and sat on it next to the handle. Ward flinched as her hand went down towards it. She let the hand hover over it, then tap-tapped at it with her index finger. Ward awaited the agony. He was rigid, every sinew taut with the expectation of pain.

'So, Mr Ward,' said Mirlande lightly. 'Do you have anything to say?'

Ward licked his broken lips. He tried to keep his head up, but it was too heavy and sagged to his chest. 'Yes,' he said weakly.

'That's good,' said Mirlande. 'What would you like to share with me?'

'Well,' said Ward breathlessly, 'I've given this a lot of thought…'

Mirlande leaned eagerly in towards him. 'And?'

'And I really do think that I picked a very bad time to give up smoking.'

Mirlande's hand went straight to the handle. Once again, Ward felt the spikes begin to nibble at his raw flesh, only this time, they went a bit further and already exposed nerve ends sent currents of pain shooting through his entire body. With every slow, small turn of the handle, it felt like they were piercing the backs of his eyes. He screamed, but all that came out was a dry rasp.

Mirlande stopped. This time she left the spikes in place. That can't be a good sign, thought Ward. She's leaving them in to plug the holes. If she takes them out…

He felt a sharp, hard slap across his face. Mirlande stood before him, tight-lipped and wild-eyed. She leaned over him and bit his left ear. She severed it. Whether she had bitten a lump off, Ward couldn't tell, but he could feel blood running from the wound, filling his ear, dripping down his neck and onto his shoulder.

'You,' she said slowly, 'are not funny.'

She wiped his blood from her lips with the back of her hand, smeared it down Ward's chest, then left the room.

Ward tried to move a tiny amount, just to relieve the pressure, but he was pinned to the chair. It felt as though he was ripping his flesh.

When she came back into the room, Mirlande was not alone. Next to her was Bill Buckley.

Ward's head dropped. He felt hope desert him. Tears filled his eyes. He tore his dry lips apart. 'Oh, Bill!' he rasped. He had no other words. Only a few hours ago he had hope for this man, told himself how much he liked him, would have been willing to lie for him to keep him free, but now all he could feel was an all-consuming disappointment.

Mirlande left the room. 'It's up to you, Bill,' she said

on the way out. 'Die slowly, die fast. I don't care.'

Bill took the chair that Mirlande had placed next to the iron monstrosity. 'Come on, Mike. Time's up, for both of us. There's no need to suffer. Just tell them what they want to know.'

Ward lifted his head and turned towards Buckley. The poor man had taken such a beating. His bottom lip was split and black. Both of his eyes were bruised, the left one with a savage cut below it. A trail of blood seeped from beneath his hairline and ran down towards his right eye. It fell down into his eyebrow and then carried on to his cheek. With the cut beneath his other eye and the loss from that, he looked like a clown.

'Piss of, Bill!' said Ward.

Buckley leaned in towards him. He stank of sweat. His breath was stale. He can't have eaten or had a drink, a non-alcoholic drink, for hours.

'I have told them all of it. Everything. I had no choice. They were going to kill me…'

'They still are,' said Ward flatly.

Buckley's head fell. 'I know, but I'm a coward, Mike. You know that. I just want to die quickly, painlessly. I am happy to pay the price for my stupidity.'

He put his hands across Ward's left hand. Ward wanted to recoil. The idea of a serpent on his skin repulsed him, but Buckley's grip grew tighter. As he did so, Ward felt Buckley's fingers fiddling, manipulating the handcuffs. The fool had sneaked in something - a hairpin, a needle, some method of picking a lock - and was working at his wrist.

The cuff fell loose. Ward didn't move.

'Did I ever tell, you, Mike, that I used to be in the Boy Scouts? I got a few badges. Nothing spectacular.'

Buckley got up and walked unsteadily across the room. He played upon it, ran his hands along the wall to steady himself and stopped to fight off the dizziness. 'The thing is, boy scout-wise, I didn't do too well. I was too highly-strung and they moved me sideways into admin. I was always good with the paperwork, Mike. Always very good.' He wheeled his way next to Ward's right side, then dropped to his haunches again. Again, Ward felt something at the cuffs and they slipped loose.

'You know, Bill,' said Ward as loudly as he could. 'You're not a bad chap. I think you just fell in with the wrong crowd.' He meant that. 'I just can't do what you ask.' He dropped his voice. 'But I can do what you want me too.'

'They never search me. No idea why.' Buckley slipped a Smith and Wesson Model 36 from his waistband. He put it in Ward's hand. 'Good luck from her Majesty, Mike. I'm sorry. I'm sorry for all of it.'

Ward held the gun in his right hand. He had five shots and a dose of street-fighting to get out of his sorry predicament.

'You're forgiven,' he said with as much kindness as his condition would allow. 'If you wouldn't mind turning that handle a notch…' Buckley went to the other side of chair. 'Anti-clockwise, Bill,' warned Ward. 'And slowly.'

Buckley turned the handle. In the time that they had been in his skin, his blood had congealed around the spikes. Ward gritted his teeth as they came away. It felt like they were peeling his skin off but, at the same time, the relief was immense. He undid the belt and immediately felt as if he could breathe again.

'Okay,' he said to Buckley. 'Now blow the candle out and get behind the chair. It'll give you some protection. The words fan, hit and shit come to mind.'

Buckley blew out the candle and made himself as small as he could behind Ward.

Ward rubbed his wrists to get some life back into

them. He had no idea what the hell he was supposed to do now. He had a five-firecracker gun and an army to fight, but Buckley had risked his all to save him, so he had to do all he could in return. He peeled the metal seat from under him. Now he understood why Mirlande hadn't withdrawn the spikes. He had stuck to the chair like glue. To move was agony. He could feel the blood start to flow again.

'Alright!' he said aloud. 'Alright! I'll do it. But I hope you know that it means we're both dead.'

He waited for some reaction.

Mirlande entered the room.

He aimed at her head and fired.

She fell to the ground.

20. Dead Eggs and Pickled Herrings

Somehow Mirlande got to her feet and ran before Ward could take another shot. She had a hand to her head as she fled. He could see blood glistening on the ground in the corridor, so he knew that he had hit her.

The air was filled with the echo of footsteps, all converging on the cell. Ward got up from the chair and hid at the side of the door. Two men rushed in. He shot each of them once in the head, then grabbed one of their rifles. He ripped the spare magazine from the other rifle, then realised he had no pockets to put it in. He dropped it to the ground and waited.

Sure enough, more guards came at a pace towards the cell. If there were only five as Ward had counted when he had been captured, that might not be so bad.

He leapt into the corridor and fired three shots. One of the guards went down. The other two ducked into rooms at either side. In the packing room there was a stunned silence as people stood with their hands in the air or lay cowering on the ground. Ward walked slowly and silently along the corridor.

Suddenly there was a shot behind him.

He raised the rifle and turned, ready to fire. Buckley was in the corridor with the pistol. In front of him lay Moise. Buckley raised the gun and fired once more at him. He was dead. He stared with horror at what he had just done.

'That's empty now,' said Ward sharply. 'Pick up a rifle.'

Buckley turned away from what he had done and gingerly grabbed the rifle next to the fallen guard. 'I'm not sure how you fire these things,' he said.

'Just point it and pull the trigger,' said Ward. 'Keep looking behind us.'

Ward moved cautiously towards the two rooms. It was a matter of seeing who would twitch first. The guards could not stay where they were forever, but he was beginning to feel cold and shaky. The shock was setting in. He didn't know how much blood he had lost, but he suddenly became very aware of his nakedness, of how vulnerable he felt.

'I don't think I can just stand here,' he said to Buckley. 'I have to keep moving or I think I might pass out.'

'A room each?' suggested Buckley.

'I can't see any other way,' conceded Ward.

They each went to a side of the corridor, pinned themselves to the wall and slid warily along. It was hell on Ward's back. He took a quick look behind him and saw his blood smeared against the rock.

They reached the lip of each room. Buckley looked terrified. Ward indicated that they should go on three. He raised a finger and counted. Buckley went early and leapt into the room firing frenziedly. His thirty rounds must have been used in a couple of seconds. The noise was horrendous. The shots exploded within the rocky walls like cannon fire. Ward threw himself to the floor and faced into the room on his side of the corridor, his shoulder to the ground, gun raised. He took three shots, then caught a flash of light from a watch and fired at it. The tiny light disappeared. He heard a body slump to the ground.

He immediately turned and went to Buckley. He feared the worst. Buckley had gone in with his eyes closed and gun blazing. It had not been a recipe for success.

'Bill?'

'Mike?' groaned Buckley from the darkness.

'Bill? Did you get him?'

'I did, you know, I did. But I think he might have got me too.'

Ward went into the room and turned on the light

switch. A single dull bulb dangled from a threadbare wire.

He made sure the guard was dead, then went to check out the High Commissioner. 'Well done, Bill. You got him. Where did he get you?'

Ward scanned Buckley's body. There was blood everywhere. Ward scrabbled madly at Buckley's abdomen for an entrance wound. He could find nothing.

Buckley held up his left hand. It was a mess. 'I think he shot my little finger off,' he said.

Ward couldn't help but smile. He helped Buckley up and told him to wait while he checked the corridor. Mirlande could be anywhere and he didn't know how badly he had hurt her. His aim had clearly been off. She was just lunatic enough to let herself bleed to death if she could get Ward first.

Ward advanced into the packing room. There were drugs everywhere. He raised the gun. 'Get out!' he ordered.

At first hesitantly and then in a rush, the workers gratefully ran past him.

Ward stepped into the heart of the giant cave. Like the cell he had been in, it had been excavated from rock. Strip lighting had been put in place. It bathed the room in a pale, yellow light. Down the centre of the room was a row of tables, each put end to end to run the entire length of it. Much like in the sewing room, there were boxes along the wall, all with 'Denimes Internationale' on the side. Ward took a look in one of them. It was full of tightly sealed bags of drugs, each bag about the size of a house-brick. The tables brimmed with plastic containers, each of those containing a powder to be transferred to one of the bags and packed away.

So, where did that pickled, vinegary smell come from? It was so potent, but there was simply no obvious source.

He walked to the end of the room, it must have been two hundred yards, but he was greeted with little more than another wall. This though was not carved from the indigenous rock from which the rest of the underground was made, but from bricks. It seemed odd to Ward that whoever had paid for this hideaway should suddenly use bricks. It had to be significant. Why build a wall in a cave when you already had the raw materials available? Yet there was no way through. The whole area was sealed tight. He stood back, rested against the edge of a table and stared at the wall. It was a perfect wall. He walked up to it and sniffed it. There was that acidy, vinegary smell, as if it had seeped through the pores in the bricks. He stood there naked and crossed his arms. He must, he thought, have looked ridiculous, but it was too late for modesty.

Then he saw that the mortar between two of the bricks had a hairline fracture in it. The crack was minute, but in such perfection the fault always stood out. He went back to the wall and took a closer look. There it was. The mortar between what was a jagged square of bricks, nine or ten feet apart, had the same hairline crack. Anyone not looking for it would never have seen it.

Ward ran his hand across the wall, looking for abnormalities in the design, for bumps and bruises that could give something away. There was nothing. He banged upon the wall in frustration.

Buckley moved forward, the rifle in his arms, glued to his belly like some raw recruit told that it was his brand-new friend.

'Mike? What is it?'

Ward shook his head. 'There's more. I'm missing something.'

Buckley put is gun down on the table and moved towards the wall. He could see nothing out of the ordinary.

He ran his hands across the bricks, searching for the tell-tale anomaly that would give the game away. Then he saw what the answer might be. He got Ward's attention and pointed out a double light switch.

Ward looked at him as if to say 'Really?'. Nothing was ever that simple. He walked to the switch and flicked the one nearest the wall. Sure enough, the segment between the cracks began to move backwards and then slide sideways.

He took a step forward to the entrance. He was astounded by what he saw. Beyond the wall was another cavern and, inside that cavern, were vats, enormous vats that held God knew how many gallons. The place reeked. It was like the bad end of a chemistry lab, a cross between dead eggs and pickled herrings. Unseen things bubbled and dripped.

'What the hell?' he said.

Buckley shrugged.

'My God,' continued Ward. 'This is a base lab, refinery and supermarket rolled into one. They've gone from import export into production.'

He walked around the perimeter of the room. So, this was where the forklift had taken the barrels. They were labelled Acetic Anhydride and had the familiar hazard symbol on them. There were also containers for calcium oxide, calcium hydroxide, ammonium hydroxide, sodium carbonate, sodium bicarbonate and calcium carbonate, among others that Ward did not recognise. There was litmus paper, ethyl alcohol, activated charcoal, hydrochloric acid, drying boxes, beakers and heat sources. It was everything needed to turn the raw imports into street value muck.

Interestingly, ward noted that there was nothing associated with cocaine production or even marijuana. He could only assume that those labs were dotted elsewhere on the island.

Buckley stepped forward and took in the enormity of

it all. 'I don't know what any of that means,' he said.

'This?' said Ward. 'This means the house on the Sussex shoreline.'

Buckley sniffed and screwed his face up. 'I hope it smells better than this.'

'You know what?' said Ward. 'I'm going to find some clothes and then burn their house down.'

21. Bloody Water

Dressed in the jacket of one of the dead guards, albeit pitted by one or two singed and blood-ringed holes, and a pair of overlarge jeans, Ward looked in the rear-view mirror as he drove the Allegro away from the factory.

As he watched, the sky was lit by a fireball of orange and red, flecked with wraiths of green and blue as the chemicals burned and evaporated, wiping out the stars and the night . It was the *Aurora Borealis* without the peace.

It was revenge, spite, pure and simple, for the damage done.

It was also the wrong thing to do. The whole jaunt had been wrong. He had walked in there with an arrogant righteousness and paid the price. If he had left it alone, been patient, asked London for advice, even for help, he might not have blown the whole operation. Now, all that was going to happen was that The Genie would move on, probably take their business to another Caribbean paradise and start the revolution there. The whole pace was a tinderbox anyway. Sparks would fly across the waters and ignite the kindling carefully placed for change. The entire Caribbean would catch fire; all those on low wages, living in tin boxes, subject to a country, any country among many - the British, the Netherlanders, the French, the Spanish - that had forced themselves upon them centuries ago and continued to exploit them for profit and power, were ready to rise.

And who could blame them? What right had anybody to impose themselves, their beliefs and cultures, upon those from a different land, with a different mentality, who maybe even lived in a different time? Some countries did not want a supermarket. Some didn't even want democracy. Some societies were happy to be led, to dwell in the shadow of a single power, so long as they could eat more then they needed, have more roof than they could share and had a few pennies left at the end of the month. Many were simply content with peace and the sunrise.

The Chief would not be pleased. He could hear his words - impulsive, immature, rancorous, self-indulgent. He would not be able to argue. He had been stupid, simple as that. He should have backed off when the perimeter fence had told him to.

Ward turned to Buckley. He was pale. He clutched his left hand to his chest like an injured bird. The wound would have already clotted by now, the healing process already begun, but behind his eyes lay turmoil and wounds that would probably never mend.

He watched the fireball retreat. It tumbled from the blackness to the ground as if it was being sucked from the sky. A halo of orange remained on the horizon. Occasionally one of the barrels of chemicals would rupture and send a lick of flame into the sky. By the time the fire was done, there would be nothing left but the bones.

He wondered briefly what had happened to Mirlande. Had she burned in the inferno? Or was she now cowering in the sugar cane? Or on her way to the next hideout, wounded, vengeful, full of hate?

'How are you, Bill?' he asked.

'It stings,' said Buckley. 'How are you?'

'It stings,' said Ward. The truth was, he was in agony. Every pothole jolted him from his seat and clawed at the holes in his skin. It felt as if he was draining away.

'What do we do now?' Buckley looked at him pleadingly.

Ward sniffed. 'Let's just get to that HC and get ourselves sorted. I need a salt bath and a scream. And both of us might need some sort of diplomatic immunity.' He paused. 'I'm sorry, Bill. I should have...' He searched for the right words but none would come.

'It's fine,' reassured Buckley. 'You can only do what you can do. If I'd had an ounce of courage, you wouldn't have been in there in the first place.'

'You saved my life tonight, Bill, twice over as I recall. You're no coward. And you didn't start all this. That's down to your predecessor and his wife. I still don't know what the hell was going on.' Ward dropped gear for a dark corner. 'Do you really not know what was going on with Lawrie Stuart? Do you really have no idea of the connection between him and the Benson-Haines woman?'

Buckley shook his head. 'For all my faults, Mike, I have no idea. It was as much a surprise to me as anybody else. I genuinely wanted to know, and I honestly went to the Prime Minister and the police in complete ignorance. I didn't realise...'

Ward cut Buckley off. 'Don't worry, Bill. I believe you. What you have done is beyond wrong, but we're not all made of steel.'

Buckley remained silent for a moment. 'Will you turn me in, Mike?'

Ward turned onto Saint Jeanne's main street. He could see the lights of the High Commission in the distance, a beacon of hope in a dark, dark world.

'Don't ask me that, Bill,' he said.

*

Mr Dragonfly and the High Commissioner were let through the gate by the same man who had greeted Ward a lifetime ago. He shone his torch into the car, then withdrew it, as if to say the blood and bruises were none of his business, then raised the gate.

Buckley took them to a side door. He knocked on

the glass and caught the attention of the attendant. The attendant jumped and opened the door.

'What the hell you doing, sir? You damned near scared the soul from my body.' He saw the state of the two of them. 'Christ almighty, you look like a couple of carrion.'

He ushered them in, closed the door, then escorted them, all the time muttering, down to the medical area.

'You haven't seen us, okay?' said Ward before the attendant left.

'No, sir.' The attendant gave them a final once-over. 'That doesn't mean I'll ever forget the sight of you though.'

Ward and Buckley walked into the ward together. At last Ward felt safe. At last the tension could ooze from him until it was only an imaginary puddle at his feet.

'I need to take a bath,' he said. 'And then I need you to soak me in iodine and dress the worst areas. Think you can do that?'

Buckley nodded uncertainly. 'I am a bit squeamish,' he confessed.

Ward chuckled. 'Wait until you look in a mirror.'

Ward went to one of three bathrooms, the largest, and ran the water. The taps gushed like waterfalls and filled the bath quickly. Steam filled the room and headed towards a vent that whirred silently in the ceiling.

Ward removed the loaned clothes. They had adhered to his skin and came away reluctantly. He threw them into the corner of the room. They sat stiffly in a pile like an animal in *rigor mortis*.

He could not focus at the moment and yet he needed to make sense of it all, needed to know where he was going; whether he *was* even going. Tonight had been disaster and triumph. He had kept some evil off the streets, but he had probably shut down an operation that would have been more useful had he left it alone. The heroin base which had just lit the horizon was gone. It would open up somewhere else, if it hadn't already. The people who ran these things were full of anticipation and rarely short of funds. They would have treated discovery as inevitable. It would cost them, but it wouldn't kill them. They were pragmatists. If it failed, rebuild it.

The only question for Ward was where they would have the next factory ready. Would they keep it on Saint Quentian or move it to a different island? Had they put all their eggs in one white-sanded, palm-strewn basket? Was Saint Quentian it? A once in a lifetime opportunity to stoke unrest gone to hell or could the revolution be started elsewhere? He didn't have a clue.

He tipped some salt into the bath. Wasn't this what they did to people who had been whipped aboard ship? Wasn't that where the saying came from? To put salt on the wound? It promoted healing, the parching of the bloody gashes, and prevented infection, despite the immediate, almost insufferable pain.

He stepped in and reluctantly lowered himself. The salt immediately bit into the backs of his legs, his buttocks and then his back. He lay in the water up to his neck, his teeth clenched and lips pale, until the initial agony had passed and he was left with a perpetual sting and a slowly reddening bath. All the same, it was a relief. He could feel the tension in his muscles subside, each one a guard given permission to stand down.

What would he do? He would have to phone the Chief again, surely, tell him that he'd blown it and await the consequences. Oh well, back to writing books.

The bathroom door swung open. 'Not ready yet, Bill,' he said. 'Need a few more minutes. You get that iodine and I'll be there in ten.'

The door closed again. Ward rubbed at his neck. It

ached. His left shoulder, where he had thrown himself to the floor, felt as if it had been dislocated and put back in place by a plumber. He hadn't dared to look in a mirror.

So, that was it. He had made up his mind. He would go home. He would take Buckley with him and on the plane they would concoct some story to save Buckley's freedom and his pension and keep him at a desk. They would be fine. The Chief would pass the whole debacle over to the Yanks, as if doing them some favour, and then move Ward onto something more within his limits; probably baby-sitting or writing pamphlets on self-defence. That move sideways was always the end. 'Put him where he can do least harm,' the Chief would say. 'That's what they do with all the useless buggers, the has-beens, the ne'er-do-wells'.

Well, to hell with that, he thought. He'd had enough anyway. He'd done his best and it just wasn't good enough. Let someone younger, someone more able, step into his shoes. Someone who didn't resort to revenge and fireballs in the late heat of a Caribbean night. He'd had sufficient anyway. He had lost an ex-wife and two women he had loved to this job. He had killed the despicable and lost friends in the process. Wasn't that payment enough?

To hell with them.

After he had got out of the bath, he would write his letter of resignation and slap it on the Chief's desk, once the old man had torn off a layer of flesh. Better to go out with a bit of dignity than let your self-respect diminish in a series of lesser roles. And his writing would be all the better for his experience. He could go where he had never been before and speak with truth.

He felt the danger before it happened rather than when it happened. That sixth sense that he had developed over time set in and forced him to raise his arms in front of him.

As he did, he felt something bite and then cut into his skin. The pressure was enormous, as if a tourniquet had been placed upon them and jerked and twisted rapidly like a bladed garotte.

There was nowhere to go. The force being applied was phenomenal and he thought that it would only be seconds before the wire found an artery.

He submerged into the deep water and strived to place his hands above his head. As he did so, the wires lost their grip and ate away a slice of each arm. But, it was enough.

He rolled like a crocodile and caught sight of Mirlande. Free of the cheese-wire, he kicked himself towards her and grabbed her hair, then dragged her into the water. Her arms flailed. The wire in her hands fumbled wildly for a grip, lost any purchase on their subject and then fell into the water as her body was yanked forward. It was no good. She could see nothing and all her wild thrashing could do nothing to release her from Ward's roaring, enraged grasp.

He knelt in the water and pulled until her head was between his legs and then, with everything he had left, he held her down until he could feel the spasms of death begin to devour her. He grabbed the cheese-wire, wrapped it around her throat and pulled as much as his faded strength would allow. Mirlande, now wild and desperate for life, kicked furiously; her fists battered at anything that came within their reach. But it was not enough. Ward crossed the wire and pulled. He felt it bite into her neck, break the skin and watched as she kicked, fought and screamed against him. Eventually, in a crimson cascade, the bath water turned a deep, arterial red. He pulled tighter, his knee in her back.

Mirlande's kicking and raging began to subside. Her arms were the first thing to slide away as she groped hopelessly for his face then, as her breath subsided and the bloody water filled her lungs, her legs kicked out and a spasm ran through her frame.

Ward held on, his raw, bleeding arms taut upon the wire, until he knew that she was dead. She shuddered twice more as her autonomic nervous system fought for air, but there was none. The wire had cut through the carotid arteries on either side of her neck and gnawed through to her trachea. Water had flooded her lungs and her brain was empty of oxygen.

He held her down. She had survived a bullet to the face. Who was he to say that she could not survive a couple of lungs full of bloody water?

Soon enough though, she stilled. The reflex twitches withered. Ward pinned her down, his breaths quivering, his eyes as wild as a cow's on the way to slaughter.

Eventually, he released her and slid from the bath. He shook, his hand to his temples, as he gazed upon the abattoir-like scene before him. He had come so close to his own undignified, solitary death, at the hands of a woman who had pursued him for no other reason than for money and reputation.

Was she any different to him? Yes. She was more determined, more skilful, better rewarded. She was his absolute nemesis. She had died by an inch, he had survived by the same inch. Now all that remained was a seaweed of black hair afloat in his blood-stained bath.

Ward could feel nothing but anger and self-doubt and guilt. He was angry because he should have known that she would be in the building. Self-doubt because he had let down his guard. Guilt because he had killed someone's daughter, he had again been forced to take the life of another human being. He could never escape from the guilt. Even when he had committed his first killing so long ago in Cyprus, he had felt guilt, and he had never forgotten the umbilicus between life and death and how he had wielded the knife which severed the two. Now here he was, racked by the same self-reproach and remorse.

He was grateful for the sensations.

Oh, he wasn't on the verge of some epiphany. Far from it. If he was going to luxuriate in her wonder and her ties and her dreams, then he might as well give up; he might as well just shoot himself now. There was no time for revelation. Just the now; just the survival.

Buckley knocked and came through the door, reading the instructions on a bottle of iodine in one hand and a packet of gauze in the other.

'I've got the iodine,' he said. 'I'm afraid this might sting a bit.'

22. Lucky

Ward awoke. He opened his eyes and wallowed in the dizziness that consumed him. He felt seasick. The whole room seemed to shift from east to west with the tiniest movement of his eyes.

An unfamiliar voice broke the silence. 'Ah, Mr Ward. Awake at last. My name is Doctor Bhatia. How do you feel?'

Ward turned his head slowly. Beside him stood an older south-Asian man with grey hair, combed back and held in place by pomade, with kind, inquisitive, brown eyes, which peered through a set of half-moon glasses. He had a bag of fluid in his hand. He changed a drip and set it off again.

'If you feel a bit woozy, don't worry, that's just the morphine. You have been through quite a rough and tumble. All cleared up now though.' He wrapped a cuff around Ward's upper arm, put a stethoscope in his ears and pumped at a rubber bulb. Ward felt the cuff tighten and then felt the relief as it was loosened and blood flowed back into his arm.

The doctor made a note of Ward's blood pressure. He seemed satisfied. 'I've come over from Nassau, me and a couple of colleagues actually. All very rush-rush, hush-hush, but there you go. It comes with the territory.'

'Bill?' asked Ward. He felt like his throat had been sandpapered. 'Is he okay?'

'He's fine. He might have a bit of a scar on his cheek and a gap where his pinkie used to be, but he'll be okay. I think he was more disturbed by what he found in the bathroom.' He looked over the rim of his glasses like a schoolteacher. 'As I said, all cleared up now.'

Ward shifted, more to test out his level of pain rather than because he was uncomfortable. It didn't feel so bad. The worst pain was in his ear. He put a finger to it.

'We stitched that back together,' said Doctor Bhatia.

'It was hanging on by a thread. I thought at one point I was going to have to bin it, but I'm quite a good seamster, you know.'

'Anything else?' asked Ward. The way his body felt he wouldn't have been surprised to hear that it had been sewn back together in its entirety.

'No. No broken ribs, no other internal injuries. Lots of bruises. I'm not going to say that you won't have scars, but all should heal. We found some slivers of your forearms in the bath; couldn't save them unfortunately. Had to graft some skin from your thigh onto one of them. That'll probably hurt more than anything else. It tends to expose the nerve endings.' He smiled. 'You've been through a hell of a lot, Mr Ward. Try to relax.'

'You should leave,' said Ward. 'It's very dangerous here.'

'Don't worry,' reassured the doctor. 'I brought some friends with me.' He pointed at either end of the ward and for the first time Ward noticed the armed guards. 'Besides, you're going home and when you go, I can go back to Nassau, back to my tough life in the sunshine.'

'Home?'

'Yes, Mr Ward. Home. In your case, back to England. You'll be going in a few days, which should give you enough time to come round a bit, find your feet.'

'But I can't go,' objected Ward. 'It's not over.'

Doctor Bhatia put a hand on Ward's arm. 'It is for you, I'm afraid, Mr Ward. On the orders of someone called the Chief. How's the pain? You want something?'

Ward shook his head. 'No.'

So, the Chief was bringing him home, as he thought he would. He could feel the coldness of his shoulder already.

'Okay, if you want anything, press the buzzer and one of the nurses will be along. I finish work at seven this evening and then Doctor Sweeting will take over until the morning.'

'Fine. Thanks,' said Ward flatly.

Doctor Bhatia put his hands in his pockets. 'You're a lucky man, Mr Ward, to have come out of this alive.'

'Yes,' said Ward. 'Lucky.'

He didn't feel particularly lucky.

He wished the doctor would go away now. He didn't want comfort talk. It was useless. He knew that he had screwed up and that he was going to pay the price. No amount of well-meaning chit-chat would change that.

'Anyway, you have a visitor. Are you up for it?'

'No,' said Ward.

Nonetheless, Doctor Bhatia turned and beckoned the visitor.

Marianne entered the room. She looked splendid. She wore a pale-yellow summer dress with a thick white belt around her waist and some low-heeled, white sandals. As ever, her dark hair fell down across her shoulders and lay across her chest. It was as if she had just stepped out of a catalogue. Behind her she pulled Ward's Samsonite case.

She walked purposefully over to the bed and kissed Ward on the lips. She held them there. They were full and soft. 'Hello, Mike, how are you?' she asked.

Ward could taste cherries. 'Lucky,' he said. 'Really very, very lucky.'

Doctor Bhatia smiled and left them to it.

'What was that for?' asked Ward.

'I told him I was your girlfriend.'

'Just playing lip service?'

Marianne didn't answer, but pulled a chair from beside the bed next door and sat down.

'How are you, really?' she asked.

'I'll be fine. Although, I think I've made a bit of a

mess of this. They're sending me home in a few days.'

'I know. Buckley told me. He has to arrange the flight and everything. He's…procrastinating.'

Ward snorted. 'Why? It's over.'

Marianne looked at Ward severely. 'I never had you down as a quitter.'

'I never had you down as a girlfriend,' countered Ward.

'Well, maybe we've both misjudged.' Marianne leaned down to the suitcase. 'Code please.'

'Nine forty-three,' said Ward.

She dialled the number in. 'And what's the significance of that?'

'Random,' said Ward.

Marianne looked at him doubtfully. 'There was a study in Sweden a couple of years ago, when all these codes started to become fashionable. Do you know what they found?'

Ward raised an eyebrow. 'What?'

'That there really was no such thing as a code. Nearly all the numbers used meant something to the person who had used them. It was the one way people could remember them.' She dialled the numbers in and flipped open the case. 'The numbers had to be significant for them to retain the information. So, if anybody trying to break the code knew enough about them, it could be broken. What is nine forty-three to you, Mike? You're not a Virgo are you?'

Ward grunted. 'No comment.'

Marianne emptied the case of clothing, transferring it to a bedside table. She then pushed the case under his bed.

'It's open,' she said.

'Thank you,' said Ward.

'Use it wisely.'

'I promise.'

'Don't promise. Just do.' She stood up and replaced the chair. 'I have to go. I'm due on shift.'

'One more kiss?' asked Ward.

She kissed him, fully and longingly, then left.

Ward watched her go. She didn't have to try. She had grace and sensuality rolled into one.

He just hoped that…

Well, there were always doubts.

Ward declined painkillers for the rest of the day. Even when the nurse had changed his dressings, he had refused. Of course, it had been maddeningly painful, especially on his forearms and around the graft area on his thigh, but he needed to stay awake. He only had a few days to put things right and, more importantly, to find out who The Genie really was.

He had no idea where to start. He thought back over the past couple of days. Is that all it had been? Just a couple of days? How absurd. On the other hand, kingdoms, nations, had fallen in hours, so this was nothing.

What was there, among all that he knew, which could steer him in the right direction?

There were two things that still disturbed him. One of them was Clarissa Benson-Haines. No matter how nasty she had been, and there was little doubt of that, she had done what she believed to be right. That was the thing with people like her. They had a distorted sense of morality. Her moral line might have been higher, skewed even, but she still had one. She, with all her convictions, would not be bent. The question was, how high up that scale of self-denial was murder?

The other thing was the complicity of the state, in the shape of the Prime Minister and the police. Moise was a prime example, but had he been only the tip of the iceberg? He had got what he deserved.

Ward thought that Buckley's conversation with the Prime Minister had been too easy, too cut-and-dried. Either Buckley really was a jelly-spined diplomat or he knew exactly what was going on and had collapsed in the face of pressure. Buckley said that he had been threatened. He was open to blackmail at the very least and if that failed, he could be disposed of. It was easy to threaten Buckley, but exactly how far did that threat go? Was it just him, the joker of the pack, or did it reach the society queen? Could it have gone as far as Benson-Haines? Ward just couldn't see it. As hideous as she was, and as much as she liked the arena, her gladiatorial prowess was limited merely to words, to innuendo, to the weaknesses and susceptibility of others. To actually pull the gladius and submit the final stroke was beyond even her. She wasn't a killer. She was a destroyer. She revelled in the humiliation, not the kill. Her mental illness was kept under control by the lithium. Her blood levels of the drug were fine, so the post-mortem said, so as far as that went, she was probably as stable as she was ever going to be when she died.

So, beyond her? Around about her? Was she caught, wittingly or unwittingly, in a hurricane? Could she do nothing but bend with the wind or break in the face of its power? Her husband was dead. She was insignificant. It was possible that she was being blackmailed, but with what? That her dead husband had been a drug addict? That they had been involved in the drug trade? By the time she had killed Stuart, she was a threat to no one. She was just an old lady living with her sins, but she had killed Stuart for a reason, however oblique that reason might be, and there still remained the question why.

When the lights were out, Ward slipped from his bed and pulled the suitcase out from underneath it. He undid the secret compartment and pulled out a new weapon. The lost Browning had to be replaced by its back-up, a Ruger Speed-

Six revolver with a seventy millimetre barrel. It was a reluctant back-up, but space allowed for one only Browning. Still, if it was good enough for the RUC, it should be good enough for him. As well as the six bullets in the chamber, there were a further twelve .357 Magnum cartridges. He dressed as quickly as his wounds would allow, in a black, long-sleeved top, a pair of black slacks and then put on a pair of lightweight shoes. He split the cartridges between two pockets.

Where he was going, he had no idea. He just knew that it was better than where he was.

23. I know, I know, I know

Ward went first to the HC's offices. It was only up four flights of stairs.

He had bypassed the guards in the infirmary quite easily. They had been sleeping or chatting, smoking outside or reading. He worried that his life might have depended on them.

The offices were in darkness. He switched on his pencil torch and searched.

He found Buckley's office, left carelessly unlocked, and entered. He went to one of several filing cabinets which were tucked away in a corner of the room. They were locked. He tilted the first cabinet and felt along the right side at the bottom. His fingers found a hole and then a metal rod. He pushed the rod upwards. The cabinet opened. It was an old trick, but it never failed.

There was little inside it of relevance. It was all memos and letters. If he had had time to read each one, he was sure it would have made fascinating reading, but time was of the essence. Once it was noticed that he had absconded, there would be lights on all over the place.

He moved to the next cabinet. There was nothing on the drawers to indicate what was inside. He tilted that cabinet too and unlocked it.

This was a bit more like it. It was the famous knick-knack vault. In the same way that every home had 'a drawer', the one where the bills and letters and superglue were kept, so was this austere, grey tombstone.

He rifled each draw. The top one was useless, full of spare pens and staples and notebooks. It was the equivalent of a stationery cupboard.

The second drawer down was more interesting, a collection of labelled, buff folders. He ran through them with his fingers, torch in mouth. It was all a bit random, but no doubt between Buckley and Miss Grace there was a semblance of order. There was nothing. He tried the last drawer.

It was, of course, a mess, with things seemingly tossed in from a height to lay where they fell.

Ward shone the torch in and turned a few bags and small boxes over. He was about to give the search up as fruitless when something caught his eye.

There were two clear plastic bags. On the bags were official-looking sticky labels. He picked them up for a closer look. One was labelled 'Lawrie Stuart', the other 'Clarissa Benson-Haines'. Underneath each of the names was written 'Personal Effects'.

He removed the bag with Stuart's name and took it to Buckley's desk. He tipped the contents out. It was all rather sad; a pair of reading glasses, a well-loved watch, a pretty decent Parker ink pen and a ticket to the local opera - La Bohème. Ward smiled. He had seen La Bohème with his wife at La Scala years ago. It was a grand affair. It was not his favourite work, a little too saccharine for his tastes but, nonetheless, he saw the appeal and had been caught up in the moment, to the point of tears. Such was the power of music.

He looked at Benson-Haines' bag. It was sparse. As these were the things that they were supposed to have had on them when they died, she naturally had very little. In fact, nothing. Nothing but a single piece of paper folded into four and creased, as if it had been stuffed inside a pocket and a fist had held onto it for some time.

Ward pulled the paper from the bag and gently opened it on the desk.

He read:

'I KNOW ABOUT YOUR HUSBAND. I KNOW WHAT HE HAS DONE. I KNOW THAT YOU HAVE TAKEN THE MONEY. IF YOU WANT ME TO KEEP THESE SECRETS, YOU MUST KILL LAWRIE STUART. KILL LAWRIE STUART. KILL HIM.'

It had been hand-written in capital letters. The writing was not particularly good - neither was Ward's if he was honest - but the content, that was odd; short sentences and repetition. Three times she was told to kill Stuart. And then, before that, it said, I know, I know, I know, again three times. Was that simply to hammer home her guilt? To exercise control over her?

How bizarre, thought Ward. How utterly bizarre. Why was something so significant tucked away in a plastic bag in a filing cabinet in the High Commissioner's office? Had Buckley seen it? If he had, did he have no concept of its meaning? And why the hell had he kept it, knowing what it could imply?

He put the note back in the plastic sleeve and replaced it in the filing cabinet drawer.

It was feasible, he supposed, that Buckley had been handed these things and that he had just dropped them, unexamined, into the drawer. The bags were clear plastic, after all, so anything inside was entirely visible. Maybe he had intended to do something with them at some point, but events had simply overtaken him. It would have been impossible not to have reacted to that note once it had been seen.

And there was one loaded question that needed to answered; who the hell had the note come from?

Once again, he didn't know if he could trust Buckley.

The man was either covering up or just plain irresponsible. He had saved Ward's life, yes, but that might simply have been a way to get into Ward's good books, so that Ward might save him from the chopping block.

Too many ifs and buts.

There were footsteps in the corridor. They walked purposefully and stopped outside the office. There were three taps at the door.

'Mr Ward, you can come out now.'

It was a woman's voice, young, decidedly British.

'Come on, Mr Ward. We haven't got all night.'

Ward took the Ruger from his waist holster and approached the door. He listened for any other footsteps. Had she brought the heavy-mob with her? There were no sounds to say that she had.

He carefully opened the door, the gun tucked behind his right thigh, ready to use it if he had to.

What he saw was a very attractive blonde with piercing blue eyes and a scowl, all wrapped up in a doctor's coat.

'Hi,' said Ward.

The woman put out a well-manicured, soft hand.

'Hello, Mr Ward. My name's Penny Sweeting.' She had a strong Australian accent. 'The Chief sent me.'

Ward took her hand. 'Are you going to take me back to bed?'

Dr Sweeting rolled her eyes. 'No, Mr Ward. I'm the transport. Let's go.'

Ward followed without hesitation. They walked quickly through the dark corridors and down dim stairwells until they reached the same entrance through which Ward had come. Tonight there was no attendant, just an empty chair and a shaft of white light against linoleum.

Ward followed Sweeting out. She led him to a car.

'Give me the keys,' he said.

'Not a bloody hope,' she said. 'Just get in and tell me where we're going.'

24. Mexico Bound

Penny shovelled Ward into the passenger seat then ran around to the driver's seat, started the engine and drove. 'Where to?'

'I don't know,' said Ward. 'I'm just making this up as I go along.'

Penny raked the car into forth and screamed out of Saint Jeanne. No one was going to follow them, she had made sure of that, but just to be away from that concrete tomb was all she asked.

'For God's sake, Ward! What are you looking for?'

She drove like a rally driver, between the fields of cane, along dark and narrow roads, following only her headlights. They rushed past factories and fields, past vast plains of volcanic stone that held onions and potatoes and turnips and cactus that forked the sky with three fingers and threw still-man silhouettes.

'Head north, said Ward.

'North?'

'North. I have to speak to someone.'

'Someone? Who? Little Miss Muffet about her tuffet?'

'Are you always this short?' asked Ward.

'Only with the long-winded. Who?'

Ward bit his tongue. Whether he liked it or not, he needed Doctor Sweeting. 'With Clarissa Benson-Haines' servant.'

Penny scoffed. 'Servant? What is this? The nineteen-fifties?'

'As good as,' said Ward. 'Let me guess, you come from a well-to-do family…'

'We did alright…'

'And you have an ethnic supermarket where

occasionally you go to browse, have no clue about what the hell they are selling, and walk out again with an apple. You're a bloody cliché. A white girl with a conscience. A Daddy's girl with nowhere to belong.'

'What the fu..?'

'True or not?' snapped Ward. 'I've spent years in these rat-holes. I have grown to love the food and the people and the culture, but their politics leave me dumbfounded. If they don't like it, they take a machete to it. There is no curtained booth where you may or may not mark your 'X'. There is a folded paper and a tin and man behind you with an automatic rifle in his hand. What is it with hot countries and the inability to understand the process? Is it too much sun?'

'You sound a little old-school, Mr Ward,' said Doctor Sweeting sharply. 'You sound like you miss the Empire. And the servants of course.'

They reached a junction. Ward pointed left.

'No, not at all, but I miss the order. Everywhere's such a mess now. All we seem to be doing is putting out fires.'

'Or starting them, if what happened a couple of nights ago is anything to go by.'

Ward relented. 'Yes, that was stupid.'

'I think that was one of the words the Chief used. Among others.'

Ward laughed. He could imagine the old man, pipe held rigidly between his gritted teeth, enveloped in a pall angry smoke. 'I'm sorry, Doctor Sweeting. It's not your fault. I shouldn't have a go at you.'

'It's Penny and it's fine. But thank you.'

'So, what are you? A doctor or a spy?'

'Both,' said Penny. 'I was born in Brisbane, actually. I came over to England to become a doctor, was recruited by the firm at Oxford, who made sure I finished my training, got all the experience I needed, then sent me out into the big, wide world.'

'And what did you have to offer that caused the mother country to need you so badly?'

'I have an eidetic memory.' Ward looked at her curiously. 'Often referred to as a photographic memory, although technically, they are two different things.'

'I see,' said Ward.

'I had finished the Aussie equivalent of my A-levels by the time I was fifteen. It was almost impossible for me to fail because I just couldn't forget what I had been taught and what I had read. Of course, I couldn't spout it all out to you today because there are now other priorities, but I think I could still pass, if I dug deep enough.'

'So by what age were you medically qualified?'

'I was twenty-one.'

Ward whistled. 'That's a lot for a young person to take on.'

'You'd think so, wouldn't you, but I never really saw it that way. I loved learning and, at that age, it's always fun to show off a bit.'

'So how old are you now? If you don't mind me asking.'

'Twenty-seven.'

'And how do combine doctoring and spying?'

'Sometimes, with a little difficulty. Nassau is my base. I specialise in orthopaedic surgery, so I can use that as an excuse to trot off to various conventions around the world whenever HM wants me there.'

'But why Nassau?'

'Well, it's bloody gorgeous, isn't it.'

'And your mother and father?'

'Dad's a sheep farmer, don't snigger…'

'I wasn't about to,' said Ward with a faint smile on his lips.

'And Mum's a teacher. She teaches English in Maleny.'

'That's quite a mix,' said Ward.

'Hard work and intellect,' said Penny proudly. 'I am of that stock!'

Ward didn't doubt it. She was made of tough stuff and wouldn't be afraid to show it.

Ward looked across at her. She seemed hard-faced to start with, but he was warming to her. She had a femininity that oozed, perhaps accidentally, through her hard carapace. She had the faintest hint of a good perfume about her, one that he could not identify but one that he would recognise from a mile away. Her hair was more than blonde. It was honey and it fell about her shoulders like a wild waterfall. She had those cobalt blue eyes, those just-a-bit-more-than-thin lips, which were eminently kissable, and a body that could have tangoed through the night. Ward wondered briefly what she would be like in bed, then dismissed the thought. Business was business. And besides, if he tried that now, he would need an ambulance.

'Are you married, seeing anyone?'

'Well, that's subtle, Mike!'

Ward tutted. 'I didn't mean it like that. God knows! I've had one marriage fail and every other relationship…' He paused. It was too much in one go. 'I would just be surprised if there wasn't somebody keeping your side of the bed warm in Nassau.'

Penny frowned. Her voice was harsh. 'No. I screw when I want to screw and then walk away. This job doesn't allow me to do much else.'

Ward was mildly shocked by her honesty. He wouldn't have given a second thought if it had been a man who had said it. Perhaps he was more shocked by his being shocked. Just how old-fashioned was he?

They pulled up outside Chaddleworth and left the car tucked away on the driveway.

'So, where to now?' asked Penny.

Ward stretched his stiffening joints. Being crammed inside a car on these roads had been a challenge.

Penny took his arm and leaned him against a wall. 'Are you okay?'

'Just struggling a bit.'

'I thought you might do.' She reached into a pocket and took out a small bottle. She opened the lid and tipped two of the tablets into Ward's hand. 'Take these.'

'What are they?' asked Ward.

'Benzedrine. You'll pop 'til you drop.'

Ward took them. He had used them before on overnight work. She was right, once you had popped you really dropped; he had slept deeply and well after each time he had taken them; until then, they would keep him very much on his toes.

'Thanks,' said Ward. 'One for yourself?'

'I already did. About an hour ago. Shall we move on?'

'Let me ask you something,' said Ward.

'Sure.'

'What effect would a combination of lithium, amitriptyline and something called ma huang have on a person?'

'Ma huang? That's just basically ephedrine. I assume from the lithium that we're talking about somebody with bipolar disease?' Ward nodded. 'It would depend on the individual. If there was already anxiety there, it could certainly increase that.'

'Could it make someone more vulnerable to suggestion?'

'Not necessarily, but if the lithium was reduced in some way, then any psychosis combined with heightened anxiety could certainly present a problem. Not only that, but combining ma huang and tricyclic antidepressants is just plain dangerous. It can mess with the cardiac cycle and cause arrhythmias. Possibly fatal.'

They moved on downhill towards the Baie de Dieu. Despite the context, it was an enchanting walk. The breeze flowed in from the bay and climbed the hillside. It carried with it the scent of the sea and myriad plants that it stroked along the way. The odour was a perfume designed to capture the heart of a man. It did. In all his time abroad, no matter the circumstances, Ward always remembered the lowering of the sun and the inshore breeze that picked up every scent and cleansed the land. It didn't matter if it was East Africa or the Indian Ocean or the Caribbean, the sweetness grasped the soul and broke it like a lover.

About half a mile down and to the right lay Dieuville. It was where the locals lived; those working for ex-pats in the expensive houses or involved in the building of new hotels or in the still underdeveloped hospitality industry around the Baie de Dieu.

There were no street lights. Clearly, local government had not got as far as to deem Dieuville worthy of such luxuries. Wait until the tourists start to flood in, thought Ward. They won't be able to throw enough money this way.

'Who are we looking for?' asked Penny.

'Henrick and Evie Chery,' said Ward.

'And which house number is it?'

Ward shook his head. 'Do these places look like they have house numbers?'

At last he could feel the Benzedrine beginning to kick in.

'I suppose not,' said Penny. 'So how are we meant to

know which one it is?'

'Apparently,' said Ward, 'there is a Ford Escort Mexico RS 1600 in the driveway.'

Penny gasped. 'Are you serious?' she asked with some excitement. 'Is it yellow? I mean, it has to be yellow. How much was she paying him for God's sake?'

'About seventy-five dollars a month.'

'What the hell?'

'It makes you wonder,' said Ward.

'Yes, it makes me wonder. What was he doing to make enough to afford an Escort Mexico?'

'What do you think?' said Ward. 'Everyone who is involved in this is making drug money, one way or another.'

'What about the neighbours?'

'The neighbours?' scoffed Ward. 'Between superstition and the fear of revenge, they turn a blind eye.'

'Superstition?'

'Yes. You know? The whole voodoo hoodoo thing?'

'Surely that's just hokum,' said Penny.

Ward sighed. 'The Catholic church tied the people of Europe in knots for centuries by threatening their souls. Kings were afraid of excommunication. If a country was expelled from the church, there were no services. If there were no services in church, there were no burials on consecrated ground. If there were no burials on consecrated ground, the dead went to hell as well as rotted in the street. People went to church, paid a tithe, all their lives, in the hope that their souls would be saved. It's all fear. Voodoo is no different. If people believe strongly enough, you own them. The difference between Hoodoo and Voodoo, and there are distinct differences, means nothing. It's a trap-all web, built upon ignorance and fear. If someone tells you that you and your family are going to hell, that's it. You do as you're told.' Ward scoffed. 'Come on. Don't tell me that Nassau is immune to this rubbish.'

'Of course not! Obeah, whatever you choose to call it, holds as prodigious a grip as any of the great terrorist organisations. I just think it's an excuse for organised crime, like the IRA or the PLO or Abu Nidal. There's no magic involved.'

'You think that because you don't live in one of these shacks and fear the goat, that these things hold no terror? Don't you believe it. Whatever Henrick and Evie have going on, no one will tell because they might just be protected, if not by the Devil, then by the machete.'

'How did you know about the car?' asked Penny.

'A man named Jacques,' said Ward fondly. 'He was a bit of a petrol-head. He told me that there was only one Mexico on the island. He was as envious as hell.'

'Why do you think he mentioned that?'

'Oh, you know,' said Ward. 'Man talk.'

'Well, that's bollocks,' said Penny.

Ward thought about it. 'It might have been. I liked Jacques. I'd like to think that…'

'What are you on about?'

'Oh, nothing. Must be the Benzedrine kicking in, making my mouth flap.'

'Well, shut up. There's a yellow Ford Mexico across the road.'

The Chery's house was no different to any other in the row of flat-rooved, concrete shacks that lined the street. Their front doors spilled out onto the main road. Their windows had the peel of age. Their concrete walls were dulled by sunlight and exhaust fumes. There were no lights on.

Ward and Penny kept low as they crept up to the property. All the windows were barred with scrolled metalwork. There could have been several reasons for that.

Many houses had the windows grilled so that they could be left open to allow a breeze to blow through without risk of theft.

It could also have been, thought Ward, to keep secrets. It wouldn't have surprised him if the main door was reinforced. If drugs or money were involved, then heavy defences were needed.

On the other hand, there was a shiny new Escort Mexico parked outside the property, and that didn't have a scratch on it. It was likely that no one would dare touch anything which belonged to the Cherys.

Ward reached the front door and gently tried it. Surprisingly, it gave way. They must have been sure of themselves to leave the door open, he thought.

He took the Ruger from its holster and held it close to his waist, then eased the door back some more with his free hand. Inside it was pitch black. There was no benefit of moonlight to even cast a shadow.

Ward looked at Penny. She had a knife in her hand. It was a new Al Mar Model 3101, made in Seki City, Japan, for the Al Mar company based in Oregon. It was a knife designed for and used by the American special forces. Quite how she had got her hands on one Heaven only knew, but Ward felt a twang of envy. It was a deadly object of great beauty.

She grabbed him at the elbow, held him back and moved past him, indicating that the knife would draw less attention should it have to be used. Ward reluctantly agreed. A knife was only as good as the person who used it and he had no idea how good Penny Sweeting was when it came to combat. You could not defend yourself with an eidetic memory.

They entered a small living area. The dark outlines of two sofas and a couple of small tables were visible. To the left was the kitchen. Ward went in there while Penny carried straight on.

It was only a small kitchen, almost like a ship's galley, but it was pristine and modern. It had a fan oven and four-ringed electric hob, all packaged in a hard white surround with a black door. Ward couldn't tell a good oven from a bad one, but could tell that this was a pretty expensive set-up.

The cupboards along the kitchen wall were wood laminate. Much like the oven, Ward guessed that they would have to have been imported.

At the other end of the kitchen was a door to a small dining area, containing a wonderful set of industrial style Bistro chairs and a horrendously expensive mahogany dining table, which had absolutely no connection with the chairs, attached to the living room, in which Penny examined the contents as she crept around.

She found the same as Ward, spic and span and modern, right down to the TV and parquet flooring. It was as if they had one day picked up a copy of Homes and Gardens magazine, cherry picked the bits they liked, then jumbled them together. There was little thought put into the aesthetics of the place - it was all about the money, about having the best available, rather than taste.

They could have bought a bigger, better house and decorated it less lavishly, but that might have drawn too much attention. Apart from the Mexico, their luxuries were on the inside. It was all a guilty secret.

Ward moved on, out of the living room and into a short corridor. There was a sweet, slightly sickly smell in the air, as if they had also imported some air freshener that had mixed poorly with the humidity.

To the right of the corridor was a bathroom. Again it was expensive and modern.

Beyond that was a bedroom, really a storeroom,

which took the overflow from the rest of the house.

The final room, the main bedroom, reeked, but the sickly sweetness had become mixed with something less pleasant; something gaseous, rotten.

Ward knew that smell. He had come across it many times in his travels. It was Nicaragua, the Belgian Congo, Eritrea, Rhodesia, Bangladesh, Afghanistan, Thailand. He took out his pencil torch.

It reflected upon Henrick's and Evie's inert faces.

But they weren't going to wake up.

And that smell?

That was death.

25. A Moment of Clarity

When they examined the bodies, Henrick turned out to be alive.

Ward started as what he thought was a corpse inhaled deeply, its chest rasping with honeycomb mucus that filled its lungs.

Henrick was little more than a mummy, his half-closed eyes sightless, his thin blue lips drawn across dry teeth. His skin had turned grey and there was barely a horizon between that and his aged hairline. As the pencil light hit him, his tongue protruded from his mouth to lick his dry lips, but it was swollen and parched and had no effect at all. His eyes, once so full of pride, were dead in their sockets. His day was done.

'Penny!' called Ward.

He heard footsteps and Penny came cautiously into the room. 'Christ!'

Ward held Henrick's hand and squeezed it gently.

Henrick lay next to his wife. Her throat had been slit. She had bled a terrible death. It had been someone's way of either getting Henrick to talk or to shut him up.

Henrick himself had been less fortunate. He was missing five fingernails from his right hand. His two front teeth had been smashed and severed his top lip. His elbows had been reduced to pulp by constant bombardment. His nose barely existed any more. His right eyeball had been slit open. There was no blood, but the flaked remains of aqueous humour, the jelly that filled the eye, lay like fish scales on his cheek. Ward looked down and saw a bloom of blood at his groin. Whoever had done this had also removed his testicles. He was supposed to exsanguinate.

He had been left to die. He had been left to die next to the body of his wife, the soaked sheets gradually growing colder and colder until her blood stuck to his arm, his shoulder, his head, his back.

His breath rasped from him like a percolator.

Ward stared with horror and, yes, some guilt. He could do little else in the face of such barbarism.

There was a glass of water next to the bed. Ward put two fingers into the warm liquid and allowed the drops to fall between Henrick's broken lips. He waited a moment, then did the same again.

'What happened, Henrick?' he asked. 'You're wife is dead and you soon will be. What happened?'

Henrick's single eye turned towards Ward. His dry tongue poked from between his lips as he tried to speak. 'Genie,' he croaked.

'What about the Genie?' asked Ward. 'What about him?'

'Mike!' said Penny. 'For God's sake! Leave him alone!'

'Shut up!' said Ward. 'What about the Genie?'

Henrick's mangled lips drew back across his shattered teeth. 'Gonna kill you,' he said. There was no triumph or defeat in his voice, just fact. 'The Genie gonna kill you like he killed me. He's a ghost, a spirit, a devil. He's gonna come for you.' With his last ounce of energy he put his thin hand on Ward's arm. 'Take care of my car.'

With that he died. He simply let out a short breath and left the world, another vacancy to be filled.

He had outlived his usefulness.

Ward rubbed his tired eyes and swore. Whoever had done this to Henrick had killed his wife in front of him, allowed her to bleed and gargle her way to death while he was forced to listen, and yet something told Ward that Henrick had refused to yield.

What point religion, he thought, when there was no

God? What point life, when all that was left was death?

He sat silently next to the dead man, his head low. Penny thought for a moment that he was praying, then realised the absurdity of the notion. This was Mike Ward. This was the same Mike Ward who had overcome the death of lovers and wives, of friends and traitors, who had taken betrayal and thrown it upon the anvil to harden his steel.

There were no prayers left in Mike Ward.

'What are you doing?' she asked.

For a full thirty seconds Ward did not reply, then he let go of Henrick's hand. 'Nothing,' he said. 'Search the building.'

Penny returned to the living room, while Ward stayed in the bedroom. There really were few places he could look. There were some bedside drawers in which Ward found a bible and some change, some underwear and socks, but nothing of relevance. There was no wardrobe. Henrick's work suits, two of them, were hung upon a clothes rail along with some white shirts, two black ties, casual trousers and a few dresses, but that was all. He searched the suits to no avail. They smelled lived in, a cross between body odour and the dampness that infected clothes in the tropics. He imagined that Henrick had been wearing the same suits for years.

He crossed to the other room which had been used for storage. It was full of odds and sods - an old ironing board, a sweeping brush, an old set of shelves upon which lay books, unread for many years and covered in dust.

'Mike?' called Penny.

'What is it?'

'You might want to see this.'

Ward left the room and went to Penny in the living room. She had a bin on a table, around which were scattered tightly screwed up balls of paper. Penny had unravelled one and held it in her hand. She handed it to Ward.

It had on it a hand-written note, the same note that Ward had found in Clarissa Benson-Haines' personal effects in the HC office. He opened another scrap and read the same. He and Penny unravelled seven balls of paper, each with the same note, each written differently, as if they had been done for practice.

'What do you make of it?' asked Ward.

'Interesting,' said Penny. 'There's a lot of repetition. It's a pretty carefully constructed message, despite the fact that it's so short. There isn't a wasted word in it.' She looked at Ward. 'Any context?'

'When I was in Buckley's office, I found Henson-Baines' personal effects.'

'And?'

'That was it. Just that note, written in capital letters.'

'Does anybody know about it apart from us?'

Ward shrugged. 'I have no idea. Whichever way you look at it, it's evidence of something and should have been treated as such. The coroner should have seen it, made a note of it in the post-mortem, but it was tucked away in the bottom of a filing cabinet, apparently unread, in Buckley's office.'

Penny sighed impatiently. 'Well, somebody must have looked at it.'

Ward crossed his arms and leaned against a wall. 'You would think so, wouldn't you. The thing is, if it is evidence and could implicate someone, you would think that someone would have destroyed it. What's the point in keeping that? It's either litter or evidence. Either way, it shouldn't exist.'

'Unless somebody wanted it to.'

Ward grunted. 'Yes, that makes a kind of sense, but who and why?'

'Well, what about the dead guy?'

'Henrick?'

'Sure. Why not? I mean he'd been with her for years. If he hadn't liked her he'd have moved on, but he stayed with her until the day she died and now it looks like he might have died for her too.'

Ward yawned. The Benzedrine was beginning to wear off and with it came the aches and pains that had been inflicted on him at the factory.

'You okay, Mike?'

Ward smiled. 'It's nothing a long holiday in a cold climate wouldn't cure.' He paused thoughtfully. 'It can't have been Henrick. Once he had given her the note, that was it. It was found on her body. That means it was present on her person at the time of death.'

'Well, the note's in his writing for sure and he would have been in a position to deliver it to her.'

Ward sat down gingerly. 'Absolutely,' he agreed. He liked the idea that he had someone to bounce ideas off. Sometimes on a job he felt so isolated. Now he felt like he could get proper feedback instead of hearing his own voice.

Penny flumped down next to him. 'Okay, how about this? You asked me earlier about lithium and ma huang et cetera.' Ward nodded. 'Let's just think about that. If Henrick was a man for all seasons, did her food, made her drinks…'

'Dispensed her medication…' interrupted Ward.

'Precisely. He might have been reducing her lithium to the point where the delusions and psychoses were creeping back, especially in conjunction with the ma huang, which might well have made her suggestible, paranoid even, certainly vulnerable. One morning, Henrick gives her this note, she reads it, her paranoia goes up ten points and, along with whatever 'they' knew, tips her over the edge. She gives Henrick the day off, grabs her husband's old service pistol, goes to the newspaper and shoots Lawrie whatshisname, because the note told her to.'

'Would you be able to tell? From her blood levels for example?'

'Well, lithium has a half-life of about twenty-four hours. It drops rapidly and rises rapidly. It does very much depend on the maintenance dose. The potential for manipulation is massive. Post-mortem I would expect it to be point six to one point two millimoles per litre, depending on how long after death the post mortem was carried out.'

'Hers was zero point two.'

'Jiminy! That's hallucination heaven right there! You can't just withdraw these things without some sort of long-term titration and I'm not convinced that would be enough. Bipolar disease is a friend forever, mate. That's it. If you don't keep it on some sort of leash, it turns feral.'

'But why would she kill herself?'

'A moment of clarity?'

'Poor thing,' said Ward. 'She didn't stand a chance.'

'There's a high suicide rate among those with bipolar disorder, as high as twenty percent or more. It wouldn't have taken much to make it happen.'

Ward shook his head. 'She was just a weapon in the end, used to do someone else's dirty work.'

'That's my theory.'

'I think it's a good one,' said Ward. 'I certainly have nothing else to offer. The question remains of course; why? Why was she used to murder Lawrie Stuart? And who pressured Henrick into reducing the old girl's medication and giving her the note?

'And what the hell was the secret she was trying to hide?'

'Her husband was a drug addict,' said Ward. 'He had been for years. She had been keeping him supplied. And there was no doubt that they had been involved in the shipment to and the selling of drugs on San Quentian. Something Buckley took over when Haines retired.'

Penny gasped. 'Really? Is that a fact? Buckley? The British High Commissioner is mixed up in the drugs trade?'

'He's a coward,' said Ward. 'They, the mysterious 'they', threatened to kill him if he didn't. He was trapped. If he didn't, he died. If he did, he was a slave to blackmail for the rest of his life.'

'Oh, well, that's for you to work out, mate. I've done the hard bit.' She slapped a hand on Ward's knee. 'I think we should go. It'll soon be wake-up time.'

She stood up.

Ward remained seated. 'What about the Mexico?'

'You can't have it. I want it.'

Ward tutted. 'I mean, why did Henrick tell me to take care of it?'

'I think he told both of us actually. Like, fifty-fifty?'

Ward held up a hand. 'I promise you, when this is all over, you can have the damned car. Why would a dying man's last words be about his car? Have you seen the keys for it?'

Penny went to a side table and picked them up. She tossed them to Ward. 'Here.'

'Okay, you take your car and I'll take the Mexico.'

'Where are we going?'

'The High Commissioner's residence,' said Ward. 'I want to speak to Bill Buckley.'

26. No More Lies

As best he could, Ward dismantled the Mexico, right down to the footplates and tyres. The wheels lay uselessly on the ground beneath each empty arch. The back seat lay crookedly behind the front seats. The boot gaped, the bonnet yawned. He had found nothing. He wasn't sure what else he could do. He stood on the gravelled driveway and eyed the car with some distaste. There was something in there. There had to be. He knew there was. A man who was dying in his wife's blood and yet spoke about his car really had something to say.

He heard footsteps upon the gravel.

'Anything?' Buckley stood next to him and gazed at the car. 'It's a bit crass, don't you think?'

Ward smirked. 'Don't say that to Penny. She thinks it belongs on a wall between two Van Goghs.'

'It looks like a banana.'

'I thought maybe a bowl of custard,' said Ward. 'Nice to drive though,' he added.

Buckley pondered for a moment. 'So why are you here at this ridiculously early hour? What have I done wrong this time?'

Ward crossed his arms and looked Buckley in the eye. 'The truth is, Bill, I just don't know if I can trust you.'

Buckley looked at the ground and drew an arc in the gravel with his foot. 'I can't say that I blame you. I haven't given you much reason to have any faith in me.'

'Oh, I wouldn't say that, but I do wonder how much of it is self-preservation.' Ward squirmed inside. He hated this. In his heart he believed Buckley to be telling the truth, but the hard-headed policeman inside wanted him in a cell.

'All of it,' said Buckley. 'I'm a good diplomat, Mike, but I'm a terrible coward. I can hide behind the flag and the government and use them for all I'm worth, but without that shield, I am a coward. The kid never left boarding school, with its bullies and its oppression and the loneliness. It's always just been survival, whatever it took. I had a good brain but a weak soul, I'm afraid.'

'What about the note? What about the note that finally sent the old girl round the twist? Why didn't you show it to me?'

Buckley appeared confused. 'Note? What note?'

'Oh, come on, Bill! The note! The note in the bottom of your filing cabinet in your office?'

'You've been through my office?'

'Yes,' said Ward flatly. 'I've been through your office. It's my job.'

'You could have just asked.'

Ward's patience wore thin. 'Don't be so bloody naïve, Bill!'

Buckley looked away. 'I'm sorry.'

'Don't be sorry. Be honest.'

'I am, Mike. I am being honest.'

'The note?'

'I never saw a note.'

'And Lawrie Stuart's personal effects?'

'They've never been returned. I asked for them at the same time that I originally asked for the post-mortems, but they never appeared.'

'That's ridiculous,' said Ward. 'So how the hell did they get into the filing cabinet? Who else has access to it?'

Buckley put his head in his hands. 'Miss Grace.'

'If you're lying…'

'Give it up, Mike. No more lies.'

'Shit!' spat Ward. 'That explains how Mirlande got in. That's cancer for you; rotten from the inside.'

'Miss Grace is a traitor?'

'Miss Grace is a bitch,' said Ward. 'She sold us both down the river.'

Buckley was astounded. 'Why?'

'How the hell would I know? Blackmail? Money? Cause? It could be anything.'

'I'll fire her,' offered Buckley feebly.

'You'll have her for breakfast!' said Ward. 'It's time for you to toughen up. Forget the flag and everything that you hide behind. Think about what matters.'

'I'm not sure I know that,' said Buckley. 'Not anymore.'

'If you didn't know that, I wouldn't be standing here right now. You know what's wrong and what's right, Bill, despite yourself. You just need to pick a side.'

'Yours,' said Buckley.

'Right,' said Ward.

'What shall we do about Miss Grace?'

'Nothing,' said Ward. 'She'll get what's due.'

'Will you kill her?'

Ward was astounded. 'Is that what you think I do, Bill? Just go around beheading the guilty? I kill only because I have to. I kill to stay alive or to keep others alive, that's it. I'm not a murderer, Bill.'

Ward knew he was wrong. He was an apologist for himself. He always justified the punishment he dished out, either in the name of his country or to save his own skin. Kill or be killed. That was it.

Many years ago he had slit a stranger's throat in the hot quiet of a Cyprus night. In the name of…what? Queen and country? Imperialism? Justice? Freedom? That man's child had seen him and, many years later, come back to haunt him. His cause had been as clear as Ward's. It was just…different.

What made right wrong and wrong right? A well paid

job and a very good pension? A sense of the moral and the immoral? The politics of the day? He had no idea anymore. He only knew that what he did was labelled 'job', and that was it. If he tried to understand it, it would drive him insane.

'Nothing in the car then?' asked Buckley.

It broke Ward out of his bleak reverie. 'I can't find anything. I've looked in everything from the glove compartment to the rocker panels.'

'Mind if I take a look?'

Ward looked at Buckley sceptically. 'Be my guest.' He handed him the keys.

Buckley went to the car and did everything Ward had already done. He checked the glove compartment, the steering wheel, beneath the seats, the door panels, under the bonnet, the boot, but still there was nothing. Finally, he sat in the front seat and scrutinised the interior.

He checked the sun-visor.

And there it was. Once the visor was lowered, it fell into his lap like a dead moth.

'What is it?' asked Ward.

Buckley couldn't help his self-satisfied smile. 'A key.'

'To?'

'A lock.'

Ward walked over to Buckley and examined the key. 'Thanks, Mr Smug!'

The key was like any other. It could have belonged to a front door, a garage, an airport locker, office furniture, even some cars; almost anywhere that took a Yale key.

'Well that's not much good is it,' said Ward.

'Let me have another look,' said Buckley. Ward handed the key back to him.

Buckley gave the key a serious examination. 'Yes,' he said. 'Not a clue.' He handed it back to Ward who took it wearily. 'Except, I do seem to remember that each key Yale made had a code.'

'Right?' said Ward tentatively.

Buckley rolled the key around in his hands. 'Well, each Yale key has a serial number and from each serial number, to an expert, you can gather the purpose of the key.'

'And you're an expert?'

Buckley looked at him from behind heavy eyes. 'No. No, I am not a key expert, Mike.' Ward sighed deeply. 'But I know a man who is.'

'Really?' said Ward. His voice alone gave away the fact that he had little hope.

'Listen,' continued Buckley. 'These people can make a shirt for you in twenty-four hours from two measurements and a pair of shoes in a half a day by drawing around your foot. In their own way, each of them is an expert. They take pride in their work and they know their stuff.'

'Fine,' said Ward apathetically. 'We might as well. We have nowhere else to go. It's just one dead-end after another.'

Ward heard footsteps behind him. He turned to see Penny Sweeting crossing the gravel. 'Morning, Penny,' he said. 'Did you get a couple of hours kip?'

'More than you, obviously,' she said, pointing out the dismantled Escort. 'I hope you're going to put that back together. It's mine, you know.'

'How could I forget?' asked Ward. 'Buckley thinks he's found something.'

'Oh, yeah?' Penny walked to Buckley who had remained in the front seat of the car. 'What have you found, mate?'

Buckley held up the key.

'A Yale key. That's great!' said Penny eagerly. 'I'm sure you can narrow its identity down by the serial number on it.' She paused and pointed at the key. 'Where'd you find it?'

Buckley in turn pointed at the sun-visor. Penny broke out into raucous laughter. 'Are you serious?' She turned to Ward. 'You didn't think to look there before dismantling my car? Mate, sometimes you think too much.'

Ward, mortified and amused, started to walk back to the residence. 'Come on, Bill. Breakfast and then your locksmith.'

Penny followed. 'And what about me?'

'If you're good,' said Ward with a wicked grin, 'I'll let you do the washing up.'

'You bloody chauvinist!' she called after him. 'Jesus! I can cook as well, you know!'

27. A Key For Every Need

Ward had pretty much collapsed once he had finished breakfast. Penny, recognising the thumping comedown from the Benzedrine, shooed him off to bed with the assurance that she and Buckley would go to see the locksmith.

Ward had been too tired to argue and had dragged himself into a guest room at the residence where he had fallen immediately into a deep, dreamless sleep.

Penny drove into the centre of Saint Jeanne with Buckley next to her in the front seat; Ward had warned her of his proclivity for vomiting when seated in the rear. Now, during the early hours, the pace in the capital was frenetic. People zig-zagged across the streets, oblivious to the traffic, each heading towards work or the market, bags slung across their shoulders, baskets balanced on their backs and heads, flip-flops flip-flopping lazily across the warming tarmac.

Once Penny had parked, Buckley took her around the small town. The market was ablaze with colour - chillis, peppers, plantains, bananas, pineapples, lichees, oranges, grapefruits and mangoes. Spices peppered the stalls – cayenne pepper, chili pepper, Scotch bonnets, nutmeg, ginger, coriander, oregano, cumin and garlic - lay like a rainbow and tempted the casual onlooker as well as the home-expert, those forced to cook for a living. People chatted and bartered and argued. Money changed hands as customers dipped fingers into purses, eyes down, counting the coins, and handed over their hard-earned pay or the weekly housekeeping.

Buckley took Penny past rum-joints and cigarette shops, which would sell singles or full packets of twenty, past mini-supermarkets who prided themselves on their red and white Coca-Cola sponsored fridge, filled to the brim with

Sprite and Orangina and Doctor Pepper and Fanta, and counters full of chocolate bars that bore no relation in taste or texture to the chocolate to be found in Europe.

They passed motorcycle repair shops, where wheels could be straightened after a pothole trauma for a few bucks and new petrol tanks could be fitted in ten minutes, past tailors and shoemakers and music shops that would sell a TDK tape, C60 usually, with half an album on each side for ten bucks each.

Telephone wires hung loosely between aged wooden poles, just waiting to be snagged by a careless lorry or bus driver, victims of the yearly hurricanes, repeatedly repaired. The road was full of potholes which Buckley was only just able to negotiate. To him it was like a rough sea. He opened the window.

They reached the locksmith, Joshua's Locks, at the end of the street.

It was a small, dark shop with 'Joshua's Locks: Locksmith' written in sun-faded, peeling paint, gold, edged with black against a green background, above the entrance.

Buckley stepped aside and allowed Penny through the door first. She was astounded by what she saw. Upon the walls, on shiny, thinning metal hooks, were keys of all types, thousands of them, some cut, some not, and on a counter there were two slanted, glass-fronted cabinets, the kind in which jewellery might have been displayed, also filled with keys. Beneath those, in the glass-topped counter, were more keys. Some of them looked new. Some of them looked Victorian, perhaps earlier. Penny guessed that this would be a collector's paradise. For half a second, she wished she cared about them.

'Just after I got here,' said Buckley, 'the residence was broken into. Nothing was taken really - a couple of lamps, a fax machine, a TV; Joshua was recommended to me by one of the maids, no doubt a cousin or some such thing. He came out and fixed it in less than an hour. Now, when we have a problem on any of our properties, we turn to Joshua. He works quietly and efficiently. He will supply everything from suitcase keys to house keys. He's phenomenal really.'

As if on cue, a late middle-aged man, his hair Brylcreemed back, with silver streaks running through it, appeared through some beaded curtains. He was only five and a half feet tall and had perhaps half his teeth, but he smiled widely nonetheless. His wide brown eyes darted like a deer's eyes, as if always on the lookout. He had a grey five o'clock shadow and the whites of his eyes were flecked with the redness of late-night rum.

'Hello, Mr Bill,' he said.

'Hello, Joshua. I'm sorry to disturb you, but I need some advice.'

'No problem, sir.' He spoke with that strange accent that was a combination of French and Jamaican. It lilted and swayed like a contented drunk.

Buckley took the key out of his pocket. 'I need to know all you can tell me about this key.'

'For sure.' Joshua took the key, popped a jeweller's loupe into his right eye and examined the key closely, meticulously, taking his time, until he was ready. 'Nineteen-sixties,' he said with certainty. 'Not a house key. It's too small. Not a suitcase key. Too big. The serial number, as my memory recalls, was given to keys used for lockers.'

'Lockers?' said Buckley. 'Like airport lockers?'

Joshua closed his mouth tightly; his lips turned into a shark-like frown. He shook his head. 'Airport lockers are different, Mr Bill. This is less worn. Airport locker keys are abused. People use them roughly, then leave them behind when they are done. There's not enough wear and tear on this.' He looked up at Buckley with the loupe still in his eyes.

'Not enough shine.'

He took an old cloth, the holey victim of many a cleaning, and rubbed the key. 'Some dirt,' said Joshua. 'But not airport dirt. Dirty hands, sweat. Sweat is like an acid. It eats away at the metal.' He pointed a bony finger at the key. 'Not here. No way. Not here. This has been used once in a while, but that's all.' He screwed the loupe tighter into his eye and re-examined the key. 'One owner. You can tell by the wear. Right-handed, had a limp.'

'Are you serious?' said an astonished Buckley.

'No!' laughed Joshua. 'How can I tell if a man has a limp from a key?' He paused. 'Definitely right-handed though.'

'And where's it from?' pressed Buckley.

Joshua pondered for a moment, going through the options in his mind. 'PO box,' he said at last.

'A post office box?' sighed Buckley. 'There must be hundreds of them. Where do I start?'

Joshua handed him back the key. 'Leave this shop. At the next junction turn right. The post office is one hundred yards down the road.' He smiled happily. 'The only one with boxes on the island.'

'You're a lifesaver,' said Buckley. He put ten dollars down on the counter. 'Thank you.'

Joshua slid the money across the counter and dipped it inside a shirt pocket. 'Thank you, Mr Bill.'

Penny looked at him with admiration. It always astounded her that the further you got away from so-called civilisation, the more inventive and knowledgeable people were. It was simply common sense with a little ingenuity.

'Thanks, Josh,' she said. 'You don't happen to have a spare key for a Ford Mexico, do you?'

Joshua stretched his arms out and circled the room. 'A key for every need, Missus. A key for every need.'

Buckley and Penny stepped back out into the sunlight.

'Post office?' asked Penny. She wondered briefly if Ward would feel the same sense of awe from such an ordinary man as she did. For all that she knew, there was so much more to learn. She found the prospect more than thrilling. That was what appealed to her about medicine – it never stood still; there was always something new to be found.

The day was almost too bright. The eager sun cast deep, dark, sharply defined shapes across the narrow road, throwing everything into relief, picking out the peeling paint on shop fronts. It hurled dusky glints from the burnished tarmac as if the road was embedded by jewels. The heat was already heavy. The sun was already high in the sky and threatened to hover like a god until the yardarm was passed. Penny felt her clothes begin to cling. This was different to the heat in which she had grown up. That was parched, dustbowl heat, the kind of heat where sweat was a luxury rather than a consequence. It brought with it, along with the big skies and endless land, an almost absurd peace of mind. This heat was a plastic bag over the head. It made her gasp, despite the fact that she had been in Nassau for several years and was familiar with the weight of God. Now it seemed that the gods wanted to crush her, to force her to be aware of the power of nature and the unknown. Like everything though, she ate it up. Everything was worth it, for good or bad, because it made the next thing better.

'Post office,' confirmed Buckley, breaking like a burglar into her thoughts.

'I bet that guy's worth a bloody fortune,' she said.

'Worth every penny,' said Buckley.

They walked the short distance to the post office. The streets shimmered with colour; exotic shirts of every hue and every pattern mated with light summer dresses; aged, red and yellow and green cars, left behind by long-dead owners, coughed along the roads and yet remained magnificent in their sharp-finned, chrome-plated glory.

Penny loved them. She had been to Cuba and seen perhaps the greatest selection of classic cars in the world. There, they were still just workhorses, but to her, they were works of art. She had been a fixer on her father's farm. When machinery broke, she was in there. When something went wrong with a car or tractor, she dived in and fixed it. It had been so satisfying to resuscitate what most thought was dead. Not unlike her day-job really.

The market thronged. It had been busy when they had first passed, but now people, mostly women, darted and slid and swayed and drifted their way through, each with a different coloured mind, a multi-coloured heart, a different destination ahead.

The post office was wonderful. Penny absorbed the Victorian architecture; the cold marble floors, the counters with carved stone aprons, lions *en passant* forever poised, foot forward, claws drawn, set in a mahogany frame. It reeked of a time where what was seen was worth more than what it actually was. It impressed. It said that the post was as reliable as the Empire, that the Home Counties were merely a sliver of paper and a twopenny stamp away. It was built upon the tragedy of Khartoum and the farce of Sevastopol, the Indian mutiny of eighteen fifty-seven, Gallipoli and Dunkirk. Each time glory had followed, either through Tennyson or Churchill, and the Empire rested uneasily for one more deep, deep, ever-weary sigh. There was greatness, true greatness, but it was singed by the foolhardiness of ambition and greed.

The whole concept of PO boxes being some sort of secret, forbidden, underground haunt, disappeared in no time. On the left wall of the post office, six feet high, twenty feet long, as grey as a storm cloud, chipped and finger-stained, stood a row of lockers, each numbered, each number worn to the point where only a disordered imagination could label it correctly.

There were one hundred and eighty-three of them. Buckley's head dropped at the thought of having to go through them. 'This is ridiculous,' he moaned. He raised the key to a locker, tried to insert it into the lock and failed. 'We should have just brought a hammer and screwdriver with us!'

Penny held out a hand. 'Just give me the key, Bill. You people are just so...' She shook her head with exasperation. '...polite.'

She snatched the key and went to a serving window. The people in the queue before her thought about objecting, but something told them not to.

'Hi,' she said to the cashier. He was young with wide brown eyes and crooked teeth, his dark hair combed neatly to the side; every now and then he blew his fringe out of his eyes, only for it to fall back down, which would make him blink.

'Could I see the manager please?'

The young man was clearly daunted by the request. 'Why?'

'Well, I want to know which locker this key belongs to and I just know, deep in my heart, that you won't have a clue. I mean, how old are you? Twelve? Come on, kid, get the manager and stop wasting my time. I need answers more than I need pizza and I am hungry as hell. Jump to it!'

The young man turned on his heel, thought better of it, and turned back. 'I can tell you.' He was clearly trying to avoid any managerial involvement. He reached across the counter. 'Key please.'

Penny pushed the key across to him. 'And don't try and steal it,' she menaced. 'I know your name! What's your name?'

'Daniel,' said the young man.

Penny rested her hand flat upon the counter. 'You see what I mean, Daniel? Do you see what I mean?'

'Yes, madam.'

Daniel looked at the key, then pulled a thick ledger, as big as his chest, from beneath the counter. He skimmed through the thick pages, his fingers running proficiently down the lined and ordered lists, until he reached what he wanted. 'Number twelve,' he said.

'Does it say who's renting it?'

Daniel ran a finger across the page. 'Mr Eigen.'

'Is there any more about him?'

'No, madam.'

He slammed the ledger shut, then placed it back beneath the counter. The breeze it caused as the pages came together reminded Penny of a second-hand bookshop in Brisbane in which she had spent many happy childhood hours. It was a glorious smell.

'Would you keep any details on Mr Eigen anywhere, Daniel? Could I contact him if I wanted to?'

'I'm sorry, madam. That's confidential.'

'You mean like twenty dollars confidential or really confidential?'

Daniel blew his fringe from his eyes. 'Really confidential. I'm sorry.'

'Fifty dollars?'

Daniel looked furtively about. The other counters were busy; no one was paying any attention to the pushy Aussie at the far window. 'One moment, please.'

He left his station and disappeared into another room. Two minutes later he came back. He had a piece of paper tightly folded in his hand and slid it across the counter to Penny.

Penny opened her hand. 'Key, please.'

Daniel gently placed the key into her palm. Penny slid fifty dollars across the counter. 'Thanks, Dan.'

Daniel grabbed the money and slyly stowed it away.

Penny turned to face the glares of the queue behind her. She ignored them and paced back to Buckley.

'Number twelve,' she said. She offered the key to him.

Buckley looked at her with no little admiration. 'Your honour, I believe,' he said. He strolled off, hands clasped behind his back, in search of the locker.

It wasn't difficult to find it, halfway down the second tier, its hand-painted numbers scratched and faded by time.

Penny slipped the key into the slot. She actually felt a thrill; a trip of her heart and tremble in her stomach. She turned the key and slowly opened the dented, chipped, grey locker door.

She was faced by a deep rectangle of darkness. She put a hand into the emptiness and felt around. She was met by warm metal walls and a fistful of stale air.

There was nothing.

'Well?' asked Buckley.

Penny stood on tiptoe and felt every inch of the locker.

'Empty,' she said. She couldn't hide her disappointment. 'Just empty.'

Buckley leaned unhappily against the lockers.

'Really!' spat Penny through tight lips. 'I don't believe this! Why the hell would this Jacques guy have even mentioned the damn car in the first place? And what about Henrick? What was all that 'look after my car' bullshit?' She slammed a fist into the locker next door. People stared at her. She didn't care. The hell with them! They constantly lived on the brink of nuclear war or the risk of invasion as they went about their ant-like lives. What the hell did they know as they stood in their coloured shirts and fashionable skirts? Every one of them was doomed, prey to the faulty neurones of a single man in a place so far away it might as well have been the moon.

'Mind if I take a look?' said Buckley.

Penny stood aside. 'Go ahead.'

Buckley leaned down and looked into the locker. There was certainly nothing to be seen. It was dark in there, but not so dark that you couldn't make out the back wall.

Penny was right. It was ridiculous that there should be nothing after all that had been said, particularly in the dark shadow of so much death. On the other hand, maybe they were just misinterpreting it all, putting a spin on words to suit their own needs. It might just have all been coincidence.

Although, it was strange how a coincidence had led them to a car, a key and a locker. Maybe it wasn't coincidence but serendipity. No, it wasn't that either; it was all too neat.

He looked in the locker again and ran his hand methodically around the walls.

As he was about to withdraw his hand for the final time, he found it. In the top back right corner was a small latch. It was easily missed unless you knew it was there.

'You don't happen to have that little torch of yours, do you?' he asked.

Penny took the pencil light from her back pocket and handed it to Buckley. 'Why?'

Buckley held the torch in his left hand while the thick fingers on his right hand fumbled at the latch.

'There's something there, some sort of fastening,' he said. He moved out of the way. 'Here, you've got smaller hands than me. Give it a go.'

Penny pushed a hand to the back of the locker. There it was! How had she missed it before? She shone the torch in. There was another latch in the opposite corner. With her fingernail she loosened first the right latch, then the left. The rear wall of the locker fell forward. It had been a false back.

She reached in and felt at the newly exposed area.

This time, there was something there.

28. Old Wooden Signposts

Ward awoke at eleven-thirty. He had had one of the most refreshing sleeps in years. The overwhelming drowsiness and the sheer weight of his body as he had fallen into bed had gone.

He took a shower in the en-suite. He allowed the cold water to drench him as he stood under the strong flow. His back, that inverted bed-of-nails, still stung with the power of the water and his ear, half eaten away by the mad Mirlande, felt as if the stiches were barely holding it in place, but it could have been worse; he might have had left only half an ear and if he had been forced to sit in that chair much longer might now have been disabled had the chair's teeth killed off any nerves.

He suddenly heard movement in the room. He didn't have his gun and cursed his carelessness at leaving it in the bedside drawer. Suppose he had been in bed, out-for-the-count whenever who it was had come in? Would they simply have killed him and carried on with their search or could they hear the shower running and just taken their opportunity.

He left the shower running and stepped out, wrapped a towel around his waist and looked for something with which he could defend himself. He picked up a new toothbrush which had been left for him and snapped it in half. He was left with a perfect shard of plastic that would find any artery it was aimed at. He wrapped a smaller towel around his left hand to fend off any knife strikes.

He went to the bathroom door and listened. Someone was padding about the bedroom, but there were doors and drawers opening and closing. They were looking for something.

He opened the bathroom door a crack. He would wait until whoever it was had come closer, then come out of the bathroom door and surprise them.

As he heard them pass, he leapt out, prepared to strike.

'Oh, morning, Mike,' said Marianne. 'You gave me a bit of a start.' She looked at his hand. 'What happed to your toothbrush?'

Ward turned around and went straight back under the cold shower to wash away the sweat which had drenched him.

*

'I thought you knew,' said Marianne. 'Buckley said he would tell you that he'd called me and asked me to bring your things over from the hotel.'

Ward pushed aside his empty plate of eggs Benedict and took a sip of strong black coffee. The eggs had been divine and were either the perfect way to end a sleep or the perfect way to start a day.

'I haven't seen him or Penny since about seven o'clock.'

Marianne straightened in the chair. 'Penny?'

'Yes, Penny. I'm sorry. I just assumed you knew.'

'About Penny?'

'Yes, about Penny.'

'Well, I didn't.'

Could Ward sense a pang of jealousy in Marianne? She certainly seemed to bristle at the mention of the lovely Doctor Sweeting.

'And what does she do?' asked Marianne tightly.

'She's an orthopaedic consultant who also happens to work for us when required. She's very good.'

'I bet she is.'

'Well, she helped save my neck, her and Bill. I'd have

been bath time sashimi if it hadn't been for Bill.'

Marianne looked at his arms. He had redressed them after the shower, but watery blood was seeping through. 'I'll dress those when you're ready,' she said.

'No need,' said Ward.

'Oh, yes there is. They look a mess. And that ear looks like it's been weeping a bit, too.'

'You should see the rest of me,' said Ward.

Marianne smiled. 'I have, remember?'

Of course she had, when he had come out of bathroom in only half a towel. He suddenly felt a little self-conscious that Marianne should have seen his ravaged back as he had returned to the bathroom.

Marianne sensed his embarrassment. 'It must have hurt,' she said softly.

'I didn't notice,' said Ward tritely. 'I was too busy screaming.'

'I'm sorry, I didn't mean to…'

Ward felt rotten. Marianne had no more meant to upset him than the hot black coffee intended to scald. 'No, I'm sorry. Thank you. Thanks for bringing my stuff over from the hotel. It's good of you.'

'Bill thought you would be safer here.'

'He's probably right.' Ward looked at her across the table. 'You look very beautiful today, if you don't mind a bit of a compliment.'

Marianne ran a hand demurely through her long blue-black hair.

Ward meant it too.

She had on a light blue dress with an ochre two inch belt and a pair of flat-healed white shoes. Her eyes were subtly made-up, just a hint of eyeliner to accentuate the almond shape and a merlot red lipstick that added weight to her full lips. Her brown, almost black, eyes added a plumbless depth. Beneath her slightly shortened nose, with round, small nostrils, was a well-defined filtrum, one which emphasised the fullness of her lips. He imagined that a kiss would last forever. Her breasts lay small and even beneath her body-hugging lightweight light blue dress.

Her whole being spoke of honesty and a passion as yet unfulfilled. There was no doubt in Ward's mind that she was loyal; loyal and desirable. There was always a moment in a man's mind as to how a woman would look when making love. Some looked ridiculous, lazy, bored, uninvolved, like a school diagram. Marianne would be none of those.

'Thank you,' said Marianne. She remained unconvinced.

'So, what about you now? Where does this leave you with the hotel?'

'I don't think my employer would object to a leave of absence.' She paused. 'Thank you for putting me to bed that night, in the hotel.'

Ward frowned. 'You were a little worse for wear.'

'You could have…'

'I wouldn't have.'

She leaned forward across the table and kissed him. Her mouth was soft and full and filled with longing.

Ward returned the kiss without holding back. It had been so long since he had felt anything, so afraid was he that it was certain death for anybody who came close to him. The frivolousness of one-night stands was behind him now; he had done it and wore the T-shirt. Now, he just wanted contact.

'I'm expensive,' she said with a smile.

'I have a gold card,' said Ward.

They were torn apart by Buckley, who emerged from the residence and burst onto the veranda. 'Oi, oi! What's this?'

'Breakfast,' said Ward without taking his eyes off Marianne. He didn't release her until he was ready. He looked into her eyes and saw nothing but acceptance. He kissed her longingly, one final time. 'We'll get our moment, I promise,' he whispered.

'I know,' said Marianne.

That would do for now, he thought. That would do for now.

Marianne retreated to her seat, her eyes still upon Ward. She had a mischievous, come-hither look in her eye.

'Hello, Bill,' said Ward affably. 'What's up?'

Buckley approached the table. 'Well, quite a lot actually,' he said.

He sat down and poured himself a coffee.

He was quickly followed by Penny Sweeting. She looked a little flustered, a little hot, a little excited.

Ward caught Marianne throwing an appraising glance towards her.

'Penny, Marianne. Marianne, Penny,' he said by way of introduction. Marianne nodded her head, her eyes narrowed.

Penny stuck out a hand and forced Marianne to shake it. 'G'day. How are you doing? Sorry to break in and all that but, you know, business before pleasure, eh.' She saw the leaking dressings on Ward's arms. 'I'll get to those in a minute, mate.'

'I've got it,' said Marianne quickly.

'Sure,' said Penny. 'They're a bit gooey though.'

Marianne threw a sideways look at Ward. 'I can handle gooey.'

Sensing that she was straying unwanted onto someone else's territory, she put her hand palm down on the table then withdrew it. She left behind what she had found in the PO box. Desperate not to be outdone, Buckley did the same, only he left a tightly folded piece of paper behind.

'Which do I choose first?' asked Ward at the show-and-tell.

Buckley and Penny looked at each other.

'Hers,' said Buckley.

'Yeah,' said Penny. 'Mine's way better.'

'It's different,' said Buckley.

Penny scoffed. 'Different but better! And just so you know, I got both of them. He's only looking after that for me.'

Amused by the silly competition, Ward looked at the two pieces of paper. 'Marianne?'

Marianne pushed the one which Penny had found towards him.

Ward picked it up and ran his eyes over it.

'I don't believe it!' he said.

'You should,' said Penny.

'Where did you get it?'

'In a false back in a PO box.' She said it with some satisfaction.

'Christ! Is this real?'

Penny shook her head. 'I don't know. It's what I found. That's it.'

Ward held the paper up. 'If this *is* real…'

Marianne took the paper from him and studied it. 'Oh, my God!' she said. 'Do you have any idea…?'

'Oh, yes,' said Ward. He took the paper back and smoothed it out with his thumb. 'A list like that? All the numbers?' He turned back to Penny. 'Do you think it's genuine?'

'It was hidden in the false back of a PO box, mate,' said Penny. 'What do you think?'

Ward held the paper before him, stretched between his hands. 'Okay.' He found it difficult to take it in. 'Names, addresses and payments.' He shook his head. 'Who are these people?'

'I know a couple of names,' said Penny.

Ward handed it to Buckley. 'Damn it!' said Buckley. 'These people. These places. The money.'

Marianne took the paper back. She looked at it with obvious distaste. 'I don't believe it,' she sighed. 'I've met half these people. They've stayed at the hotel!'

Ward picked up the other piece of paper, the one Daniel had passed surreptitiously to Penny and which Penny had passed onto Buckley for safekeeping.

He opened it slowly.

'That,' said Penny, 'is who owns the box.'

Ward looked at it and shook his head. 'I don't know who that is,' he said flatly.

'I do, said Marianne. 'Felix Eigen. He owns the casino in Saint Jeanne and is heavily involved in the building of the new hotels in the north of the island.'

Penny snapped her fingers. 'I knew I knew that name! He owns the Hotel Christophene on Jacob's Island.'

'Jacob's Island?' asked Ward. He had never heard of it, despite several previous visits to the Bahamas.

'It's just a tiny island a few miles east of Nassau. He built a hotel on the northern tip of the island a couple of years ago. It was a bit controversial; everything up there was pretty unspoiled, home to some rare bats and birds.'

'So, how did he get permission to build on the island?' asked Buckley.

'You know,' shrugged Penny. 'Sense walks when money talks. He bought the island and became the lord of all he surveyed. You can only get there by taking a plane to Nassau International Airport and then a private boat to the island.'

Ward tossed the piece of paper into the middle of

the table and leaned back in his chair. 'This makes no sense to me at all. What the hell does this man Eigen have to do with any of this? And how is he connected to the list of names found in the PO box?'

Nobody offered an answer.

'Only the fact that he rents the box,' said Penny eventually.

'And the names on the paper found in the box?'

Ward looked at each of them in turn. They seemed deflated after returning to the residence with their finds.

'Marianne,' prompted Ward. 'You said you knew some of the names. So did you, Bill. Tell me about them.'

Marianne picked up the list and studied it. 'Okay.' She picked the first name on the list. 'Remy Lorah. Lived on Saint Quentian. Paid sixty thousand dollars.'

'Who is he?' asked Ward.

'He was the Attorney General,' said Buckley.

'Was?'

'He's dead. He died seven years ago in a car accident.'

'Accident?'

'Apparently.'

Ward turned to Marianne. 'Who's next?'

'Carey Orr. Lives on Saint Quentian. One hundred thousand dollars.'

'Christ!' said Buckley. 'He's the Governor-General.'

'Now?' asked Ward. 'Today?'

'Yes,' said Buckley. 'He was appointed by Perry Abadie when he became Prime Minister.'

'When?'

'Years ago.'

'How many years?'

'Fourteen,' said Buckley. 'The next election is a year away.'

'And who's the Attorney General now?'

'Hawthorne Vickers,' said Buckley.

'Let me guess; for the last seven years?'

'I would guess so.'

'On the list?' Ward asked Marianne.

'Yes,' she said. 'Lives on the island. Eighty-five thousand dollars.'

'He must have been in the sales,' said Ward sourly. 'He was cheap. You say, 'lives on the island'. Do we have an address?'

'Yes.'

'For all of them?'

Marianne nodded.

'Who else?'

Marianne's eyes followed the list. 'Ministers for Agriculture, Aviation, Finance, Economic Affairs, National Security, Tourism and Labour. Some others I don't know.'

'Each with an address and a price tag?'

'All of them.'

'Is the Prime Minister on the list?'

Marianne examined the list. 'No.'

Buckley breathed a sigh of relief. 'I'm glad about that.'

'Why?' asked Ward. 'The last time he saw you he all but dismissed you.'

'I know,' said Buckley. 'And it made me feel very small, insignificant, but there was something about that meeting which simply wasn't right.'

'Such as?' pressed Ward.

'When I had met him previously, he had been warm, inviting, welcoming even. Not all the leaders of the commonwealth countries feel that way. He had talked to me for at least half an hour, about everything from golf to tailors, tucked away in the corner of his residence, asking me about where I was from and what it was like and was England as peaceful and countryfied as all those old films he had seen. I had to disillusion him a little, but he wasn't far wrong. There are still woods and fields and old wooden signposts and village pubs and duck-filled ponds and cricket fields and the smell of late spring cut grass. It's all marvellous really and he made me feel quite homesick, but then I remembered the doom of winter; the snow, the ice, the cold, the darkness. I told him it was a good place to visit in summer.'

'So what had changed?' asked Ward.

Buckley pulled his gaze back to the present. 'He was remote, cold, as if he was somehow keeping me at arm's length. I don't even think it was a subconscious thing; it appeared to me as if he was making a real effort to keep his distance, to say as little as he could get away with. Well, you know how that meeting went.'

'Did you get no inclination as to why he had changed? Nothing at all?'

Buckley rubbed his chin. He could feel a couple of days' stubble. 'No,' he said. 'Just that he wanted me out of there as soon as possible.'

'So he might have been hiding something?' suggested Ward.

'Perhaps,' said Buckley without conviction.

'And then the delay with the post-mortem reports.'

'That was Moise,' said Buckley. 'There's no doubt about that. It was your presence that prompted him to hand over the post-mortem reports, not my visit to the PM.'

Marianne rested her chin upon her hand. 'So why was the PM so evasive?'

'Because he had something to hide,' said Buckley.

The four of them stared at each other, each hoping that one of them had the answer.

'Wanted,' said Ward. 'A lodger to share the bills each Wednesday. Phone 610-121495'.

'What the hell does that mean?' asked Penny.

Ward smiled. 'You're not the only one with a good memory. It was the advertisement left in the *Gazette*. I think it means,' said Ward, 'that he was the one who put the advert in the paper. I think that he was Lawrie Stuart's contact.'

'How'd you figure that?'

'Well,' Ward ran his fingers through his hair. 'The code for the island is 610.'

'It is,' agreed Buckley.

'Which leaves,' said Ward, '121495'.

Marianne asked first. 'Meaning?'

'A is one. B is two. A is one. D is 4. I is 9. E is 5. A-B-A-D-I-E. Abadie. It's the simplest, most effective code on earth. A letter for a number. So ridiculously simple it makes the Enigma code look pretentious.'

'Abadie was ready to make contact?' said Marianne.

Ward tilted his head. 'It would seem so. The fact that he was ready to show himself, and on a regular basis, meant that something was in the offing. Every Wednesday could have meant anything, not just every Wednesday. Twice a week, three times. Who knows? A lodger? Someone close at hand? Maybe.'

Ward wasn't yet prepared to share what the Chief had told him. If there was revolution afoot, if there really was the chance of another Cuba, then clearly that point in Saint Quintian's history was looming.

'So what was he going to say to Stuart?' asked Penny.

'I don't know,' said Ward. 'That's for us to find out.'

29. A Very Red Flag

Ward sent a telegram to the Chief. He wanted to know all he could about Felix Eigen. He knew that the Chief would set the new Chief-of-Staff, Colin Simner, onto it. Simner had risen through the ranks, had done the field work and shadowed the Chief for long enough since Peter Brooks, the previous, corrupt, C-O-S had been shamed and named and taken to task. Ward liked him. He was about five years younger than Ward but had proven himself to be twice the administrator Ward would ever be and had done exceptional work in the field.

It had just been a little more than he could take. He had been seriously injured on his last mission in the Irish Republic in 1976, when he had been turned in by a local landlord and had been forced to fight his way out of the pub. In the process he had lost three fingers to his left hand and ended up with a glass eye, as well as a three-inch scar down the left side of his face. He had hidden out for two days before making it to a checkpoint and safety. It must have been agonising with those wounds. He had the permanent stain of a palsy upon him and yet remained buoyant and alert and involved. Ward liked him tremendously. More importantly, the Chief liked him. He knew that he had suffered at the hands of the Republicans and still come back alive. Gradually, along with the ever-faithful Mrs Thornton, the Chief was getting a new family together and he appreciated it. He would like to have put the days of mistrust behind him; he couldn't of course, but it was something to strive for.

It took little time for Simner to reply. It was a full and precise fax which landed in the residence office.

FELIX EIGEN. BORN 1935. OF GERMAN

EXTRACTION. HIS FATHER WAS A SERGEANT IN THE EINSATZGRUPPEN IN WORLD WAR 2 AND WAS NEVER REALLY ABLE TO ACCEPT THE DEFEAT OF NAZI GERMANY IN 1945. HE WAS A PART OF THE EINSATZGRUPPEN WHICH ENTERED EJSZYSZKI, A SMALL TOWN NOW IN LITHUANIA. IN A TWO DAY ORGE OF KILLING, JEWISH MEN, WOMEN, AND CHILDREN WERE LINED UP IN FRONT OF OPEN PITS AND SHOT. FROM THERE HE WENT FROM SQUAD TO SQUAD - THE FOURTEENTH ARMY, THE TENTH ARMY AND THE EIGHTH ARMY, TRAINING EINSATZGRUPPEN SQUADS AND TAKING THEM INTO AREAS OF RESISTANCE WHERE THE POPULATION WERE INTIMIDATED INTO BETRAYAL OR SIMPLY MURDERED FOR THE SUSPECTED HARBOURING OF FUGITIVES. THERE ARE NO JEWS IN EJSZYSZKI TO THIS DAY. SUBSEQUENTLY, HE REQUESTED A POSTING TO AUSCHWITZ AS PART OF THE SS-TOTENKOPF. AFTER THE WAR, HE WENT TO WORK FOR AN ACCOUNTING FIRM UNDER THE NAME JOHAN MEYER IN MUNICH, TAKING HIS FAMILY WITH HIM. IN 1952, HE WAS CAPTURED BY THE ISRAELIS. HE WAS KILLED WITHOUT TRIAL. WE DID NOT, REPEAT, DID NOT, INTERVENE. HE LEFT BEHIND A WIFE, LINA, AND A SON, FELIX. LINA DIED IN POVERTY OF TUBERCULOSIS IN 1953. FELIX THEN PURSUED AN INTEREST IN NEO-

NAZI GROUPS UNTIL, IN 1958, HE MET AND FELL IN LOVE WITH GALINA LAGUNOV, A COMMITTED MEMBER OF THE COMMUNIST PARTY IN MUNICH, WHERE HE HAD BECOME A RIGHT-WING BOOK-SELLER FOR THE SHOP DER RICHTIGE WEG (THE RIGHT WAY), A POPULAR SHOP WITHIN THE BURGEONING FASCIST REBIRTH AT THAT TIME. LOVE CONVERTED HIM. HE JOINED THE COMMUNIST PARTY IN SEPTEMBER 1962 AND BECAME A WRITER FOR *DAS ROTE ERWACHEN* (THE RED AWAKENING) MAGAZINE. HIS FANATICISM DROVE GALNIA AWAY. IT WAS ALL OR NOTHING FOR FELIX. WITHIN SIX MONTHS HE HAD MOVED TO MOSCOW AND TAKEN ASYLUM. HE BECAME A PART OF THE PROPAGANDA MACHINE AND WROTE NUMEROUS ARTICLES FOR *SOVETSKAYA ROSSIYA*, *PRAVDA* AND *IZVESTIA*. UNDER THE COMMUNIST REGIME HE BECAME WEALTHY. THERE WERE CERTAIN 'PRIVILEGES' AFFORDED TO THOSE WITH THE EXPERIENCE AND INTELLECTUAL KNOW-HOW TO REJECT WESTERN IDEOLOGY AND REINFORCE THE COMMUNIST IDEAL, ESPECIALLY ABROAD. HE WROTE FOR *RED RAG*, OSTENSIBLY A WOMAN'S MAGAZINE IN THE UK, UNDER THE NAME MARY WINT, AND FOR THE *MORNING STAR*, THE *DAILY MIRROR* AND THE *NEWS LINE* AS WELL AS THE *SOCIALIST WORKER*. BY 1969, HE HAD

MADE ENOUGH MONEY TO LEAVE THE SOVIET UNION AND, WITH THEIR BACKING, BOUGHT HIMSELF JACOB'S ISLAND NEAR NASSAU AND BUILT THE CHRISTOPHENE HOTEL. THE COMMUNIST PARTY HOLDS SHARES IN THE CHRISTOPHENE TO THIS DAY AS THEY WERE HIS PRIME BACKERS. FROM THERE, HE DECIDED TO SPREAD HIS WINGS AND BOUGHT AN AREA OF LAND ON SAINT QUINTIAN, UPON WHICH THERE ARE PLANS TO BUILD A FURTHER COMPLEX OF HOTELS. HE IS SUSPECTED, REPEAT, ONLY SUSPECTED, OF DRUG-DEALING, BLACKMAIL AND MURDER IN ORDER TO SUBJECT THE ISLAND TO COMMUNIST RULE WITH A VIEW TO CREATING A 'NEW CUBA' FROM WHICH A SUBVERSIVE OR OVERT ATTACK ON THE UNITED STATES MIGHT BE LAUNCHED. END OF TRANSMISSION.

Ward put the article aside and considered its contents. It could have been the story of any number of German kids, the descendants of fervent Nazis, searching for a cause in the wake of their parents' failures. There were tales of religious conversion, but when the religion followed didn't quite have the fanaticism required to fill a soul, they went off and transferred their allegiance to something else, this time for love, for money or power or, once in a blue moon, genuine belief.

Eigen was a combination of all of them. He needed belief for identity, something his parents had lost in the destruction of Berlin in nineteen forty-five. He needed some form of religion, something to follow, something less ethereal than God, under any guise. And he needed it to be everything or nothing. He needed the fanaticism to drive his mind and steer it onwards, either towards world-conquering success or that brick wall of inevitable failure. He never considered failure, of course. People in his position, the well-off communist or fascist or conservative or socialist, never considered failure. Money and the protection it afforded was enough for him and his cause.

So long as he had it all, Communism was his moat to his castle, his trench, his essence. It had made him what he was – rich and powerful. So long as Brezhnev was in the Kremlin, he would be fine. After that, he would be fine too. He had staying power. He had staying power because he had money. So long as the KGB was happy, he lived another day. God help him if he lost it all. He would be lucky to survive twenty-four hours.

The Chief really was playing his cards close to his chest. If this was in the fax, then they must have had a file as thick as a doorstep on Eigen. Why were they forcing Ward to walk through the mire when they already knew what they were dealing with? Was there simply no evidence to confirm it all? No matter what a man believed or where he lived, that was no evidence of guilt. You could suspect all you wanted, but without evidence, there was nowhere to go. All they had at the moment was suspicion and coincidence. So what if Eigen had communist partners? Half the world was attached to Communism in some way.

To Ward though, with Eigen's name on the PO box, the paper hidden inside the box and now his involvement in the new hotel complex at Baie de Dieu, as well as the communist involvement in the Christophene, it raised a very red flag.

There still remained the question as to where Clarissa

Benson-Haines was involved in all of this, as well as Buckley. For all he knew, Buckley might have been a consummate liar, a sociopath or just a con artist. If he could retire at fifty-five and find his West Sussex haven, then it might just have been an opportunity too good to miss.

Neither did Ward know where he stood as far as the blaze at the factory was concerned. The bodies would have been found by now and probably identified. So far, all he had done since then was covert, kept his head under the radar. For all he knew he was the most wanted man on Saint Quintian. What would have happened if it had been him that had gone to the post office and not Penny? Would he and Buckley have ended up like Butch and Sundance as they exited the building, silenced forever by a hail of bullets?

He needed to find out. Marianne was the answer to that prayer. She could easily find out if he had been tagged. And even then, what would that mean? That he was never a suspect? That only Moise had knowledge of him? That Jacques hadn't spilled the beans? That Mirlande had enough self-pride that she shared her failures with no one but Moise? He didn't see how it was possible because someone had always known he was there.

But who? Who would have been in a position to know the comings and goings, the gossip and the lies, the half-truths and dirty little secrets of anyone who came to the island?

Penny and Marianne walked into the small office. Suddenly they seemed the best of friends, the thin lips and narrowed eyes a thing of the past.

Ward handed Penny the fax. 'Interesting,' she said. 'You think that's our man?'

Ward's fingers rolled out a tattoo upon the chair arm. 'I think it's possible.'

'There are an awful lot of coincidences if he's not.

What about you, Marianne? What do you think?'

'The same as you,' said Marianne. 'Everything that has happened so far has led to this.'

Ward linked his fingers and leaned back in the chair. 'Am I clean, Marianne? Has my name come up in connection with the explosion or anything else?'

Marianne looked at Ward in astonishment. 'Of course your name has come up, Mike. That's why people have been trying to kill you. Ever since you set foot in the Hibiscus, you've been known.'

'And the explosion?'

'Nothing. They're still sifting through the debris, but your name hasn't come up. Either someone doesn't want it to or nobody knows that you were there.'

'And who wouldn't want it to?' asked Ward.

'Stuart's informant,' said Penny.

Ward sighed deeply and rested his chin on his fingertips. 'The Prime Minister?'

'That would make sense if he's the informant.'

Buckley came into the office. He had showered and changed his clothes and shaved. He looked like a new man.

'Bill?' said Ward. 'Could you get an interview with the Prime Minister again?'

Buckley puffed his cheeks out, then went to a filing cabinet and pulled out a bottle of the island's Green Diamond rum. He emptied some into four glasses, dished them out, then put a bottle of Coke in the middle of the table. 'I suggest you leave the Coke,' he said. 'It ruins this fuel.' He sat down behind his desk and thought about what Ward had asked him, then took a large sip of the rum. His lips drew back across his teeth as the alcohol hit the back of his throat. 'I think I'd be lucky,' he said at last. 'The last meeting didn't go so well, as you know.'

Ward sniffed at the glass of rum. The fumes burned

the inside of his nose, but the odour wasn't unpleasant, surprisingly sweet and fruity. He took a sip. The taste was far, far stronger than the smell, but Ward liked it. It was quite light and refreshing. It would be nice with lime juice, he thought.

'I appreciate that,' he said. 'But we have got to make contact with him and commit him somehow. If he runs shy, we'll have nothing but speculation.'

'I'll try my best,' said Buckley.

Ward turned to Marianne.

'You, Marianne, have a problem. Did you know that my room at the Hibiscus had been bugged? I found two devices, one behind a painting and another in the room's phone.'

Marianne was horrified. 'Of course I didn't know!'

Ward continued regardless. 'You say that you've seen many people on the list at the hotel and also that people knew when I had arrived.'

'Yes,' said Marianne cautiously. She flushed, afraid that she might be under suspicion.

'I think I might know who your little quisling is,' said Ward.

30. Too Many Lies

Ward entered the Hotel Hibiscus as if he had never been away. Marianne pretended to do the paperwork as he came in, her ears alert to his every step, longing to raise her eyes to look at him.

'Mr Ward. Welcome back. We were about to let your room go.'

'I'm sorry,' said Ward. 'I've been out and about. The ladies, you know. Single man. Lots of time.'

Marianne smiled tightly. 'They must have been whores,' she said acerbically.

'Not all of them,' said Ward. He winked at her.

Marianne rolled her eyes. She dropped Ward's key on the counter like a hot nettle. 'Have a good evening, Mr Ward.'

'I hope so,' said Ward. 'Could you send a bottle of Green Diamond to my room, please?'

'Certainly, sir.'

'Two glasses,' said Ward. He caught a whiff of her perfume. It was citrusy, with a touch of rose and musk. He guessed at Rive Gauche. With her hair tied back and her stern appearance, with the severity of the hotel uniform, Ward found her arousing. He wanted her more than ever.

Marianne glared at him from behind wide brown eyes. 'Two glasses?'

'I'm thirsty,' said Ward. 'Parched.'

'I know the feeling,' she said.

'And perhaps a conch salad?'

'It's late. Haven't you eaten, Mr Ward?'

'I'm hungry,' said Ward. 'What time do you finish?' he asked.

'Ten,' said Marianne, her pupils wide.

'Oh,' said Ward as he went to leave the desk. 'I seem

to have forgotten my key. Could someone open up for me?'

'I'll open up for you, anytime,' said Marianne. 'I'll see you at ten-thirty?'

'Perfect.' Ward leaned on the counter and inhaled her scent once more.

Marianne rang the bell.

Pierre, the bell-boy, appeared.

'Ah, Pierre,' said Marianne. 'Mr Ward appears to have misplaced his key. Would you take him to his room while I get a spare please?'

Pierre bowed dutifully. 'Of course. Follow me, Mr Ward.'

Ward followed the young man up the stairs. 'This is very kind of you, Pierre,' said Ward.

'No problem, sir. People often misplace their keys. Too much happy-time. Drink. Food. Ladies. I understand.' He was awfully aware for a sixteen year old; a bit cocky, thought Ward.

Ward allowed him to open the door to the room. Pierre, out of habit, followed him in.

Ward quickly closed the door and grabbed Pierre by the scruff of his well-starched collar. He threw him across the room. This was no time to spare the rod. As Pierre landed next to the French windows, there was an audible crack and a strangled yelp as he landed clumsily and snapped his wrist. Even from where he was, Ward could see the classic fork-shaped bend of a Colles fracture. He felt a pang of regret; he had not intended to cause such pain, only to intimidate.

Pierre grabbed his crooked wrist and cradled it. Within seconds he was crying.

Ward picked him up again and threw him towards an armchair. It broke his fall but tipped backwards and the boy tumbled to the floor.

'Why?' said Ward. 'Why did you betray me and

Marianne? I'm used to it, but she trusted you. She trusted you with her life and yet you sold her out. Why?'

Pierre cried. It wasn't just the pain. It was the humiliation.

No one had told him about this, only about the glory that came with an extra hundred dollars a month and the chance for him and his friends to break free of their chains forever. There was splendour in their words; equality, brotherhood, money, money, money. That money would remove his mother from subservience. That money would give them goat *and* fish each week, that money would distance the unchanging Catholic God and bring the sharp-edged sword of puritan fellowship within his reach. Was this about Communism? It had been mentioned, but he had no idea. All he knew was that he and his mother would eat, that his meagre wage would not merely bring fresh fruit and vegetables to his table, instead of the withered specimens that they could afford, but the crack of fresh food and the chance to silence the borborygmi of hunger. He might have even had the chance to drag himself from subservience, get a job in one of the new hotels, perhaps as a waiter, a receptionist, a manager. He was born low to reach high.

'Who recruited you?' demanded Ward. He was in no mood for lies. 'Pierre, I will break your other arm if you don't tell me. I will have you arrested and thrown in prison for at least thirty years. What will happen to your mother without you, Pierre? How long do you think she will last without you?'

Ward despised himself for such behaviour, for such pain, but in the heat of the moment, as the world stood on the edge of yet another crisis, anything went. He would kill Pierre if he had to. The boy, by his actions, had become a man and he had to take the consequences. God knew how many lives he had cost by his actions.

'Well?' said Ward. 'Who recruited you?'

'Jacques,' said Pierre through tears and snot. 'He told me to tell him who came here. He told me to put the microphones in your room. He told me to report all you did.'

Ward stared at the kid. It was all too easy to fall. It was all too easy to get drawn in until there was no way out, because either fear or reward kept you where you were.

'Tell me about Jacques,' said Ward.

Pierre rocked back and forth with the pain in his arm. 'I don't know what to say. He gave me money. I told him stuff. That's it.'

'Did he say why he was doing this or for whom?'

Pierre shook his head. His face was soaked by tears, his eyelashes melded by moisture, his nose red. His hands trembled and his eyes, closed most of the time, fluttered like a man in a deep, deep sleep. He was lost.

'Who did Jacques work for?'

'I don't know.'

'He never told you? Anything?'

'He said that once I accepted the money, that I was in and could never leave. He said that if I tried, they would kill me and my mother and leave me begging on the streets.'

'They? Who were they?'

'I don't know.'

Ward suddenly felt less sympathetic towards Jacques. He had assumed that Jacques was as trapped as any man, but it turned out that he was just a pimp, no more, no less. He sold souls for cash and reaped the rewards.

'And tell me about the people who stayed here. The ministers, the politicians.'

'They attended meetings in the conference room. That's all I know.'

'You didn't hear any of it?'

'No! I'm in pain.' He leaned forward over his arm

and pressed it to his chest. No matter what he did, it was going to hurt. 'Let me go! Please!'

Ward ran his hands through his hair. He felt frustrated and angry, both with himself and with those that had driven him to break a boy's wrist. He felt no guilt for his actions, he did what he had to, but those dark people in the shadows didn't care what happened to the likes of Pierre, so long as they were safe.

'Jacques gave you money to do bad things. Do you see that?'

Pierre's face contorted as a wave of pain shuddered through his wrist. 'No, I do not. I liked him. He was funny. He was kind. He helped me care for my mother. Who will care now, Mr Ward? Who will care now?'

'No one,' said Ward. 'You did this. You did this to yourself. It's your responsibility.' Even he didn't believe that. 'I'll tell you what,' said Ward. 'If you work for me, for the British government, for Marianne, we will give you your one hundred dollars a month, plus twenty dollars. And I will have your arm fixed by one of the best doctors in the world. All you have to do is tell Marianne all that you hear, all the bad words said against this wonderful island, against America, against Britain. What do you say?'

Pierre considered the offer for a quick three seconds. 'Okay.'

'Okay,' said Ward, a little surprised by the rapidity of Pierre's decision. He had expected a harder bargain. 'Now I need you to tell me all about the people who came here and what they said. It's important. These people mean to harm Saint Quintian.'

Pierre looked sceptically at Ward. Who could blame him? Would you trust the man who had just snapped your arm? Somehow though, he knew that choice was not an option.

And anyway, this wasn't about sides, this was about his mum.

'They all came here. All those people I see on the TV. The big guys with big smiles and big lies.'

'Lies?'

'How do I believe them, Mr Ward? They say one thing and do the other. Worse, they say one thing and do nothing. People like me, we pay taxes, we come to work every day and we work hard. Jacques worked hard. He mixed with some bad people, but he didn't like drugs, so he arrested them. He took what he earned and made a better life.'

'He stole from what he had confiscated from them,' said Ward. 'He took the drugs and just sold them again. What good is that?'

'He did what he had to do, sir.' Pierre moved his arm into a more comfortable position and winced. 'You have to survive.'

'Really?' said Ward. 'At any cost?'

Pierre's eyes froze. 'At any cost,' he said coldly.

Ward rested two fingers against his temple and rubbed. There was a headache on the horizon, brought on by too much heat and too many days of tension.

'So who were they? These people who came to the hotel?'

'Men from the government,' said Pierre. 'The ones I see in the newspapers and the TV.'

'Like whom? Hawthorne Vickers perhaps?'

Pierre seemed genuinely surprised that Ward knew the name. 'Yes, sir.'

'And others you have seen on the television?'

'Many others,' said Pierre.

Ward took a breath. 'What did they say?'

'That they would kill my mother if I listened to them.'

'But you listened anyway?'

'What would you do, Mr Ward? They threatened my mother. They gave me money. I hated them and I was grateful for them.'

'You could have asked for help,' said Ward.

Pierre looked at Ward as if he was an idiot. 'Where? Where could I ask for help? What am I, Mr Ward?' His eyes were red with tears. Ward knew that the boy felt nothing but shame for his own inadequacies. He constantly balanced on a taut string of despair. 'I am nothing. I am a nothing with nothing to say.'

Ward retreated. 'Let me get you to a doctor,' he said. Pierre nodded gratefully. 'On the way, perhaps you could tell me what you heard.'

'Yes, Mr Ward,' said Pierre sadly. 'What about my mother?'

'We will take care of your mother,' said Ward. 'I promise.'

He picked up the phone, spoke to Penny and arranged for her to meet him at the HC ward.

*

As it turned out, Pierre's mother was dead. She had died as Ward had talked to Pierre.

She had been stabbed in the right flank, severing her renal artery, in itself fatal, and then, as she had slowly exsanguinated, every one of her senses had been tortured. Her ears had been perforated by three inch nails, hammered into place. Her eyes had been slit, plucked from their sockets and squashed underfoot. Her tongue had been, for all appearances, dropped into a shredder. Her fingers had been dipped in acid; the tips were blistered and burned. Her nose had been broken and severed. It lay open upon her face. The blood had congealed and it looked like little more than a giant blood clot through which protruded bloody slivers of bone.

To add a sickening, perverted twist, her skirt was lifted above her thighs, her knees raised and her privates made available for the world to see. It was the ultimate degradation. It was humiliation for the one who died and revulsion for those who saw it.

Ward stared open-mouthed at the debris left behind. It took a special kind of sadist, of sickness, to inflict such horror. She must have suffered, in whichever order the damage was inflicted. The message was clear; don't talk, don't hear, don't even suspect; not you, not yours.

Pierre, had been dropped off home by Ward after Penny had treated him. After seeing him safely through his front door, Ward had driven away, back to the hotel.

Now Pierre knelt next to his mother's body. His free hand hovered warily over her, afraid of the blood which soaked through the thin sheet that now covered her, longing for touch. His newly plastered arm, restricted by a sling, seemed magnetically drawn towards her.

The only reason Ward knew about this was that Pierre had told the attending police officers to contact the hotel. They had stuttered and delayed but in the end called the Hibiscus. Ward had called Buckley and picked him up on the way.

Ward sat in an armchair with tarnished wooden arms, a seat with broken slats, and stared at the body. It was brutal. It was too much. It was torture.

If you're going to kill a person, it only took one stroke of the knife; it didn't take a thousand cuts to every square inch of flesh. Ward knew this. It was impossible to tell which wound had been inflicted first and which last, but the imagination was a great interpreter of such things. Each wound was designed to humiliate and hurt. No one wanted her to talk, only to suffer. If this did not make her errant son come to terms, nothing would.

But how had they known? How had they known to take Pierre's mother and make her suffer for his transgressions? Every woman's fear was there in her corpse, from mental torment to physical assault. What purpose this? Ward asked himself. Would it cause Pierre to retreat, knowing that he could in some way suffer the same? Or would it make him realise that he had nothing to lose any more, that his fall had merely been an excuse to stand tall? That to lose all was to gain so much more? He was a pathetic teenager who had thought he knew it all but realised that he knew nothing, that it was all too big, too much for his narrow mind, too much for his pathetic greed. He had thought that he would make life better for the only woman he had ever loved; instead he had killed her. Those wounds were his wounds; that guilt was his.

Ward leaned back in the chair and coldly examined the scene. Enough was enough. He had broken the boy's arm, inadvertently or not, and felt sick at his actions and yet what the boy had done, in his grasping innocence, had killed his mother. His need to keep her had led to her demise.

Buckley stood next to Ward with his hands in his pockets. 'We did this,' he said. 'We made this happen.'

'We?' said Ward. He didn't look at Buckley. 'Not me. Definitely not me. This was you and Haines and all those involved in this petty war. For Christ's sake, Bill. Take some responsibility.' Ward waved a hand at the corpse. 'Look at her. Just look at her. In the end she was just meat, not someone's mother, wife or young lover back in the mists of time. Just meat, all because of the games that you and Haines and Clarissa bloody Benson-Haines played. Because of you all, the communists are about to get a grip on another island in the Caribbean. They are about to launch another Cuba, only this time with better weapons, with more determination, with the war-tired world ready to submit. No one wants another Cuba, another Korea, another Vietnam. Nobody wants to have to hide under their school desk in the case of nuclear attack. Nobody wants underground shelters with row upon row of tinned beans and bottled water and the everyday cold war paranoia that comes with it. People just want to live, that's it.'

Buckley hung his head. 'So what now? What do we do?'

Ward tutted impatiently. 'What do you think we do? Do we have a choice?'

'I suppose not.'

'I want to find out who did this,' said Ward resolutely. 'Somebody knew every step, every conversation. Who swept the HC?'

Buckley looked uncomfortable. 'Miss Grace.'

Ward sighed. 'Is Miss Grace English?' The question had only just occurred to him.

'Hell, no,' said Buckley. 'She's local; San Quintian mother, English father.'

'Oh, Bill you complete arsehole. Did you not think of sharing that with me? You knew that the odds were that she had let Mirlande back into the building to kill me and now this? She's not a traitor. She's a bloody rebel! Didn't you at least have her shadowed?'

'No,' muttered Buckley.

'No? You thought you'd leave her with access to the HC knowing what you know?'

'There was no evidence,' snapped Buckley.

It suddenly dawned upon Ward. 'Oh, sweet Jesus! You're screwing her, aren't you!'

Buckley looked coyly at the ground. 'I love her.'

'Of course you do,' said Ward 'Of course you do.

Even though she let in Mirlande who nearly sliced and diced me! Even though she helped Mirlande escape after killing those two medical workers? You might have provided the knife to cut her restraints, but she opened the door! Oh, Bill!' Ward put his head in his hands. 'Have you known all along that she was working for the other side?'

'Yes,' said Buckley. 'I have.'

Ward considered the human Passchendaele that was Bill Buckley one more time. What a wreck he was. 'We need to go,' he said.

'Where?' asked Buckley.

'Away from here.'

'Okay.'

Ward led the way through the mess. He wanted to say something to Pierre, to assuage the damage done, but there was nothing.

He and Ward stepped outside into the warm night. The sky was speckled with stars that glinted like sequins. Shooting stars occasionally crossed them, here one second, gone the next, on the road to who knew where.

'Get in,' said Ward as he reached for the keys.

Once unlocked, Buckley stepped inside the car and pulled the seat belt across him. 'Where are we going?' he asked.

'I need to check something out. Bear with me.'

Ward started the car. It bellowed in the dark street like a lion.

A few miles away, Ward pulled up next to the debris of the Jeans Genie factory. He got out. 'Come on,' he said.

'What are we doing?' asked Buckley. He got out of the car and walked into the sugar cane with Ward.

'There's something I've been meaning to do,' said Ward. 'You go first. Head towards the factory.'

Buckley did as he was asked.

Ward took out his gun and shot the High Commissioner through the back of the head. Buckley's legs folded and his body collapsed.

He wouldn't have known.

Ward gazed at the pitiful figure. He had been lost, self-involved, greedy, disingenuous, a traitor. He knew that Buckley had told somebody about Pierre. He had informed on the boy's mother. He had done business with Jacques. He had written the note to La Folle. He knew about the list. He knew about Eigen. He had made it easy for Mirlande. He had done nothing but save himself when he thought that the tables might be turned.

In turn they, whoever they were, had sent somebody to kill the boy's mother. Buckley had caused Ward's capture and torture by Mirlande, despite taking a beating to add authenticity to his lies. The only reason he had given ward a gun was because he wanted redemption. He thought that Ward might save him. They would have killed him eventually. He was in too deep. So many people had died because of him so that he could save himself; the medical team in the HC ward, the poor girl who worked at La Folle, Jacques, the Cherys. Even those who had been peripherally harmed could find Buckley within six degrees of separation.

Too many lies.

Ward left the body where it was. By the time it was found among the thick, unbending cane, it would be soup.

He climbed back into the car and headed back to the Hibiscus.

31. Unbroken

Ward stood in the shower and allowed the luke warm water to pummel him. His hands lay flat against the tiling, his eyes closed, his arms taut, his torn back muscular as the water flowed in torrents over his ravaged skin. Tears were washed away by the water. Guilt fell into the whirlpool at his feet.

When was the last time he had killed someone simply because he…wanted to? Casta? Brookes? Not so long ago. He couldn't deny the satisfaction, nor could he deny the small part of him that craved humanity. Slowly, he could feel that compassion slip away.

His father had been a vicar, with his own little parish in a quiet village in Norfolk. What would he feel now? Shame for his son? No doubt, shame.

Eric Ward had been through Juno on that unpleasant June morning and had survived while those about him were mown down by the German guns. He had survived because he had run. He had ducked and dived between tank traps, hidden behind bodies, taken the chance while the machine guns were diverted and mowing down those around him. Finally, he had negotiated the sparse beach grass and taken out a German pillbox.

He had saved so many men and yet he spoke of it with dishonour, of the families that he had denied a husband and a father, of the futures he had stolen. His humanity had never left him. Perhaps it had been increased by what he had seen, by the useless deaths and the blind bodies he left behind.

After the war he had turned to the church, perhaps only for redemption, perhaps because he had been through hell and now saw only light.

What was there for Mike Ward? He had no religion, no faith. He had nothing to cling to in grave times. All he ever had was tears, regret and the eventual subsidence of guilt via the practiced suppression of emotions. With habit it had improved, no doubt. The first kills had left him bereft. Over time, that bereavement had diminished to regret, then to sorrow, then to merely tears in the shower, washed away.

He heard the door open and close. The sound of a trolley stopped, then the sound of plates and glasses being placed.

Marianne came into the en-suite and took off her clothes. Finally, she shook her hair free, slid back the shower curtain and stood next to Ward. She cradled his head on her shoulder. He shuddered.

She knew it. She knew that Buckley was dead. She knew he had killed him. She knew that Buckley had deserved to die, if only for the familiar souls which he would meet in purgatory. She understood that with each death, a piece of Ward died too. He was a statue in the rain. With each sulphurous shower, a little more of him melted away. With each summer heat he grew more brittle. Life chipped away relentlessly until what was left resembled little of what had started.

Ward kissed her. He felt her breasts against him, her nipples hard. She put her hand down and caressed him and with each stroke he felt his whole world centre upon her. Every pent up emotion, every desire he had for her, was released in a moment. He gasped, his body trembling as he felt the tensions flow from him. She put her hand to her groin, then touched herself as she had touched herself so often in the past, waiting for a man like Ward.

He searched her body with his fingers. She was firm and moist. She held him to her and whispered in his ear while his fingers searched. She lifted a leg and wrapped it around him, her breath hot upon his cheek, her lips full upon his.

They left the shower and fell wet and eager upon the bed. There, Ward made love to her, her legs enfolding him, his body crashing like waves into her. She came and with that release, tears rolled from her eyes. Ward came too. He felt the rush inside her as she clasped him to her. She pulsed, as if to drag every last ounce from him. He collapsed, still inside her. She rubbed her nails through his hair, desire and compassion flowing through the tip of every finger.

Finally, they fell breathlessly apart.

Still, they locked hands, reluctant to be apart.

The silence was enchanting. All that could be heard was their breaths. In the distance they could hear the gentle lapping of the sea as it brushed against the sand. The night breeze carried all ashore.

'You killed Buckley,' said Marianne. There was no question in her voice.

'Yes,' said Ward.

Marianne turned on her side and lay a hand across his hard abdomen. 'I understand,' she said.

'Could you understand for two?' asked Ward.

'Yes,' she said softly. 'Yes.'

*

They both slept through until a gentle breeze from the French windows stirred the room and the day turned from a ruby dawn into a gilded tomorrow.

Ward was the first to wake. Marianne lay next to him, her chest rising slowly with each breath. She was beautiful. Her blue-black hair cascaded untidily across her shoulders and lay upon her tawny skin. Her full, soft lips invited attention. Ward leaned over and kissed them.

Marianne stirred and a contented smile crossed her face. 'Good morning, Mike.'

'Good morning, Marianne. I don't suppose you fancy a conch salad for breakfast?'

The meal lay untouched on the trolley.

'Most certainly not.'

'Then I shall order eggs Benedict for two, some hot, black coffee and some fresh orange juice. How does that sound?'

'Make my eggs scrambled on heavily buttered toast,' she said sleepily. 'While you do that, I'll have a shower.'

She got out of bed and walked with the confidence of someone who understood their beauty and wasn't afraid to show it.

Ward picked up the phone and ordered the breakfast. Then he phoned London. Once past the switchboard, he was answered by Colin Simner, the Chief-of-Staff.

'Westie,' said Simner, a name they had agreed to use if they spoke. 'How's the holiday going?'

Ward laughed. 'It's a busman's holiday, you know that. Listen, I'm afraid the old BBHC has had to retire. We could do with another lorry asap.'

Simner only hesitated for a moment. 'I see, he said. 'That's a shame. Anything else you need?'

'I was thinking of doing a bit of sightseeing, taking the girlfriend along. Could I take a few day's leave?'

'I don't see a problem with that. Going anywhere nice?'

'I was thinking of going to see Charles in town.'

'Well, that'll be pleasant. Have a good time. I'll let the boss man know all of this and get something sorted.'

'Thanks. See you in a week or so, all being well.'

'Fingers crossed. Bye.'

Ward had told Simner all he needed to know. Another lorry was another Lawrie Stuart, a trouble-shooter, someone to step into Buckley's shoes for a while. Nassau was originally called Charles Towne, hence going to see Charles in town. The boss man was the Chief. He was not going to like the fact that Ward had become judge and executioner, but he would understand that Ward will have done what was necessary.

Marianne came out of the shower. Her hair was wrapped in a white towel and she wore one of the white hotel gowns, which finished just below her knees, cinched at the waist by a thin white belt .

'Did you order?' she asked.

'I did,' said Ward. 'I also phoned home.'

'Oh? What did they say?'

'That they would sort things out. I also told them I'd like to take my girlfriend to Nassau.'

Marianne sat at the table just outside the French windows and soaked in the warmth. 'Girlfriend, eh?'

'Oh, don't worry,' said Ward with a smile. 'It's just a code word.'

Marianne took one of her hotel slippers off and launched it at Ward.

32. Jacob's Island

Through the aptly named Nigel Reason, the deputy HC, Ward had gained admission to the Prime Minister of Saint Quintian, Perry Abadie.

He was not as Ward expected. He was in his late forties, thin, clean-shaven, about five feet ten with a full head of hair which faded to grey at the temples and intelligent brown eyes. He was a modest man who presented a moral high ground, though not in any way superior.

When Ward had presented him with the advertisement from the *Gazette*, he had held it in his hand as if it was the Holy Grail itself. He had been visibly moved.

'I'm sorry about Mr Buckley,' he said.

'Don't be,' said Ward.

The PM looked at him with glazed eyes. 'Why?'

Ward was reluctant to tell the truth. He found it distasteful, nauseating. You don't shoot a man in the back of the head without some residue of revulsion. 'How did you know about Buckley?' he asked.

'He is not here; if here were alive, Mr Reason would not have been the one to arrange this meeting and you would not be here without him. Therefore, he is either fired or dead,' said the Prime Minister.

'I need to know,' said Ward.

'What?' asked Abadie. 'What is it you need to know, Mr Ward? What is it that you don't already know?'

'I don't know how you have remained in power when those about you have taken inducements to look the other way.'

Abadie's eyebrows collapsed. 'Really?'

'Yes,' said Ward. 'Most of your cabinet are involved in this and yet I can find no connection to you. Why not, Prime Minister?'

The Prime Minister sighed deeply. 'I'm a wealthy man, Mr Ward. I made my money by investment in Western stock. I was born poor, Mr Ward. My parents worked the fields and my father died with an abdomen twice its normal size due to liver failure. My mother brought in sewing, did cleaning, cooked for special occasions for the diplomats, she even…' He choked.

'Say no more,' said Ward.

'She paid for me to go to college, to university, where I studied politics and realised that most of it was bullshit.' He snorted a laugh. 'We pretend, Mr Ward. We pretend that the end justifies the means. We pretend that all those promises will mean something, that we will abide by them, but in the end it's all compromise. Worse still, it's compromise with the big boys; the arms dealers, the pharmaceutical industry, the land developers, the drug dealers and manufacturers and suppliers.'

He knitted his hands together. His fingers were white with the tension. 'So I remained silent. I watched, I listened, I made notes. In the end I was able to record all that had happened, including who, from my cabinet, had taken what. They were vampires, Mr Ward, sucking the blood from this country while this country simply did nothing but lie down and bleed.'

Ward took out the list that had been found in Eigen's PO box. Abadie looked at it. 'Those are my words,' he said. 'This is my writing.' He sighed deeply. 'My nephew, Daniel, works there. I told him that someday, someone would come; for whatever reason, someone would come. And they did, in this case, Mr Buckley and Dr Sweeting.'

'And they found your list,' said Ward. 'Hidden in the back of an empty PO box belonging to the man you knew who was behind this, Felix Eigen.'

'The Genie,' said Abadie with a tired smile. 'Eigen.

The Genie. It's an anagram. It takes only a moment to see.'

'And yet a lifetime to understand,' muttered Ward. 'What was his plan?'

'His plan? I have no idea, Mr Ward. I can theorise, if that would help.'

'It would,' said Ward, not unkindly.

Abadie pulled of bottle of Green Diamond from the bottom draw of his desk, along with two tumblers, and filled them. Ward was grateful for the drink.

Outside, the sun was beginning to fall. The whole world was submerged in a golden-orange afterglow, stained by the red wine of sunset.

The office in which they sat dimmed, fed only by the light that fell through the old Georgian window. It fell in rectangles across the Prime Minister's desk and splashed the office floor.

The Prime Minister took a long drag upon the rum and then lit a cigarette. He offered one to Ward. Ward declined.

'You might have noticed, he said, 'that the island has been in the midst of a drug epidemic in recent years. It has been flooded. Children are failing school, people are not turning up to work, the number of homeless has tripled. Drugs are cheap, Mr Ward. Do you know why drugs are cheap?'

'I can guess,' offered Ward.

Abadie took a long slow draw upon his cigarette. The paper crisped loudly as it burned. Ward envied him. 'Drugs are cheap because they are a weapon. They are no different to guns or propaganda or religion. They weaken the will. They take away the essence of a person and replace it with a shadow. The communists hoped that if they saturated the island, that they would weaken its spine, that no one would have the energy, the inclination, to object once they arrived.'

'And what do you think?' asked Ward.

'I think they were right. Money and drugs solve most problems. I refused to be a part of it, but quietly. I found out through contacts how much each member of my cabinet took to look the other way, to be among the communist elite…' He scoffed at the idea' '…and hid the list, via Daniel, in the PO box. It was the only thing I had. The only link. I only had hope that you would arrive, Mr Ward, before my home was devoured by the communist regime.'

'Weren't you offered anything?' asked Ward. He was surprised that Abadie was even alive.

'Oh, of course. Riches beyond my wildest dreams and I almost gave in, until a friend and colleague was murdered…'

'Remy Lorah,' said Ward. 'Your former Attorney General.'

'Yes,' said Abadie. 'There is no doubt in my mind that he was murdered because he was about to openly divulge the link between the government and the communists.'

'Shades of Bobby Kennedy,' said Ward.

'Indeed,' agreed Abadie.

'So, how did you stay alive?' asked Ward bluntly.

'I took their money,' said Abadie matter-of-factly.

Ward's face fell. 'You took their money? But you said…'

'I had little choice *but* to take their money.' Abadie saw the disapproval on Ward's face. 'Oh, don't worry, Mr Ward. I didn't keep it. I'm paid well enough and have invested wisely enough not to need more. I started the Bons Mots Foundation to educate children in poverty. I thought I might as well do something good with their money.'

'What then?'

'Then, over time, I had built up enough evidence of

what was going on to approach the British Government, in the form of your High Commissioner, who passed the information onto London. This couldn't be dealt with internally. It needed an outsider to come in and clean up.'

'Hence Lawrie Stuart.'

'Exactly. When I was ready to share everything, I put the advert in the *Gazette*. Unfortunately, on the very day it was published, Mr Stuart was killed by Mrs Benson-Haines.' He paused thoughtfully. 'I still don't understand why she did it. As far as I know they didn't even know each other.'

'They didn't,' said Ward. 'She had mental health problems. Her medication was tampered with by her servant, to the point of delusional paranoia, and then she was handed a trigger, in this case a fake note, apparently from Stuart, saying that he knew about her and her husband's games, the implication being that he was going to run a story.' Bond took another slow slug of the Green Diamond rum. 'So what is all this about?'

'As I have said, the drugs are a way to undermine our society, it's as simple and as evil as that. Drugs and money are poison. Once enough people were addicted or using or buying and selling, then the foundations would be gone. Then the more respectable people would want change, any change; then Saint Quintian would be ripe for revolution. Then the communists, controlled by Moscow and Felix Eigen, would take over and Russia would have a view through the Americans' back window. Eigen's already getting his bonus in the form of the hotels being built at Baie de Dieu. He paid for the privilege by bribing the right people in my cabinet and will reap the considerable rewards. Who knows, he might then move on to other islands; Haiti, Jamaica, Puerto Rica, Trinidad, smoothing the way for another Russian takeover. He has a small army at his disposal.' He clenched his jaw and rubbed the back of his neck, shaking his head. 'What disappoints me, is that it has nothing to do with communism or fascism or any other -ism. It has nothing to do with the will of the people or the good of the people, Mr Ward. It's simply about territory and resources. America is as guilty; Britain is as guilty. I, we all, simply have to choose the least worst of them.'

'That's politics for you, Prime Minister,' commiserated Ward.

'It's the way of the world,' said Abadie. 'It always has been and always will be. You will never change human nature.' Abadie finished his drink. 'You must be hungry by now, Mr Ward. Let me make you a good Caribbean curry to soak up that rum.'

Ward held up a hand. 'No, I couldn't put you to that trouble,' he protested.

'Mr Ward,' said Abadie. 'Two things. You are going to give me back my country; now *that's* going to some trouble. I think a curry in exchange is very little.'

'And the other thing?' asked Ward.

'I make an amazing curry.'

*

Nassau International Airport was much the same as all the other tropical island airports Ward had passed through over the years. It had the large, high, green-eyed control tower at one end of a rectangular building with two floors. There was a viewing balcony, a pair of entrance/exit doors laid bare to let the slightest breeze run through the hot an overcrowded departure/arrivals lounge and an apron where planes seemed to park themselves randomly to disgorge their contents.

Ward and Marianne came down the steps of the Bahamasair BAC 1-11 looking every inch the tourists in love.

They held hands and chatted animatedly, looked longingly at each other, Ward's white jacket slung over his arm and a specially adapted Samsonite brief case held in the hand below, while Marianne was poured into an explosion of floral colour, with white sandals on her feet and an elegant straw hat atop her head, with a hyacinth held in place by a white ribbon. She had a small red handbag slung across one shoulder, which bumped and swayed with each swing of her hips.

Ten yards in front of them was Penny Sweeting. She wore white slacks, a pale yellow shirt with a black knitted tie, very loosely secured around her neck, a pair of black cat eye sunglasses, a pair of Salvatore Ferragamo black, calf suede shoes and carried an attaché case. She was striking to look at, both tough and beautiful and clearly someone who meant business.

She was the perfect distraction from the doe-eyed lovers trailing her.

Behind him, Ward could hear the clatter of a baggage cart as the first suitcases were thrown unceremoniously from the plane's hold and then driven behind a tug to the baggage area.

Hot tarmac, tiny airports and blue skies still thrilled him. There was an innocence about them when compared to Schiphol or Heathrow or Charles de Gaulle. It was as if they hadn't quite caught up with the twenty-four hour consumerism which was stealing across the West and Europe like a fog fed by greed.

Inside the terminal it was cool; desk fans spun and a light breeze blew in from the apron. Air conditioning soaked up the sweat and body heat.

Ward and Marianne picked up their cases and went to passport control.

The customs officer smiled as they handed over their

passports. 'Mr and Mrs Chance. Welcome to Nassau. Are you here for work or pleasure?'

Ward grinned at Marianne. 'Oh, definitely pleasure.'

'Just married?'

'This is our honeymoon,' said Marianne excitedly.

'And where will you be staying?'

'At the Christophene Hotel,' said Ward.

The customs officer's face fell. 'Really? For long?'

'Just a week,' said Ward.

The official wrapped his hands around the passports. 'I will need to photocopy these,' he said.

'Really? Why's that?' asked Ward.

'Protocol,' replied the officer. 'A record of who comes in, in case of problems.'

'I see,' said Ward.

He knew that the man was lying through his teeth. As soon as he heard the name of the hotel, his demeanour changed. And as for photocopying passports; Ward noticed that nobody else had their passports copied; they were just glanced at and handed back.

It took a five full minutes for the officer to return. That was time enough to take photocopies and fax them onward or make a phone call. It was not an auspicious start.

Passports returned, they moved through customs. At the other side stood a man with an enamelled sign, black letters shiny on a white background, held high saying: CHRISTOPHENE HOTEL.

Ward noticed Penny take some instruction from him and disappear out of the airport doors.

'That's us,' he said. 'Our transport to the boat.'

'They think of everything,' said Marianne.

Their names were ticked off on a list and they were instructed to go right out of the doors where a coach was waiting to take them North West to Prince George Wharf.

From there it would be a twenty minute boat ride to Jacob's Island, a couple of miles to the west.

Ward caught the back of Penny as she climbed onto the bus, then he and Marianne followed. It wasn't really a coach, more of a small twenty-seater with the hotel's name on the side, emblazoned with a deep blue sea and a bright orange sun. It was all part of the service, all a part of the razzle-dazzle of any expensive hotel. They didn't want hot, bothered and tired guests, who would rather go to bed than spend money, turning up.

After ten minutes the driver arrived, with no acknowledgement of the expectant onlookers, and pulled away.

The bus had all the windows open, but this just caused the warm air to flow resolutely around the cabin with no relief. Everybody was red-faced and shone. Some of them batted a leaflet in front of them, but it wasn't enough. The only hope for them was the open sea, the fresh air, the draft of speed as the boat skimmed the tiny waves and swept them onwards towards Jacob's Island.

The reality, of course, was different. The boat slammed clumsily from wave to wave. Water cascaded over the sides and soaked anything on deck. There was the stench of diesel in the air, a stench which seemed so weighty that it settled on deck and whirled in small, invisible hurricanes into everyone's nostrils. Several of the guests threw up over the side. One threw up on her own feet.

Ward figured that it was all part of the experience. Marianne clung to him like an octopus.

By the time the boat pulled into the concrete dock, they had all had enough. Some vaulted onto dry land, others weaved haphazardly, supported by a crew member, onto the hot landing.

Ward and Marianne held hands and stepped together

onto the dock. Their suitcases followed them, lifted from the boat by an incredibly muscular man who refused to meet anybody's eyes and yet picked up and landed each piece of luggage as if his life depended on it. Ward gave him ten Bahamian dollars for his care. He had no idea if this was enough, but the man broke into a tight-lipped smile and tucked the money into his pocket with pride.

Another small coach awaited them. It had the same rather crass decoration upon it that the bus at the airport had. It was more welcome though. The heat on the dock was oppressive. The concrete was hotter than a barbeque. The balmy inshore breeze gave no relief.

The bus was not much better, but with all the windows open, at least the air was allowed to circulate. It was a short journey anyway.

The island was fairly lush. Ward could understand the objections raised by those who had opposed the building of the hotel. It was little short of paradise. Either side of the purpose built road that led from the dock was essentially sub-tropical dry forest. Ward recognised none of the trees and plants, but the verdant, intertwining beauty of the place enchanted him. There must have been thousands of creatures taking shelter beneath the broad leaves. It would be easy to believe how many undiscovered species lay in the shadows. Ward wouldn't have been surprised if it hadn't just been bats and birds that had been rendered homeless by Eigen's relentless pursuit of profit and power.

However, there was no denying the stunning architecture of the hotel. It was constructed to look like the sails of a cutter, even to the point where a mast propped up each building while the rooms billowed out at either side. The smallest of the 'sails' must have been about one hundred and ten feet in height, while the largest must have been thirty or forty feet higher. The 'masts' had a glass lift attached and on each floor was a glass bridge where the passengers could cross to their rooms.

The main accommodation of the hotel was in the bigger, slightly squarer first 'sail', while the other two sails swept up from the ground and rose to a single penthouse at the top of each. Each was tucked into the other as if a strong wind had filled them, lifted them from the sea and placed them on dry land. Blue windows dotted each sail and reflected all around them. Anywhere else, it would have looked tacky; here against the blue sky and cobalt sea, it looked magnificent. If Saint Quintian got anything half as good, the tourists would flood in.

Beneath the sails was the main part of the hotel, designed as the sleek body of a cutter, even to the point of having a bowsprit - the purpose of which was not immediately clear - which held the main reception, several different dining areas and no doubt a sauna/spa/pampering area and indoor swimming pool. Ward was mildly disappointed that this was work and not play.

As the newest guests stepped into the climate-controlled reception, they were each offered a glass of champagne, guided to the main desk and booked in. The whole operation was smooth, calming, with none of the hysteria often associated with arriving tired and bad-tempered at a hotel.

Mr and Mrs Chance checked in and were delighted to find that they had been transferred to the Honeymoon Suite (second sail) at no extra cost to themselves. Naturally, the young lovers were thrilled. They were escorted to the very top of the sail to a room which was its own floor. There was nobody at either side of them and above them was a glass roof that looked out upon the heavens. Their escort showed them that, should it prove too hot or too bright, the glass could be covered by blinds, of which there were three layers, three densities, which could be used in any combination, each providing a greater degree of shade.

The bell-boy left. Marianne was about to speak when Ward put a finger to his lips. He went to his case and removed his bug detector.

'Look at that view, darling,' he said as he moved methodically around the room. 'Isn't it magnificent?'

'It is,' said Marianne as she watched Ward work. 'Aren't we lucky?'

The detector picked up a device. 'We don't know how lucky we are,' said Ward with a grimace. 'Why don't you go ahead and unpack, pick out some prime wardrobe space, while I take a good look at the view.'

Marianne picked up her case and started to unpack, all the time humming *(I Love You) For Sentimental Reasons*.

By the time Ward had finished two slow scans of the room, he had found four devices; one in the phone - as ever, one behind a painting of a cutter at sea, one hidden in a lamp and one within the air-conditioning control, just next to the enormous slider window which opened onto a small balcony, which was protected by thick safety glass. That way, Ward assumed, they would hope to pick up any external conversations.

So, the customs officer at the airport had been very thorough. After he had contacted the hotel, it would have taken very little time to install the devices, that's if they weren't already installed.

The question was whether to leave them intact or to render them ineffective. If he did anything to them, then whoever was listening would know and immediately throw suspicion upon them. It was best to leave them in situ and be careful what they said.

He went into the bathroom and ran the taps at full throttle. Marianne followed him in. 'We're bugged alright,' he said. 'I have no idea if it's for us or just anybody that uses this room, but it's a bit more than a coincidence that we were moved here, wouldn't you say?'

'Of course. We will speak only as lovers on honeymoon, but if you think you're going to make love to me with them listening...'

Ward smiled wickedly, turned the shower on full pelt and closed the bathroom door. 'They won't hear a thing,' he promised.

33. An Invitation to Dine

Ward stood on the beach, a secluded cove bound by palm trees, and gazed at the horizon, a hand shielding his eyes from the sun. His swim had been refreshing to say the least. The waters were warm, but they had just enough freshness in them for him to take a snorkel and mask and skim the coral and allow the cool waters to finger his skin. It would be healing, he knew, for his wounds.

It was a beautiful journey. The sun filtered through the meniscus of the sea and fell like pieces of eight upon the sand. It had been a long time since he had swum for pleasure and to do so had been liberating.

He had seen chub and parrotfish and angel fish and, a couple of times, a stonefish, the like of which had, in the past, saved his life. He had also come across blowfish. They hadn't reacted to him, merely waddled along like boxes. They still turned Ward cold, to see something so beautiful, so apparently harmless, and know that it could kill.

The return journey to shore had been as colourful as the journey out. The coral had glistened with fish which darted in and out of their hiding places as his shadow passed. In turn, Ward had marvelled at their colours and their bravery, at the way they nipped his legs once he had passed and coloured the water again with their courageous rainbow.

As he approached the beach, the coral had dissipated and he was left with the occasional glimpse of a trumpet fish and, hidden under a bit of debris or beneath a stray coral, a deadly lionfish, whose fins, if they touched the skin, could bring about a very unpleasant and painful reaction.

On the beach, stretched out upon a blue lounger with a Rainbow Paradise cocktail, full of grenadine, rum, coconut and pineapple, on a table next to her, lay Marianne. She wore an orange bikini. It highlighted her dark honey skin. Ward knew what was beneath those triangles of thin linen and wanted her again.

He towelled himself down and ran his fingers through his blond hair. Sensing his shadow, Marianne opened her eyes and gazed upon his lean, tight body.

'Here,' she said softly. 'Now.'

Ward fell upon her.

*

They had chosen the Sables D'or restaurant to eat in. It was the only one which offered an open menu. Le Poisson, as the name suggested, was limited to an exclusively fish menu. Les Specialtiés offered only local cuisine. Ward was not against either of these, indeed resolved to occupy a seat in both over the coming nights, time and events allowing, but tonight he needed a steak. He needed a large rib eye, where the fat had melted and been absorbed by the meat and tasted out of this world. It was something for which he rarely had a hankering, but steak with fries and pepper sauce was what he needed most; the hell with the vegetables.

Marianne ordered swordfish with roasted fingerling potatoes, artichokes and salsa. Ward could see that she was excited by the choice. 'It's expensive,' she said.

'Don't worry,' said Ward. 'Her Majesty will pay. The Chief will raise his eyebrows and tut once he sees the accounts, but I think, to save the world, it might be worth it.'

He ordered a red wine. He had no idea what he had ordered, but it sounded expensive. His love of alcohol left little to discretion. He knew a cheap wine from an expensive wine, for sure, but did not know a Shiraz from a Merlot. He knew which whiskies he liked, which rums but, if put to the test, would probably not be able to discern one from another. He drank because he liked to drink. He drank because he liked the warmth, the fuzz and the relaxation that came with it. He never drank too much, not while on duty, but if he could just for one moment lessen the edge, he would take it. When alone at home, in his London flat, he would drink and read until his eyes could no longer stay open. He always treated himself to a couple of large Glenfiddichs, with a cube of ice, and be glad that he was alone, just him and his habits. He sometimes wished that there was someone to share the moment with him, but had tried that once and failed miserably. He was probably too set in his ways by now to reopen any doors.

And on an evening like this, there was always that temptation to smoke; that would never go away, according to those he had talked to, but he didn't want to slow down yet, not too soon. He was still a few years from being taken off the active list, chained to a desk with pen and paper for handcuffs, and wanted to make the most of them. Besides, Marianne abhorred cigarettes. It was the one thing about Jacques she had disliked.

As the starters arrived, Chiquetaille De Morue for him and Shrimp Bruschetta for Marianne, the waiter gave a little cough and bowed his head.

'Mr and Mrs Chance,' he said with a flourish. 'Mr Felix Eigen has noticed that you are the only honeymoon couple to attend the hotel this week. Therefore…' He held his index finger up to stress the importance of what he was about to say. '…he has invited you to dine with him in his apartment tomorrow night. All courses from all restaurants will be made available to you and if you can find nothing to meet your tastes, he will have it flown in by helicopter. If you could let him know any special requirements by ten tomorrow morning via the reception, it will give him time to source your needs.'

Ward took a double-breath. It was bare-faced, he had to admit that. How could he refuse? Really? If he said no, then Eigen would find another way to get to him. Saying yes meant that the games were afoot, that Eigen wanted to play with him, to show his intellectual and physical superiority. Like all good sociopaths, he had to prove himself superior.

Ward played it cool.

'Well, that's very kind of him,' said Ward. He took a sip of wine and lifted his eyes to Marianne. 'What do you say, darling?'

Marianne's cool, steady eyes said it all. However, she agreed. 'That so kind,' she said. 'Is there any particular time?'

'If you go to reception at six forty-five, you will be taken to his quarters.'

'Well then,' said Ward. 'We must accept his very generous offer. Please, thank him for us.'

The waiter tilted his head. Ward was sure that he had snapped his heels together. 'Of course, Mr Ward. Please, enjoy your meal.'

The waiter left, his back straight, his buttocks firm, his footsteps unerring.

'Eat up,' said Ward. 'This is going to cost a bloody fortune.'

Marianne sunk a knife and fork into her seafood bruschetta.

*

Marianne slept beneath a light silk sheet. Ward could see the outline of her figure - the line of her breasts, the ripple across her flat abdomen and the enticing dip in her groin and down her thighs.

Her right hand rested against her cheek, her neck was slightly tilted. Her hair fell haphazardly about her shoulders and rested upon her breasts. Her chest rose deeply and evenly and Ward thought that he could see a smile upon her soft, full lips.

He grabbed a bottle of Chivas Regal with three cubes of ice – a drink that, for all his ignorance, he knew was good – poured himself half a tumbler and sat upon the balcony.

The glass balustrade protected him from an inebriated tumble into the pool below, but the gentle breeze still found a way around it and raised some goosebumps as the hairs on his body shimmered in its wake. Above him the sky, first seen through the glass ceiling in the suite, glistened and shimmered against the velvet black. The sea hushed gently against the shore and threw silver back at the moon.

He took a sip of the whisky and let it rest on his tongue, then sucked some air into it. It exploded in his mouth and sent tangs of vanilla and fruit and citrus and smokiness flying across his palette. For all the troubles in the world, it was the little things that mattered.

He had forbade himself from thinking about Marianne beyond the mission, but the longer they were together, the more his mind wandered towards her.

He wondered if she would like his world; the hustle and bustle and dirt of London, theatres, cinemas, restaurants, Ronnie Scott's and the Marquee, the distinctive seasons, the hope of spring, the joy of summer, the multicoloured decline of autumn and the Christmas and New Year celebrations of winter, followed by the low of January and February until the crocuses and daffodils could be seen again and hope returned.

Or could he resign and return to Saint Quintian, live the rest of his life out on golden sands beneath blue skies, live off the street food and play dominoes at night with a glass of rum at his side?

Were there children? Was there a home? Was it enough to drag him away from the thrill? To steal his independence? His freedom? Was he now too selfish to share his life with anyone? There was still a place for a married man in the civil service, still good pay and a good pension and the probability of a nice house in the suburbs, maybe even on the edge of the countryside.

But part of him recoiled at the thought. It was never enough to settle; to simply settle. There was enough time to settle when dead.

His mind turned to Felix Eigen. What kind of a man was he? Successful, without doubt. Charming, without doubt. He would have held all the attributes of a sociopath and a narcissist; good looks, a firm body, a regime that put a temporary stay on the encroachment of age. He could, as the old adage went, sell coals to Newcastle. Old ladies would hand over cheques and young ladies…so much more.

But he could not pass a mirror without a sideways glance, could not shower without self-adoration, could not believe that any woman who saw him did not want him; and many times he was right.

His charm smothered even the most immune. He could laugh with them and cry with them, sympathise and empathise, walk a mile in their shoes until they were convinced that this man would give his own life for them. But, in the end, only one thing mattered; Felix Eigen. He believed in the myth of the Genie, he believed himself magic, a jinn, an ancient power which could devour flesh and bones, snatch children or influence the living with merely a whisper.

He had built an empire based on superstition and fear. He had got others, such as Mirlande and Jacques, to carry out his work, merely for money. There was no Aladdin's cave, only an unfound bank account that shifted with the political winds.

And now he was so powerful that he had his own small, private army. Now he was so powerful that he could pull Russia into his schemes like a magnet pulled iron.

He was a nihilist. He didn't care about Russia or democracy or any other belief. He had seen his father murdered for his broken beliefs and his mother die solitary and afraid because they had to pay for the sins of his father.

Ward was sure that Felix Eigen believed in the communist cause. He would also have believed in the fascist cause if he could make a profit from it. He was the remora to the Soviet shark. He would take their crumbs which slipped from between their jagged teeth and grow strong on them. Eventually, perhaps, he might turn his own eyes upwards and bite the belly from the shark and move on to the next predator in line.

Money talked, belief walked.

Word will already have got back to him about the disaster at Jeans Genies. How much would he have lost? Ward had no idea. A million dollars? Two million? And that was only in assets destroyed. Long-term, with the vast income generated by the fine cutting and bulking of the drugs with agents such as laxatives or creatine, baking soda or flour, which would see the distribution go further and the profits raise by ten, fifteen or even twenty times, who knew?

By inviting Ward and Marianne to dinner, was this his way of saying he knew about them? That he now had them where he wanted them? Ward and Marianne could walk into a trap and never be seen again. Or were they genuinely the only newly-weds at the hotel this week? Was this Eigen's habit? It would be impossible to tell until they sat down with him and ate.

Ward drained his glass and set it upon the table. He needed to sleep. He needed to feel the warmth of Marianne's body and hear the sighs of her sleep. He wanted to wake her and make love to her, but he was forbidden, thanks to the men with big ears.

He reached for the bottle and poured himself another drink.

Their time would come.

34. The Price of Bread

The fire alarm went off at two am. It rattled and echoed shrilly through the buildings and caused an outpouring of tired, shuffling and irritated guests and staff onto the beach.

Everyone stared up at the concrete sails, the moon and stars reflected in each dark window, and searched for a lick of flame to justify their broken dreams. There were no flames. An air of disappointment rippled through the crowd. At the very least, sleep disturbed, there should have been some sort of drama to keep them amused.

The night-manager, loud hailer in hand, apologised to the crowd and promised them champagne, which the waiters were in the process of distributing. Unfortunately, he added, nobody could be permitted to enter the building until it was declared safe by the fire brigade. They would, sadly, have to come to the island by boat and then weave their way along the narrow roads to the hotel. The crowd groaned. Fires were rapidly lit upon the beach and music spilled from invisible speakers. Hors d'oeuvre were served with the champagne and, for those who didn't like the bubbly, there were always the finest spirits available.

'Let me assure you, ladies and gentlemen,' said the night-manager, 'that we are prepared for any event and will always put your comfort first. Now gather round the fires; drink, eat, dance, sing and talk.'

It was all said with the dramatic flourish of the ringmaster.

As research had told the owners of the Christophene Hotel, people could be induced to anything, given the right rewards.

Inside the hotel, Penny Sweeting walked brazenly through the corridors, a Lone Ranger mask around her eyes, blue latex gloves upon her hands, her hair pulled tightly back and pinned until it became androgynous and flip-flops on her feet. Partly, it was her sense of humour and partly it was because she knew she would not be recognised by stray people or any internal cameras. If anybody challenged her, she could deal with them with little more than a thumb but, after setting off the alarms, she knew that there would be nobody around. These places, whoever owned them, would never risk a lawsuit and therefore were unrelenting when it came to health and safety. Every room would have been checked and everything with a heartbeat ushered outside.

It would have made more sense to build a fire station on the island but, what with the environmentalists and the sprinkler systems and the advanced firefighting architecture within the hotel, it was thought unnecessary. Not only that, but at least twelve men would have been employed on each shift to simply swing from a hammock in the hope that something had the decency to ignite. So the fireboat brought the fire engines to the fire, in the hope that the already installed fire prevention would delay the damage.

What was Penny hoping to find? She had no idea. She had managed to acquire some blueprints of the hotel and had, that afternoon, with the blueprints spread across the floor of her room, decided which would be the most important places to visit.

There were two; the manager's office and the executive suite.

The manager's office would be easy. It might have appeared safe, but it would, as with all these places, be all trousers and no willy, as Penny liked to say. It was the appearance of security and quick prayer that kept things safe.

The executive suite, Eigen's quarters, would be a greater challenge with possibly the best rewards. She had a very good idea of the layout but, once the blueprints were approved, there was little anyone would do once he had made changes. What was done was done. There would be yearly inspections by various authorities of course, but they wouldn't care about where the proprietor stayed; it was all about the guests' quarters and restaurants and the pool areas and the spas. They would even examine the beach to see that it had been cleared, on a daily basis, of dangerous materials. God forbid they should find a dead snapper on the sands.

The powers that be could object to the change in the situation of his swanky new kitchen or the bathroom add-ons or the latest sauna in the extension, but they would do little about it. So long as there was no risk of damage to the tourist market, certain things could be let go.

Penny tried the door to the manager's office. The night-manager had failed to lock it in his haste to ensure an orderly evacuation. She opened the door and slid in. The lights were on. His cigar dwindled to a smoky halt in the ashtray, leaving behind half an inch of fat ash as it died. She curled a lip at the soggy end. The idea of anyone holding a spit-sodden wedge of dried leaf in their mouth was not attractive.

She went to a filing cabinet (ubiquitous, it seemed, in every den) and opened it without a fuss.

She went for the most recently labelled drawer and opened it. She picked a file at random. It was an astounding find. For each guest there was a file. Each file was at least one quarter of an inch thick and told their story.

Penny picked a file at random and read it. It was about Thomas Wyszynski. Thomas worked at Asgaard Tyres in Woodridge, Illinois. His commission on each sale helped pay the bills, his basic wage little more than two dollars above minimum wage. He had a wife, who worked as a teaching assistant at the local high school, and two children, Maisie and Clarke, and barely lived within his means. Each month he had dipped into his overdraft, not because he was extravagant, but because he had costs. They had worked hard and saved hard for this break, while the kids spent some time with the grandparents.

He had no secrets. Not one. He paid his credit card off bit by bit, the minimum each month, ate sensibly and made his clothes last. Most of his money went on the kids; school trips, birthdays, Christmas, pocket money, treats. They had an account at Hamblett's, the local department store. He paid eight percent of his monthly wage in repayments so that the kids could be dressed for school, could have birthday parties, could attend birthday parties; could be kids.

He was a good man, apart from the regular fifty dollar a pop payment (in cash) to someone. It turned out that this was a bimonthly appointment at the Happy Hippo, a brothel on Chicago's east side, where he got his kicks at the beginning of route sixty-six.

Penny fingered the files adeptly. She scanned them and remembered them, each file gluing itself to her idetic memory.

Then she found the file belonging to Ward and Marianne -the Chances. Cutely, it was a joint file, dedicated to the newly-weds, to the love-lorn. Ominously, the sections were in their real names - Ward and Knightly, her father's name.

She opened Marianne's file first. It spared no detail, from first love (Roman Glassberg, later a DA in Florida) to school qualifications (all As). It detailed her parents; the Saint Quintian mother who had fallen for the English ex-pat one New Year's Eve next to the swimming pool, had made love to him in the cool waters and married him with all her heart. He had been a priest, a member of the Anglican church, sent out to promote The Word, one of many, scattered across the world, who had found their fallibility in the flesh and spread more than their word.

But they had been happy and lived and died together, two years apart, on the island, he a teacher, she a dedicated housewife. They weren't so old, but they had loved each other deeply; they held hands wherever they walked, she had indulged his quirks and he had indulged her obsessions. Once one had lost the other, life had become a countdown.

As for Ward, it had little more to say. His father, a vicar in Norfolk, his mother a vicar's wife, all scones and jam and jumble sales, until she had died of breast cancer and been buried in Saint Cuthbert's church. He had followed her ten years later at the age of seventy-eight.

It spoke of Ward's army service, his time in the Dorset and Devonshire Regiment, his discharge, his journalism, even a couple of his early articles (they seemed naïve) and his recruitment to the firm after the island affair. It even spoke of Rose Trelawney and Raven Temple, names not known to her, but significant enough to be on file. Eve Ward, née Balston, the daughter of Ralph Balston, professor in history at Durham University and Ellie Balston, celebrated modern artist, was even given a mention.

Felix Eigen knew it all. He had compiled dossiers on everyone he believed to be a threat to his sanctuary, to his powerbase, to his cause - that cause being himself. He, in his paranoia or his infinite need for privacy, perhaps even his wisdom, had a file for everyone who had come to his hotel and might, just might, have been more than they seemed. It was compiled by date, then alphabetically. Accompanying it was a rolodex of names and addresses.

He knew it all. Either he never slept or he had one hell of a dedicated team working for him. Penny suspected it was half money and half fear that drove his staff, but she also suspected that Eigen was an obsessive that knew no bounds, that didn't, couldn't, sleep with a task undone. He would never wilt, never display exhaustion. He galloped tirelessly across his realm, like Henry II, ready for rebellion, ready for war.

Penny closed the cabinet.

She really needed no more. Eigen was a power-hungry capitalist ready to exploit anyone who was ready to be exploited. In desperation, the Soviet Union, that bastion of equality, had turned to him in the hope that, inch by inch, he could take the Caribbean, much as Japan had worked its way down the far east in the Second World War. This was more subtle, less overt, but the result was the same. Power by any means. Control by any means.

She replaced the folder and closed the cabinet. Somehow she had to warn Ward and Marianne. If she didn't, not only were they doomed, but the entire Caribbean would become a centre for communism.

Out of curiosity, Penny looked for her file. She opened it and read about things that even she had forgotten; the schools she had attended, the university, her grades, her first lesbian experience, her recruitment to the service and her work in the orthopaedic field. It told of her idetic memory and her knife skills - she always refused to carry a gun - and the countries to which she had been as doctor and agent.

Penny was filled with both horror and admiration for the man. He was going to be one of those people that the world rarely saw and yet, once seen, never was never forgotten. He would change borders, nations, leaders. He would present a benign capitalist face to the world while at the same time crushing it within his iron fist.

This was no more about creating a new Cuba than it was about the price of bread. This was about him and only him. The world would in the end succumb to his power and wealth and he would create a totalitarian state where allegiances no longer mattered, but obedience was all. He was Hitler and Stalin, Pol Pot and Mao Zedong or any number of mother-obsessed, father-battered children who wanted revenge for their perceived abuses as a child.

She left the room as she found it, with everything she had read stored in her memory.

She decided to skip the inspection of Eigen's suite. It was nearly time up; she had spent too long with her nose buried in the files. It wouldn't be long before the fire brigade turned up and declared the place safe.

She took a fire door out the back of the building and then a circuitous route to the beach, where she mingled among the crowds, all happy and chatty by the fires with their complimentary champagne and hors d'oeuvres.

She searched for Ward and Marianne and found them sitting at the water's edge with their backs to the crowd. She went for a walk along beach and, as she passed them, clicked her fingers loudly. They did not immediately acknowledge the sound but, as Penny walked away from the flickering firelight and into darkness, they sauntered like lovers towards her and all three disappeared into the shadows.

35. Clean the Chalk from the Blackboard

Ward was stunned by what Penny had to say. There were so many implications, not least that just about every security service in the world had been compromised, including MI6 and possibly MI5.

Whether this had been done from the inside or the outside was, at this stage, impossible to say. Attacks upon what were thought to have been safe and secure systems had been happening since 1903 when Marconi's telegraph system was broken into with Morse code. There was no reason not to suspect that someone had somehow crashed the levels of security to steal information. Certainly, local authorities, judging by the very ordinariness of the people compromised, had something to answer for. It wasn't perhaps so much outside forces hacking into the systems as people selling information from within but, with the advance in technology, came an advance in the ability to manipulate that technology. The bad guys were always quick to latch onto weaknesses and it wasn't until those weaknesses were exposed that the good guys did anything about it. It was reactionary, not anticipatory. And it wasn't just Britain that was culpable. The Christophene welcomed all nations and all nations had people and all people had a dark side.

Whether Eigen had ever considered people's proclivities as a possible source of blackmail and therefore income was unclear, but the potential was there. Poor old Thomas Wyszynski might already have been contributing to party funds for all Ward knew, along with the thousands of others with secrets to hide.

What a network he had. To be able to suck the marrow out of one country was something, but it seemed that anyone from anywhere was as susceptible to such surveillance as Thomas Wyszynski might have been, to potentially be able to prise money from his guilty hands in the hope that his wife would not find out about his deviances.

Maybe Ward was thinking too far ahead, full of conjecture, that this had not occurred as yet to Eigen and his communist bedfellows, but he doubted it. The communists had spent years refining their ability to get what they wanted, from honey-traps to death threats. A close look at people's accounts might well show a regular payment to the 'Dog Defence League' or some other 'charity'. He doubted that the Russians or Eigen would miss such a chance. There was no point in being outraged, British intelligence had been doing it for years. The call was, 'don't get angry, get even'.

In the meantime though, he was only a couple of hours away from dinner with one such possible future. He had brought nothing formal with him to wear, so he went with black slacks and a white polo shirt. He couldn't have been more bland, more ordinary. He asked Marianne to do the same. She wore a pale yellow blouse with navy slacks and still looked stunning. Next to her, Ward looked like a parking attendant.

'You look lovely,' said Ward, partly for the people listening in, partly because he meant it.

'Well,' said Marianne, playing the part. 'It's not often a big hotel owner invites you to dinner. Do you think he'll have champagne and caviar?'

Ward pulled a face at her. 'I have no idea, my darling. Let's just make the most of it.'

'I had a rich aunt,' said Marianne out of the blue.

'Oh, yes?' said Ward, determined not to be thrown. 'What happened to her?'

'Well, she fell in love with an entomologist from Iowa.'

'Did it work out?'

'No, turned out he was a real louse!'

Ward smiled. Marianne must have been nervous as hell and yet she still put on a brave face.

'Shall we report to reception?' he asked.

'Sure,' said Marianne. 'Is my makeup okay? I don't want Mr Eigen to think I'm not good enough.'

Ward kissed her slowly and with love. 'Never,' he said. 'Never in a million years. If he doesn't fall in love with you like I have, then I'll beat him with one of his silver spoons.' He ran a finger through her hair and then placed a palm upon her cheek. 'I love you,' he said.

'And I love you,' replied Marianne. Her eyes shone with the lightest of tears.

'Then let's go eat with the compliments of the owner of this grand hotel'.

*

Ward and Marianne were guided from the main reception to the executive suite by a handsome young man in an expensive suit, not so well tailored that the slight rise at the back of his right hip where his gun lay, didn't go unnoticed.

He didn't talk, merely asked Ward and Marianne to follow him and led the way through a key-padlocked door which, in turn, took them into a maroon-carpeted corridor with rooms at either side. None of the doors were open. Ward could only guess that they might have been offices, that they were passing through the administration area of the hotel. Above them was thick, tinted glass which let in a surprising amount of light and yet kept the temperature at a bearable level. Combined with air conditioning, the corridor was not as claustrophobic as it might have been. Through the glass, Ward could see the day die as the sun raced to the other side of the world and left in its wake an onslaught of colour.

At the end of the hallway was another keyed padlock attached to a magnificent ebony door. Ward tried to make a note of the number keyed in, but their escort worked fast and obscured his view.

Once keyed in, the door opened automatically. It opened onto a large living area, steeped in deep burgundy carpet and a charcoal grey three-piece suite. It was expensive, Ward could tell, but he had no idea who had made it, only that he would never be able to afford it. Beneath his feet the carpet sighed, gave way gently beneath his feet and then returned to where it had been.

There were several Tiffany floor lamps strategically placed around the dimly lit room, most of the light coming from a huge picture window, filled by the most extraordinary, blazing sunset as if Eigen had ordered it from God himself. The still sea caught the light and fractured it. It seemed almost like a mosaic that shimmered and shifted as the giant sky above it whirled with the lowering of the sun.

When the day had finally gone and a full moon spilled its heart upon the oily waters, Ward imagined it would be beautiful.

They moved as one towards the centre of the room. To the left of the vast living area was a dining area. It was equipped with contemporary designer furniture; Ward guessed Italian but really had no idea. Culturally, he was in over his head. The table was glass upon chrome legs, the chairs steam-bent wood upon the same legs. They were nice enough, he thought, but to him furniture was functional, no more. His only collection was about two hundred and fifty vinyl albums and a Technics hi-fi player. It had cost him a pretty penny, but it was more than worth it in his downtime. He would relax in his flat, his legs stretched out upon the sofa, a tumbler of Glenfiddich with just two ice cubes balanced on his chest and lose himself.

It wasn't that he didn't appreciate fine things; anything well-made with a story behind it was worth ten minutes of his time but, despite his time in that rather precious, pretentious public school all those years ago, he found it difficult to carry the affectations of the supposedly intellectual. What good was a Ferrari that couldn't cope with the weekly shop?

'Good evening, Mr Chance.'

The voice, a strange, deep mixture of Russo-European, came from their left as Felix Eigen emerged from the shadows.

Marianne instinctively stepped behind Ward at the same time that he moved in front of her.

The figure remained in obscurity. 'I've startled you, Mrs Chance, forgive me.'

Marianne said nothing.

Eigen emerged into the half-light of the fading day, most of him in the shadows, the rest of him ignited by the volcanic fracture of the sky.

The message sent to Ward by Simner had transmitted none of the horror of the man.

The most obvious thing to strike Ward was Eigen's height; he must have been at least six feet seven. As he stepped slowly into the room, it became apparent that he had no hair; no eyebrows, no eyelashes, not even a trace of stubble. His eyes were enormous; the whites encircled his irises and left them like two black discs in a sea of milk. It made him look at once both startled and furious. On top of these he wore thick-lensed glasses which magnified his eyes further, made them even more disproportionate. When he blinked, which was not often, it seemed to be an effort, as if he had to make himself do it, that he simply didn't have the reflex that others had. Everything about him was oversized. His giant head was almost square and riven by deep wrinkles, similar to a Shar Pei, and his ears seemed lost in the folds of flesh but for enormous, melted lobes. His nose, long and at some time broken, stood out like a pyramid in the desert. His lips were thick and moist and seemed to pout. He sweated profusely and had to constantly run a handkerchief across his face.

His hands protruded like shovels from a white silk shirt, semi-transparent with sweat, and once again, the skin fell in folds across hammer-like knuckles.

He emerged fully into the room.

He was broad. His shirt lay unevenly over his torso and adhered to the wet areas of his skin, no doubt a victim of the same wrinkles that affected the rest of him. In the end-of-world sunset, he appeared to be from Dante's Inferno or something from Hieronymus Bosch's visions of Hell.

Yet he moved lightly on his feet. Ward had expected him to lumber under the weight of all that skin, but it was clearly a coat in which he had grown to be comfortable.

'They give it the rather quaint name of Wrinkly Skin Syndrome. I am a rather extreme version of the disease.' He walked to the window. 'The alopecia is a bonus, I suppose, as is the constant sweating. Perhaps I am paying for the sins of my father.'

He turned to Ward and Marianne. 'Forgive my appearance please. I am luckier than most. I have been able to have surgery to alleviate the prominent rolls of skin over my eyes. It leaves me looking a little…surprised, especially with the severe myopia that accompanies the disease and the necessity for these very strong glasses. I have to go back to Switzerland and have them redone now and again. They tell me that there is nothing else to do about the rest of my body. I know it's hideous.'

He walked over to a drinks cabinet. 'What can I get you? You look like a whisky man, Mr Chance and Mrs Chance seems…a rum kind of woman.' He paused as if he expected his weak pun to bring about howls of laughter. When it didn't, he carried on pouring the drinks, as if his guests' answers had been irrelevant.

'Most people with this disease are small, fragile creatures, inflicted with the most horrific side-effects.' He smiled falsely. 'These teeth are not my own. They were so small and rotten, I had to have them removed.' He gave Ward and Marianne their drinks and poured himself a glass of Robinson's Lemon Barley Water. 'I cannot join you in a drink, I'm afraid. I don't drink alcohol. It sends me a little crazy; as if the wires in my brain had caught fire. I tried it when I was younger and was unable to walk for a couple of days. Such is life. Please, sit. Admire the sunset.'

'It's a beautiful place you have here,' said Ward in an attempt to lighten the tone.

Eigen ignored him 'When I was about seven years old, my father took me and my mother to live in Auschwitz concentration camp. As a child it meant nothing to me. I was segregated from the business of the camp and my parents never spoke of what really went on there. However, I later found out that my father had an ulterior motive for taking me there. You see, Auschwitz was a place of great scientific value. The work being done into twin studies and eugenics, the work being done to help the recovery of the injured soldiers, was remarkable. Wirths was there, as well as Mengele, Schumann and Clauberg - all great men doing great work, not just for the Reich, but to further humanity.

My father gave me to them and asked them to cure me, by any means possible. Most people like me would have been exterminated, but I was protected by my father and I intrigued the doctors; a challenge I suppose.'

A man in chef's whites quietly entered the room and whispered into Eigen's ear. Eigen nodded and the man left. 'That's good,' he said. 'Five minutes until we eat. I hope my choice of menu will delight you. We are going to start with crushed avocado on toast with a poached egg on top. It's all very creamy. I'm a sucker for creamy. The main course will be...' His lips turned up at the corners as if something funny had occurred to him. He clasped his giant hands together with pleasure. 'Fish, of course. What else could it be? Yellow fin tuna steaks and a Caribbean salad with a honey lime dressing. And finally, one of my favourites, Caribbean bread pudding. There will of course be a spiced rum sauce for you both. I will settle for double cream.'

He unclasped his hands and laid them upon his knees. They lay there like naked mole rats. 'Anyway, these doctors batted me between them and gradually, with the help of some very lengthy and painful procedures, managed to make me a little more...' He grimaced. 'Normal. Unfortunately, things went a little too far and they overcompensated, turned me into the Frankenstein's monster you see before you now. It also left me with this hyperhydrosis which, as you can see, causes me to sweat excessively. I exercised, lifted weights, constantly applied myself to becoming....' He hesitated. His brow furrowed. 'To becoming something. It was enough to let me live, but perhaps not enough to let me live a normal life.

My father was captured by the Israeli secret service and murdered in nineteen fifty-two. It's funny, don't you think, how they thought they were saving the world by murdering my father? He was just a man living a peaceful life with his wife and son, the war over, and then he was gone. He was just an accountant, that's all. A harmless, hard-working accountant. My mother died not long after. We had no money; we scratched out an income wherever we could.

I was eighteen when she died. I found her one morning in bed, frozen in rigor mortis. There and then I took everything we had and ran.'

Ward wanted to tell him to stop this self-indulgent bullshit. It was the same story told over and over again by someone out to justify their crimes. But, it was absorbing; even Marianne seemed to have been sucked in by the horror of it all.

'Anyway,' continued Eigen. 'I ran. I had a suitcase full of belongings, mostly old clothes and nothing else. I got to…'

He stopped as a door opened and the food was brought in by the same man who had given Eigen the five-minute warning.

'Shall we?' he offered. 'I don't know about you, but I'm very hungry. This morning I had some toast with lots of butter and strawberry jam and some sweet black tea for breakfast. Nothing since. I noticed that you, Mr Chance, had eggs royale for breakfast and your lovely wife had scrambled eggs on toast.' His large eyes wandered towards Marianne. 'Lots of butter, I hope.'

The man in the chef's coat led them to the table. There was a glass of red wine already poured for Ward and Marianne. He pulled out a chair for Marianne, then for Ward. Eigen did not wait, but pulled out his own chair and sat down. Before Ward had picked up his cutlery, he was into his crushed avocado. With each mouthful he gave out a satisfied 'mmm', as if he had never eaten before and ate so quickly that Marianne and Ward had barely taken their first mouthfuls by the time he had finished.

He put his knife and fork at precisely six o'clock on his plate and then carried on speaking as if there had been no interruption.

'I lived rough for while in Munich and, just to get a roof over my head, followed a street vendor home and killed him for his money. He had everything he had made that day in a money belt around his fat waist. He had done well that day too. I spent the night in his house, ate from his fridge, took drinks from his larder and slept in his bed. I think that it must have been one of the best night's sleep I had ever had.

The next day, I did the same thing and doubled my money. The man ran a newspaper stall. I grabbed him as he walked home and crushed his head in these very hands.' He held up his gigantic paws and gazed upon them with wonder. 'It popped with a sloppy crack. Like a water melon. He had his address on him, on his driver's licence, so I went there with the intention of another good night's sleep. I could not stay at his house because, when I went to it, it was occupied. I spent the night in a rather seedy hotel and the next day met some people who were right-wing sympathisers. They seemed okay, so I joined them. I wrote for their papers. I didn't believe in their words, to be honest, but they paid me and gradually I became more popular, more in demand and was able to build myself a nice little nest egg.'

Marianne put down her cutlery and pushed the plate away. She had taken perhaps three mouthfuls. Ward ploughed on. It was too good to waste.

Eigen looked at Marianne's plate. 'Not to your liking, my dear? Too bad. Perhaps the tuna will be more to your taste.'

Ward drew attention away from Marianne. 'Why are you telling us all this, Mr Eigen. It's not exactly light-hearted dinner chat now, is it.'

Eigen linked his huge hands and rested his chin upon them. He pondered for a moment. 'Mr Ward. Miss Knightly. I'm sorry. We shall give up the pretence. You know who I am and I know who you are. Mr Ward has come all the way from London, presumably to kill me and thwart my plans to take over the world. A bit cliched, but not so far from the truth. Miss Knightly is hanging onto your coat tails. She is very out of her depth. You both are.'

'Well, seeing as we're being honest,' said Ward, 'Let's be clear. Your father was a torturer and a murderer. There is no redemption for him as there is none for you. You talked about the sins of your father, it couldn't be any clearer. You're as insane as he was; a sociopath, amoral, unscrupulous and narcissistic. You're a nihilist. You believe in nothing but yourself. You'll take a mark or a rouble from anyone.'

Eigen remained silent. Their plates were cleared away and the tuna course arrived. Ward noticed the familiar bulge of a gun in the server's pocket.

When the server had left, as if Ward had never spoken, Eigen dived into the meal in much the same way as he had leapt into the first course, with all the same animalistic 'mmm's and oral vacuuming as he had before. Marianne didn't touch anything. Ward tucked in. If he was going to fight, he would need sustenance, if he was going to die, he was sure as hell going to enjoy his last meal.

Eigen cleared his plate and placed his knife and fork ritually at six o'clock. His eyes scoured the plate. 'Splendid,' he said, to no one in particular.

'It's not actually about me,' he said calmly. 'It's about the world. There is only one way this world will survive, at least with humans on it, and that it to sift the weak and elevate the strong. It is about control. Humans are stupid. They are the only species, in the history of the earth, that will destroy itself. We pollute, Mr Ward, we pollute indiscriminately and we acquire profit and comfort. We pump oil and waste into the seas with no regard for consequence. We give sealife plastic to eat. We discard our waste in beauty spots and hope that they will somehow dissolve. We don't care. Out of sight, out of mind. Every government, every country, has its own set of rules by which it abides, each with its own agenda, regardless of the effect upon its neighbours. There are too many of us and it is growing. There are four and a half billion humans on this planet right now. If we multiply at the rate we are, by 2023 there will be eight billion people. The world will suffocate. People will slip into the sea and drown because there will be no land left to stand upon. One war will see the world starve because we are now so interdependent. How did Britain survive World War Two, Mr Ward? It dug, it dug its heart out and persuaded its people to live on carrots and potatoes and eight ounces of ham a week. Could you see that now? Could you see modern Britain living on anything but McDonalds and ready-made meals? Would they fight for belief? For God? For their way of life?'

Eigen shook his head and sighed. 'No, Mr Ward. They would do as your spivs did. Profit for themselves and the hell with the rest. Except now, instead of the few, it would be all. Anarchy, Mr Ward. Anarchy.' He looked Ward in the eyes. His glasses magnified the thoughts that lay behind his black eyes.

'Christ!' said Ward. 'It's not about Saint Quintian or the Caribbean, is it. It's about the world. You hope to push a nuclear war between America and Russia and you will pick up the pieces. This has nothing to do with hotels or another Cuba. My God! How can you gamble with our future like this?'

Almost, but not quite,' said Eigen with a hint of triumph. He frowned. 'I haven't gambled with anything,' he said. 'You did. You and all those who decade by decade have allowed self-fulfilment to rise above the needs of the earth.

By simply surviving, you have eaten away at the skin of the earth with mining, with oil, with things that make your calculators calculate and your watches glow, by using mercury, cyanide, sulphuric acid, arsenic and methyl mercury to mine these commodities. We must start again. We must go back a thousand, two thousand years to put this right. The world needs time to recover.'

'So you're going to let the Greeks and the Egyptians off the hook are you? What about the iron age? Would you wipe that out? The bronze age? Are you going to abandon every advance ever made? The Industrial Revolution? Where will you draw the line? The extraction of gold or silver? The production of copper? No aluminium? No magnesium? No chlorine? No barium or plutonium? No advances in medicine? No antibiotics? No home comforts? No cars? No planes? No wireless?'

'None,' said Eigen without a flicker of emotion. 'I will peel back the layers until we get to the core.'

'And nuclear fallout. Will that not exist in your world? The Soviet Union and North America, plus a substantial part of Europe, will be left uninhabitable for centuries. How are we meant to cope with that? How will we survive?'

Eigen leaned forward. His massive arms leaned against the table. 'We won't,' he said. 'We will start again. The world will cleanse itself. Nature always wins.'

'You're mad,' said Ward. 'You can't make things better by making them worse.'

'Clean the chalk from the blackboard, Mr Ward, and you have a clear space to write.'

Ward realised that no reasoning would change this man. If he wasn't killed, then he would destroy everything he knew for the chance of a willow crown. 'You're a sick man, Eigen,' he said.

Eigen sat back in his chair. 'That sunset,' he said pointing a fat finger at the window. 'That is not mine. That is created by man. It is full of unnatural gases that have broken through the ozone layer and now diminish our atmosphere. It is a creation of the gases we have released from beneath the earth's crust by our constant mining and use of fossil fuels. It is coal fires and oil and natural gas. It is the things that are made with these fuels - electronics, plastics, clothes, iron, steel, fuels.' He opened his hand pleadingly towards the window. 'It is an angry sunset, fired by stupidity and greed.'

'And you think destroying all we know will make that better?'

Ward pushed his plate away. It was empty. It had been the perfect meal, with citrus and mandarin and butter lettuce and onions. It had been topped off with sesame and chia seeds. He felt a pang of guilt for enjoying it so much, especially when Marianne had pushed her plate way (which he now wanted to pick at with all his heart).

'And after the bread and butter pudding which, incidentally, will not in any way compare with my mother's bread and butter pudding - so you're onto a loser there - what will happen then? Are you just going to fold that extra fifty pounds of skin up and walk away or is there more? Bear in mind that Mirlande, that demon you sent to kill me, failed, despite herself. What about you? Do you intend to make us talk?' he shrugged. 'You already know everything we know. Do you intend to make us suffer simply for the sake of suffering? We can take it. All suffering is gone after death. Wiped out. Meaningless. We can scream and cry and curse in our suffering, but it will be rendered meaningless by sleep. To hell with you.'

Ward drained his wine. Eigen refilled his glass. 'That is a Château Le Crock nineteen fifty-nine. Please, do not let it pass you by.'

'I am,' confessed Ward, 'a man of little taste. I like or I do not like. That's it.'

'And this wine?'

Ward took a sip and filtered it with his lips. The act felt pretentious and yet it split the wine and flooded his mouth with an infinity of flavours. 'I like it,' he said.

'That,' said Eigen flatly, 'is the difference between wealth and poverty.'

'Really?' said Ward. 'You being such a communist and all, I thought that you mind find basic nutrition to be the difference.'

'Any man can grow and eat potatoes and marvel at his swollen abdomen,' said Eigen.

'But knowing the difference between a cheap wine and a good wine is the mark of a man?'

'One of many,' said Eigen.

The bread and butter pudding was delivered. Silence reigned as the server placed the full plates meticulously and left two jugs, one of double cream and the other of rum sauce.

'Would you mind if I had both?' asked Ward. 'Rum sauce and double cream is too much of a temptation.'

Marianne kept her hands in her lap. 'How can you eat?' she asked Ward. 'This is not a game.'

'I'm hungry,' said Ward coldly. 'I'm not going to starve because I don't like the table cloths in a restaurant.'

'I like your principles, Mr Ward,' said Eigen.

'It's not principles,' said Ward. 'It's pudding.' He dripped rum sauce onto his plate, followed by a generous spill of cream. He split it with a spoon and took a mouthful. He had loved his mother, but this was superb.

Eigen chuckled. 'We all have our price.'

Ward swallowed. 'You think this is my price? You think I can be bought with some fish and a delicious rum sauce? You think you can bully, bribe or intimidate me the way you did Bill Buckley or Raphael Moise or the Saint Quintian cabinet?' He shook his head firmly. 'No, Eigen. You're just a freak with a pipe dream. You think that you can disguise your ugliness with power and oppression. But you never will. You're a freak of nature and Nazism, a collision of catastrophes. No matter what you do, people will be afraid of you and hate you and eventually replace you, because that's human nature.'

Eigen put his hands across his cheeks and rubbed slowly. They looked like fat spiders on his face. 'Then I'll persuade you.'

'You can't persuade me. You can kill me if you want, allow the Americans and British to come for you after me, because they know everything I know, but in the end you will be broken by your own sick dream.'

Eigen sighed deeply. His massive eyes consumed Ward. 'Well,' he said softly, with barely disguised restraint. 'Let's see what your price really is, Mr Ward.'

He clicked his fingers. A door behind him opened.

Penny, dragged between two men, beaten and bruised, hog-tied, was thrown onto the floor between Ward and Eigen. 'What do you say now, Mr Ward? How about her life for your cooperation?'

36. Then, I Will Be King

Penny, gagged and bound by Gaffa tape, was able to do little. Her eyes, with cuts on her cheeks linked by a gash on the bridge of her nose, looked at Ward and shook her head. He could hear her voice in his head, threatening him not to do it but to sacrifice her.

Marianne knelt down next to Penny and attempted to undo the ties. She was dragged back to her seat by those who had dragged Penny into the room.

Eigen grunted. 'Just sit,' he said.

Marianne defiantly shrugged her shoulders and shook her captors away. Tears rolled down her cheeks, but they weren't tears of fear, only of anger and frustration. Until this moment, Ward had never seen the killer in her eyes but, at that moment, that was all that was left. She looked at the knife on the table in front of her. Ward felt his heart leap. It would be a bee sting to a bear. He shook his head minutely. It was enough.

Eigen shooed the men away. They retreated, footsteps unheard, destination unknown.

'It won't be long until the stars appear.' His black eyes gazed absently at something that could not be seen. 'You see how the blush of day gives way to the gentle bruise of night? Soon we will see a black velvet sky, enriched by the distant dusty deaths of suns from a thousand years ago, and it will be beautiful.'

'And how will it look through the dusty sky of a nuclear winter?' said Ward.

'Like hope,' replied Eigen. 'A second chance. It will be the war to end all wars.'

'I seem,' said Ward, 'to have heard that phrase before.'

Eigen paid him scant attention. 'Do you know how many conflicts we have had so far in the twentieth century alone? In this century of madness? Hundreds. Small wars, world wars, civil wars, rebellions, uprisings, crises. Never a decade has gone by without one. Britain and the United States have been involved in the majority of them. Russia and China have also provided funds and supplies to many of them. No one is innocent. Go back in time and you will find no different. Every great empire, the Roman, the Ayyubid, the French Colonial empire, the Dutch empire, the Normans, the Vikings.' He raised his giant hands and let them fall heavily upon the table. Everything on it shook; wine shimmered, cutlery bumped heads, plates leapt in surprise. 'Humanity, since the dawn of time, has been incapable of peace, of sharing, of compromise. It has always been about land and resources, not to share, to give the benefit to humankind, but to keep and shield and wield over supposed adversaries.' He stuck his thick bottom lip out. 'I despair, Mr Ward. I really do. Democracy and politics have proved to be useless. The democracy we practice is a fallacy, given human nature, and politics is merely games, musical chairs, a never-ending dance in which partners are swopped liked cheap lovers, like whores.'

'And how will you be different?' asked Ward. 'If you oppress, you will crush freedom of thought and deed. If you crush thought and deed, you will foment rebellion. If you democratise, you will be swept away by popular vote. You won't win either way.'

Eigen's chest swelled. 'I will be the opium of the masses. I will be the benevolent father. It will not be religion or football or philosophy or alcohol, it will be me. I will ensure that if people cannot be controlled by the baton, they will be controlled by drugs. I will inveigle myself into every aspect of their lives and they will grow to love me or fear me, like Stalin or Hitler or Cromwell or William the Conqueror.'

'Also known as William the Bastard, I believe,' said Ward.

'What's in a name, so long as that name brings compliance?'

'Truth?' offered Ward. 'People will find you out and come at night with torches in their hands to burn the monster from his shelter. People are not as compliant or as stupid as you think. What about those who will not take the drugs or hide beneath their bed in fear? There is always a Boudicca, a Spartacus, a Nat Turner or a Joan of Arc.'

Eigen wrinkled his nose as if he smelled something unpleasant. 'And they were all defeated. Every last one of them. If anything, their deaths gave their opponents strength. It united those dissolute empires and rekindled their fires. History is littered with martyrs, the only problem for you is that martyrs die while their killers thrive. Personally, I love that. If there is no obedience there is no spine, no strength, no opposition. Rule with a big stick and thrash those that step out of line to within an inch of their life…' His black eyes burrowed into Ward. 'Or beyond.'

'And what happens when there is nobody left? When you have killed all those who oppose you?'

'Then, I will be King, Emperor, Pharoah, Emir, Lord of all.'

'God?'

'Oh, yes!' Eigen could barely restrain himself. 'God!'

'The power of life over death? The power to create something in your own image?'

Eigen scratched his head impatiently.

'That's quite a picture,' continued Ward. 'All you need is a couple of bolts in your neck. Can children be born with bolts in their neck? Perhaps you could stitch a couple of kids together, you know, from the best bits of a classroom.'

Eigen's palm made contact with Ward's face so quickly that Ward could do nothing to stop it. He was thrown from his chair, hit the carpet with a gasp and did not stop until he hit the large window. He had been slapped by a giant hand, but it had been more than a slap; it had lifted him for his chair and thrown him across the corner of the table, Fosbury-style, his back arched and his legs trailing uselessly behind him. He hit the window with the side of his forehead. The glass remained intact; his head did not. The dizzying speed with which he hit the window split his forehead. For a moment he passed out and was only brought back by a sharp yelp from Marianne.

He pushed himself up and looked woozily towards Eigen.

Marianne sat open mouthed, her eyes wide, her nostrils flared. Her hand sat near the knife, fist clenched, knuckles white.

As Ward rocked onto his backside, he could feel the warm treacle of blood as it flowed down over his left eye.

He put a hand up and wiped at it. It smeared across his face like a brush of paint. He looked at his hand. It glistened in the bright explosion of day's end.

He licked his lips and then spat. A stream of blood flowed from his mouth. He couldn't feel a thing, but he wouldn't have been surprised if he hadn't lost a couple of teeth. His tongue searched his mouth.

'Go ahead,' said Ward. 'Do what you want. It doesn't make you right. It just makes you mad, bad and dangerous to know. You are, when all is said and done, a con artist and a murderer.'

Eigen stood and lumbered towards Ward. He wrapped his hands around Ward's head and yanked him from the ground.

Ward tried to pull the colossal hands away, but it was like trying to prise a limpet from a rock. He lifted a leg and kicked Eigen in the groin. Eigen didn't flinch. He tried again and again made no impact. Whatever the Nazis had done to him, they had made a eunuch of him. The man had no balls.

Ward felt the muscles in his neck stretch as Eigen pulled him from the floor. His head was filled by the sound of rushing blood as fingers pressed down on his arteries. A swell of dizziness rolled over him. His body wanted to sleep.

Suddenly, Eigen let go and dropped Ward. Ward saw the two girls, Penny to the left of Eigen and Marianne to the right, with raised and bloody knives as they stabbed into Eigen's fleshy body. Penny still had the remains of tape around her wrists. Marianne had worked fast to free her while Eigen had been distracted by Ward. Ward tried to say no, to stop them. They were just making the bear angry. Sure enough, Eigen flipped around and with a single gesture put the heel of each hand into each girl's chest and sent them reeling. They crashed, winded and dazed, into the far wall.

The same guards ran back into the room, weapons drawn and held them upon Penny and Marianne.

Eigen's white shirt was spotted by blood, some of it leaving broken trails as it rolled down the folds of loose skin. Penny and Marianne had probably done little more than scratch his fleshy armour. The knives they had used, obviously good enough to cut Penny's arms free, simply weren't long enough to reach any major organs on Eigen.

The guards dragged the girls to their feet. Their hands were clasped to their chests as they fought for breath. With his power, Eigen could easily have broken some ribs or cracked a sternum. At the very least, they had had the wind severely knocked out of them.

They were dragged away by the two guards, bodies bent, guns pressed to the backs of their heads.

Ward tried to stand, to go after them, but his legs would not let him leave the floor.

Eigen grabbed him by the scruff of his collar and flung him into a chair, only this one was in the living area and a damn sight more comfortable. Eigen's huge, squid-like eyes seared into Ward, a mixture of hate and fascination, like an ant beneath a magnifying glass.

He poured Ward a whisky and an orange juice for himself and sat down next to him, as if they were two friends having a chat.

'Well, congratulations,' said Eigen. 'You've just killed your friends. What my men will do to them before they die, I dread to think. I tend to leave these things to their discretion. I suppose it doesn't matter. They were going to die anyway, as are you; it's just unfortunate that all your actions have led to a slow retribution rather than a swift bullet to the head.'

'I wouldn't call a blowfish rammed down the throat a quick bullet in the head.'

Eigen raised his arms hopelessly. 'Well, that's hired help for you. You have to compromise sometimes. How's your back, by the way? Healing?'

He took a drink of his juice and savoured it as it passed his slug-like lips.

Ward took a sip of his drink. It hit every wound in his mouth. He might as well have sucked a lemon. He threw the glass across the room in disgust. It shattered upon the wall and the shards buried themselves in the deep carpet.

'Sorry,' said Ward. 'It slipped.'

Eigen grabbed Ward's face, pushed his head back in the chair and prised his jaw open. He grabbed the bottle of whisky and rammed it into his mouth. Ward felt it burn its way into his throat. He choked as it entered his airway and scorched his lungs. It overflowed from his mouth and stung his broken lips and drenched his shirt.

Eigen removed the bottle, punched Ward in the nose and then shoved him into the back of the chair. 'Sorry,' he said. 'I slipped.'

Ward leaned forward and coughed the whisky from his lungs. He could see blood drip from his nose, wetly merging with the burgundy carpet.

Eigen grabbed his hair and pulled his head up. His lips were tight with fury, his black eyes like wormholes. 'What is it with people? I'm trying to be civilised. I'm trying to make you realise what is best for you, for the world. No more wars, one government, no envy, no greed.'

Ward raised his eyes. 'You're an idiot, Eigen. You're naïve. People don't want shared accommodation, they want a castle; they don't want portions, they want it all. They want their back gardens and their allotments and their cars. They don't care about the rising of the sea or the belligerence of the minority, they just want to *be*. They want to be left alone with their wives and their daughters and their sons and they want to be content.'

Eigen sneered. 'Contentment is settling, no more.'

Ward shook his head. He felt like it would fall off if he was too vigorous. 'Contentment is all, Eigen. It's not settling, it's accepting and taking to your heart. It's your pillow against the world. If you cannot see contentment, which is far greater than any fleeting moment of happiness, as somewhere to rest your head, you are lost.'

Eigen contemplated Ward's words for a moment. 'No,' he said. 'Contentment is merely compromise. If you are married, you eventually assimilate, take the most acceptable from each, become one, and settle. If you are single, you do what you can for a peaceful life, what the government says; you pay their taxes, you follow their rules, you vote for the least worst of them. If you take that concern, that periodical worry from them, then they will feel free to continue as they have. They might even find happiness, maybe you're your longed-for contentment, in their humdrum existence. Or merely the unconscious comfort of the gene, floating through life in alpha mode, oblivious to anything other than the fulfilment of the senses. Either way, they will not scratch like cats at the all-seeing eye of the benevolent father.'

'No,' said Ward. 'They will fight like lions to remove you.'

Ward saw Eigen's fist fly towards him and felt a stab in the temple. He passed out.

37. The Greatest Spy

Ward could hear a hiss of air, the low rumble of engines; the white noise, he knew, of an aircraft cabin. He opened his eyes.

Eigen sat in the seat opposite him. 'Welcome back, Mr Ward.' He looked towards the back of the aircraft. 'Coffee for Mr Ward, strong and sweet,' he ordered. His eyes fell back upon Ward. 'Something to eat? A sandwich perhaps? Some cake?' He chuckled. 'That was a lie. We have no cake, I don't like cake, but we do have sandwiches.'

Ward rubbed a hand across his face. Every part of him ached. 'Anything,' he said. 'I'm starving.'

'Well,' said Eigen slowly. 'That's an overused phrase and a bit offensive to those who really are starving, but I get your drift.' He nodded at the person making the coffee. The smell of the strong coffee pervaded the cabin. It was one of those irresistible smells, like bacon being cooked on a campsite in the early morning or onions at a neon-lit fair.

A large mug of black coffee and a thick ham sandwich was placed in front of him by an aged woman in a dowdy grey dress. 'Girlfriend?' he asked.

Eigen shook his head with disappointment. 'You can't help yourself, can you. Here I am doing something nice for you and once more you spit in my face.'

'It's a face worth spitting at,' snapped Ward. He pushed himself up the chair. 'What now then?'

Ward bit into his sandwich. It had mustard on the succulent, thick-cut slices of ham. Under any other circumstances, it would have been delicious; today it stuck in his craw, but he needed food and drink if he was to be of any use.

Eigen rubbed his hands together. 'Well, hold onto your hat because it's going to all get very exciting. You see, the United Kingdom has secretly, for many years, had nuclear weapons on Saint Quintian…'

'Don't be ridiculous!' snapped Ward.

Eigen's wide eyes, incapable of anything other than horror or surprise, burned into Ward. 'Oh, no, Mr Ward, it's true. You have had your own little Cuba, tucked quietly away at the tail end of the Caribbean, for years and no one knew. The Baie de Dieu is the perfect place from which to launch nuclear weapons. You have been to Chaddleworth. You have seen the building taking place on the coastline below. The ministers in charge of things paid scant attention to what I was doing once their children were at boarding school in England or they had invested in the markets or paid off their mortgages or lived a life of unlimited debauchery. They all thought it was just to get some hotels built and to skip a few regulations. Their greed blinded them.'

'So you haven't been building hotels at the Baie de Dieu?'

Eigen snickered. 'Of course we have. Every now and then an inspection takes place and we pass with flying colours, not because we have paid any more bribes or because there are no hotels to see, but because they failed to look beyond what they saw. There are miles of tunnels, with sleeping quarters and bathrooms and places to eat or relax, to grow food, labs in which to experiment.'

'And where do these weapons come from?' asked Ward. He had no doubt of their existence, only their provenance.

'The USSR, of course. Four SS20 Mod 2 missiles.'

Ward polished off his coffee. If Eigen spoke the truth, it scared him. The damage he could do would not simply be limited to where he aimed. The entire world would suffer. Everything familiar - every daily habit, every home, every season - would change, simply dissolve in the afterburn. It didn't matter where you were on the planet, your life would be changed forever - if you lived.

'And what does any of this have to do with me?'

Eigen seemed thrilled that Ward had asked the question. 'Well, obviously, you will be the one who bombed America.'

'I see,' said Ward. His stomach knotted. He knew where this was going. 'Why? Why would I want to do that?'

'Because you and your lady friends were communists.'

'I'm not sure people will believe that.' That wasn't true; the sheep would go wherever the wolves led them.

'Of course they will. They will see your body, shot in the heat of battle as the local army tried to halt your madness, a broken hero of the Soviet Union, your two female comrades lying dead at your side, and you will go down in the new history of the world as a liar, a communist, a traitor to the West, but a hero to the all-conquering USSR, to the new world; the greatest spy. That will be your epitaph.'

How Eigen had smuggled these warheads onto the island was anybody's guess. They were fifty-five feet high and five feet wide. Now that the right people were looking the wrong way, it was probably easy to conceal them and pass them off as building supplies; concrete supports or groundworks.

'It takes thirty minutes minimum for a missile to travel from the USSR to the USA. How long would it take from Saint Quintian?' said Ward. 'Four minutes perhaps? Depending on the target. At most. Even the Americans would struggle to put countermeasures in place in such a short time.'

For the first time, Ward saw sheer joy upon Eigen's face. His eyes lit up, his lips broadened beyond his outsized, patently false, teeth. He chortled like a child who had stepped on his first fly.

'If you launch an SS20 from here,' said Ward, 'it could make it to the West coast, the North West, pretty much anywhere in the US and at a little under eight kilometres per second, it wouldn't take them long to reach their destination.'

'You know your missiles, Mr Ward.'

'It's a basic in my line of work. I also know that you need to launch them from a Maz TEL. Those are big transporters to hide, so I must assume that you have brought them through various friendly ports, in bits, and then had them rebuilt on site. That's an expensive and complicated business. You would need to have engineers and scientists at the site to put them back together, but that's feasible.'

'You're a clever man, Mr Ward.'

'No. Just well-informed.' Ward paused to think. He had to admit to himself that he was scraping the barrel of his knowledge. There was winging it and then there was Icarus.

'Now each missile,' continued Ward, 'is an MIRV, which means that it can carry three one hundred and fifty kiloton warheads, each one ten times the power of the bomb dropped on Hiroshima. That gives you a potential twelve targets. At a guess I would say, by wealth and population,' Ward closed his eyes and counted down on his fingers, 'San Jose, San Francisco, Washington DC, Boston, New York, Baltimore, Seattle, Minneapolis, Philadelphia and Chicago. And a couple of others which don't spring to mind. Hopefully Disneyland and Disneyworld.'

'That's very good, Mr Ward,' said Eigen. For the first time he seemed hesitant. 'I would also go for Philadelphia and Memphis. Just because of the population. And because I dislike Elvis Presley.' He paused and smiled. 'Though I would also consider both the Disney brain-drains, truth be told.'

'For once, we agree,' said Ward. 'Except about Elvis.'

He gazed out of the window and could see the old, scratched film of the Enola Gay dropping the bomb on Hiroshima and the devilish, grey cloud of death with burning bowels that loomed over it and which eventually descended in a radioactive blanket to coat the decimated city. The world should have learned a lesson from that, but it had failed. It hadn't been an endpoint but a beginning.

'So, all this for what is essentially a heist. You're no ecowarrior. All that bullshit about starting again was just that - bullshit. You don't give a damn for the planet. You're going to rob America of its wealth, its land and most of its people. But to what end? Just to make the USSR top dog? You know, Eigen,' said Ward, 'I don't think that you are a nihilist. Far from it. I think you're a communist through and through. You run red.'

Eigen swivelled his wrinkled head towards Ward. With his enormous black eyes and furrowed flesh, he reminded Ward of some sort of undersea predator. He let out a stuttered laugh. 'What makes you say that?'

'Something you said; 'That's an overused phrase and a bit offensive to those who really are starving'. And you meant it. You despised the Nazis, the brainless right-wingers that came after them and you despised your father for what he did to you and your mother. You both paid the price for his crimes.'

Eigen listened tetchily, but Ward knew that as long as he was the subject matter, then he would hear, because he was fascinated by himself.

'You fell in love with a communist, then you fell deeply in love with communism; you wrote for the communists, spread their propaganda. You moved to Russia and started your life anew. You were handsomely rewarded. They made you king of all you surveyed so long as what you surveyed was theirs, and the rewards were too great to resist. But, believe me, there is no equality in communism; just false piety, soundbites and a massive pay gap. Would you really be happy with the true democracy that comes with real communism, where what's yours is mine and what's mine is yours? Where everybody shares equally with others, where there is no master and no slave? Never mind the fact that the very core of that concept is too fragile to hold up to human nature? We need leaders, Eigen. We need capitalism. We need reward. We need others to fail to make our own successes seem greater than they really are. We need people to drive us and we need to be driven.'

Ward was enjoying himself. He was needling Eigen, getting him to listen to him.

'What difference will it make to the world if there is no more America? Humanity will adjust. The US would be replaced by the USSR and someone else, probably China, will grow to resent them and the madness would start again. What will you do then?'

Eigen didn't respond. He simply waved a giant dismissive hand in Ward's direction.

Ward pushed on. 'And even if you only target America, there will be global temperature drops, anarchy among the survivors, crop failures, the sun blocked out for years, not to mention all the slow deaths from nuclear fallout, carried in the waters and on the winds around the earth, even into the heart of Russia. All that money you have tucked away in secret accounts would become worthless because there would be a global economic collapse. That will be *your* epitaph. Destroyer of worlds.' He shook his head. 'You are genuinely round the bend, Eigen. That's not a dream, that's a nightmare. Where will you be in all this? Where will you hide? How will you stave off famine?'

Eigen's jaw tightened. 'I will be the King in my castle.'

'Castle?'

'Of course. Me and others for whom I have some value - a small obedient army of about five thousand, scientists, doctors, educationalists, engineers, as you surmised, and some breeding couples, among others - will live beneath ground until we can emerge into the new world and start again under a true communist banner. I would have more power than ever. Communism will have its first God.' Eigen put the tips of his fingers together and rested his chin upon the steeple. 'Also, the USSR, the new USSR, will be the dominant world power. I will be so rich, so powerful, that I might, one day, succeed the sodden inebriates that rule the union today and a new form of communism will be born, where everyone has access to free healthcare, free access to the law and a free education.'

Ward narrowed his eyes in disbelief. He couldn't quite accept what he was hearing and yet he knew it to be true.

'Out of curiosity…' he said.

'Yes?'

'Is all this because you have no balls?'

Eigen looked out the plane's window. He blinked slowly, forced his lids together like a child being told to shut his eyes before a surprise. Ward could see he was finding it difficult not to retaliate; the clenched jaw, the balled fists, the tightly sealed lips.

'I could drop you off here, you know.' He didn't look at Ward. 'I could simply open the door and throw you out.'

'You could,' said Ward, 'but you won't.'

Eigen sneered. 'Don't be so sure.'

'But I am. You need me for your tragic little history lesson. You need my dead body to shine the light of innocence upon you so that your disciples can follow you without question and you can pretend that none of it is your fault. Besides, you want to punish me, don't you?'

'Why do you say that?'

'Because I have compelled you to bring your plans forward. This wasn't meant to happen quite yet, was it? In fact, it wouldn't surprise me if the Russians didn't even know about this. They just want the missiles there as deterrents, as a last-ditch effort to subdue the Americans, as a rabbit to pull out of the hat in case of emergency. I bet they have no idea what's going through your worm-riddled head. But I've forced your hand and, for that, you want to punish me. Am I assuming too much?'

Eigen's gaze returned to Ward. 'No, Mr Ward, you're not assuming too much.'

Ward leaned forward, fingers locked, his elbows on his knees. 'Couldn't you simply have left that poor old woman in Chaddleworth alone? If she hadn't killed Lawrie Stuart, I wouldn't have come here and if I hadn't come here, then we would not be here now having this absurd conversation at ten thousand feet. Why did you do it?'

Eigen drew in a deep, stuttered breath, impatient at having to explain himself and yet drawn to do so because he could not resist the opportunity to boast of his achievements. 'She was nosey. She was watching. Every day she would be in her garden with her binoculars looking down upon the building site. It would only be a matter of time before she saw something she shouldn't. And I had to get Stuart out of the way. He was a smart man. He would have found out about me the same way you have and still brought me problems. And, above all, I wanted her house. We had tunnels beneath of which she was unaware. It would make the perfect view from which to watch the start of the rebirth. It will be my castle and I will look down upon my realm.'

'So, you manipulated a mentally ill old lady into killing a stranger so that you could take her house?'

Eigen nodded his head slowly. The folds of flesh on his neck bellowed with each movement and squeezed out drops of dirty sweat. 'Yes. The deeds are done.' He smiled to himself. 'It's already mine. It turns out that lawyers have fewer scruples than politicians. Who'd have thought it? I had hoped that the deaths would simply be treated as an isolated case of murder, that Inspector Moise would make sure that it was all kept under wraps. On this, I was wrong.'

'Oh, you were, very wrong,' said Ward. 'You upset my boss, Lawrie Stuart's cousin, though they were more like brothers. You couldn't have picked a worse man to hurt.'

'How about you? How about your lady friends?'

Ward refused to allow his true feelings to the surface. He would do what he always did, supress them, push them down into the dark recesses of his mind and mourn on his own time and in his own way. 'I'm fine and they're out of it. At least they won't have to listen to you bleating on anymore.'

Eigen cackled. His massive shoulders rolled. 'Oh, I'm afraid they will. They're not dead yet, Mr Ward.'

Ward stifled any relief, but his breath and heart fluttered. 'Not dead?'

'No, they were taken to Saint Quintian last night after they had attempted to be heroic. They were an annoyance. I wanted them out of the way, so I sent them to bed without supper. I'll find something else to do with them. I have a respected orthopaedic consultant and an accountant with an IQ almost as big as mine. I could make good use of them when the new day dawns.'

Ward's heart leapt. He could feel a weight lift from his shoulders. Marianne was alive! She was hope. She was something tangible to fight for. Something, someone, for him, after this mess was over.

The voice of the pilot, all short vowels and staccato English, interrupted them. 'Twenty minutes to landing, Mr Eigen. I'm starting our descent.'

Eigen's naked, wet, undulating head turned to Ward.

'And so, Mr Ward, the countdown begins.'

Beads of sweat fell into his eyes. They looked like tears.

Ward hoped that they stung.

38. Great Men In Grey Surroundings

They were swept from the late night airport like kings in a Daimler DS420, full of leather and wood and more carpet than would be found in the average house.

The roofs of the airport were crenellated by the shadowed bumps of heads, coal against the starlit, moonlit skies, each one armed and ready to ambush anyone who dared to encroach.

As the Daimler exited the apron gate and slipped gracefully onto the main road, Ward saw guards, all bald, dressed in unadorned black jackets and black trousers, with AK-47s; they marshalled them from the airport, their fingers just an inch from the triggers, their eyes tight upon the car, ready for anything.

The roads were empty. Every now and then they would pass a stray person, frozen in the headlights, who was rushing home, eyes to the ground, short, rapid footsteps intent upon their destination, determined not to become embroiled in whatever it was that had suddenly, violently, shaken their world.

When they passed through Saint Jeanne, the streets were deserted but for more guards dressed in black, armed with Kalashnikovs, each a hundred yards apart, alert, rigid, ready to fight, their dark uniforms and hairless heads stealing their identity and creating stark clones. They weren't all locals either; there was black, white, Chinese, South Asian, East Asian, European, a whole mix of ethnicities, each united in a single cause, each without origin; despite this, it was difficult to tell them apart, as if they had become denatured, desaturated and shared only their grey anonymity.

After the capital, they turned North West, towards the Baie de Dieu. Every door of the vehicle was locked and every window lowered an inch. Ward could smell the change from town to country to coast. There was the shift from dusty diesel and the lingering odour of street food to clear air, the smell of bougainvillea or the ubiquitous hibiscus or yellow bells drifted through the windows and filled the car, then onto the smell of the sea, so distinctive anywhere in the world, now assisted by the shift of the night-time breeze. It was still warm, but it carried with it a mournfulness, as if there were no tomorrows, as the sea hushed upon the shore and the wind whispered through the palm trees and made them clap until dawn.

It took about thirty minutes to reach Baie de Dieu. The journey had been smooth, uninterrupted. Nobody had wanted to be out tonight. Before it had shut down, the San Quintian Broadcasting Company had issued a warning that anybody found on the streets after eight pm would be arrested or shot. A curfew was in place, the population now too afraid to step beyond the threshold. It said that there was a new government in town, that the media and ports and airports had been taken over, but that there was no need to worry because the revolution had the interests of the people at heart.

At the skeletons of the new hotels in the Baie de Dieu, their steel beams criss-crossing the sky like a monstrous web, the Daimler pulled up opposite some bomb-blast shutters and waited as they rose like a steel eyelid. Ward noticed a door next to them which remained closed. A shaft of light stole from beneath. Once high enough, the Daimler slid inside, into the belly of the hill which eventually led to Chaddleworth four hundred feet above, the shutter falling as soon as the chrome rear bumper had cleared it. The street outside fell back into darkness, the only relief the light of the moon as it plated the scene in silver.

The car stopped in the middle of what appeared to be a huge concrete reservoir. The silence that fell after the engine was turned off was immense.

The driver, squat with broad shoulders, with not a hair upon his head, not even eyebrows, got out of the car and walked around to Eigen's side of the vehicle. His footsteps echoed against the concrete walls, made it sound as if a dozen men were closing in upon the car from every direction. Even the metallic click of the door handle threw itself suicidally upon the walls before it eventually died.

Eigen stepped from the car. His footsteps slapped against the ground and ricocheted.

He walked around to the rear door and opened it for Ward. The driver stood behind him with a pistol in his hand.

'If you do anything but walk,' said Eigen, 'Baris will shoot you.'

Reluctantly, Ward got out of the car. The place was as sterile as the concrete bunkers of the war, the underground shelters in which Churchill and his cabinet hid and from which they ran the country. Great men in grey surroundings. All echoed, all was bland, cold, dead, functional. It reminded Ward of the graffitied pedestrian subways in London which rumbled with the weight of the traffic above and threw back the scuff of every footstep, the reverberation of every tin can, the high-pitched scream of every kicked stone.

Ward closed the Daimler's door behind him. The door was so heavy, so well built, that its sound barely registered.

They walked on. There was another blast door ahead. Eigen tapped at a keypad and the shutter opened. To the side of the shutter was a door. Next to it was a small black button. Ward guessed that once the code was put in, the door would open once the button was pressed.

At either side of the long corridor were rooms, their doors open. Ward saw bunks, some of them occupied, much like he had seen in his time at boarding school, all steel tubes and hard mattresses, a single pillow, a grey blanket, no windows, just a clean-air vent, without which the occupants would have been suffocated or poisoned in their sleep. In the middle of the ceiling was a white strip light which shed an unnatural brightness into the room.

'Those lights,' said Eigen as he heaved his massive frame through the tunnel, 'stimulate the production of vitamin D. Every employee is expected to spend at least half an hour a day beneath them. This helps muscles, bone density and, most importantly, helps the user avoid the depression that comes with such living.'

They passed several offices and then a surgical theatre, the operating lights, like something from an HG Wells novel, loomed over an empty table. Each table was headed by an anaesthetic machine, silent in the darkness, ready to illuminate at a moment's notice.

'And how are those lights powered?' asked Ward.

'By a generator,' replied Eigen, as if it was obvious.

'And how is that generator powered?'

Eigen's impatience surfaced with a small tic of the lips. 'By biofuels, Mr Ward, made from sugarcane and corn. I understand what you are trying to do, to undermine my efforts, but I have thought of everything. I am so far ahead of the rest of the world.' His huge eyes devoured Ward. 'Baris, take Mr Ward to his quarters would you?'

Baris nodded submissively.

'I shall see you after we have both rested. Maybe for some brunch. That's an exciting word, don't you think, brunch? The melding of breakfast and lunch to create something new. Did you know that there are up to five thousand new words invented every year, many of them portmanteaus in the vein of brunch? Biofuel. There's another. The Oxford Dictionary, that bastion of the English language, accepts about one thousand of them. Every new event, every new invention, brings with it a new language. You could probably track the changes in history by the words that have come and gone. I find that fascinating.'

He turned away. The conversation was over. With his hands still clasped like spider crabs behind his back, he wandered off into the concrete maze.

Baris spoke into a radio. Within twenty seconds he was joined by three other guards, all armed with Kalashnikovs and dressed in black, unmarked clothes, similar to theatre scrubs, presumably for their lightness; most sinister of all, they too were hairless. It would have been funny had it not been so disturbing.

One of the guards took the lead, while Ward was flanked by the two others. Baris trailed behind, his Makarov pistol held at waist height and aimed at Ward's coccyx.

Ward was guided through the corridors. He wasn't going to do anything because he wanted Penny and Marianne to come through the affair intact. He did once swerve to the right, just to see what would happen, but all he got for his pains was the butt of an AK-47 in his kidneys.

Eventually they reached his apartment. A keypad opened the door and he was shoved into his quarters and the door immediately closed. It clicked softly behind him.

Had it been a two-star hotel, he would have been pleased, but considering that he was being locked inside little more than a cave, he was astounded.

It was a magnificent room with a large en-suite, a music system connected to a quad sound system, a selection of vinyls (Ward was pleased to notice Pink Floyd's Dark Side of the Moon among them) and a drinks cabinet that would have delighted any discerning alcoholic. It was tempting to dive in, but he resisted.

On the walls were what appeared to be original works of art: a Pollock, a Giger, a Veselka, a Mistry, of the most beautiful Asian woman playing sitar among the fishes. There were also books, classic and contemporary, running along an entire wall. They ranged from F Scott Fitzgerald to Shakespeare (folios from the turn of the century, noted the journalist in Ward), and pulp fiction, from Mickey Spillane to Ian Fleming, Eric Ambler and Harold Robbins, along with Graham Greene, Stephen King, Edgar Allan Poe and Jackie Collins. The thing that attracted Ward to them was that they were pretty much all first editions. The hardback first edition of *Casino Royale* on the shelf, published by Jonathan Cape in 1953, written by Fleming, was worth about twenty-five thousand pounds. In a few years it might be a good deposit on a house. There was something for everyone. It was clearly part of Eigen's long term plan, to keep the masses placated, take their minds off everything but the truth. There was even a plethora of VHS tapes, movies from every decade and of every genre. Clearly, Eigen had prepared thoroughly for tomorrow and the tomorrows that followed.

He looked inside the mirror-fronted wardrobe and found that the clothes, little more than surgical scrubs, red, blue or green, were his size, along with some plain white, light slip-on shoes.

He found a door. He tried the handle and found that it gave way. He opened it. Who knew where it led? It might well have been some sort of trap, but just how trapped could he be?

He listened and heard nothing. Part of him wanted to go through; part of him told him to be grateful for what he had, to sit tight and see what happened.

He edged the door open. The door shushed against the thick carpet. As he pushed the door further, he saw Penny and Marianne, sitting in deep armchairs, legs adrift upon the arms, heads and necks lolled against the sumptuous backs, misery etched upon their faces, a little worse for wear, but alive.

Marianne noticed him first. 'Mike!'

She leapt from her chair, ran towards him, flung herself into his arms. He held her tightly and wallowed in the smell of her hair and the feel of her body. There was no other place he would rather be.

Penny gave them a moment and then took her turn to embrace Ward. 'Where the hell have you been, mate?' she whispered.

Ward put his fingers to his lips for the girls to be careful what they said. There was every chance that the rooms were bugged.

'Busy,' he whispered in Penny's ear.

'I'm so glad to see you,' she said.

'And I you,' said Ward. He pulled her tighter to him. 'You convict!'

Penny laughed and pushed him away. She didn't know what to say. She was bursting with questions, but she knew she could say nothing if they were being heard.

'This bloke's off his head!' she said.

'No doubt,' said Ward. 'Barking like a dog.' He hoped that his words would be fed back to Eigen.

'Have you had the full tour yet? Some creep called Baris showed us around.'

'I haven't been that lucky. Good is it?'

'It's a humdinger, mate. We had it as soon as we got here. I remember a lot of it.'

Ward shot her a curious glance. 'Well, you'll have to jot it all down sometime. I'm sure it'll make fascinating reading.'

'Will do, mate.'

Marianne wrapped her arms around him. 'I'm so happy to see you.'

'Good,' said Ward. 'I've come an awfully long way to see you.'

Ward kissed her, with desperation and longing, with relief and fear. There would always be Eve and Rose and Raven, God knows, they were tattooed onto his heart and they would be with him wherever he went, but they were gone and Marianne was here and he had a wound that needed to be healed.

'Jesus!' whispered Penny harshly. 'Get a room!'

'In time,' said Ward, his eyes fixed upon Marianne. 'I need to sleep.'

Marianne put her lips to his ear so that she would not be heard by anyone outside the room. 'Want some company?'

Ward held her at arm's length and smiled. 'Desperately, but not today.' He took Marianne's hand and kissed it. 'Our day will come. There will always be tomorrow.'

'Promise?'

'No,' said Ward. 'I never make promises. They're too frivolous and too easily broken. I give you my word.'

With that, torn in two, he retreated to his room, his head full of Marianne, his spirit full of vengeance.

He had to somehow stop Eigen, stop the missiles, stop the end of the world.

When he got to his room, he had a cold shower and then dressed in a pair of red scrubs. They were light and comfortable. The shoes were very light, almost as if he had nothing on his feet.

He sat down in the tanned leather Vetra Eames armchair and crossed his legs. It was more comfortable than the bed in his flat.

His mind raced. He knew that if he tried to sleep, he would fail. He would have to play the precocious lover, pretend that sleep was not needed, that there were plenty of other armchairs in the world to sit in, that being awake was in fact what he wanted.

He got up and looked at the whiskies. He didn't want to have to rely on alcohol to help him sleep, but the right amount would nudge him in the right direction.

He settled on a Haig's Dimple. It was delicious; smoky with caramel, with a hint of citrus and vanilla. He had tried it a couple of times, usually at someone else's expense, but was never prepared to pay the exorbitant prices it demanded. Now that he could sup it as a sleeping draught…well…it would have been rude not to.

He was happy to admit that he had underplayed his hand, if only a little, when talking about the wine to Eigen. He wasn't the kind of man to filter alcohol through his teeth and lips, but on occasion he would do so and was always pleased by the payback. He had spent many a long hour exercising his palate for wine and spirits and, although a long way from being an expert, most certainly had his preferences.

He picked up a hardback copy of *Field Work* by Seamus Heaney. He liked Heaney, his gentle sense of humour, his melancholia, his humanity and his ability to make the reader work and then give reward. There was no pretentiousness, just Celtic honesty with a dark, lyrical heart.

He sat back down in the sumptuous chair, read the book and drank the entire glass of whisky in three delicious chugs. That was a couple of hundred pounds down his throat and out of Eigen's pocket.

He fell asleep quickly and didn't dream.

39. Smoke And Mirrors

Ward was awoken by the soft voice of an American woman. 'Mr Ward?' It came through the speakers on the wall and filled the room. 'Mr Ward? Good morning, sir. This is your wake-up call. Your meeting with Mr Eigen is in half an hour. You will be collected in twenty minutes by two of our escorts who will take you to Mr Eigen.'

Ward's eyes flickered. For a split second he thought he was in his flat in London, that it had all been a dream, indeed was prepared to tell himself exactly that. Many a time he had woken from a nightmare and reminded himself, with great relief, that none of it had been real.

Now, it was. He looked at the open Heaney on his lap. He vaguely remembered reading *Casualty* and then drifting in *The Badgers*, unable to finish them because of the whisky and his sheer exhaustion.

He wondered what time it was. Wasn't brunch a mid-morning thing that bored housewives or estate agents did? Something to fill the empty first half of the day while the toddlers made papier mâché pots or to give that wily crocodile a chance to entrance his victim?

That meant it was still reasonably early, maybe ten o'clock. When someone like Eigen used a word like brunch, it was never an accident.

Ward had a shower and a shave then dressed in fresh red scrubs, slipped on some of the comfortable white shoes, then sat down with Heaney until the guard arrived.

Sure enough, almost startlingly, the door opened and two guards arrived. The younger of the two, although it was difficult to tell in their hairless state, carried a Kalashnikov rifle slung loosely across his chest, while the other had his fist wrapped tightly around a Makarov. Ward make a note of it. One was sloppy, one was tense. These little things mattered. Sloppy was brash, arrogant, inattentive; tense made one liable to mistakes.

'Good morning,' he said to the younger man. 'I can only assume it is morning, mainly because I was invited to brunch, a snack that apparently takes place between breakfast and lunch. And, if I remember rightly, a fine portmanteau.' He stood up, book in hand and looked at the younger guard. 'I also know this because of the rather cheap Timex on your wrist.'

The younger guard automatically looked down. He had no watch on his wrist. Again, Ward made a mental note of this; easily distracted.

Wordlessly, the guards directed Ward towards the door.

He was escorted the same way he had come in. It was difficult to tell in all the concrete, but here and there was a chip out of the wall caused by a careless electric cart or an errant forklift or a fluorescent light that flickered in warning of its imminent death. There was always something to tell you where you were, if not when.

Eventually, after perhaps three minutes brisk walk, they changed tack and reached yet another keypad. The older guard tapped in a number and the shutter door opened. Again, Ward noticed a door with a black button next to it. Quite why they simply couldn't use that was unclear. Perhaps they didn't work. Perhaps the guards had just got used to tapping the key pad and waiting for the blast door to rise.

Beyond it was an altogether different world. They entered a hangar-sized building, too big to see from one end to the other, where all was green, all was steamy, all smelled of peat and soil and roots and the petrichor that came with hot summer rain. It was like walking into a glorious, giant hothouse, fed by high-intensity lighting that purred above their heads.

There were tomatoes the size of pumpkins and pumpkins the size of babies. Cucumbers stood proud from their vines as if Priapus himself had raised them and enormous carrot tops fell heavily upon the soil like hippy-hair. Runner beans plunged like lamb's tails and apples, heavy enough to cause the branch from which they hung to bend like a salmon-filled fishing rod, grew from carefully manipulated trees, much like giant bonsais, only these had no love, just restraints to allow for the limited space and time available.

If such a population were to thrive, then all four seasons had to be annulled and produce that which would have basked in the heat of July or the half-light of February, would have to be carefully reproduced. Ward could smell each one of them. It had the raw smell of subsistence, of earth, of the beginning. A misty haze filled the building as if the seas had boiled over and spilled man upon the land, still gilled and flippered, ready for evolution to take hold and create history anew.

The air was filled with citrus and dirt and the moisture of carbon dioxide, a heady mixture of rebirth.

Ward gazed upon it and thought it genius, the kind of genius that only a wealthy madman could achieve.

'Have you slept, Mr Ward?' Felix Eigen stepped out from behind a tree bursting with papaya. Ward started. 'I'm sorry,' he said. 'I didn't mean to…'

'You didn't,' said Ward quickly.

Eigen showed his fake teeth inside a fake smile. 'Good.' He raised an arm in a sweeping gesture at the environment. 'Welcome to Eden. What do you think?'

Ward looked casually around. 'I think that once the entire water system on the planet has been polluted with radioactivity that this rather lush pretence at self-sufficiency will wither and die.'

Eigen linked his hands and let them hang. 'You think that this didn't occur to me?' His arrogance oozed from him like sweat. 'We use carbon filters and reverse osmosis to clean the water. It remains mildly radioactive, but not so much that the hardier among us will be affected.'

'And the less hardy?'

Eigen's top lip twisted. 'Survival of the fittest, Mr Ward. Anyone who succumbs at such an early hurdle is not worth keeping. There are many kinds of filter, Mr Ward.'

'You're a jerk,' said Ward.

Eigen raised an eyebrow. 'Maybe, but I'm a very rich jerk who will outlive you.'

'And many others,' said Ward.

Eigen's mouth twitched dismissively at one corner. 'As I said, survival of the fittest.'

'And what will happen to those who do survive?'

'They'll come to me, of course. I will be the oasis in the desert. Where there is a well of water, there is life. I will be their well. I will give them life.'

Ward move closer to Eigen and looked him in the eye. There was a heavy smell of stale sweat in the air. 'How many out of the billions alive right now do you think will survive? Four? Five? Maybe ten? A dozen? There will be millions left, Eigen. You won't be able to cope with that, not with this overblown greenhouse.'

Eigen tutted. 'They will not all be welcome, they will not all be eligible, they will not all survive. But that's okay because the fewer the people, the more chance of survival. I can take perhaps thirty thousand. That's enough to start again. We shall have wheat, not chaff.'

Ward puffed out his cheeks and shook his head. He held his thumb and index finger a centimetre apart. 'That tiny Nazi part of you, that genetic, mostly lab-born fuck-up, isn't quite dead yet, is it. You can call it communism all you want;

egalitarianism, classlessness, but it's totalitarianism, in any colour you want. You think you're saving the world. I think you're moulding it to your twisted ideal.'

Eigen sighed. 'Maybe so.' He dropped his head and smiled to himself. He had expected intransigence in the face of the obvious. All except him were so fixed in their beliefs that they could not concede an inch. He would forfeit a world for his dreams. 'Would you like a tour of the rest of the facility, Mr Ward? I mean, you might as well see what you're dying for.'

It was the last thing Ward wanted; the proud jabbering of a lunatic as he trotted merrily through his kingdom, so happy to share his delights, his philosophies and his nightmares.

After leaving the garden area, which Ward had to admit to himself was impressive in its planning, in its size and ambition, he followed Eigen through another key-padded blast shutter into the next area.

The contrast could not have been more different. They passed through a misted decontamination chamber and, once they had been salted and peppered, were allowed to progress.

The isolation door slid open. They were greeted by the sight of people in white lab coats, face masks and hairnets, hunched over microscopes, a single eye dissecting the contents of test tubes and petri dishes. Bunsen burners licked at the underside of glass beakers. Condensated Erlenmeyer flasks, those thin-necked, fat-waisted, flat-bottomed darlings, the icon of the lab, hissed and steamed, filled with everything that hubbled, bubbled, toiled and troubled.

It took Ward back to the school chemistry lab. It was wonderful, mysterious and beyond him. The smells were still the same and those same odours turned to taste and that taste turned into a well of nausea, of helplessness and ignorance. Give him a pen and he would shine and yet science would eclipse him.

Ward shook himself out of his thoughts. 'And this,' he said, 'is presumably the alchemist's lair, where you desperately try to turn base metal to gold and simply get a handful of rust.'

Eigen's shoulders moved up and down as if he was amused. 'It's an interesting analogy, Mr Ward, but wrong. This lab, I suppose you could say, is the heart of the operation.' He walked on, his hands again knitted behind his back. 'The area, the ground floor, four acres in total, is divided into sections, each set within its own quarantined area, bordered by a decontamination area. The Health Quarter, where we can investigate any health issues that might occur and look at ways to improve the performance of the entire team. Then there is the Technology Quarter, where we can maintain and improve upon the tech that we already have, look into alternative sources for energy and then the Environmental Studies Quarter to look at our interaction with the environment with a view to solving complex problems, including the future. Finally, here we have the Food Research Quarter. This is where we find new, healthier strains of food, where we can, by the use of computers, predict need and over-indulgence and preserve a balance, maintain a stock count, look at the likelihood of plant and human survival, assess numbers for the cull or increase the breeding pairs, where we can splice various varieties of foodstuffs to produce a superfood; all this among other things, of course.'

Ward looked perplexed. 'A superfood? What the hell's a superfood?'

Eigen ambled over to a desk. 'It's very easy,' he said condescendingly. 'In the garden area through which we have just passed, we are for example, splicing goji berries with blueberries. The blueberries are full of antioxidants and phytochemicals, as well as plenty of vitamin C, vitamin K and manganese. The goji berries have many times the oxidants of blueberries and can help in the fight against disease. That research, the mathematical and chemical work, is done in this lab, both by traditional methods and by the computer systems that you see, the plans of which I bought from an employee at one of America's largest computer companies and improved by my tech team. There will be no food served here that is not beneficial.'

'No fish and chips then?' Ward was desperate to burst his bubble.

Eigen shook his head. 'No fish, no meat. We eat a vegan diet. There is no livestock, so there are no eggs, no milk, no steak.'

Ward couldn't stop his curiosity being pricked. 'So how do you substitute, for example, milk?'

Eigen smiled patronisingly at Ward's ignorance. 'We produce soya milk. Soya milk is good for bone density; it supplements the antioxidants from the berries while being rich in protein and vitamin B.'

Ward moaned inwardly. There would be no more Berni Inns in which you could eat a prawn cocktail and steak and chips by the half-light of a poorly shaded forty watt bulb. There would be no more barbeques, no more fast food outlets, no more bacon sandwiches or pork belly roasts.

'No wine, I suppose?'

Eigen stuck his chin out. 'All drugs are banned. No alcohol. No caffeine. None of the chemicals which today fool us into believing all is well as we slowly poison ourselves.'

'It sounds dull,' said Ward.

Eigen crossed his arms and rocked on the balls of his feet. He was not one for criticism. 'To you, yes, because you have become inured to the pull of the false high. Chemicals rule us, Mr ward. In our fast food, in our meat, in our vegetables, in our drinks. No more. All that we eat…'

'Will be lab grown,' interrupted Ward. 'Of course, there's no genetic sampling or manipulation going on there,' he added caustically. 'Nothing like splicing to interfere with the natural process.'

Eigen stopped. He wiped the sweat from his head and neck and turned his huge frame turned to Ward. 'You can mock as much as you like, but in the end the population will be healthier, more productive, less prone to disease and malaise.'

'And how do you propose to feed the five thousand, Eigen? Even you can't turn stones to bread. If you have breeding couples, as you claim, your population is going to get very high very quickly.'

Eigen covered his mouth as if hiding a smirk. 'Do you understand the principles of dairy farming, Mr Ward?' His tone was condescending.

'Not entirely, no.'

'Well, after the cows have birthed a few times, their milk production reduces or even ceases altogether. It costs more to keep them alive than the profit provided by their milk. So, they go to slaughter at anything between three and six years. The farmer takes a meagre profit from their death while still maintaining a population for breeding. It is one of the many circles of life.'

'A sort of *Logan's Run* then?'

Eigen grimaced. The comparison had thrown him. 'I don't know what that is, but I'm sure you're right. Everything has a useful life, so what point is there in keeping something alive after it serves no purpose?'

'Well, by those rules, you'd have been dead some time ago.'

Eigen raised a fat warning finger at Ward. 'You're not funny, Mr Ward.'

'I don't intend to be funny,' said Ward. 'I only want to highlight your hypocrisy. And what about the bodies? You can't bury them, not so long as the outside world remains poisonous.'

Eigen's black eyes glowed with enthusiasm. 'Recycling, of course. It takes about thirty days to turn a human body to compost; stick it in a leakproof container, mix it with a few woodchips, a bit of sawdust, hey presto. The remains can be used to enrich the soil of the plant life here. Once we are left with the bones, they can be ground down and used as bone meal. No one will be wasted. They will continue to be useful, even after death.'

'And how do you propose to execute them?'

Eigen shrugged nonchalantly. 'Well, the Nazis had a few good ideas, no?'

'No,' said Ward flatly. 'They didn't.'

Eigen snorted. 'That's just a matter of perspective.'

Ward ignored him. 'So, by means of culling, you maintain a steady population?'

'Absolutely.'

'Any other lunacy you'd like to share with me?'

'No lunacy, just genius.' Eigen pointed somewhere in the distance. 'Beyond this are the living quarters. They are, I assure you, up to hotel standard. The people want for nothing. Of course, there are dorms rather than individual spaces and all facilities are shared. The only private areas are family areas for breeding where the mother can bring up a healthy, functional child.'

'And the fathers?'

'Well, once they have fulfilled their duties, they go to work. When they are required again, they will be used.'

'And at what age do the children go to work?' asked Ward.

'That depends upon the child. Five, perhaps six? As soon as they can contribute.'

'How very Victorian.' Ward's eyes wandered the lab. 'You've got it all planned out, haven't you. Your own Little Red Book, full of inequalities and lies and duplicities, all designed to give you a few moments at the top of a broken chain. It's meaningless.'

Eigen was coldly philosophical. 'Life is meaningless, Mr Ward. You're born, you live, you die. It's what you leave behind that matters. Look at the Egyptians. They are eternal in what they have created. We speak of Nefertiti and Tutankhamun as if they were still alive. The pyramids, the tombs, the beauty of their art are their epitaph. The same with the Romans. Look at what they left behind. Every great society, every great instigator of these societies, lives for ever. And so too will I.'

'You'll still be dead.'

Eigen narrowed his eyes. 'And who will remember you, Mr Ward, after your time is up?'

Ward reflected on the question. 'Those who know me, and then they will die and, like all living things, even you, I will fade from memory and this world will continue to turn until, one day, it's swallowed by the sun, ironically the one thing that sustained it for so many millions of years; then even this planet will be forgotten. As you said, circles of life.'

Ward followed Egan to the far end of the room. Again there was a keypad. Eigen tapped in a number and a blast door, sturdier than the others they had passed through, lifted. As it lifted, so a two metre thick concrete wall parted, sliding left and right, accompanied by the soft hiss of hydraulics and the echo of rollers against concrete, though it was impossible to tell where they had receded to.

They entered an empty area. It seemed to have no purpose other than to just be an empty room.

'And the purpose of this?' asked Ward.

Eigen looked at him smugly, his heavy, dewy eyebrows raised like mountains, and crossed the room. It must have been the size of a football pitch and took Eigen a good thirty seconds to walk from one end to the other.

Ward stayed where he was. He had seen enough keypads to last a lifetime. He watched as Eigen tapped in a number. Nothing happened immediately and Ward felt a moment of joy as he thought something had at last gone wrong.

His joy was short-lived.

The end wall, another massive concrete barrier, slid away with all the daunting grace of the preceding wall. This though was bigger and opened up onto a sunlit, glass-roofed warehouse and, glinting in the bright light of high noon, piggy-backed upon their launchers, were four canisters containing SS20 missiles.

That explained the empty room. It was a cushion between the launch area and the inhabited zones.

'How?' asked Ward, astounded by the sight in front of him. 'How were you never seen by satellites, by reconnaissance planes?'

Eigen laughed. 'Smoke and mirrors, Mr Ward. It's all just smoke and mirrors. Well, no smoke and two-way mirrors actually, each mirror four inches thick and made of reinforced glass. The total weight is five thousand tons. This side, as you can see, is covered by the same substance that they use on polarised sunglasses. It stops the temperature becoming unbearable.'

The room was essentially a concrete aircraft hangar. The four launchers sat side by side. Each one approached forty feet in length and ten feet high. Each of its twelve wheels was about sixty inches wide, but none of them touched the floor, raised as they were by four stabilisers, the launcher ready to fire. On their backs sat the cylinders containing the triple-headed missiles, inert, asleep, soon to wake enraged and tear the world apart.

'If you arrange the mirrors, in a certain way,' continued Eigen, 'you can hide what lies beneath. It's just a centuries old magic trick. What people see, from any angle and from any height, is the reflection of the hillside. Of course, it requires mathematical precision. If a single mirror is half an inch out of place, the illusion is ruined.'

'And how do you release the beasts?' asked Ward, unable to pull his eyes away from the launchers. 'Do they simply smash their way through?'

Eigen wagged a finger. 'No! They wouldn't get through. Once erect, they are only ten feet from the ceiling. They would not have built up enough thrust to enable them to pass through the reinforced glass. They would simply crash and blow up. Their warheads would not have been activated, but there would be an explosion that would tear the heart out of the hills and cause all this to collapse in upon itself.'

'So? What do you do?'

Eigen went to a small bare concrete room tucked away in a far corner. Ward followed. Eigen took a key from his pocket and unlocked a cabinet. Inside was a single red button. 'Press this button and it releases small explosive charges built into the roof. The mirrors will shatter, leaving space for the missiles to be fired. It is a one-time-only affair, I'm afraid, but then I suppose one time is all I will need. Of course, anybody in here when those mirrors break will be shredded. Once the missiles are launched, this area is lost to us. The concrete wall behind us is sealed and we give this area back to nature.'

'I'm sure she'll be grateful,' muttered Ward.

Eigen crossed his arms and contemplated the room with satisfaction.

'Now,' he said. 'Brunch.'

40. Kill the King

The brunch had been a quiet affair. For once Eigen appeared to have run out of words and was happy to hoover his food as noisily as ever.

Ward was repulsed by him. Sweat ran from his head onto his plate and he would mop it up with the food. Occasionally Eigen would take out a soggy handkerchief and run it across his face and neck and it would come away black with the filth that lay in the deep crevices of his skin folds.

The food did little for Ward; aubergine lasagne which was as bland as elevator music. He ate it because he had to. No matter how he felt about the fare, he needed the sustenance. He pitied the poor fools who were going to have to eat the insipid slop and drink mildly radioactive water for the next thirty years - they would be begging for execution after a while.

'So what's next?' he asked. 'A bullet for me and the girls? Fling our bodies over the wall so the world can see our guilt?'

Eigen voraciously slurped up the last forkful of lasagne. It smacked against his thick lips and left a trail of sauce down his chin. He wiped it away with the same soiled handkerchief. 'Well, you know, I've been thinking about that. After all, history belongs to the victor, so history will be mine.' He lay his cutlery at six o'clock, ensuring that the ends of the knife and fork touched and that the handles were perpendicular to each other. 'I think perhaps I would like to see you suffer. After all, you've been quite an annoyance. You know, I would have been quite happy to give this world another twenty or thirty years while I inveigled my way across the Caribbean, controlling it by drugs and violence and, in the end, the willing subservience of the population. Who knows, I might even have been able to create a new world without destroying the old one. But you came along and left me with little choice, so now I must do what I must do and take a little extra pleasure in the deed. It came to me as I explained the mirrors to you. I think I'll let you suffer death by a thousand cuts then, once the roof is gone, I can launch the missiles and incinerate your body.'

'And where will you be when this happens? Sitting in a deckchair with your sunglasses on, waiting for the bang?'

'No, Mr Ward, I will be in Launcher One, ready to press the button as soon as the glass breaks. We will have to be quick. I cannot risk any last second detection. Me and my men will launch all four missiles, protected in the cabs of the launchers and then walk past your crispy remains and through the bomb doors to safety.'

'Sounds like a plan,' said Ward. 'And when do you intend to do this?'

'Well, if I said that tonight will be your last supper, would that be a clue?'

'I see,' said Ward. 'It's a Big Bang breakfast then, is it?'

Eigen drank the remainder of his orange juice. 'It is. Nine a.m. So, I will send menus to yours and the ladies' rooms for you to decide what your final feast will be. I have saved some meat and wine for the occasion and you have the bottles of spirits in your quarters, so you'll all be able to have a jolly send-off.'

'I might oversleep and miss the fun,' said Ward dourly.

Eigen exposed his large teeth. His fat lips sat like leeches across them. 'No you won't. I promise.' He clicked his fingers and Baris appeared with another guard behind him. 'Take Mr Ward back to his quarters, Baris. Let him listen to his music and drink his alcohol and make love to his woman.' He got up from the table. 'Until the morning, Mr Ward.'

As he turned, Ward launched himself at Eigen. He put enough power into the charge to bring him down and land some palm strikes to the bridge of his nose. Taken by surprise, Eigen put his hands up to shield himself against the speed of Ward's assault.

Baris and his colleague kicked Ward in the ribs and dragged him away. Ward let them. He had done what he wanted to do.

Eigen scuttled away like a spider. His eyes were full of tears and his nose bleeding.

'You see, Eigen,' spat Ward. 'You bleed just like the rest of us.'

Baris whipped the butt of his Makarov into Ward's solar plexus. Ward fell breathlessly to his knees and, before Eigen could react, was dragged away.

He felt triumphant.

*

Ward turned the stereo on and put *Long Live Rock 'n' Roll* by Rainbow on the turntable. He had until the last track, the subdued *Rainbow Eyes*, to make himself heard.

He went next door and beckoned Marianne and Penny to his room. They came through without hesitation, full of trepidation, and each stood next to a speaker.

He whispered to each of them. Their faces remained grim. Occasionally they nodded. Finally Ward instructed Marianne, his hands upon her shoulders, despite her attempts to shrug him off and then kissed her.

He pulled the key to the cabinet which contained the red button from his shoe and explained it to them. The tussle with Eigen had been worth it, so long as he didn't realise the key was missing.

Marianne threw her arms around him; her face pleaded, her eyes brimmed with tears. Penny pulled them each to her and flung an arm around them. Finally, she tore them apart and as *Kill the King* played prophetically and filled the room, dragged Marianne away, back to their own quarters.

Ward took to the shower and allowed his tears to mingle with the water once again. Never was goodbye so hard. He had said goodbye to Eve, to Rose and to Raven, and each time it had felt as if his soul was being wrenched from him. Now, here it was again, that cold sensation down the spine, that sickness in the stomach, that resignation to fate.

When the menus arrived and they chose their food, they would decide upon that final meal as if it represented their lives, themselves, what they were and had been.

Ward had made up his mind; black pudding (soft inside, a tinge burned outside, many fatty bits for flavour, times a link), bacon (singed, times many pieces), sausages (cheap and juicy, also singed, times three), fried eggs (soft yolk, crispy edges, no snot, times three) and fried bread (white bread, two halves); his own, bespoke, Full English.

When this was all done, he would walk into a greasy spoon and order just that, and Marianne, (scrambled eggs - loose - toast, lashings of butter) would be there to show her disgust, her indulgence and her love.

Before that though, he had to bring the hillside down on Eigen and end the nightmare the madman had begun.

41. Black Pudding and Death

Ward dressed in fresh red scrubs, slipped on some of the comfortable white shoes and then sat down with Seamus Heaney and a weak G and T until the guards arrived.

Eventually, the door clicked open. Two guards, both in black scrubs, the younger one with a Kalashnikov in hand, the other with a Makarov pistol wrapped tightly in his fist, came into the room.

They brought with them a trolley with his meal upon it. It smelled delicious and, as these ingredients always did, brought back very fond memories.

Each ingredient was in a separate container so that no taste could corrupt another and Ward could pick as he pleased.

Ward stood, the Heaney still in his hands, and went to the trolley. He raised a random lid from a container and sniffed. It was the black pudding. He relished it.

'Thank you,' he said. 'I hope, when you die, you get the chance to experience such splendour. It is simple, I admit, but those little things matter when the big things fall.'

He moved round the trolley, raising each lid and savouring each smell until he was next to the younger man with the Kalashnikov.

Without warning, Ward rammed the spine of the book twice into his nose. He went down immediately, his legs melted and his eyes blind from the assault. Before his companion with the pistol could react, Ward turned and planted the hard edge of the book in his throat. The man stumbled backwards, disorientated, and blundered to the floor. Without thinking, Ward followed on; two blows to the nose and another to the trachea.

He watched fascinated as the guard flailed upon the floor, his legs climbing an invisible ladder, his hands scouring at his neck until his nails had clawed into his raw skin, his flesh blue until, finally, he ran out of air and succumbed to the inevitable, his pupils pinpoint, the whites of his eyes fractured by a ripple of red, as the capillaries burst with the pressure.

The other guard, struggling to stand, raised the Makarov. Ward kicked his wrist and saw the gun fly, then planted the tip of his foot into the man's throat. He was dead before his head hit the ground.

The whole episode, but for a couple of bumps and wheezes, had remained silent and taken less than thirty seconds.

Ward carried the corpses into the bathroom and dumped them in the shower base, their bodies entwined, spidery, hauntingly still.

He grabbed the Kalashnikov and a spare magazine of ammo, along with the Makarov and a spare clip. It was, thankfully, a PPM model that held twelve rounds. Then he took an electronic room card from each of the dead men. At least now he could find a way out.

He went through the doors to the adjoining room and tossed the Kalashnikov and its spare magazine at Penny.

'What's going on?' she whispered.

Ward kept his voice low. 'I've got an idea, but it might not work. If worst comes to worst, use the gun and try to get out; until then do nothing and deny me if you have to. If all goes to plan, I'll be back in time for breakfast.

Penny thrust a piece paper into his hand. 'Here,' she said. 'Key codes. I'm Mrs Memory, remember? Key in the code then press the hash for the blast door to open, press the black button for the door.' She hugged him. 'Be safe.'

With a lingering glance at Marianne, if they spoke he might stay, Ward ran back to his room.

Cautiously, he slid the card into the slot next to the door. The door clicked softly and then slid open without a sound.

Gun held high, Ward stepped out.

42. Sorry Will Never Be Enough

Ward retraced his steps from earlier in the day. The garden was empty, silent, with only the sound of misters hissing like snakes as he passed through

He keyed in the number which Penny had given him, then pressed the black button. The door to the side of the blast door hushed open. He walked through the decontamination area through which he and Eigen had passed earlier that day. The misty sanitiser fell upon him and then the door opened.

. The Food Research Quarter was empty but for the occasional green halo of light where computers remained on and the indiscriminate flash of lights against the walls, calculating and monitoring, on constant watch.

Ward looked at one of the screens. It was gobbledygook to him. No matter how long he stared at it, it would make no sense.

He moved on and found the keypad at the end of the room. In the dark corner, he fed the numbers into the keypad and pressed the black button. Again the door gave way. He once more found himself in the large empty concrete room, the cushion between the interior of the building and the blasts of the rockets.

There was no one in the room. The only sound was the occasional scuff of Ward's feet as he tried to quietly cross the floor and approach the next barrier.

Once again, he read Penny's paper and keyed in the pad, then pressed the black button.

The door yawned and Ward passed through.

It was still a most impressive sight, the launchers silhouetted by the light of the moon that fell through the thick mirrored windows and reflected inside the room like a kaleidoscope, the light falling at angles, quenching the scene in rays of silver which criss-crossed the room like the beams of a hundred distant lighthouses.

He went to the small concrete room in the corner of the room and found the box. He opened it and examined it. There was no obvious way to disconnect the red button which protruded like a clown's nose in middle of it, certainly not without extensive damage and certain detection. He put the stolen Makarov in the cabinet, then closed the door and put the key back in his pocket.

Before he left, he went and looked at the launchers. They were immense, hunched like dragons, ready to wake and breathe fire at a second's notice.

Satisfied that he had done all that he could do, he made his way back to his quarters, one slow foot at a time.

He again passed through the Food Research lab. The stop/start, tic-tic of reel to reel tapes, the voice of the computers, sounded like insects against the night, the dark shadows of the huge mainframes lined up against the wall, crenellated like a stronghold in the shadows. Lights flickered and jumped like fireflies as information collated then moved to memory, to be replaced by another minute alteration in the feed.

It was a hell of a set up. With ideas stolen from one of the biggest computer researchers and manufacturers in the world, then expanded by Eigen's own team of masterminds, of number crunchers and programmers, there was nowhere he couldn't go and nothing he couldn't do in this modern world.

Quite how the modern world would splice with Eigen's new world, he wasn't sure. All these twentieth century wonders might be made redundant by the sheer crudeness of the apocalypse. It would be a struggle for sure. But in the intransigent mind of a crazy man, anything was possible, anything at all, even immortality, in some form.

Ward wandered back to the door that led to the research room and went through the decontamination area.

Then he was back into the hallways, the lighting subdued, Ward supposed, to save resources when not in use.

He soon came to his room and slid the passkey into the slot. The door slid open.

As soon as he stepped into the room, he knew that there was little he could do about what awaited him.

*

'There are dead men in your shower, Mr Ward,' said Eigen. 'Their guns and pass keys are missing. Where have you been?'

He was flanked by Baris and two other guards.

'Oh, out and about,' said Ward. 'It was all beginning to feel a little claustrophobic.'

Eigen hit Ward with the butt of a pistol. He felt his cheekbone split as a cloud of dizziness enveloped him.

'Where are the guns and passes?'

'I left them with the concierge.' He smiled tartly. 'He even gave me a ticket for when I wanted to retrieve them. I'll show you' He went into his pocket and pulled out a middle finger.

Eigen grabbed it and broke it. It snapped like a twig. Ward screamed. The finger jutted at forty-five degrees and had already began to swell. He cradled it in his other hand and, with a single, wretchedly painful pull, straightened it. It hurt. It was perhaps worse than the iron chair had been, so focused was the pain, so visible the damage.

'Where,' repeated Eigen, 'are the guns and the passes?

Ward fell to his knees, overwhelmed with pain, his broken hand tucked beneath his right armpit. With his free hand he pulled out his one pass from his pocket and tossed it at Eigen's feet. 'That's it,' he said. 'The guns and the other pass are in the garden somewhere. I tossed them. I only needed this one pass to get back into my room.'

'We have searched the women's room...' began Eigen.

Ward's heart trembled. If Eigen had found the Kalashnikov and the other pass in there, they were done for. 'Oh yes? I bet you found little more than two frightened women.'

Eigen paused before answering. 'This is true. Which means that you're not lying. What were you doing out of your room?'

'Looking for a way to escape,' said Ward.

'There is no way,' snorted Eigen, as if it was obvious.'

'I know that now,' said Ward. 'That's why I came back.'

'In the hope of what? Some sort of heroic act in the morning? What were you going to do? Jump on one of the launchers and tear down my world?'

'Something like that,' said Ward.

'Fool.' Eigen went down on his haunches and put his hand under Ward's chin. 'You have a torrent of blood streaming down the left hand side of your face, Mr Ward. That is your flag of failure. Tomorrow, you will be chained to a launcher, with your companions, and fried. You think it won't hurt? Those few moments of agony before ignition will be the most painful of your life as you look your cohorts in the eye and know that it is all your fault. Sorry will never be enough.'

He stood. 'Baris, bring the women in here. Keep them together until it's time for them to leave. If any of them misbehaves, maim them. They can hobble to their death.'

Baris went to the adjoining room and hustled Marianne and Penny through. They looked exhausted but had the glare of defiance in their eyes. Good for you, thought Ward. Don't reward him with fear.

Baris locked the door to their room and pointed at a couple of chairs. They sat.

Eigen ran a handkerchief over his head and face. It did little good. Globules of sweat immediately rose to replace those wiped away.

Ward pulled himself up and sat on the edge of the bed. He could already feel the swelling below his left eye. His left middle finger competed for the pain.

'Right,' declared Eigen. 'That will do for now. Mr Ward, ladies, I will see you in a few hours. Please, feel free to use the facilities, but bear in mind that more pain will be inflicted should you do anything foolish.'

He inserted his card into the slot and left.

Ward looked at Penny and Marianne. 'I'm sorry,' he said. 'I tried.'

'Forget it,' said Penny. 'You can only do your best.'

'Well,' said Ward. 'I shall keep pressing those buttons until the last. I'll keep ducking and diving. You should too. Both of you. Now will be as good a time as any. It's the only weapon we have, to keep pressing that little red button until the end.'

Penny and Marianne looked at each other.

'Was that crack in the head a bit much, mate?' asked Penny. 'You keep up this mumbo-jumbo, you'll have us all running for cover into that little concrete room in our heads.'

A wave of relief flooded Ward as he realised that she understood. He looked at Marianne. The corners of her mouth were turned up into a narrow smile. She gave the slightest nod of the head to indicate that she too understood.

Baris stood attentively in the corner of the room where he had a view of all of them. 'Shut up would you?' he said. 'You're just spouting shit. Enough. Just…shut up.'

'Sure,' said Ward. 'No problem. Be a good man and get me a tot of that Haig's Dimple, would you?'

'Get it yourself,' said Baris.

'Fair enough. Ladies? Anything?' They shook their heads. Ward held up his broken hand. 'Purely medicinal,' he said.

He went and poured himself a large shot of the whisky and downed it in one. Then he went and looked at the books that lined the opposite wall. After that he went to the bathroom. The eyes of the guards followed him but no one tried to stop him closing the bathroom door.

He went to a cabinet and searched for some painkillers. There were some paracetamol, so he washed down a couple with tap water. They would have to do.

He flushed the toilet and went back into the room. No one had moved.

That was good. They would hopefully maintain that overconfidence until they got to the launchers.

He lay on top of the bed. Penny and Marianne watched him.

He winked at them.

They smiled and relaxed back into their chairs.

43. The Remains Of A Dream

'Baris. Bring them to me.' Eigen's voice filled the speakers like the toll of the final bell.

Baris went to a duffel bag and pulled out three chains and two padlocks. 'Stand,' he ordered.

He gave his gun to one of the other guards and proceeded to wrap the chains tightly around each of their waists, then padlocked them, with Ward in the middle. The three of them were now inextricably bound.

'One runs,' said Baris, 'you all run. You won't get ten yards before being shot.'

He opened the door with his card and ordered the two other guards to lead them out into the corridor.

Baris remained behind them. There was one guard in front of them and one to the side.

They passed through the garden area, then through the decontamination area into the Food Research Quarter. No one looked at them. There was tension in the air, knowledge of what was soon to come, absolute concentration upon the work before them. It had suddenly all become real.

They came to the door. The guard in front fumbled the code on the keypad.

'It should be a seven,' said Penny. 'Not a four, you bimbo.'

The guard sneered at her and re-entered the number and pressed the black entry button. The door opened and the six made their way through to the large empty area that shielded the main building from the blast area.

Again, the guard entered the code and they finally stood in the launch room.

Beside each launcher stood a man dressed in black, except for the furthest launcher, beside which stood the colossal Eigen. He too wore the black scrubs of the guards but, in a stroke of vanity, had added his initials in gold braid onto its chest.

'Welcome to your tomb, Mr Ward.' He barely had to raise his voice. It carried through the room and bounced off the bare walls with ease. 'In a moment, Baris will chain the three of you to the back of this launcher and I will have the pleasure of turning you all to cinder. After that, each launcher will send its missile to its predetermined destination and my new world will begin.'

'There's still time to change your mind,' said Ward. 'I'll put a good word in for you.'

Eigen showed no emotion. 'Why don't you just stop now? All this bravado, all these words, they are wasted. Try to go with a little dignity.' He nodded to Baris. 'Bring them forward'

As they started towards the launcher, Ward pulled Marianne and Penny towards him and wrapped his arms around them. 'Now!' he said.

They ducked into the small concrete room as bullets flew around them and pock-marked the walls. Ward reached up, opened the cabinet door and removed the pistol he had hidden there. He tossed it to Penny. She held it ready to shoot anybody who ventured too close.

'Reflect upon this, Eigen,' he shouted at the top of his voice.

He pressed the red button and heard a series of small thunder claps as each small explosive in the glass ceiling detonated.

As it did so, Eigen looked up. The four-inch thick glass shattered and rained down on all.

Ward didn't dare to look out for fear of decapitation from the shards of glass.

Baris ran into the small room for protection. Penny shot him and he stumbled back out. Ward watched as a thousand slivers of sharpened glass cut into him. His body shuddered with each new wound. The sound was horrendous; an ear-splitting, high-pitched, relentless cacophony.

As quickly as it had started, the downpour stopped. Ward grabbed Baris' foot and dragged him towards the shelter. He was in shreds. There wasn't a centimetre of him that had not been pierced, right through the fatty layer of his skin and through to his major organs. There can have been no blood left in his body. Ward fumbled through his bloody pockets until he found the padlock keys and tore off the restraints.

He took the gun from Penny. 'Stay here,' he ordered them both.

He walked out of the small room. There were bodies everywhere, each in the same state as Baris, defleshed almost to the bone, all framed by their own blood.

Ward walked cautiously towards Eigen's launcher, the gun held ready between his hands. It was impossible to move quietly as his feet ground the glass beneath them.

He found Eigen propped up against one of the enormous wheels of his launcher. His clothes had been torn from him. His flesh had been macerated, his naked head now little more than ribbons of skin. Large pieces of glass protruded from the folds of flesh that fell about him like butter. Once again, his major organs had been protected by his deformity, but blood seeped from every cut, from the arteries in his wrists and legs. It pulsed weakly from his wounds, slowly but surely subsiding with each dwindling beat of his heart. He had little time left.

His remaining eye swivelled toward Ward. 'What have you done?' his voice was barely audible through his severed neck.

'I've killed you,' said Ward. 'I have put the mad dog down.'

'But, the new world!' stuttered Eigen.

'I like the old one,' said Ward.

Eigen licked at his dry lips. 'At least have the decency to put me out of my misery.'

Ward kicked glass aside until there was an area of the floor for him to sit on. He lowered himself wearily and leaned on the wheel of the launcher next door.

'No,' he said. 'I'm all out of decency. I'm going to sit here and watch you die, Eigen. You've killed some good people. Now, it's your turn.'

Ward watched on as the life slowly seeped from Eigen. Two minutes later, he was still, a formless, shattered giant, the remains of a dream.

44. That Square Inch Of Blue

Ward had been to surgery to have his fractured cheekbone repaired. Thankfully he was under the care of one of the best orthopaedic consultants in the world. While under the knife, she had also repaired the two fractures in his finger. They would, she assured him, be as good as new.

It had been two days since Eigen's death. The Americans, at the request of the British, had gone in to tidy up. They had, quite naturally, been somewhat put out by all that had gone on without their knowledge, but they were grateful for what Ward had done. The island was back in the Commonwealth's hands and America, for now at least, was safe.

Penny removed the dressing under Ward's left eye. The bruising was still considerable, but the wound was healing and she thought it unlikely to scar.

'Thanks,' said Ward. 'I knew you'd come in useful one day.'

'Cheeky bastard!' said Penny with a smile. 'You'll be fit to fly in a couple of days. Back to the wind and rain and the snow, desperate for the sight of a daffodil and a square inch of blue sky.'

Ward sighed. She was right. After all this, he would go back to his flat and his job and carry on with life in grey as if none of this had ever happened. 'You're a comfort, Ms Sweeting.'

'Don't you bloody know it?' She held his hand and then kissed it. 'I didn't get a chance to thank you properly.'

'You don't have to,' said Ward. 'Without you I would probably never have been able to stop Eigen.'

'All the same…'

'It was my pleasure,' said Ward. 'Really.'

Penny swallowed her emotions. 'Listen, Marianne's outside. You ready to see her? It's been a couple of days, what with all that bloody anaesthetic and surgery going on.'

'I'm very ready,' said Ward.

'Okay. I'll give you two some space. See you later.'

Penny left and closed the door.

The room was silent, sterile, discomforting. It was only a hospital room, he knew that, but it had no heart. He needed heart.

There was a knock on the door and Marianne came in. She looked beautiful, her hair pulled back into a pony-tail, a lemon shirt atop a white skirt and those wide, seductive, brown-almost-black eyes.

She leaned over and kissed Ward. She smelled like heaven. He held her for a moment and inhaled the same Rive Gauche as he had smelled at the Hibiscus Hotel so very long ago.

Marianne pulled away. There were tears in her eyes.

'It's okay,' said Ward. 'It's all over now.'

She buried her face in his chest. 'That's what I'm afraid of,' she wept.

Ward ran his hand through her hair. The light from the window rippled across it like a dark wave. It was soft and yielding and Ward wanted to swim in its velvet blackness forever.

Perhaps he should.

Perhaps he would.

The End

Also by Christopher Bradbury

Mike Ward Adventures:

The High Commissioner's Wife
The Devil Inside
Catfish
No Time to Repent
Semper Occultus

Mayflies
Eidolon
The Stilling of the Heart
The Ghost of Dormy Place and Other Tales
The Ashes of an Oak
A Kind and Gentle Man
Earthbound
Earthbound Part Two - Hellbound
Chine (Horror)
Uncomfortably Numb (Play)
The Scarlet Darter (fiction for children)
Unton's Teeth and Other Tales of Wordful Mystification
(poems for children)
Phoenix - A Look at the Causes of World War Two
A Beginner's Guide to the Wars of the Roses
A Beginner's Guide to Creative Writing
A Beginner's Guide to Death
Praxis (Sci-Fi Fantasy - with Ian Makinson)
Praxis - Part Two: Regeneration Paradox (Sci-Fi Fantasy -
with Ian Makinson)
Praxis - Part Three: The Liar's truth - (Sci-Fi Fantasy - with
Ian Makinson)